# DEADLY DISTRACTIONS

## A STAN TURNER MYSTERY

# Other Books by William Manchee

*Brash Endeavor,* A STAN TURNER MYSTERY

*Ca$h Call,* A STAN TURNER MYSTERY

*Death Pact*

*Plastic Gods,* A RICH COLEMAN NOVEL

*Second Chair,* A STAN TURNER MYSTERY

*Trouble in Trinidad: A Tale of Love, Politics, and Betrayal*

*Twice Tempted*

*Undaunted,* A STAN TURNER MYSTERY

# DEADLY DISTRACTIONS

## A STAN TURNER MYSTERY

by
**William Manchee**

**Lean Press**

Portland, Oregon

Editor: Michael Ryder, Portland, Oregon
Proofreader: Kelly Anderson, Portland, Oregon
Cover design: Lorraine Millard and Nicole Schnell Creative Group,
    Portland, Oregon
Composition and page design: William H. Brunson, Typography
    Services, Portland, Oregon

ISBN: 1-932475-02-8


This Lean Press quality paperback was printed by Malloy Litho,
Ann Arbor, Michigan


Lean Press
www.leanpress.com
1-503-595-5400


06 05 04   1 2 3

This is a work of fiction. Any similarity to actual persons, living or dead, or to actual events, is purely coincidental.

*This book is dedicated to my sister-in-law,*
*Patricia Mello, who has been there*
*from day one cheering me on.*

# STANDOFF 1

Never call your office while you're on vacation. That's always been one of my hard and fast rules. Several years earlier I had made the mistake of calling the office to make sure one last detail had been properly handled. When Jodie heard my voice she was panic-stricken. A client had called claiming we hadn't filed an answer to a lawsuit and the plaintiff had taken a default judgment. It was untrue, the client had never contacted me about the suit, but the accusation was enough to spoil my vacation. Although, we continued on our trip, I had this nagging knot in my stomach the entire time. When I got back from the trip and called the client in, he admitted he wasn't sure he had sent the citation to me, but he thought he had!

Paula, my new partner, however, insisted before we left that I provide her with a written itinerary of our travels. I tried to explain to her that we didn't plan our vacations in great detail and usually just wandered around at will. This bothered her so much, I finally agreed to call her every other day to make sure everything was okay. You would think having a partner to cover for you would make life easier, but so far that hadn't been the case. Whereas I used to do as I pleased, now I had to consult with Paula before I made even the most trivial decision. It was like having two wives. But she had provided needed capital for the firm and claimed to be an astute businessperson, something the firm desperately needed, so I bit my tongue and patiently complied with her requests.

It was early afternoon on Friday, July 11, 1986. It was a comfortable seventy-eight degrees, twenty degrees cooler than it was when we left Dallas. We were five days into our long two-week Colorado vacation and were staying in a cabin at Estes Park, Colorado. The kids and I had just returned from white water rafting down the Cache La Poudre River. It had been an awesome trip through some class II and III rapids and we were all as high as the bald eagles we had seen circling above us all afternoon. Rebekah, who had opted to stay in the cabin and read the latest Danielle Steele novel, rushed outside when she heard our van pull up. She hadn't been pleased with the idea of us going white water rafting despite the guides assurances that it was perfectly safe. The thought of her baby, Marcia—now age eight—out there on the raging river, was particularly troublesome. Marcia, however, put up such a stink at the idea of her staying back at the cabin, that Rebekah finally shrugged and said she could go.

Rebekah was all smiles once everyone had been accounted for and appeared to have all their limbs.

"So, how was it?" she asked.

"It was so cool," Reggi said.

"We almost capsized," Mark said.

"No, we didn't," Peter snickered.

Rebekah frowned. "You almost capsized?"

"Not really," I interjected. "It got a little rough, but the guide knew what he was doing."

Rebekah put her hands on her hips and shook her head. "You guys are crazy going out there on the river. You should have just gone fishing."

"Don't worry, we're gonna do that too," I said with a wink.

Rebekah gave me a dirty look and then said, "Oh, Paula called. She said for you to call her just as soon as you got back."

My heart sank as I feared my vacation was about to take a nose-dive. "Can't they leave me alone? All I want is two weeks of peace and quiet."

"I know. I asked her if it couldn't wait until you got back. She said that it was your call, but that she needed to brief you on what was coming down."

"Wonderful," I said, as we went inside the cabin. After grabbing a beer from the fridge, I collapsed on the sofa. Marcia snuggled up next to me.

"This little girl is quite the sailor," I said. "You should have seen her paddle."

"Bull," Mark said. "She splashed me every time she put her oar in the water."

"I did not," Marcia protested.

"Okay," I said. "It didn't much matter. We all got soaked anyway."

Rebekah gave me a hard look.

"What?" I said.

"Aren't you going to call Paula?"

I took a deep breath. "I'd rather not."

She shook her head. "She said it was important."

"Okay, okay. I'll call her," I said as I got up and went to the telephone. I dialed the number and waited.

"Law office," Jodie, my secretary, said.

"Jodie, this is Stan."

"Oh, thank God! Paula needs to talk to you."

"What's up?"

"Haven't you seen the news?"

"No, we don't have a TV up here."

"It's Dusty Thomas. They say he shot an IRS agent. They were trying to seize his tractor. They're not sure if the Agent's gonna live. The FBI has him cornered in a barn. Martha wants you to go out there and talk some sense into him. She's afraid they're gonna kill him."

Martha was a sweet lady. She and Dusty had been married for nearly twenty years and were very happy despite a string of bad luck that would have destroyed most marriages. I was torn between my family and duty calling, as usual.

"But, I'm in the middle of Colorado."

"I know, I told her you were on vacation."

"Oh, God. Poor Martha. She and Dusty have the worst luck of any people I know. Do you have a number for the FBI agent in charge?"

"Yes."

Jodie gave me the number and then put me through to Paula.

"Have you talked to the FBI?" I asked her.

"Yes, they're not in a hurry to storm the place. I guess they figure he has no way to escape so they can afford to just wait it out."

"That's good. I wonder why he hasn't surrendered already. Dusty's not exactly the violent type."

"He's probably afraid they'll kill him if he shows his face."

"With his luck, they probably would."

"What do you mean, 'his luck?'" Paula asked.

"Dusty's mother died in childbirth. His father deserted him at age three. His grandfather and grandmother raised him on the Double T Ranch. Jodie and I call it the Double Trouble Ranch. When Dusty was eleven he was riding his pony out in the pasture when a storm came up suddenly. He took cover under a big tree and was nearly killed when the tree was hit by lightning. At twenty-five he married the woman of his dreams who promptly spent his life's savings on clothes, cosmetics and a boob job. Unfortunately, she didn't hang around long enough for him to enjoy her new boobs and before she divorced him she had managed to max-out a half dozen credit cards to the tune of $50,000."

"Jesus, he is unlucky."

"Oh, that's just his early history of bad fortune. Just since I've known him his house has been blown away by a tornado, the IRS has seized most of his ranch, he broke his leg falling off a tractor, he had a heart attack, and now he's about to be arrested for murder."

"Oh, my God. What are you going to do?" Paula asked.

"I don't know. I doubt I could get there before morning. By then it will probably be too late."

"Wait. There's a special bulletin coming on the TV. . . . Oh, my God!"

"What is it?"

"The IRS agent just died."

"Shit! . . . Okay, I'm on my way."

I hung up the phone and gave Rebekah a disappointed look. "I guess you heard."

"Dusty Thomas killed an IRS agent?"

"Right."

"They ought to pin a medal on him," Rebekah said with a grin.

I smiled. "I doubt the FBI will see it that way."

"So, why do you have to go back? Can't Paula handle it?"

"Ordinarily she could, but Dusty doesn't trust too many people. He doesn't know her. His wife thinks I'm the only one that might be able to talk him into surrendering. I'd feel pretty bad if he were killed and I hadn't at least tried to help him."

Rebekah sighed. "Okay, we'll pack up the van and hit the road."

"Actually, I have a better idea. Maybe the FBI will come get me. You guys can continue the vacation without me. Once Dusty is safe, I'll come back."

"Yeah, good idea," Reggi said. "I don't want to go home yet. We just got here."

"That's right," I said. "There's no use all of us going back."

"All right," Rebekah said. "Call them and see if they'll do it."

I explained the situation to the FBI agent in charge in Princeton, Texas where Dusty had his ranch. He agreed to send a helicopter to come get me. About two hours later, I climbed aboard the big black FBI chopper that had set down in the spacious RV parking lot adjacent to our resort. After I buckled up and put on my headset, I waved to Rebekah and the kids and we were off. It was a beautiful ride over the Rocky Mountains, across the Texas panhandle and then along the Texas-Oklahoma border. The pilot put on some classical music along the way to drown out the hum of the engine. It would have been an incredible ride under normal circumstances, but knowing Dusty might be shot at any moment had me on edge. What was I going to say to him? Did he really kill the IRS agent? It didn't sound like Dusty. But if a man is pushed too far, there's no telling what he might do.

When we got to the Red River, it was nearly dark. The pilot followed the river awhile until we got to Gainesville where he turned southeast. Soon we were over U.S. 75 just north of McKinney, Texas. Princeton was just a few minutes away and I was beginning to get nervous. What if Dusty was on drugs or something? What if he wasn't happy to see me? Would he kill me? I didn't think so, but with a dozen FBI agents and hundreds of other law enforcement officers surrounding him, who knows what he would do. The thought even occurred to me that I might become his hostage.

As we approached Dusty's ranch, I saw several banks of floodlights that had been set up on the edge of the driveway to illuminate the crime scene. The Double T Ranch once had more than 1,000 acres but the IRS had seized all but the 200 acres Dusty had claimed as his rural homestead. The IRS could have taken the homestead portion too, but had a policy not to seize a homestead until the taxpayer died. The main house was about half a mile from the farm to market road that ran on the southern border of the ranch. It was a modest, 1,800-square-foot house in desperate need of repairs. The old house, occupied by the previous owners, was on the left side of the driveway at the front of the lot. Dusty used it for parties and special occasions. The land itself was flat and planted with a hybrid Bermuda specially formulated for grazing cattle. Unfortunately the Service had seized most of Dusty's cattle. The barn where Dusty was held up was on the northwest corner of the ranch and was used to keep the horses that Dusty and his wife loved to ride.

As the chopper set down two agents came over to greet us. One of the agents helped me out of the helicopter and introduced himself.

"I'm agent Ronald Logan and this is Agent Jennifer Giles," he shouted over the noise of the chopper. I forced a smile and shook their hands. As we stepped away from the chopper it took off and we were able to talk in a normal tone of voice.

"So what's the situation?" I asked.

"He's been in there since early this morning. The sheriff got a phone call from a wrecker driver who found a white, middle-aged male body lying in the driveway. He had been shot and was already dead when the body was discovered. It turns out he was a revenue officer from the Sherman office of the Internal Revenue Service who was there to seize a tractor. The wrecker driver was supposed to meet him there."

"Jesus. They just couldn't leave him alone," I said.

"What do you mean?" Logan asked.

"The IRS has been after Dusty for ten years. They just won't lay off. They say he owes a quarter million dollars, but I personally think it's bullshit."

"Well, bullshit or not it didn't give him the right to kill anyone."

"True. Did anyone actually see him kill the revenue officer?"

"No, but Thomas was standing over the body with a shotgun when the wrecker driver pulled up. When he saw the driver he ran. The driver called his dispatcher and reported the murder. When the sheriff's deputies arrived about ten minutes later, the driver pointed them in the direction Thomas had fled. They found him at the stock pond. When he saw them coming, he ran. They told him to stop but he kept on running until he got to the barn. He went inside and took up a position in the loft. When the deputies got too close he fired a warning shot, so they've been holding back. There's no point in endangering the lives of any of our agents or the sheriff's deputies. Thomas isn't going anywhere."

I shook my head, still not believing what Logan was telling me. "This is so unlike Dusty. He's the nicest, laid-back country-boy you'll ever meet. I've really grown fond of him these past few years."

"I hope the feeling is mutual for your sake. I don't know if I'd go in there if it were me."

"I'm not worried. He wouldn't hurt me. Right now I'm the only hope he has."

"So, how do you want to play it?" Logan asked.

"Can you communicate with him?"

"He doesn't have a phone. The bullhorn is the only way to talk to him and it's strictly one way," Logan said and then handed me a walkie-talkie. "Take this in with you so we can talk once you make contact."

"Fine, just let him know I'm coming in so he won't shoot me."

"Okay," Logan said, and motioned to a sheriff's deputy to bring him the bullhorn. With the bullhorn in hand, Logan moved as close to the barn as he dared. He lifted up the bullhorn and said, "Mr. Thomas, your attorney, Stan Turner, is here to talk to you. He's unarmed and he'll be coming inside in just a minute."

Everyone looked at me as I mentally prepared myself to enter the barn. I took a deep breath and started walking toward it. Agent Logan grabbed my arm and whispered, "Do you want a vest?"

I looked at Logan and wondered if that would be wise. My gut feeling told me it might spook Dusty. He might think I didn't trust him. "No, I guess not," I said and continued walking. As I stepped inside I scanned the interior looking for Dusty. "Dusty? Where are you?"

There was movement above me to my left. I looked up and saw Dusty, with shotgun in hand, staring down at me.

"There you are. Should I come up there or are you coming down?"

Dusty glanced outside toward the crowd of sheriffs' deputies and FBI agents. Then he quickly made his way to a ladder and climbed down.

"So, what happened?" I asked. "They say you shot a revenue officer."

"It's a damn lie. I didn't shoot anybody."

"But they have a witness who saw you standing over the body."

"That's true, but I came out of the house after he had already been shot."

"Really? Do you have any idea who might have shot him?"

Dusty shook his head no. "I wish I did."

"Why did you run? Now they think you did it."

"I was hoping to get away. I knew they'd never believe I was innocent."

I sighed. "So, what now?"

Dusty shrugged and replied, "Hell, I don't know. Maybe I should let them kill me. It will probably be the only way I'll ever get them off my back."

"Don't talk like that. If you're innocent, we'll find a way to prove it. Don't worry. Why don't you lose the shotgun and we'll both walk out of here right now?"

"No, I can't do that."

"Why not?"

"It wouldn't be right. I'm an innocent man."

"If you don't surrender, you'll be an innocent dead man!"

Dusty looked away. I wondered if he was serious about dying. I couldn't imagine how he figured he could escape. "Come on, Dusty. There's no way out of this. You don't want to die. Think about Martha."

Dusty's face became grim. "It doesn't matter, either way she's lost me. Why prolong the agony?"

"You say you're innocent and I believe you because you're an honest man. So, let me prove it. Don't give up before the battle has begun."

The walkie-talkie crackled. "Stan, everything okay in there?" Logan asked.

I pushed the talk button and replied. "Yes, I'm fine. Just having a little chat with Dusty."

"Okay, let me know if you need anything."

"I will. Thanks. Bye."

Dusty took a deep breath. "What happens if I surrender?"

I smiled sympathetically and replied, "They'll take you to a holding cell, probably at the Collin County Jail where you'll stay until you are arraigned. If we are able to post bond you won't be in jail more than 24 hours."

"How much will the bond be?"

"I don't know. It's a murder charge so it could be pretty steep."

"So what you're telling me is I might not get out?"

"If you can't post the bond, that's true. Do you have any relatives who might help you raise the bond?"

"No. No rich relatives."

"Well, I know time in jail isn't going to be much fun, but it's not the end of the world. I've been in jail before and I survived."

Dusty rubbed his forehead like he was in great pain. I could feel his agony and wished I had some way to relieve it for him.

"Listen, Dusty. You're in a long tunnel and either way you go it's going to be pitch dark for quite a while. If you go out there with me right now, I'll do everything in my power to bring you to the light. If you go the other way there's nothing but darkness."

Dusty smiled. "You don't believe in heaven?"

"I do, but I'm going to hang around on earth just as long as I can and I'd recommend you do the same."

"Okay, Stan. I'll do it your way, but you sure as hell better get me off."

# SURRENDER 2

A rush of relief washed over me, but it didn't last long. I now had the seemingly insurmountable task of proving Dusty Thomas innocent of murdering an agent of the Internal Revenue Service. He had motive, opportunity and the whole world already knew he was guilty. Just the kind of hopeless case I always seemed to attract. Everyone would expect me to lose, but I couldn't lose this one. I had promised Dusty I'd lead him to the light and I damn well planned to do it.

I pushed the button on my walkie-talkie and said, "Logan. We're coming out."

Logan responded, "Copy." He raised his hands and yelled to his troops, "Hold your fire, they're coming out!"

We walked out of the barn with our hands over our heads. I made Dusty leave the shotgun inside. Two deputies rushed over and pushed Dusty up against the barn. They cuffed him and escorted him to a waiting squad car. Logan and Giles came over to me and patted me on the back.

"Nice job, counselor," Giles said. "You may have saved his life."

I shrugged. "Perhaps. I just hope I can keep him alive."

Giles nodded sympathetically. "That could prove difficult. We've already been given the word that this is a high-priority case. The justice department wants your guy nailed. They can't have revenue officers becoming the targets of unhappy taxpayers."

Logan asked, "Did he have anything to say to you?"

"Yeah, he had a lot to say, but you know I can't talk about it. I will tell you one thing, though. He's claiming to be innocent."

Logan laughed. "That's a good one."

"Well, anyway, I'm putting you on notice that he's my client and I don't want anyone talking to him without me or my partner Paula Waters present . . . understand? "

"Loud and clear," Logan said.

I watched as the crime scene crew entered the barn. They put the shotgun in a long plastic bag and carried it to a waiting van. There was a commotion behind me at the perimeter of the crime scene. I heard

Paula arguing with a deputy. They finally let her through and she joined us."

"What jerks." Paula said. "I've been trying to get in here to see you for twenty minutes."

"I'm surprised you made it at all," Logan said. "The perimeter's been closed all day."

I said, "Paula, Agents Robert Logan and Jennifer Giles from the FBI."

"Nice to meet you," she replied. "I just came from the morgue. I didn't learn much, but I did find out the wound was from a 12 gauge shotgun."

"Really?" I said. "I wonder what kind of shotgun they took out of the barn."

Giles looked at Logan and he turned and walked over to the crime van. He talked to someone there and returned.

"It's a 12 gauge Remington and it's been fired recently."

"Shit," Paula said.

"Sorry guys," Logan said. "It's not looking good for your client."

"You got that right," Paula replied. "We better get going, Stan. Martha is waiting for us at the house."

"Oh, okay," I said. We thanked Logan and Giles and took Paula's car back to the main house. The FBI had already completed their search of the place and Martha was straightening up the mess they had left. She was a thin, dark haired Irish woman of about fifty-five. She looked tired and worn out from the ordeal she had been through. Despite everything, she offered us coffee, which we accepted.

"Did the FBI find anything, Mrs. Thomas?" Paula asked.

"I don't think so. They took all his tax records, most everything in his office, and all his guns and ammunition."

"Were there any other shotguns?" I asked.

"Yes, he had several."

"Do you know what kind?"

"God, no. I stay away from guns."

"Where were you when this all happened?" Paula asked.

"Shopping in McKinney. They have a great dress shop near the old courthouse."

"Did your husband know the IRS agent was coming by today?" I asked.

"No, I don't think so. He didn't mention it to me and I'm sure he would have. He hates the IRS and if anything is going on with them he'd have been ranting and raving about it."

"Do you think Dusty killed the agent?" Paula asked.

"I don't think so, but it's possible, I guess," she replied.

"What makes you say that?"

"He said he was going to kill that bastard someday, but it was just talk—at least I thought it was."

"Do you know of anyone else who might have been around your ranch today?" I asked.

"No, we had to let all the hands go after the cattle and the land were seized. The only person who visits us these days is Dusty's son George and his wife Connie. They live up in Paris. They usually come down to see us at least once a month."

"Were they here today?"

"No, I don't think so. They usually come on the weekends."

"What about your neighbors?" Paula asked. "Did any of them come by today?"

"No, but we see our neighbor across the road quite a bit. We have to go by their place when we come into the ranch. Sometimes they're outside working in the yard or sitting on the porch. We say hi and chat a little occasionally. As a matter of fact I did talk to Emma Lou this morning when I left to go to McKinney. I asked her if she wanted to go, but she had company coming for lunch."

"Emma Lou," Paula said. "What's her last name?"

"Marshall. Her husband's name is Fred."

"Okay, we'll check with them. Maybe they saw something," I said. Martha's energy seemed to be fading so I stood up. "We should go. You're tired."

"I am a little bit," she said. Paula and Martha got up and we walked to the door. "Do you think you'll be able to get Dusty out on bail?" she asked.

"The judge will set bail in the morning, but it will probably be very high," Paula said. "I don't know what you're—"

"They don't have anything!" I said. "IRS took everything of value except the house and 200 acres. Since there's a federal tax lien on the house and acreage, they won't be able to use it as collateral."

"Can I visit Dusty in jail?" Martha asked.

"Of course, they have regular visiting hours. He'll be in the Collin County jail for now. You'll be able to see him a lot before the trial," I said.

"Good. I'll visit him everyday. I know he must be very scared," she said. She began to cry. Paula took her in her arms to comfort her. "I'm sorry," she said. "I miss him so much already!"

Tears began to well in my eyes as well and I could see Paula was also crying. It was a difficult moment and I wondered if there was any way we could actually prove Dusty innocent. It seemed there was no doubt he was the killer, but when he looked me in the eyes and told me he was innocent, I believed him.

On the way back to Dallas we discussed how to proceed with Dusty's defense. Paula convinced me that there wasn't anything I could do for Dusty in the next ten days and that I should return to Colorado. She said she'd handle the arraignment and help Martha try to raise the bail money. Reluctantly, I agreed and she took me to the airport. I thanked her for covering for me and she left.

While waiting for my flight, I tried to forget about the events of the day and get my focus back on our vacation, but Dusty and I were all over the news. I couldn't help but watch the TV monitors showing Dusty and I, with our hands raised, walking out of the barn. Then someone recognized me and suddenly I was the focus of everyone's attention. People were talking and pointing at me. It was very unsettling and I was glad when they finally let us on the plane where I took refuge behind the latest in-flight magazine. I knew this was just a taste of what was to come. Paula and I would be under a microscope for the duration of the trial and it wouldn't be pleasant.

Rebekah and the kids met me at the Denver airport. They were excited to see me and full of questions. The kids had seen the footage on the TV screens in the waiting area and were anxious to tell me they had seen me on TV. Rebekah was relieved, as she had been worried sick as usual. As we walked out of the terminal to the van, I fielded all their questions.

"You'd have thought the FBI would have had the decency to fly you back to Estes Park after you saved their ass," Rebekah said.

"Yeah, that would have been nice, but they didn't offer and I was too busy to worry about it. Martha was pretty upset."

"Yeah, I can imagine. I know how she must be feeling."

Rebekah was referring to the two times I had been in jail. The first time I was in the Marine Corps and I faced a court martial for allegedly killing my drill sergeant. The second time I was held in contempt of court after the Sarah Winters' trial and had to serve thirty days in the county jail. Luckily both of those incarcerations were short.

"So, what did you guys do today?" I asked.

"The kids went swimming this morning and we went on a nature trail this afternoon."

"Oh, great. Sounds like you had fun."

"We did," Reggi said. "They have a humungous pool."

"Really? Cool," I said. "I'll have to check it out."

"The kids had fun, but I missed you," Rebekah said.

"I missed daddy too," Marcia said.

I smiled and took Marcia's hand.

"I missed all of you, I said. . . . At least I was able to come back right away—thanks to Paula."

"Is she going to be all right without you?" Rebekah asked.

"Yeah. I should think so. She knows a lot more about criminal law than I do. Dusty's in good hands."

We arrived at the van and the kids climbed inside. Rebekah put her arms around me and said, "Good, because I don't want any more interruptions. I want you all to myself."

We kissed as the kids watched us intently.

"You can't have him every minute," Mark said. "Dad promised he'd teach us to fly fish."

I shook my head, smiled at Rebekah and said, "You're the one who wanted a big family."

When we got back to Estes Park it was late. Although it was summer the night was cool. Marcia was asleep so I carried her inside and put her to bed. The rest of the kids managed to stagger inside and jump in the sack on their own. After the kids were in bed and fast asleep, Rebekah and I went outside to look at the stars. In the city they barely shone but up here in the mountains they were bright and beautiful.

"I'm glad you're back," Rebekah said. "I was worried about you."

I put my arm around her and replied, "It was no big deal. I knew Dusty wouldn't hurt me. This whole thing makes no sense. I can't see Dusty killing anyone, even if it was an asshole like Bobby Tuttle."

"Maybe you didn't know him as well as you thought you did?"

"Maybe. It wouldn't be the first person I've misjudged."

We continued to wander through Colorado another week and ended up in Steamboat Springs. We had just returned from a jeep ride through the backcountry. The tour company had taken us up to an old abandoned mining camp where we were fed a big steak dinner. It was a rough ride but the landscape was spectacular and along the trail we saw deer, elk, and a big brown bear. When we returned to our cabin I noticed the message light on the telephone was blinking. "Shit!"

Rebekah jumped. "What!"

"There's a message for me."

"Oh, no. What now!"

"I don't know, but I better check it out," I said and picked up the phone. I dialed the number to get my messages and waited. After the explanatory remarks I heard a familiar voice. It was one of my best clients, Tex Weller. 'Stan, I'm in Ecuador concluding a little business venture. I need to wire some money into your trust account. I took the liberty of calling Jodie and getting wiring instructions. I hope you don't mind. I'll explain everything when I get back to Dallas next week. Sorry to bother you on your vacation, but I didn't want you to be surprised when you got your bank statement at the end of the month. Bye.'"

Rebekah looked at me expectantly. "So, what's up?"

"Oh, nothing important. Tex was just letting me know he was wiring me some money—some business venture he's winding up in Ecuador."

"Ecuador? I didn't know he did business in Ecuador."

"I didn't either. I wonder what in the hell he's doing down there."

"Why didn't he wire the money into his own account?" Rebekah asked.

"I don't know," I said. "It is a little strange but if it's a new venture he may want to set up a new corporation, get a tax ID number, and open up a bank account. From a bookkeeping standpoint it makes sense."

"Have any of your clients done that before?"

"No, but there's a first for everything."

"How much money is it?" Rebekah asked with a wry smile.

I laughed. "I don't know. He didn't say."

"How does he know you won't spend it?"

"I think that's why he called. He wanted to make sure I knew who it belonged to."

"Well, at least he didn't want you to rush back to Dallas."

"Thank God."

The next morning my curiosity got the better of me, so I called the office and asked Jodi about the wire transfer. Not that it mattered, but I was curious if the money had come and how much it was. She put me on hold while she called the bank.

"You won't believe this," she said.

"How much?"

"1.8 million."

"1.8 million? Holy shit! Did Tex say anything about what kind of deal he was into?"

"No, not a word."

"Okay, thanks. I'll see you in a couple days."

Tex had a little money and I had helped him set up a few small ventures, but this was way out of his league. I knew he was a sucker for any kind of get-rich-quick scheme that came down the pike. I wondered if one of them had finally panned out. I assumed Tex would have a reasonable explanation for how he got the money, but I couldn't help but feel a little uneasy about having it in my trust account. What if it were illegal? Was Tex using me to launder his money? I didn't think he would do that, but what if I was wrong about him?

# OBSESSION 3

You probably wonder why I am obsessed with Stan—why I can't just leave him alone. Well, I'll try to explain it, although you still may not understand. Ever since high school I have been searching for an intelligent, mature, and sensitive man that I could live with the rest of my life. I thought for sure I'd find that man at Highland Park High School or at UT, but it just didn't happen. Most of the boys I dated were immature and were threatened by my intelligence.

I was getting worried, by the time I got into law school, that I wouldn't ever find that man. Then at SMU I met and got to know Stan Turner. He was the man I had been looking for all those years. The only problem was he was married, had a family, and wasn't remotely interested in a romantic relationship with me.

Even so, I still found myself repeatedly trying to get his attention. But he was totally oblivious to my flirtations and vain efforts to lure him away from Rebekah. So, I tried just being a friend, but the more I got to know him, the more I wanted him all to myself. Maybe I'm a rotten person for even thinking of stealing a man away from his wife, but Rebekah is no saint either. She deserted Stan during his Marine Corps court martial and nearly divorced him. What kind of woman would do that? She's constantly complaining and whining about him working long hours and working too hard, yet she knew all along he was going to be an attorney and that long hours and hard work came with the territory.

After we graduated from law school I didn't see Stan for several years. We both went our separate ways. My search for a soul mate continued, but still with no success. What happened was, I found myself comparing every man I met with Stan and they'd always come up short. Then I started reading about him in the newspapers. He was getting all these great cases and the media loved him. I read everything they wrote about him and was sick that I wasn't a part of his life. Then fate brought us back together and I told myself; this time he would be mine. Well, it didn't work out exactly as I planned, but here I am smack dab in the middle of his exciting life.

Will I ever lure him to my bed? Well, the jury is still out on that one, but I know he likes me. I've caught him watching me many times and if I wear a sexy outfit to work, he can't keep his eyes off me. I like to tease him by getting up close and putting my hand on his shoulder or his arm and smiling affectionately. Sometimes I'll sneak up behind him and rub his back. I'm sure he enjoys it because he never tells me to stop. One day he'll come to the Condo and then—well, who knows what might happen.

I glanced at the clock and noticed it was almost nine o'clock. My fantasizing had to stop. I needed to be at Dusty Thomas' arraignment at ten. Earlier I had contacted the bail bondsman to see what the prospects were for getting Dusty a bond. It didn't look good as the only assets Dusty and Martha had were their home and land which was useless as bond collateral. At the hearing the judge cited the ruthless nature of the murder and the lack of any other suspects as justification for a $250,000 bond. Our bondsman wanted $25,000 in cash and assets worth at least $225,000 as collateral to put up the bond. This didn't appear to be possible so I informed Dusty that he might have to stay in jail awhile.

"But how will I pay my bills?" he complained.

"I don't know. Do you have any savings?"

"Shit, no. If I have to stay locked up we'll lose our ranch and Martha will be out on the street."

"Don't you have any relatives you could stay with?"

"No, my son lives in an old mobile home with just two bedrooms. The three eldest sleep in one room. He and his wife and the baby in the other. There is no way Martha could stay with them."

"Well, there is one other possibility." I said. "It's not a very attractive one but—"

"What is it? I just can't stay in jail."

"Well there is an organization that has contacted me and offered to put up your bail and pay for your defense."

Dusty's eyes widened. "Who would do that?"

"It's an organization called the Citizen's Defense Alliance or CDA. They are a radical, anti-government organization that champions the right of citizens to bear arms, less government control over our lives, and contends that the Sixteenth Amendment was never properly ratified."

"So, why do they care about me?"

"Well, the Sixteenth Amendment to the U.S. Constitution is the authority for our modern day income tax laws. They contend that the Sixteenth Amendment was never ratified and therefore the income tax is illegal. They like your case because, to them, it appears you are the first person to exercise your right to bear arms and defend your property against an illegal income tax."

"Yeah, but it's not true. I didn't kill the IRS agent."

"They don't care. It's what the public perceives that's important to them. They figure they will get millions of dollars of publicity from your case."

"So, what should I do?"

"It's probably not a good idea to be associated with a group like that. If you take their money it will appear you are guilty and believe that killing an IRS agent is justified."

"That does bring up a good question though."

"What's that?" I asked.

"How am I going to pay you guys?"

That *was* a good question and one that Stan and I should have carefully considered before taking on the case. Unfortunately, Stan rarely considered the economics of a case before plunging forward with it. Nor did he consult me about it. Of course, that was partially my fault because I didn't object to taking it on. I guess I got caught up in the excitement of it all and forgot I was supposed to be the guardian of the firm's pocketbook. Oh well, so much for fiscal responsibility. As I thought about it, this CDA offer was looking better and better.

"Didn't Stan discuss that with you?"

"No, it never crossed my mind until right this minute."

"Hmm. Let me talk to the CDA. If I make it clear to them that you are innocent and do not endorse or agree with their organization's tenets, and they still want to pay for defense, well, why not let them?"

"Okay, that sounds good to me. I'll do whatever it takes to get out of this place. I can't leave Martha alone another night."

"All right, then. I'll talk to their leader tomorrow morning, and if he agrees, I'll have you out by the end of the day."

"Oh, God. Thank you, Paula. I'm so glad Stan found you and brought you into the firm. You're a hell of an attorney."

I smiled. "Well, thank you Dusty. Be sure and tell Stan that, okay?"

"I damn sure will."

Raymond Farr, the Chairman of the CDA, was elated that Dusty was going to take him up on his offer. He said he'd have his finance chairman contact the bail bondsman and arrange for the necessary collateral and he'd put a check in the mail to us for $50,000 that day. I knew Stan would be pissed that the CDA had gotten involved in the case, but I figured I could blame it on Dusty. After all it's a free country and how the client gets the money for his fees is none of our business. The important thing is that Dusty would now get the best possible defense and we would be able to concentrate on proving him innocent without being distracted by our own financial problems. My ace in the hole, if all hell broke loose, would be Rebekah. She would be on my side on this one.

Now that I had dealt with Dusty's bail and our fees, I started thinking about how we were going to defend him. This was a critical period in the case as memories tended to fade over time and evidence often disappeared. I needed to start talking to witnesses and make an inventory of the evidence in the case. The FBI and the Collin County Sheriff's office had all the evidence.

This was kind of a strange case because of the federal involvement. I wondered if the Feds would invoke jurisdiction and take over prosecution of Dusty. I hoped that didn't happen as I knew the Texas judicial system much better than the federal. I also had a lot of friends in local law enforcement, which would make it easier for me to conduct discovery. I figured it was time to call the Collin County District Attorney's office and see what I could find out from them. Fortunately I knew an assistant DA who worked in that office. His name was Bart Williams and he and I had dated briefly when he worked at the Dallas DA's office. I called him.

"Paula, how are you?" Bart said.

"Great, I'm in a partnership now with Stan Turner."

"I heard. How's that going?"

"Well, I guess you know we got the Dusty Thomas case."

"Yes, good luck. You guys gonna plead him out?"

"Good God, no. He's innocent."

Bart chuckled. "Innocent? Okay. . . . Whatever you say."

"Hey, I've got to come up there and check out some evidence. You want to get a bite to eat?"

"Sure, I'd like that. You're not seeing anyone?"

"Not on a regular basis. Been too busy."

"Right. I can imagine."

"Twelve o'clock at the hospital cafeteria?"

"Sounds good."

The only decent place to eat in McKinney was the Collin County Hospital cafeteria. They had a trustee from the Collin County jail working there at lunch who used to run the kitchen at the Mansion. When he got arrested for possession and had to serve time in the Collin County jail, they put him to work in the hospital cafeteria. At lunch each day there were more business people eating there than patients and employees. I arrived a few minutes early and found a spot at the end of one of the long tables. Bart was short, muscular and well tanned. He was good in bed but had few other redeeming qualities. But being in the Collin County DA's office made him invaluable to me so I decided it was time to rekindle our relationship. I spotted him walking in the door so I waved. He looked over at me, smiled and made his way to where I was seated.

"Hi, Paula," he said taking a seat across from me.

"Thanks for meeting me," I said. "I really didn't want to make contact with your office without knowing a little bit about what was going on."

"Makes sense. What do you want to know?"

"At the arraignment there was some talk about the feds taking over prosecution of the case. What's the status of that?"

"It's not going to happen."

"Why not? I would have figured the feds would want to try Dusty."

"Yeah, but we talked them out of it."

"Why?" I asked.

"You know the last time they executed a federal prisoner?"

"Oh. They want Dusty to die."

"Exactly. They have to set an example here. We've promised to ask for the death penalty."

"Well, I appreciate you sharing that information with me. Have they assigned a prosecutor yet?"

"Yes, Trenton Lee. He has the most experience and the best track record. He'll be assisted by Sara Leon, a black girl who grew up in south Dallas and is tough as titanium."

21

"I've heard of her. She worked her way through law school shooting pool, didn't she?"

"That's what they say."

After we ate lunch we got a room at the Holiday Inn and had incredible sex. It was just like old times and I was getting a lot of great information. Bart had never been able to resist me so I took advantage of my power over him to get all the information I needed. It's not like I was doing anything unethical or illegal. The prosecution is supposed to share all their evidence with the defense anyway. I was just getting it much earlier in the game and without having to jump through the usual hoops. Of course, if Bart blurted out a few secrets along the way, I couldn't help that.

"Well, I had a great time this afternoon, Bart. We'll have to do this again sometime."

Bart smiled and nodded. "Absolutely."

"Oh, I was wondering, did your lab guys come up with anything that would prove for sure that Dusty's gun was the murder weapon?"

"No, you know shotguns. The bullets shatter and scatter. We do know, though, that your guy had a Remington and the shooter used a Remington. We could tell by the plastic wads bearing the Remington mark that we found in the body. The shell casings the FBI found all over the ranch and the live ammunition they confiscated from Dusty's house all matched and were consistent with what they pulled out of Bobby Tuttle's chest.

"But, you don't have conclusive proof that Dusty's gun was the murder weapon?"

"No, not conclusive, but pretty convincing."

Dusty took me to the Collin County DA's office and introduced me to Trenton Lee and Sara Leon. I was on my best behavior and told them I was looking forward to working with them. They gave me a list of their evidence and they made arrangements for me to inspect it later in the week. Included in the evidence, I was told, were dozens of bitter letters from Dusty to the IRS. He was very angry and apparently had threatened Agent Tuttle on more than one occasion.

Other supposedly damning evidence were gunshot residue found on Dusty's hands after his arrest (which he claimed was due to the warning shot he had fired early in the confrontation) and witness statements from several agents and law enforcement officers who had seen altercations between Agent Tuttle and Thomas over the years.

Depression overcame me on my drive back to Dallas. No matter where I looked it seemed everything pointed to Dusty's guilt. Maybe Stan's gut feeling about Dusty's innocence was wrong. Maybe Dusty's long battle with the IRS had finally driven him to murder. Could we plead temporary insanity? I wondered. When Dusty saw the agent on his property was he so enraged he just snapped? This was Collin County, where Candy Montgomery chopped her husband into little pieces with an axe and successfully claimed temporary insanity. I made a mental note to talk to Stan about that possibility.

When I got back to the office there was a message from Stan. He was at a motel in Steamboat Springs, Colorado. I wondered why he would be calling me. I didn't expect to hear from him for another couple days. I picked up the phone and dialed the number. The motel operator answered. She rang Stan's room.

"Hello."

"Stan?"

"Paula, hi," Stan said. "What's going on?"

"Oh, I just got back from the Collin County DA's office."

"Did you learn anything?"

"They're going for the death penalty."

"I figured they'd have to. . . . Listen, I heard some rather disturbing news on the TV a little while ago."

"What's that?" I asked.

"There's a report the CDA is putting up Dusty's bond."

A chill came over me. "Yeah, that's right. Dusty just couldn't handle it in jail so he jumped at their offer to put up the bond. I told him it was crazy and could jeopardize his case but—"

"Crazy? It's suicide! The feds are going to go berserk over this. Not only that, they'll be after us too. If they think we are in any way connected or sympathetic with the CDA, they'll put us on their hit list and make our lives miserable for the next hundred years. You've got to stop this right now."

I took a deep breath. I figured Stan would be mad, but this was more than I expected. "It's too late. The bonds already been put up and Dusty's going to be on the street in twenty minutes."

"Oh, my God. How could you have let this happen! . . . We're on our way home." The phone went dead. I stared at it a minute in shock. Stan was a very mild mannered man and it was so out of character for him to hang up on someone, let alone me. I felt sick.

Jodie walked in and gave me an inquisitive look. "Did I hear you talking to Stan?" She asked.

I forced a smile. "Right. He's coming home early. He'll be here the day after tomorrow."

Jodie gave me a hard look. I guess she saw the fear in my eyes. What had I done? "Is everything all right?" she asked.

Another forced smile. "Yeah, Stan's a little upset that the CDA is putting up Dusty's bond."

"The CDA?"

"Yeah, wait 'til he finds out I just deposited a $50,000 check from them into our account."

Jodie's mouth dropped. "You didn't?"

"Listen, Jodie. You've got to help me out here. I've heard you complain that Stan's too easy on his clients and often works for nothing, right?"

"Yes. But the CDA is a terrorist organization."

"Well, do you think Dusty could have paid us to defend him?"

She shrugged. "I guess not, but—."

"So, when the CDA offered to fund the case I jumped at it. Nobody's going to think badly of us because we took the CDA's money. It doesn't mean we support them or have anything to do with them. Attorneys take money from criminals and drug dealers every day. It's no big deal."

"It will be a big deal to Stan. I think I'll be sick the rest of the week."

"Fine, desert me. I'm just trying to do what's best for the firm. I guarantee you won't be getting any more calls from creditors as long as I'm part of this law firm. . . . Shit, you're probably due for raise, aren't you?"

Jodie gave me a tentative nod.

"Well, I know Stan thinks of you not so much as a secretary, but as a personal assistant and confidante."

"What do you mean?"

"He likes you a lot and, if it weren't for Rebekah—"

"That is ridiculous! Stan has never made any—"

"Calm down. I'm not suggesting anything has gone on between you two. I'm just saying you are very important to him and if you side with me on this issue it would be very helpful. . . . And I'll see to it that you get that raise you deserve."

"I don't need a raise," Jodie protested. "I just don't like Stan having to worry about money all the time."

"Because you care about him, just like I care about him. He's a kind and generous man and people take advantage of him. We have to protect him from those people and himself."

"All right. I'll try to help you out, but I'm not doing it for me. I'm doing it for Stan. You're right, this case could break him financially. I don't want that to happen."

I didn't have to force the smile that came over me this time. "Good girl. You're making a wise decision."

# CDA 4

Rebekah and the kids were pretty upset that we had to cut our vacation short. We had planned to take the train through the Royal Gorge and everyone had really been looking forward to it. I hated coming home early, but I was so sick over the CDA involvement in Dusty's case that I couldn't sleep or ever think about anything else. I had to get home and try to undo what had happened in my absence. Paula just didn't understand what it would mean to have the CDA supporting Dusty. Neo-Nazi anarchists who'd just as soon slice your throat as say good morning, ran their organization. The CDA had one overriding tenet: the overthrow of the United States Government. Obviously, if they could drum up support for the proposition that the income tax was illegal, it would create chaos in Washington and give them the opportunity they were looking for to seize power. It was a pretty ridiculous idea, but the people in charge at the CDA were not very realistic. We drove straight through and got back home to Dallas in the middle of the night. I carried Marcia in and put her to bed. Then I went back for Peter who was still asleep in the backseat. Reggi and Mark helped me unload the van and then went upstairs. As I climbed into bed I looked at Rebekah lying there asleep. She was so beautiful and I loved her so much. Why did everything have to be so hard for us? It scared me to think of what lie ahead.

Although exhausted from the long drive, it took me forever to fall asleep. When I awoke it was daylight outside. I looked at the clock radio and was shocked to see it was eleven o'clock. Rebekah was nowhere to be seen, so I wandered around the house looking for her. I found her washing clothes.

"Well, look who's up," she said

"Why did you let me sleep so late?"

"You needed it after driving twelve hours straight."

"Yeah, I guess. Where are the kids?"

"The boys are still asleep. Marcia is in her room playing with the Indian dolls you bought her."

"Hmm. Got any coffee made?" I asked.

"A pot is on the stove."

I headed for the kitchen, found a cup and poured myself some coffee. As I sat down at the kitchen table I noticed the newspaper laying there still in its plastic wrapper. I pulled off the plastic and the paper unfolded before me. The headlines took my breath away.

## CDA TO FUND DUSTY THOMAS DEFENSE
## TURNER LAW FIRM GIVEN $50,000 RETAINER

I read the story incredulously. Paula hadn't mentioned the CDA paying us. What was going on? How could she not tell me that little detail? I was outraged.

After quickly getting dressed, I kissed Rebekah goodbye and raced to the office. Fortunately, I had cooled down a little before I got there. *Okay, let her explain. Don't be an asshole.* Jodie gave me a sympathetic smile as I walked in. She asked if Rebekah and the kids had enjoyed Colorado.

"Yes, they loved it. It's so beautiful this time of year and so much cooler than around here."

"I bet. I'm sorry about all the interruptions."

"It's all right. Just one of the joys of practicing law," I said trying to keep my cool. "Anything *else* happen while I was gone I need to know about?"

"No. Other than Dusty and Tex it was very quiet. . . . Oh, we may be getting a new corporate client. A representative of a Fortune 500 company called and said we were under consideration for some contract work. He said he was looking at several firms, but that we had a good shot at it. I gave him our reference list."

"Good. Some steady contract work from a client who can actually pay for it would be great. What company was it?"

"He didn't say. Apparently the search is hush-hush until a decision is made."

"Hmm." I smiled at Jodie and then walked into Paula's office.

She looked up but didn't smile. "So, we've got a fat bank account now," I said.

Paula frowned. "I was going to tell you, but you cut me off. Dusty didn't have the money to pay us and we can't try this case for nothing."

"You don't feel like a slimeball taking their money?"

"No, not at all. I'm only thinking of Dusty. His life is at stake and he's gonna die if we can't prove he's innocent."

Jodie appeared at the door and swallowed hard. I glanced at her and then looked back at Paula. "Once you get in bed with these bastards your reputation turns to shit. We'll have every scumball in the world knocking at our door. Worse yet, the government is going to think we're corrupt and they'll be bugging our phones and following us everywhere we go."

"Your overreacting," Paula said. "Everyone has a right to defend themselves. Reputable law firms can defend criminals. It happens every day."

"I don't like it. We could have raised the money from other sources. I'm sure Dusty's church could have helped raise some money."

Paula laughed. "Right, we're gonna do this case for $5,000?"

"She's right," Jodie said. "It'll take a truck load of money to win this case. You can't be worrying about paying the rent every month. You won't have time for that."

I looked at Jodie and then Paula. Was I being too idealistic? It felt wrong to take the CDA money and I was sick about it. But Paula and Jodie were right about one thing. I couldn't afford any distractions if we were to have a prayer of saving Dusty's life. The question was: If we failed, what would be the consequences of our alliance with the devil?

# THE DEPOSIT 5

On Monday, July 21, I starting digging around my desk which was cluttered with mail, files, and messages that had accumulated during my vacation. It was a task I didn't relish but had to face. As I sorted through the phone messages I came across a telephone message from my bank officer, Billie Jo. She usually called because we were overdrawn in our bank account, but I knew that couldn't be the problem since Paula had just deposited $50,000. Curious, I placed the call.

"Billie Jo. You called?"

"Yes, we were just wondering if you wanted us to invest your excess funds overnight. You can usually make a little interest on your money if we do that."

Suddenly I remembered my conversation with Tex and the money he had wired to my account. I had been expecting ten or fifteen thousand dollars, not 1.8 million. What in hell kind of venture had he gotten into? It occurred to me I'd be raising a red flag if I acted surprised about the money so I said, "Oh, yeah. One of my high-rolling clients is going to buy a small apartment complex. Ah, is there any risk if you invest the money overnight?"

"No, it's fully guaranteed and secured. We do it all the time for our customers."

"Okay, I guess he'd want his money earning as much interest as possible."

"I'll take care of it," Billie Jo said. "Oh, and Stan, Robert Winger, our President wanted to know if you'd like to go to lunch next week?"

That blew my mind. Robert Winger normally wouldn't give me the time of day. Now that I had over a million sitting in his bank, he wanted to take me out to lunch. I should have said no, but suddenly I was curious about what he'd have to say.

"Sure, sounds like fun. Just tell me where and when."

"Okay, I'll coordinate it with Jodie."

The invitation to lunch with the bank president nearly made me forget it was Tex's money sitting in my bank account. I called Tex at his office but his secretary said he was still out of town. Apparently he was due back but hadn't shown up. I called his house to see if his wife Toni knew when he'd be back.

"Gosh, Stan. He was due in yesterday but something must have come up. Frankly, it's not that unusual for him to delay a return from a business trip but he usually calls and lets me know when to expect him."

"He hasn't called then?"

"No, not yet."

"Did he tell you where he was going?"

"Yes, to Ecuador. He was working on some kind of loan for a client."

Tex was more than an insurance agent. He was a financial consultant, business advisor and confidant. Once a business owner became his client he was there to help solve any problem that might come up. It was not unusual for him to act as a loan broker either. He had lots of connections and often could help out in that regard. The problem with Tex, however, was that he was a sucker for any get rich-scheme that came down the pike. He'd often call me to tell me about the latest pyramid he had joined or silver mining stock he'd bought. I would always tell him it was a scam, but he'd do it anyway and get burned. Over the years Tex referred to me considerable business, and I had grown very fond of him and Toni. They often came over for dinner and always were the first to arrive at our annual Christmas party. Now I was worried. *Where are you Tex? What have you been up to?*

"Ecuador? That seems like an odd place to get a loan."

"I know. It seemed strange to me, but I've learned not to question him. He gets very upset if I get too inquisitive."

"Well, apparently he was successful. He wired some money into my trust account a day or two ago. That's why I called. I wanted to let him know the money arrived and find out what he wanted me to do with it."

"Oh, well. That's good news. He should be back here soon then."

"I'm sure he will. I'll talk to you tomorrow."

It didn't seem prudent to tell Toni the amount of money that had been wired. That would have really shaken her. I wondered if I should contact the authorities and report Tex missing, but what if he was into something illegal? I didn't want to get him in trouble—particularly since the money was in *my* bank account. I figured I better wait and pray that Tex showed up. If he didn't, I'd have to go looking for him.

Paula walked in and reminded me that Dusty was coming by in twenty minutes to work on his defense. This was going to be our first real opportunity to question him thoroughly on the events of July 11. Hopefully he would provide us with some leads as to other suspects in Agent Tuttle's murder. He was dressed in blue jeans and a red shirt when he walked into the reception area. Jodie showed him into my office. Paula then joined us and the interrogation began.

"So, how are you holding up, Dusty?" I asked.

"I've been better."

"How about Martha? How's she doing?"

"She's really scared I'll be convicted. She's a strong woman but when I was locked up and she was alone, she nearly died. It's a good thing you got me out when you did."

"Well, we've got a lot of work to do if there is any hope of keeping you out of jail."

"I know it's gonna be a hard case, but you've got to believe me when I tell you: I didn't kill that cocksucker. I thought about it a few times, but I'm not a killer."

Paula said, "You need to be careful how you characterize Agent Tuttle. If someone hears you call him a 'cocksucker' or any other derogatory term, it could come back to haunt you."

"That's right," I said. "I know you hated him, but from this day forward you've got to forgive and forget."

Dusty shrugged. "Whatever you say. You're the boss."

"Now, it's important that you not talk about the CDA. If anyone asks you about them your response is, no comment. If anyone asks you about the case your response is, no comment. Understood?"

He nodded and said, "Got it."

"Tell us everything you remember about July 11th. Start from the moment you got out of bed."

"I got up about six. Martha fixed me breakfast and we watched "Daybreak" for a spell. The weatherman came on and said it might rain. That upset me 'cause I had a mowing job scheduled that day. One of my friends is a county commissioner and when he heard about my IRS problems he offered me some mowing work for the county. Since the only thing the IRS hadn't taken was my tractor, it was about the only work I could get. Anyway, the job was gonna take me most the day, but if it rained I might not finish. I don't get paid until the job is done so I was praying it wouldn't rain.

"About ten past seven I loaded the tractor and pulled it over to the location where I was supposed to start. I was only able to mow about an hour and a half before the rain came. If it had just rained a little it wouldn't have been any big deal, but it was a gully washer. So, I put the tractor back on the trailer and drove home. After parking the trailer in the driveway, I went inside. Martha had gone somewhere so I made myself a sandwich and watched the noon news. After eating, I got my shotgun and walked the perimeter of my property. Fortunately, it had stopped raining. I walk the property at least once a week to check for holes in the fence."

"Why did you take your shotgun?" Paula asked.

"Just a habit, I suppose. You never know what you'll run across out there—coyotes, wolves, bobcats, trespassers or the like."

"Did you see anybody or anything?" I asked.

"No."

"Then what happened?" I asked.

"When I got back to the house I went inside to see if Martha was back. She wasn't, so I was about to turn on the TV when I heard a shot. It startled me, so I grabbed my gun and went outside to see what was going on. The agent was lying on the ground with blood gushing from his chest. I looked around to see who had shot him, but I didn't see anyone. Whoever did it was long gone."

"Did you see or hear a vehicle?" Paula asked.

Dusty thought a moment and replied, "Not that I can recollect . . . Unfortunately, the wrecker driver showed up about that time and all I could think about was how it must look with me standing over the body with a shotgun in my hand. I know it was a mistake to run, but I was just plum scared. I just wanted to get away where I could think things through."

"When you ran, did you see anybody or anything?" I asked.

"No, there were some fresh tire tracks on the driveway that I hadn't seen before. Since it had been raining they were really easy to spot. I'd guess they were from a big car or a pickup."

"You sure they were fresh?"

"Oh, yes. They were still wet."

"I wonder if the FBI or the sheriff's crime scene crew found those tracks?" I said.

"I don't know, there were so many vehicles out there that night they may have run right over them," Paula said.

"Why don't you see if the tracks are still there, Dusty?" I suggested. "If they are we can send somebody out there to make a plaster imprint."

"They're gone. It's rained hard since then."

After our interview with Dusty ended, Jodie brought me a message from Toni. She had found something in Tex's office that I should see. She wanted me to come over immediately. Tex lived in Grand Prairie, so it took me an hour to get there. They lived in an old, English-style home that had been built in the late 70s. Toni was an interior decorator by trade, so the home was a showpiece. An Hispanic woman, still quite attractive at age fifty-five. Toni seemed much more upset than she had been earlier on the telephone. She led me inside to Tex's office.

"I was going through Tex's desk and I found this letter," she said. It read:

14 July 1986

Victor Alfaro
Credit Officer
United Peoples Bank of Ecuador
1 United Plaza
Quito, Republic of Ecuador

Dear Mr. Weller:

I write you this letter of assistance with a great sense of honor and responsibility. The decision to write you was arrived at after a critical consideration of the urgency of this transaction. Before I go further, let me seize this great opportunity to sincerely apologize for shock this letter will certainly cause you as we have not had any correspondence in the past.

Let me introduce myself. My name is Victor Alfaro and I am a credit officer with the United Peoples Bank of Ecuador. I came to know you from a private search for a reliable and reputable person to handle a confidential transaction, which involves the transfer of a large sum of money to a foreign account requiring maximum discretion. I shall very much appreciate your kind consideration of this proposal and stand ready to provide further enlightenment on this issue as you might require.

A U.S. citizen, the late Dr. John Wells, a mining engineer working for the Federal Government of Ecuador, died during the coup instituted against Gen. Guillermo Rodriqes Lara in 1977. At his death he had a balance with our bank of $1.8 million U.S. The money remains at the bank in expectation of a next-of-kin as beneficiary.

Frantic efforts have been made by the United Peoples Bank of Ecuador to get in touch with any of the Wells family or relatives but to no success. It is because of this perceived possibility of not being able to locate any of Dr. Wells's next-of-kin (he has no wife or children that is known to us) the management of our bank, under the influence of the Chairman and the Board of Directors, has determined that the funds should be declared unclaimed and turned over to the military dictators now in control of the government. In all certainty these funds will end up in one of the general's pockets. To avert this negative development, some of my trusted colleagues and I now seek your permission to have you stand as next-of-kin to the late Dr. John Wells, so that the fund US$1.8 million will be released and paid into your account as beneficiary's next of kin.

My colleagues and myself have made several attempts at locating persons that could be remotely related to Dr. Wells and we have been doing this diligently since his death. We are therefore requesting for your help and we will be immeasurably grateful if you would be willing. We have access to most of what it will take to transfer the money. The only thing we do not have is someone who will work with us and act as the late Dr. Wells' next-of-kin. We will provide you with answers to all the security questions that you will have to answer to acquire possession of the money. You will also be given answers to questions that only a person related to Dr. Wells would know. At the end of the transaction you will stand to get 35% of the fund with the rest for me and my colleagues. If you are interested and agree to work with us, then contact me immediately at my private number +112-555-474-9143.

Our sincere thanks for your consideration of this proposal and your anticipated assistance.

Best Regards,
Victor Alfaro

"You don't think he accepted the proposal, do you?" I said incredulously.

"Well, you know Tex and he did go to Ecuador. I found a credit card receipt for the plane ticket—Dallas to Miami and then to Quito, Ecuador."

I did know Tex and the $1.8 million also coincided with the amount of money that was deposited into my trust account. I couldn't believe Tex would get involved in something so clearly fraudulent and illegal. But the fact that he actually got the money was the real shocker. Rarely do these types of schemes pay off.

"Apparently the scam worked. The 1.8 million is sitting in my trust account," I said.

"Oh, my God!" Toni said.

"I just wonder what went wrong. Tex should be back by now."

"What should we do?" Toni asked. "I'm so worried."

"I don't know. I've got to think this through. Let me take this file and I'll call you if I figure anything out. If you hear from Tex, call me immediately, okay?"

"Yes, the minute he calls . . . thank you so much for coming over."

"No problem. I'm just sorry all this happened. If you need anything call me or Rebekah. We'll be happy to help."

My mind raced as I drove home trying to sort out Tex's scam. Something must have happened after he had the money wired. Was it a double-cross? Did Mr. Alfaro and his colleagues kill Tex once the money was transferred? If so, how would they get the money out of the bank account? Or was Tex trying to keep all the money for himself? Maybe that's why he sent it to my trust account . . . All these questions gnawed at me the entire evening. I didn't know what to do. I couldn't go to the authorities without compromising Tex—and perhaps myself. Like Dusty standing with his shotgun over the body of a dead IRS agent, here I was in possession of $1.8 million in stolen money. We both were innocent, but was there a chance in hell anyone would believe us?

# THE AUDIT **6**

Within a few days of the announcement of Dusty's acceptance of financial assistance from the CDA, I noticed I was being followed. A blue Chevy Cavalier shadowed me wherever I went. When I got to my destination and parked, the two young FBI agents inside slid back in their seats and waited. I was tempted to go up to them and say hello, but figured they might not appreciate so bold a gesture. It bothered me that I was being watched. I wondered if my telephones were also being tapped. That would be a breach of the attorney-client privilege so I was fairly confident no judge would sign off on such a request, but I wasn't one hundred percent sure. As a precaution, Paula and I agreed not to communicate about the case by telephone. This was extremely inconvenient and annoying.

The first real strike from the IRS came when we got notice of an audit. This was such an obvious dirty trick, I couldn't believe the IRS even tried it. Had this been just a routine audit, I might have overlooked it, but this was a comprehensive audit asking for thousands of documents and records that would have taken months to gather. After discussing the audit at length, Paula and I decided we couldn't let the IRS get away with this tactic. We filed an emergency application for a TRO in Federal District Court to quash the subpoena and audit of our records on the grounds that it was harassment calculated to interfere with our criminal defense of Dusty Thomas. Several days later a hearing was held on the application in the courtroom located in the Earl Cabell Federal Building in downtown Dallas. Anthony Lopez, an assistant U.S. Attorney for the Northern District of Texas, represented the Internal Revenue Service. The Honorable Winston Stanton was on the bench.

"Your Honor," I said. "As the court is no doubt aware, this firm represents Dusty Thomas, on trial for the alleged murder of Bobby Tuttle, special agent for the Internal Revenue Service. Several weeks ago it became public knowledge, through several media stories, that the Citizens Defense Alliance had provided financial assistance to Dusty Thomas for his defense of these criminal charges brought against him. It's common knowledge the CDA has been under the close scrutiny of several federal agencies including the IRS and FBI. The day after these media stories came out, my associate and I noticed that we were being followed and were the subject of electronics surveillance. We don't know if this surveillance has been legally authorized or if it has been done illegally, but it is our firm belief that, in either event, it violates our client's right to a fair and impartial trial, infringes on his constitutional right to counsel, and violates the confidential relationship between attorney and client."

"In addition to this outrageous interference with the defendant's right to counsel, our firm now has been singled out by the IRS for a full administrative audit calculated to distract it from its defense of Mr. Thomas. The Service, I'm sure, will contend that we were randomly picked, but we are not so naive to believe it is just a coincidence. We are prepared today to put on testimony and evidence to support these allegations and request the court to quash and enjoin this unconscionable conduct of the government."

"Thank you, Mr. Turner. Mr. Lopez, what does the government say about this?" the judge asked.

"Your Honor, ordinarily the government would not concern itself with the activities of the attorneys for a criminal defendant. But in certain circumstances where it appears that the attorneys themselves may be involved in criminal conduct, the state has the right to watch those attorneys and gather evidence of their criminal pursuits. It is true that Mr. Turner and his associate have been under surveillance, but such surveillance was duly authorized by appropriate court order. We are prepared today to present evidence of criminal conduct by the Turner Law Firm including the receipt by wire transfer of $1.8 million from Georgetown, Cayman Islands. Perhaps Mr. Turner would like to enlighten the court on the source of those funds and for what purpose they have been received."

Fear and outrage swept over me as Lopez issued his challenge. I hadn't anticipated the government monitoring my trust account. Banking was supposed to be private, so I had thought. So much for *that* illusion. I knew I had to respond vigorously now or the court would suspect the government had hit pay dirt. I took a deep breath and looked into Paula's troubled eyes. I wondered if she now regretted our partnership.

"Your Honor, I would be delighted to enlighten the government as to the $1.8 million dollars in my trust account except for the fact that it would violate my client's attorney-client privilege. I will represent to the court that this money has nothing to do with Dusty Thomas or the CDA. This is money wired to my account by a different client for legitimate business purposes. Your Honor, this is just another example of the government's flagrant trespass on our right to privacy and the right to have a confidential relationship with our clients."

Judge Stanton replied, "Mr. Lopez. I'm inclined to agree with Mr. Turner. It seems the government is assuming guilt by association. Unless you have some concrete evidence of criminal conduct or some direct evidence linking the $1.8 million to some criminal activity, I'm going to enjoin the surveillance of the defendant's counsel. As to the audit, unless you are prepared to show me how the Turner Law Firm was randomly picked by audit, I will quash the subpoena and abate the audit until the criminal prosecution has been concluded. Do you want to put on your evidence, Mr. Lopez?"

Lopez looked over at a man seated in the gallery. The man shook his head. Lopez turned and addressed the judge. "No, Your Honor."

I breathed a sigh of relief and smiled at Paula. After the judge left the bench, we packed up our briefcases and left the courtroom. Reporters mobbed us as we exited the elevators.

"Mr. Turner, do you support the CDA?" a reporter asked.

"No," I replied.

"Then why did you accept money from them?" the reporter asked.

"I didn't accept money from them. Our client did. It was his decision," I replied.

"Does your client support the CDA?"

"No more questions please. We have no further comment," I said as we made our way through the crowd and out onto Commerce Street. Much to our shock and disgust the CDA was just outside the door picketing in full force. One sign read: "Dusty is our hero!" Another read: "Strike Down the IRS!" A television crew that had been filming the demonstration turned its cameras on us as we walked across the street to the parking lot. After escaping from the melee, Paula and I stopped at El Chico on McKinney Avenue for a drink. I was still reeling from events and needed to calm my nerves.

"Who was that guy with Lopez?" I asked.

"That was his boss, Rupert Meadows," Paula replied.

"The U.S. Attorney?"

"That's right," Paula replied.

"You'd think he'd have more important things to do than babysit his prosecutors."

"This is a big case. He's under a lot of pressure to nail our collective ass."

"I hate it when I'm a target. It takes the fun out of the case," I said.

"Yeah, you got that right," Paula said before taking her drink and draining it.

I finished off my drink as well, and we ordered two more.

"Well, now at least we can use the phone," I said.

Paula raised her glass, smiled, and said, "Here's to Ma Bell."

I nodded, raising my glass in turn. "So, it appears I'm going to have to go find Tex and get him back here. The FBI and the IRS aren't going to forget about the $1.8 million in my trust account despite Judge Stanton's ruling."

Paula gave me a solemn look and replied, "Do you think he's alive?"

"I hope so. I can't figure how it would benefit them to kill him. They need him alive so they can retrieve their money."

"If you go down there, what will you do?"

"I've got a contact at the bank. My only link to Tex. I hope to hell I can find him."

"Maybe you should just report Tex missing and let the authorities find him," Paula said. "I don't want *you* disappearing on me."

"I'm not going alone. I'm not *that* stupid. I'm bringing Monty Dozier with me. He's a good private investigator and he speaks Spanish. Since we've got cash in the bank now, I can afford to do this first class."

"Are you doing this on your own or is Toni hiring you to find Tex?"

"We haven't discussed money. We'll sort that out later."

Paula raised her eyebrows and shook her head. "No, you always discuss money first. Clients don't have much incentive to pay you after the job is done."

"Well, I'm sorry," I said, perturbed. "I just couldn't bring that up when she was in such distress."

"I know . . . anyway, I'll work on the Thomas case while you're gone. Hopefully it won't take you long to find him."

"Hopefully."

I felt bad about leaving Paula alone in the middle of a murder investigation, but I had no choice. If I didn't find Tex, nobody would. I figured the quicker I got down to Ecuador the better. I hadn't contacted Monty yet, so I gave him a call. He seemed excited with the assignment and agreed to meet me at the DFW Airport in the morning. That night I broke the news to Rebekah.

"Ecuador? Why in the hell do you need to go down there?" Rebekah moaned.

"Tex got in some bad shit down there and I've got to go find him. Monty's coming along, so I'll be safe."

"Oh, God. I'm going to be worried sick. Can't Monty go by himself? He's a PI. You stay home."

"He doesn't know Tex and isn't familiar enough with the case to go by himself. Besides, it's better for two people to go. It's less likely anyone will give us any trouble."

Rebekah, knowing it was no use arguing, turned her attention to helping me pack and otherwise prepare for the trip. While she was packing, I called the airlines and bought our tickets. I was starting to get excited about the journey ahead even though it wasn't exactly a vacation. For some reason, I was sure Tex was alive. I just couldn't understand why he hadn't returned home or at least called. Was he having to play the role of the heir of Dr. Wells for a while? Was that it? I put a picture of Tex that Toni had given me in my briefcase along with copies of the correspondence from Victor Alfaro. It was precious little to go on, but it was all I had.

As Rebekah cuddled up next to me in bed that night, I wondered where I'd be in twenty-four hours and if I'd feel nearly as secure as I did at that moment. Was I a fool for running off to a third-world country looking for a lost cowboy? If I was killed or kidnapped, what would Rebekah and kids do without me? I had taken out a million-dollar life insurance policy, so they wouldn't be destitute if I died. That gave me some comfort, but the thought of losing them made me tremble. I rolled over and pretended to go to sleep so Rebekah wouldn't feel my anguish. It was a time to pray, something I didn't often do. But tonight I needed God's help if I were to find Tex and return us both home safe and sound.

# THE EX-WIFE 7

Stan's sudden departure for Ecuador on July 25 left me stunned and shaken. We were partners after all and I didn't expect him to desert me in the middle of the biggest murder trial to hit North Texas in twenty years. I understood that Tex was a good friend, but he didn't have any obligation to go searching for him on another continent. I regretted not objecting more to Stan's departure. Maybe had I verbalized my displeasure to him in no uncertain terms, he would have reconsidered. Now it was too late. Dusty Thomas' fate was in my hands. As I sat at my desk, I made a list of the witnesses I needed to visit.

> *Maureen Ruth Tuttle – Bobby Tuttle's ex-wife*
> *Stella Tuttle Morris – Bobby's sister*
> *Robert Perkins – Bobby's supervisor at the IRS*
> *Roy Jenkins – Bobby's best friend*

I didn't know what kind of reaction to expect when I called Maureen Tuttle. Chances were she still had feelings for Bobby so she probably wouldn't be anxious to talk to me. When I called her she was cool but agreed to meet me for lunch. Since she lived in Highland Park we met at a little café in North Park known for its luscious desserts. She was a tall brunette, slender and good looking. I wondered if the big diamond ring on her finger was a remnant of her marriage to Bobby or the promise of things to come. We were escorted to a small booth and given menus.

"This is a dangerous place to eat," I said. "I'm addicted to strawberry cheesecake."

"That's why I work out every day, so I don't have to watch what I eat," Maureen replied.

"God, I wish I had the time to work out. It just seems like I'm always under the gun."

"Well, that's what you get for being a career girl. As for me, I'm old fashioned. I believe a woman's place is at the mall."

We laughed. The waiter appeared and took our orders. Soup and salad for me, spinach quiche for Maureen. I wondered how to discreetly steer the conversation to Maureen's deceased ex-husband. She didn't seem to be in mourning so I took a gamble that she had gotten over his death.

"Listen, I hate to bother you with a bunch of questions so soon after Bobby's death, but my client insists he's innocent. You know how that is. They all claim to be innocent no matter how damning the evidence, right? Anyway, I'm duty bound to investigate and see if there is any evidence to support his claim. Can't have an innocent man convicted of Bobby's death."

"No, but I seriously doubt you'll find any evidence to support his innocence. From what I understand your client was caught red-handed."

"It does appear that way, but appearances can be deceptive. Let me start by asking you to tell me something about Bobby. Describe him—give me a little background information on him."

"Sure. Let's see. Bobby was a Leo. He was a leader and liked to be in control. Of course, he was very intelligent, had a big ego, and was exceedingly self-centered. That's why we're not married anymore. He treated me like I was his personal love slave—always giving me orders and telling me what I could or couldn't do. "

"Why did you marry him? That kind of personality is hard to disguise."

"He's very good looking and can charm a girl out of her pantyhose, if you know what I mean. I fell in love and as they say, love is blind."

"Where did Bobby grow up?"

"California—the Bay Area. His father was a salesman for IBM and his mother managed a bookstore. He joined the Army when he was seventeen, and after serving four years as a quartermaster left the service and went to college under the GI bill. He got his Associate Degree from Richland College and then joined the IRS."

"So, how long were you two married?" I asked.

"Six years. Fortunately, we didn't have children. It was a joint decision. Neither of us wanted to be tied down. We wanted to enjoy life while we were young. In retrospect it was probably a mistake. Our life never seemed to have purpose."

"So, how did Bobby like his job?"

"He absolutely loved it. He liked wielding power over peoples' lives. He assumed every taxpayer he was assigned was a tax evader and it was his job to prove it. I personally wouldn't have had the stomach for the job, but Bobby got off on it."

"Was your divorce bitter?"

"No, not any more than usual."

"What made you finally break up?"

"One too many nosebleeds."

"He beat you up?"

"Nothing serious, but he'd knock me around a little from time to time to show me who was boss. I finally decided enough was enough."

"So, did he knock anybody else around that you know of?"

"What do you mean?"

"Well, it seems to me a guy like your ex-husband might have made a few enemies over the years."

She nodded. "He had his enemies."

"Do you know who they were?"

"There was another revenue officer, Donald Hurst, who didn't like Bobby. I never knew why exactly but I witnessed a few verbal exchanges between them. Bobby would never talk about it, so I can't tell you what it was about."

"What about taxpayers?" I asked.

"Taxpayers?"

"Yes, did he ever talk about taxpayers that he didn't like or who might not have liked him?"

"He talked a lot about Dusty Thomas. He was on the top of his hit list, as he called it."

"Hit list?"

"Yeah, it's a list of cases that he has where he suspects fraud or criminal activity. He devoted eighty percent of his time to those cases."

"How many are on the hit list?"

"A dozen or so, I think. I didn't pay that much attention to it."

"Do you know where he kept the list?"

"In his office at work, I believe."

"Do you remember any names that your ex-husband had on the list other than Dusty Thomas?"

"Frank Milborn ... you know, the professional golfer. He audited him for the last three years and turned up a lot of bogus deductions.

Frank got rather irate one time and his CPA had to intervene to prevent a fight between the two."

"Really? Any others?"

"Well, there was some charitable foundation. I don't remember the name, but Bobby thought it was a sham and was gathering evidence to prove it. The leader of the organization was a self-righteous ignoramus and was always sending Bobby incoherent letters trying to justify their activities."

After eating lunch, including a piece of cheesecake, I thanked Maureen and returned to the office. It had been a very interesting lunch, and I had learned a lot about Bobby Tuttle. He definitely was a man who had enemies. Enemies who could have killed him just as easily as Dusty. I wrote more names down on my legal pad.

> *Donald Hurst — revenue officer*
> *Frank Milborn — golfer*
> *charitable foundation — possible front for other entity*

It was late in the afternoon and I was tired. As I was preparing to leave, Jodie came into my office. She seemed despondent.

She said, "Did you hear from Stan?"

"No," I said. "Did you expect him to call?"

"Well, Rebekah and Toni have both called several times today wondering if we heard anything. I told them I hadn't, but that I'd check with you."

"No, not a word," I said. "He got there okay, didn't he?"

"Yeah, he called Rebekah when he got to Ecuador late yesterday. He told her he and Monty were going to the bank first thing this morning. They were just hoping he might have called."

"Are they in the same time zone?" I asked.

"No, I think it's an hour or two earlier there."

"Well, I bet he'll call Rebekah at home tonight. Anyway, I wouldn't worry about it."

Jodie nodded and went back to her office. She stuck her head in a few minutes later and said she was leaving. I started to gather my things to go home as well when the phone rang. I considered whether to answer it or let the answering service pick it up. On the last right I picked it up.

"Turner & Waters," I said.

"This is the oversees operator. I have a collect call from Tex Weller. Will you accept the charges?"

"Yes, of course."

"Hello," Tex said.

"Hello."

"Jodie?"

"No, this is Paula—Stan's new partner."

"Oh, is Stan there?"

"No, he's in Ecuador looking for you."

"You're kidding."

"No, where are you?"

"I'm in jail in Quito. They finally let me make a phone call. Would you tell Stan I need his help?"

"Yes, just as soon as he calls. What are they charging you with?"

"Theft, forgery, and a long list of other charges. Please tell Stan I'm in a jail in Quito, Ecuador. It's in the old city and they say they're going to move me to a prison nearby in a few days."

"I will. I'm glad you're okay. Stan will figure something out. Don't worry."

I hung up, shaken by the conversation. It didn't surprise me so much that Tex was in jail, since he was involved in an illegal scam; what bothered me was that Stan had the money. The feds might think he was involved with him. I had to get in contact with Stan and warn him. Unfortunately, I didn't know how to reach him. I would just have to wait. In the meantime I called Toni.

"Toni?"

"Yes."

"This is Paula Waters—Stan's new partner."

"Oh, yes. How are you?"

"Okay—listen I just got a call from Tex."

"Oh my God! Is he all right?"

"Yes, he sounded fine."

"Oh, I'm so relieved. You can't believe how worried I've been! So when will he be back?"

"Listen, I'm sorry to have to tell you this but Tex is in a bit of trouble." I explained the situation to her.

"I told him not to get involved in any more shady deals. We don't need the money."

"Well, Stan is down there so just as soon as he calls I'll have him go see Tex. Maybe he'll be able to straighten things out."

"Oh, God. He's got to help him. Should I fly down there?"

"No. Don't do that. Let Stan handle it for now."

"Okay, but I'm so worried. I won't be able to sleep until he comes home."

"I know. I'll keep you posted. I'm sure everything will work out."

That was a lie. I had no idea how Stan was going to handle this one. He knew nothing about the criminal justice system in Ecuador, nor did I. Tension was building in my neck and my head was starting to ache. It was time to retreat to the condo and a hot shower. Maybe I'd call Stewart or Bart to come over and give me a massage. I didn't feel like being alone. They would help me keep my mind off of Stan. Why hadn't I heard from him? He should have called by now. I prayed he was okay.

# KIDNAPPED 8

As we cruised at 35,000 feet over the Caribbean in a big American Airlines jet, I thought about Tex and all the great times we had enjoyed together. Although Tex was twenty years older than I, he had a youthful spirit and a great positive attitude. Many times when he would call he'd find me depressed over a difficult case or poor finances. Each time he would quickly pick me up and have me laughing before he hung up. When I first started practice, he got me off to a quick start with dozens of referrals and lots of encouragement. Rebekah liked Toni, too, and always looked forward to our get-togethers over the years. I prayed that our mission would be successful and I could return Tex to his home and family.

Monty seemed excited by the assignment and eager to get to Ecuador. He was a Vietnam vet, an expert on weaponry, and had converted his garage into a gun shop. An ex-Dallas cop, he liked action and wasn't afraid of anyone. He had lost his job due to his inability to control his temper. The straw that broke the oxen's back was his assault on a pimp who had beaten up one of his girls. Monty didn't cut any slack to men who beat up women. He made the pimp look twice as bad as his lady of the night. Internal affairs made him a deal—resign or get fired and be charged with assault and battery.

Monty was tired of following unfaithful spouses and dishonest employees. He longed for some real action like that he saw on active duty. As we neared our destination we discussed strategy. I handed Monty a manila envelope.

"Toni managed to get me some credit card receipts from Tex's Citibank Visa account. One is for a Café Cultura for about $80, another one for an establishment called Il Grillo for $3.95, and the last one is to a store in Jardin Shopping Mall for $8.99."

Monty opened the envelope and studied the receipts. "This will give us something to do if we strike out with the banker. I can't believe Tex was so stupid to fall for this scam."

"He's always been a sucker for this kind of stuff," I replied. "Last year it was a silver mine in Mexico. I thought I had talked him out of it, then I learned he had sent the promoter $10,000."

Monty shook his head. "If he's been kidnapped we'll have to find him and break him out."

I laughed. "We? I washed out of the Marines, remember?"

"Right. What I mean is, I've got a contact, if need be, where I can get a few mercenaries to help out ."

"Really? I don't think I want to know about this."

"Okay. We never had this conversation."

I smiled and turned my attention to my carry-on bag, where I had stuck our tickets and a travel brochure. As we approached Quito's airport I began reading the travel brochure about Ecuador that I'd managed to get from AAA the previous day.

> Quito, the capital of Ecuador, was founded in the 16th century on the ruins of an Inca city and stands at an altitude of 2,850 m. Despite the 1917 earthquake, the city has the best-preserved, least- altered historic centre in Latin America. The monasteries of San Francisco and Santo Domingo, and the Church and Jesuit College of La Compañía, with their rich interiors, are pure examples of the "Baroque School of Quito," which is a fusion of Spanish, Italian, Moorish, Flemish and indigenous art.

Interesting as the travel brochure was, somehow I didn't figure we'd have much time for sightseeing. After we deplaned we were herded into a large room where there were three long customs lines. Armed guards stood at each exit of the building. After an hour journey through customs, we were directed to a baggage claim area where all the luggage from the flight had been delivered. More armed guards were strategically placed throughout the airport—which I found to be a little unsettling. Finding our luggage wasn't an easy task, as hundreds of bags had been dumped in the middle of the room without any attempt at organization. Fortunately I had a distinct SMU decal on my suitcase, making it easier to spot. Monty traveled with a suitcase and golf bag. The golf bag was full of guns and ammunition I feared might be discovered. If it was, our rescue effort would end before it started. I had suggested he buy his weapons once he got down to Ecuador, but he said he wouldn't trust anything made in South America.

The taxi driver—who won a spirited battle with three other drivers to get our business—was named Juan. He said he would stick with us during our entire stay in Ecuador. He explained that, with the current state of unrest in the country, it wasn't safe to take the *trolebus*, particularly in the Old City where rebels were known to be hiding. As Juan drove us through the city I noticed guards armed with shotguns at every bank, every shopping center, and many of the buildings that we passed. Jeeps full of soldiers with machine guns were patrolling the streets and police cars were everywhere. It seemed we had ventured into a war zone.

We asked Juan for a hotel recommendation. He surprised us when he said, "Café Cultura," which apparently was a hotel as well as a restaurant. Tex must have got the same recommendation. The hotel was a postcolonial two-story building with a white terracotta tile roof. It was actually the former home of one of Quito's older families that lived there thirty-five years earlier, and subsequently it became the French Cultural Centre. The building had been carefully restored, with special detail devoted to maintaining the unique characteristics of the original interior. It was surrounded by a beautiful, lush garden, with secluded seating areas for relaxing or watching the resident hummingbirds do their thing—at least that's what the postcard they were selling proclaimed.

After we checked in, Juan took our bags to our room and said he'd hang around the hotel lobby until we needed him. I asked him what I owed him. He said not to worry about it. We'd settle up at the end of each day. Once we were settled I called Rebekah to tell her we had arrived, but I got the recorder. I left a message telling her where we were staying and then we went down to the hotel restaurant, the Café Bistro, for dinner. I asked Juan to join us. He declined at first, but finally agreed when I told him I wanted to ask him some questions. After we ordered, I showed him Tex's picture. He said he hadn't seen him. We asked him about the United Peoples Bank of Ecuador.

"It's a big bank not too far from here. I can take you there in the morning," Juan advised.

"Do you know anyone at the bank?" I asked.

"Si, I drive Señor Lantz to his favorite restaurant once a week."

"Who is Señor Lantz?"

"Why he is the assistant cashier—the second in command of operations."

"Good. We need to meet with Victor Alfaro, a credit officer at the bank. It might be helpful if you introduced us to Señor Lantz."

"Of course, I'd be happy to do so first thing in the morning."

"Good. I think we're done for today. What do I owe you?"

Juan pulled out a small pad of paper and started doing some calculations. After a minute he said, "$16.00 U.S."

I nodded, handed him a $20 bill, and said, "Keep the change." He thanked me and left with a promise to meet us at 9 A.M. the following morning. Before going upstairs to our room I stopped by the front desk and showed everyone on duty Tex's photograph, asking if anyone remembered him. One of them remembered him vaguely, but didn't know much about his stay at the hotel. Apparently he had been there only one night and hadn't made any friends. They suggested I check in the afternoon when the rest of the staff would be on duty.

We were beat after getting up at 5 A.M., a nine-hour plane ride, and two more hours to finally get to our hotel, so we decided to go to bed. It was only 9 P.M. but felt much later. Before we crashed I called Rebekah, as I had promised to do, to let her know we had arrived safely. She was greatly relieved to hear from me, as she was an incessant worrier when I traveled. I promised her I'd call her again the following day.

When my head hit the pillow I fell into a dreamless sleep and didn't stir until sunglare woke me the following morning. I stretched, looked over at Monty. He was snoring. I fumbled for my watch and was shocked to see it was already 8:30 A.M. "Shit!" I exclaimed as I stumbled out of bed. Monty opened his eyes and looked over at me.

"Time to get up. Only thirty minutes until Juan gets here."

Monty moaned and rolled over. I laughed and headed for the bathroom. Miraculously, at 9:00 A.M. we were downstairs drinking a cup of coffee when Juan arrived. We asked him if he wanted to join us for breakfast. He declined, stating he'd already eaten with his wife and family. After promising him we'd be only ten or fifteen minutes, he went back outside to wait.

"So how are we going to play this?" Monty asked.

"I don't know. Should we be honest and straightforward, or play it close to the vest?"

"I don't think we should tell him we know about the scam or the money. Lets just ask if he's seen Tex and see what he says. We can play it by ear after that."

"Okay, I agree," I said. "I'll go tell Juan we're ready to go."

The ride to the bank was as exciting as a roller coaster ride at Six Flags. Traffic was brutal and Juan darted through it, tailgating the cars in front of him, slamming on his brakes and changing lanes incessantly. I breathed a sigh of relief when he pulled up in front of the United Peoples Bank of Ecuador and parked. We all got out and walked into the bank. The lobby was spacious, with a high ceiling supported by thick wooden beams. It looked like it had originally been built as a church. Juan stopped at the reception desk and spoke with the receptionist. She got up and walked into an interior room. A few moments later she returned followed by a short, thin man with a mustache. He was wearing an expensive suit and a Rolex watch. The man shook Juan's hand like he was an old friend and then Juan turned to us.

"Gentlemen, this is Señor Lantz."

We all shook hands. I said, "It's a pleasure to meet you. It's a beautiful facility you have."

"Thank you," he said smiling, "it was once a monastery. The bank bought the building when the monks moved to the countryside in 1957."

Juan excused himself and went out the front door. Lantz said, "So, gentlemen. What can I do for you?"

I looked at Monty and said, "Well, I'm an attorney from Dallas and I'm searching for a client who seems to have disappeared." I pulled out the picture of Tex and showed it to him.

Señor Lantz looked at the picture and nodded affirmatively. "Yes, I know this man. This is Dr. Wells' brother from Texas. Dr. Wells was a long-time customer. His death was so tragic. Did you know him?"

"No, Tex never mentioned him."

"It's a shame. He was actually a half-brother. They were not close, apparently. It's unfortunate that you never met him. You would have liked him. He was a most honorable gentleman."

"I bet I would have," I said. "When did you last see Tex?"

"A week or ten days ago. After he wired his inheritance to his bank in the Cayman Islands, he left to go back to America."

"Was there some kind of probate procedure or something that he went through before you turned over the money to him?"

"Of course. He had the appropriate papers to prove he was the next of kin and sole heir of Dr. Wells' estate."

"Did you handle the transaction?" Monty asked.

"No, Victor Alfaro handled it. He's our assistant cashier."

"Is he around?" Monty asked. "Tex might have told him something that would help us locate him."

"Of course, but unfortunately Señor Alfaro is no longer employed by the bank."

"He's not?" Monty said.

This wasn't a shock to me, as I had suspected Señor Alfaro wouldn't want to be around when the bank found out they'd been robbed. Besides, he had to go collect his cut of the inheritance. I wondered if he'd gone to the Caymans. That might be the next place to look for Tex.

"No, he resigned to take a position with another institution," Señor Lantz replied.

"Do you have a home address for him?" Monty asked.

"Yes, but I'm afraid I can't give you that information."

I said, "Señor Lantz, I understand your reluctance to provide personal information, but my client is missing. His wife is sitting at home worried sick about him. Victor Alfaro may know where he is. We need his address and the name of the bank where the money was wired."

"Well, I will give you his telephone number but not his address. The name of the bank is no problem."

"Thank you. We really appreciate your cooperation."

"I'm only helping you because I was very fond of Dr. Wells. He was a true comrade and if I can help you find his brother then, of course, I would want to do that."

"Of course," I said.

The bank in question, NCB, had been around since 1886. We borrowed a telephone and called the number that Señor Lantz had given us, but the number had been disconnected. We thanked Señor Lantz and went back to the hotel. There was a message from Paula to call the office. I did so.

"Paula?"

"Stan! I'm so glad I caught you. Are you two all right?"

"Yes, we're fine. How's everything there?"

"Okay, listen. Tex called here a few hours ago. He's in jail at a police station in the Old City. You need to get there soon. He says they plan to move him to the Garcia Morena Prison in a few days. He's been told once he's moved there he may never get out."

The news that Tex was in jail hit me like a Mack truck.

"Why is he in jail?"

"I don't know. He only had a minute to talk. That's all he told me."

"They must have figured out he wasn't Dr. Wells' brother."

"God, I hope not," Paula said. "Is there anything I can do here?"

"No, just tell Toni that we'll do everything we can to get him out of prison."

"All right. I will."

"How's your investigation going?"

"Fine. I've been interviewing witnesses trying to find out who else had a motive to kill Tuttle."

"Any luck?"

"Yeah, he wasn't Mr. Popularity. I'll tell you about it when you get back."

"Sure. I'll call you if anything positive develops."

"Please keep in touch. We're all worried about you."

Now how in the hell was I going to deal with a client in prison in Ecuador for bank robbery? How was I going to explain how I ended up with the loot? A loud banging on our door interrupted my contemplation.

"Policia! Abrir! Policia!

The door burst open and half a dozen armed policemen stormed into the room. Two of them grabbed Monty and slammed him against the wall. A third tackled me and pinned me to the floor. Terror swept through me as I felt the cold steel of handcuffs around my wrists. We were both rudely jerked to our feet and escorted downstairs to a waiting police van. Monty looked at me with anguish in his eyes as he stepped inside and took a seat. I felt the need to puke.

# THE JEALOUS AGENT 9

I was glad I had been able to get in touch with Stan. Now at least he could find Tex and perhaps talk to him. It sounded like Tex was in serious trouble and would need a local attorney to defend him. I was sure Stan could find Tex an attorney and then get his ass back home to help me defend Dusty. My investigation was just getting started and there was lots of work to do. I needed his help desperately. In the meantime I had to keep moving. The clock was ticking. Although no trial date had been set, I knew the Justice Department would be anxious to close this case. The CDA was getting tons of publicity from their involvement in the case, and that had to be giving a lot of people in Washington ulcers. In fact, Raymond Farr, the president of the CDA, was to be interviewed on "20/20" that very night.

I flipped open my notebook and reviewed my witness list. The name "Donald Hurst" jumped out at me. He was the revenue agent who didn't like Bobby much. Although I doubted the animosity between them would be enough to cause Agent Hurst to gun down Bobby in cold blood, I couldn't ignore the possibility. He certainly would have been in a position to know about the tractor seizure and the history between Dusty and Bobby. If he didn't have any alibi he'd have to go to the top of our list of suspects. Either way, he certainly would have a lot of dirt on Bobby and probably wouldn't mind sharing it with me in light of the bad blood between them. I called Hurst and secured an appointment for that afternoon.

His office was downtown in the Earl Cabell Federal Building. The CDA picketers were still out front trying to stir up support for their position that the income tax laws were unconstitutional. One of them stuck a pamphlet in my face as I walked by. I looked at it and was shocked to see it was all about Dusty Thomas and his battle with the IRS. I tucked it in my purse and entered the building. I looked up at a smiling picture of Ronald Reagan hanging on the wall. It suddenly occurred to me that he would probably be getting weekly briefings on the Dusty Thomas case. The thought of that nearly took my breath away. Wow! I had moved up in the world in a hurry thanks to Stan. Suddenly I became sick with worry. I wished Stan had never gone to Ecuador. It was such an unstable country. There were frequent riots and talk of an impending coup according to the magazine articles I found at the Dallas County Library. Damn you, Turner! Why did you go?

As I entered the IRS Collections' Office I felt a little uneasy. I had never had a problem with the IRS myself, but I had heard enough stories about lives being ruined by overzealous revenue agents to be a bit nervous. I signed in at the front desk and waited. Ten minutes later a door opened and a man walked out and surveyed the reception area.

He said, "Paula Waters?"

I stood up and walked over to him. We introduced ourselves and he took me back to his office. Agent Hurst was a middle-aged man, short and trim, with dark hair. He looked like he could have been a wrestler or swimmer in college. His office was a mess, piles of loose papers, files, and books scattered about. He cleared off a chair so I could sit down. He remained standing.

"So, did you see the army of dissidents you and your client have unleashed upon us?"

"Yes, I'm really sorry about that. I had no idea they would take advantage of the situation like they have."

"Oh, you thought they'd fork over a quarter-million dollars for the sake of justice."

I shrugged. "Honestly, I was just worried about Dusty getting a good defense. In retrospect, I guess I was a little naive."

"Naive? No, I don't think so. You knew exactly what you were doing. Greedy is the word I think would apply here."

I stood up. "I beg your pardon! Murder trials are expensive. Stan and I are not going to get rich over this. We just need enough capital to put up a good fight. I'm sure the government will outspend us ten to one."

"No, little lady—more like a hundred to one." Hurst laughed. "You don't know what you got yourself into. You're messing with the federal government here and you're not going to get away with it."

I took a deep breath. The interview had gotten off to a bad start. Hurst obviously hadn't agreed to the interview in order to answer my questions. He was using my visit as an opportunity to vent his hostility toward Dusty Thomas, lawyers, women, and everyone else he obviously hated. I struggled to keep my composure.

"Agent Hurst, I can understand why you don't like me and that's fine. It's a free country. But as I told you, I came here to ask you some questions about Bobby Tuttle, if you don't mind."

Agent Hurst threw up his hands then sat in his chair. He settled back and said, "Shoot. What do you want to know?"

"Thank you. I've heard you and Bobby didn't get along very well."

"We weren't friends, if that's what you mean."

"Were you enemies?"

"No. I wouldn't say that. It's true I didn't like Bobby too much. He was a know-it-all and always had to run the show, but that was just a personality conflict—nothing more."

"Other than being a know-it-all, what was it that made you hate Bobby?"

Agent Hurst gave me a thoughtful look. I wondered if he was going to level with me or tell me to get lost. He had no reason to cooperate—whatever he told me might come back to haunt him. It was a long and awkward silence. I was about to give up and terminate the interview when he finally said, "Bobby's father is a former District Director of the Internal Revenue Service. He and I started with the Service about the same time, yet Bobby has moved up the ladder much faster than I have because of his father's *connections*. That kind of pisses me off, to be perfectly honest with you."

"I see. I appreciate your candor. So, for the record, where were you at the time Bobby was murdered?"

"I was on a special assignment in Fort Worth."

"Doing what?"

"Pouring over business records that had been subpoenaed in a tax fraud case."

"Were you alone?'

"I was in a lawyer's office. They set me up in their conference room with twenty-two boxes of records. It was so much fun."

"So you were alone in the conference room?"

"Yes, except for a few visits from the receptionist. She brought me coffee. I didn't have time to drive to Farmersville," Hurst snickered.

"Are there others in the IRS who might have had a grudge against Bobby?"

"Sure, he wasn't a very popular guy. Try Laura Blair. She accused Bobby of sexual harassment once."

"Really? Does she still work here?"

"She's on maternity leave."

"Is it Bobby's baby?"

"How should I know? Neither one of them confided in me."

"Can I get an address or telephone number."

"Sure. Why not? We at the IRS always aim to please."

After agent Hurst gave me Laura Blair's address I went back to the office. Hurst was a true-blue SOB. I didn't know what to make of him. He certainly had ample animosity toward Bobby Tuttle, but his alibi seemed pretty tight. I reached for my purse to get a Kleenex when I noticed the brochure that had been handed to me by the CDA picketer. I began reading.

> Dusty Thomas
> Vs.
> The United States of America
>
> Will David bring down Goliath?
> As Dusty prepares his slingshot the IRS trembles!

I chuckled and turned to the second page. There was a picture of me conferring with Dusty before his bond hearing. It wasn't a bad shot but I wished I'd worn a better outfit. I made a mental note to pay more attention to my wardrobe, since there apparently would be many cameras clicking wherever I appeared. The caption read: "Dusty Thomas talking to his street-savvy co-counsel Paula Waters." Street savvy? I wondered where that came from! I read on.

### Dusty Thomas' Long Battle with the IRS

> In 1972 Dusty Thomas was a rancher raising cattle and growing hay to feed them. To make ends meet he also operated a bulldozer and was helping to clear land for a new housing development in McKinney, Texas. He worked 60 hours a week just to feed his family and pay the bills. While on the job he learned from one of our members that the federal income tax was illegal. He talked to his co-workers on the construction site and

found out that very few of them paid taxes. Convinced that the federal government didn't have the right to tax him, as the Sixteenth Amendment had never been ratified, he didn't file a tax return for 1972.

Three years later he was contacted by Revenue Officer Bobby Tuttle. Tuttle rejected his claim that the income tax was illegal and filed a tax return for him and assessed him taxes of $7,322.47 for 1972, $6,311.42 for 1973, and $5,742.14 for 1974. Barely being able to pay his bills and keep food on the table for his growing family, Dusty was unable to pay the nearly $20,000 taxes illegally assessed against him.

By June 1976 the tax bill with penalty and interest had mushroomed to nearly $37,000 and Agent Tuttle issued wage garnishments against Dusty and his wife, who was working as a school teacher. The IRS took over $1100 dollars per month, leaving them only $900 a month to live on. After nine months of living near the poverty level, Martha quit her job and tutored students for cash. When Dusty's McKinney job played out the garnishment of his wages came to an end.

Harassed by IRS Revenue Agent Bobby Tuttle, Dusty, under protest, filed his 1976–79 income tax returns and paid the taxes the government claimed were due. In 1980 Bobby Tuttle seized 800 acres of the Double T Ranch and all the cattle, leaving Dusty and his wife, Martha, with only 200 acres and their small ranch house. Despite wage garnishments of nearly $10,000 and land seizures valued on the tax rolls at over $80,000, Dusty's tax bill rose to $87,801 by the end of 1981.

In 1982 Dusty and his wife were referred to attorney Stan Turner, who immediately filed a chapter 13 bankruptcy to rid them of as much tax liability as possible. Unfortunately Tuttle had filed a federal tax lien, which remained as a lien against Dusty's rural homestead. To get these taxes paid the Chapter 13 plan provided payments of $542 per month with $420 going to the IRS. But in 1983 Dusty had a heart attack and couldn't work for six weeks; the bankruptcy had to be converted to Chapter 7. The effect of the bankruptcy discharge was to relieve Dusty and Martha of any personal liability for their taxes, but the federal tax lien remained in effect.

Since the value of the Double T Ranch had increased dramatically, Dusty and Martha were reluctant to surrender it to the IRS. In the spring of 1986 Agent Tuttle decided it was time to harass Dusty Thomas one more time. He personally visited the Double T Ranch for the purposes of locating additional properties to seize. When he spotted Dusty's tractor he advised them that he was going back to the office to issue an attachment for the tractor. Dusty was outraged and the two got into a screaming match and nearly came to blows. During the altercation Dusty threatened to shoot Agent Tuttle if he came back to take the tractor.

The story was followed by a commentary lauding Dusty Thomas' courage and patriotism in putting his life on the line for the Constitution. On the back page of the pamphlet there was information about the CDA, contact information, and a plea to send money for the "Dusty Thomas Defense Fund."

I shook my head in disbelief. *Wait until Stan sees this.* I wondered if the CDA realized how much damage this kind of propaganda would do to our efforts to save Dusty's life. Now I wondered if I'd made a mistake taking their money. "Damn them!" I blurted out.

Stewart walked in and said, "Did you call me?"

I smiled. "No, I'm just talking to myself. This case is getting more and more complicated every day. I wish Stan were here. I'd feel a lot better."

"He'll be back soon, I'm sure," Stewart said with a reassuring smile. "You need a back rub?"

"No, thanks. I've got too much to do right now. Later, maybe."

Stewart left. I got back to thinking about the case. I decided to follow up on Bobby's girlfriend, Laura Blair. She lived on Turtle Creek Boulevard at one of those ritzy high-rise condominiums that were springing up everywhere. It took me twenty minutes to get there.

The doorman rang her room. I heard her over the intercom tell him to let me up.

I took the elevator, and when the door opened I could hear a baby crying. After knocking on the door, I waited quite awhile. Finally Laura opened the door and invited me in. She was a dishwater blond, mid-thirties, not bad looking. She was a bit disheveled, and the place looked like she'd had a bad morning. She was carrying the baby in her arms, rocking her, and patting her gently on the back trying to get her to go to sleep.

"I really appreciate you agreeing to see me on such short notice," I said.

"No problem. Please excuse the mess. The baby is teething and I haven't got a wink of sleep all week. You don't want an infant, do you?"

I laughed. "No, not quite yet. In a few years I might be interested."

She sat down and held the baby on her lap facing me. "Too bad. Today I'd give her away cheap."

"She is so cute. I think you'd miss her."

She gave the baby a hard look. "Ah, you're probably right. I guess I'll keep her . . . So, what can I do for you?"

"As I told you over the phone, I'm with Turner and Waters. We're defending Dusty Thomas in the Bobby Tuttle murder case."

"Right, I've been following that on TV."

"I understand you knew Bobby Tuttle."

"Yes, unfortunately," Laura said.

"How did you meet him?" I asked.

"Well, I'm a secretary at the Internal Revenue Office downtown."

"Right."

"Bobby was a revenue agent and I did work for him from time to time. I made the mistake once of agreeing to go out on a date. I knew at the time it was a bad idea, but Bobby had been hitting on me and pressuring me to go out with him for a long time. I really didn't like him that much but he caught me in a weak moment and I said yes. What a mistake."

"So, where did you go?"

"We went to a Ranger game and then to a club afterwards. We drank a lot and then he took me home. I didn't invite him up to my apartment, but he came anyway. I tried to keep him out but I was too drunk to be very effective."

"Did he rape you?"

Laura didn't flinch. "Not exactly. I was too out of it put up much of a fight."

"You didn't want sex, though?"

"No, I didn't even like Bobby. If I hadn't been drunk it wouldn't have happened."

"So, did you go to the police?"

"No. I didn't want to lose my job and, like I said, I didn't put up much of a fight."

"So, did you go out with him again?"

"No. He asked several times but I politely declined. One day he became insistent and I had to threaten him with a sexual harassment charge to get him to leave me alone."

"Laura, I know this is a rotten thing to have to ask you, but I must. Is this Bobby's baby?"

"No. No way. I had a steady boyfriend before I went out with Bobby—Chet Conway. We had just broken up. That's one reason I agreed to go out with Bobby. I was a little depressed because of our breakup."

"So, is Chet part of your life now?"

Laura smiled. "Yeah, we got back together when I found out I was pregnant."

"Where were you on the day Bobby was murdered?"

She hesitated. "Home sick."

"Were you alone?"

"Just me and the baby."

I wasn't convinced that Bobby wasn't the child's real father but I didn't press the issue. Chet had to be added to my list of suspects. If he found out what Bobby had done to Laura, he might have been outraged enough to murder him. Even if I couldn't prove it, it would give a jury some doubts about Dusty's guilt. I thanked Laura and left. It was late so I went straight to the condo. I was tired and depressed, so I was glad to see Stewart's car parked out front. Some food, a good massage, and a little sex would make me feel much better.

Stewart had dinner just about ready when I strolled in and kicked off my shoes. "Whoever invented high heels ought to be strung up," I said. "My feet are killing me."

"Sit down. I'll rub them for you, love," Stewart said. "I'm sorry you had a tough day."

I sat down in a big overstuffed chair and Stewart sat on an ottoman across from me. He put my feet in his lap and started to do his magic. "Actually it wasn't such a bad day . . . ahhh! That feels so good. Ohhh . . . I've got . . . oohhh . . . two new suspects who had plenty of . . . ahh . . . motive to kill Bobby Tuttle."

"Wonderful. You can tell me all about it over dinner."

Stewart and I were lovers but we weren't in love. We had met in grammar school and been good friends ever since. We had experimented together with sex in high school but more as clinical study than passionate love affair. We both had other relationships from time to time, but none lasted. We agreed that no matter what happened we'd be there for each other. Stewart was a ceramic engineer and when he got laid off I asked him to be my secretary until he could find another job in his field. He agreed and had been with me three months now. I was getting used to him being around and I wasn't looking forward to the inevitable day that he would leave me.

"It was so nice of you to cook me dinner."

"Anything for the boss. I'm good at kissing ass, you know."

I smiled and winked at him. "Yes, I know. If you ever need a reference, I'm your gal."

"Good, I'll put that down on my resume."

I shook my head. "You dirty boy."

He pushed my feet aside and stood up. "Okay, dinner's ready."

After dinner we sat on the deck of my condo to talk and finish the bottle of wine we had opened. It was a pleasant night and the stars were bright, at least as bright as they get in the middle of the city. I was thinking about Stan—wondering where he was and why we hadn't heard from him. Stewart sensed my worry.

"So, no word from Stan?"

"No, not since I talked with him yesterday. I'm surprised he didn't call. He must have seen Tex by now."

"Why don't you call his hotel? It's only nine o'clock. He'll still be up."

I smiled. "That's a good idea."

I got up and went inside to retrieve the telephone number. I dialed it. The overseas operator came on and took the office phone number so they could bill the call there. I waited for what seemed a good ten minutes before the hotel operator answered.

"I'd like to talk to Stan Turner, please."

Fortunately the operator spoke English. She replied. "Do you know his room number, please?"

"Yes, room 224."

"Thank you. I'm sorry, Señora, but Mr. Turner is no longer in that room."

"What do you mean? Did he check out?"

"He must have. I don't show him as a guest in the hotel anymore."

"Can I speak to the manager, please?"

"Yes, Señora. One moment."

After a long minute a man's voice came on. "May I be of assistance?"

"Yes, I'm trying to reach my partner, Stan Turner. He was a guest in your hotel. I talked to him yesterday."

"Oh, Señora, I'm sorry to have to tell you this but Señor Turner and his companion were apprehended by the policia yesterday."

"What! Where did they take them?"

Tears welled in my eyes as I tried to comprehend what had happened. The manager gave me the name and telephone number of the local police. I was beside myself with fear. Stewart heard me crying and rushed in.

"Thank you," I said.

"Señora, what should I do with Mr. Turner's belongings?"

I told the manager to keep the luggage for a few days and that Mr. Turner would likely come to claim it. If not, I'd send someone by to have it shipped to Dallas. After I hung up, I dialed the number of the police station. The person who answered the telephone didn't speak English. He put me on hold to go find someone who did. While I waited I explained to Stewart what had happened. He shook his head sympathetically. Finally, a male voice came on the line.

"Yes?"

"Hi, this is Paula Waters. I'm calling from Dallas, Texas and I understand you've arrested a Stanley Turner and Monty Dozier."

"One moment, please. I'll check and see."

He put me on hold. He was gone a long time. My mind whirled as I tried to imagine every scenario that might explain why Stan had been arrested. Did they think he was mixed up with Tex's scam? Or had Monty been caught with all his guns? I had told Stan not to let him take any weapons, but Stan had insisted that Monty knew his business and shouldn't be second guessed. Finally the man returned to the line.

"I'm sorry Señora, but there is no one in the jail under that name."

"But the manager at the hotel said he was taken there."

"Forgive me, but I have thoroughly searched our records and he was not brought here."

Terror swept over me. Where could Stan have been taken? Had the police really arrested him or had he been kidnapped? I grabbed Stewart and looked up at him.

"Stewart! Somebody has Stan! What am I going to do? Oh, God! How could this have happened? What if he's been kidnapped? What if they kill him?"

# PRISON 10

It was a long, hot, bumpy ride through the streets of Quito in the windowless van. My shirt quickly became saturated with perspiration. When the van finally came to a halt we had no idea where we had been taken. The back door opened and two guards pushed us out onto a cobblestone driveway. I looked around and saw tall white walls surrounding a large courtyard. Guard posts high up at the corners were each manned with two armed soldiers. The guards pushed us toward an open door, and we were led down a long, lightless corridor. The policeman in charge barked some orders to his men and they stopped us in front of a tall wooden door. A guard opened the door. Monty was shoved inside and the door was locked behind him. They escorted me two doors down and threw me into another room. I fell hard on my left shoulder; pain radiated quickly down my arm.

As I heard the door latch behind me I looked around the barren room. There were iron wristbands attached to the walls where I could be restrained if they so desired. I crawled over to the corner and perched myself up against the hard-baked brick wall. There were no windows. It wouldn't be an easy place to escape. I noticed a video camera mounted high on the back wall, peering down at me.

On the way to my prison cell I had contemplated all the possible reasons for my arrest. I had concluded it was because Tex had wired me his money and somehow the authorities had traced it to my bank account. They must have thought I was stupid coming down here looking for Tex when I could have just taken it all for myself. I wondered how I could possibly explain to them that I wasn't involved in this conspiracy—that I was just an innocent bystander trying to help a client in distress. I closed my eyes and rubbed my aching shoulder.

Several hours passed before the door opened again. A soldier set down some food, then left. I inspected it carefully. A chunk of bread, a bowl of beans, and a glass of water was to be my midday fare. Feeling very hungry, I ate everything. When I was done I walked over to the video camera and stared at it. I could feel someone watching me.

I wondered who it was and what they wanted from me. Finally, I took a deep breath and went back to the corner of the room where I sat down. Suddenly I felt tired. My eyes closed.

Later that afternoon the door opened again, waking me from my shallow slumber. This time the guards came in, yanked me to my feet, and ordered me to follow them. I obeyed, hoping finally to find out why I'd been incarcerated. They led me down the corridor and back out into the courtyard. We crossed the courtyard and entered another doorway. Inside there was a small waiting room with a table and two chairs. The soldiers pushed me over to the table, sat me down, then left, locking the door behind them. Ten minutes later a tall man—maybe thirty-five years old and dressed in military garb—unlocked the door and joined me. He had long black hair, an overgrown mustache, and a full beard. Myriad bars and other decorations on his uniform telegraphed his importance.

"Señor Turner. My name is General Raul Moya. Please forgive my men for the way they have treated you. They have been told you are a spy for the CIA."

I frowned. "Is that what you think?"

"No, of course not. I know who you are. You are a lawyer from Texas, in the middle of a very important case."

"You've heard of Dusty Thomas' case?" I asked in bewilderment.

"Why of course. Any enemy of the United States of America is my friend and ally. And since you are defending Dusty Thomas and the CDA, I would like to consider you a friend as well."

General Moya extended his hand. It didn't seem prudent not to shake it, so I did. He seemed genuinely glad to meet me. It was obvious he misunderstood American lawyers. He just assumed that, since I had been paid by the CDA, I supported their movement. I went along with the charade, figuring it was my best hope of regaining my freedom.

"Thank you. I can use all the friends I can get."

The general laughed. "So, let me explain why you were dragged from your hotel and detained."

"I do wish you would."

"Yesterday you went to the United Peoples Bank of Ecuador and met with Señor Lantz. He reported his conversation to the police as you had mentioned Señor Weller, who was in custody for bank robbery and conspiracy. They placed surveillance devices in your room and on your telephone hoping to get evidence that you were co-conspirators with Señor Weller."

"We're not. We are just trying to find him and help him out if he's in trouble."

"I understand, but you seemed interested in where the money was wired. It seemed the money was your primary concern."

"No, it wasn't. At the time we met with Señor Lantz, we didn't know Tex was in jail. Your surveillance tapes ought to substantiate that."

"They are not my tapes, Señor Turner. They belong to the police. I am not responsible for your detention. I have called in a favor from a friend who works at the jail to arrange this confidential visit."

"Really? Why?"

"Because I want to help you escape."

"Why would you do that?"

"Like I told you. You're a friend and I believe in helping my friends if I can. If I help you escape, do you think you will be able to save Señor Thomas?"

"I don't know, it's a very difficult case. I'm certainly going to do all I can."

"You are very modest. I have heard of your reputation. I have no doubt that you will succeed.

"In a few days the guards will come before dawn to see your body-guard, Señor Dozier. They will carelessly let him escape. I trust he will then come and free you as well. You will have five minutes to come to this room. There is a passageway out of the prison. I will show it to you before you leave."

General Moya's intention to help us escape was so shocking and unexpected that I felt uneasy. Was I missing something? Did he really care about Dusty Thomas? Did he really believe there was any chance the CDA could be successful in overthrowing the United States government? The more I thought about it the more unlikely it all seemed, yet the opportunity to escape couldn't be ignored. I had no choice but to go along with it.

"What do we do after we escape?"

"Go directly to the airport and fly back to America. There is a flight to Miami every morning at eight. I will be sure your escape is unnoticed until after your plane has left."

"What about Tex Weller?" I said, fearing his answer.

"I'm afraid I cannot do anything for Mr. Weller. He will be tried and most certainly sent to prison. Few men survive long in our prisons."

My heart sank. The thought of Tex rotting in a Quito prison made me sick. The idea that he might die there sent shivers down my spine. How could I ever face Toni if I let that happen?

"Listen, I can't believe Tex would intentionally steal money. I've known him for years and he's an honest, decent man. There must be some explanation for what has happened."

General Moya raised his eyebrows. "Perhaps, but there isn't anything I can do," he said, "unless—"

"Unless what?"

"Unless you can manage to wire me the 1.8 million dollars that Señor Weller has stolen."

My heart leaped for joy and I almost laughed. Now everything made sense. He was the general waiting to seize the unclaimed money. Trying to keep a poker face, I said, "Where am I supposed to get that kind of money?"

"Don't think I'm a fool, Señor Turner. The money was wired from Señor Weller's account in the Cayman Islands to you. In Dallas."

I didn't know where he had gotten that information, but I could hardly dispute it.

"Right. Tex didn't tell me where he got it. It was a lot more money than I expected."

"Yes, he was only authorized to keep a third, but he got greedy and now he'll get nothing."

"Okay. I'll wire all of the money just as soon as I get back to Dallas."

"Good. When the money is in my account, I will see to it that Señor Weller escapes and makes it home to Dallas."

The general wasn't a good liar. I knew he wouldn't release Tex after he got the money. My mind whirled trying to come up with a way to be sure Tex would get home safely.

"No, I'll wire half the money. When Tex steps off the plane in Dallas, I'll wire the other half."

The General shook his head disapprovingly. "No! You'll send it all or Mr. Weller will rot in prison."

"If I send you all the money you'll just kill him as soon as you get it. After all, he betrayed you, and your supporters would demand that you kill him. I must insist on doing it my way."

The general stroked his beard while he considered my terms. "You are in no position to be bargaining, Señor Turner."

I shrugged. The general stared at me intently for a moment and then said reluctantly, "I am told you are a man of your word. Very well, we'll do it your way, but do not dare to double cross me. If you do, I promise you that I will send an assassin to punish you and Señor Weller for your betrayal."

I swallowed hard and said, "Right."

The guards took me back to my cell. Several days went by without further contact. The temperature in the room must have been above 100 degrees. I got very thirsty. Each day a guard brought me a cup of water, some bread, a bowl of beans, and occasionally some rice. It was not enough to quench my thirst or keep the hunger pangs away.

After a couple days I became weak and lethargic and slept most of the time. I wondered when we'd be allowed to escape. Then it occurred to me that the whole episode with General Moya might have been a charade. What if he wasn't a general but just a detective trying to trick me into admitting my complicity in Tex's crime? If that were true I had been a pushover, admitting that I had the money.

I worried about Rebekah and the kids—what they must be going through. The FBI would be involved by now. I worried about them snooping around my affairs. They were likely to find out about Tex and try to tie me into his illegal enterprise. I didn't regret trying to help Tex. He was a friend; I couldn't have just ignored his plight. It was now in God's hands. There was nothing I could do but wait and see what He had in store for me. A sense of tranquility came over me as I leaned back against the wall and closed my eyes.

# NOSY NIEGHBORS 11

On Thursday, July 31, we were all seated in the big conference room that we used for depositions. Ronald Logan, the FBI agent in charge of the Dusty Thomas case, sat next to Agent Jennifer Giles, his assistant. Rebekah and her parents sat across from them. I was at the head of the table, and Jodie was serving coffee. We had gathered to discuss Stan's disappearance and find out what the FBI was doing about it. It had been nearly a week since Stan and Monty Dozier had been heard from. The press didn't know that they were missing yet. Everyone had agreed to keep it quiet, hoping they would turn up. The FBI had set up taps on Rebekah's phones at home and they'd wired everything in the office just in case it was a kidnapping and a ransom call came in. Rebekah's parents were staying with her and the kids to keep her company and provide emotional support.

Jodie said, "Anyone need anything else?"

Logan shook his head and said, "I think that will do it. Thank you, Jodie. Okay, I know you are all anxious to hear the latest news. We've been in contact with the U.S. Ambassador to Ecuador, Travis Bolivar. His investigators still haven't been able to identify the persons who abducted Stan and Monty. Whoever they were pretended to be local police and staged a bogus arrest. No one interfered because they believed it was a legitimate police operation."

"Has this ever happened before?" I asked.

"Yes, apparently so. There is a rebel group down there that uses this technique to kidnap foreign nationals and hold them for ransom. This is what we believe happened."

"But why hasn't there been a ransom demand?" Rebekah asked.

"Well, that's a good question," Agent Logan said. "It could be that the people who kidnapped Stan didn't realize he was such a high-profile individual. They may be assessing how much money to demand. The fact that the press hasn't got wind of the kidnapping has made it harder for them to get the information they need."

"So, this isn't a bunch of thugs who did the kidnapping?" I asked.

"No, this is a highly trained, well-organized rebel organization that gets a substantial amount of its revenue from abducting foreigners and holding them for ransom. We're dealing with professionals who know what they are doing."

"Can't the elected government help us at all?" I asked.

"If they could, they would. But these rebel parties have been operating with impunity in Ecuador for decades. I'm afraid there isn't much we can do but wait and see what they demand."

"I can't believe there isn't anything that can be done," Rebekah moaned. "Can't we hire some private investigators to look for them?"

Logan shook his head. "That would be throwing money away. The national government and the local police have assured me they are doing everything in their power to find Stan and Monty. There's nothing a private investigator could do that isn't already being done. I'm afraid we'll just have to wait."

"What about the press?" I asked. "How much longer can you keep it under wraps?"

"Not much longer," Agent Logan said. "I think we should have a joint press conference in a day or two and advise the public of what's happened. Hopefully the kidnappers will contact us by then."

"Well, thank you Agent Logan for the briefing. If there is anything else we can do to help, let us know. In the meantime we'll just wait for a call."

Everyone stood up and prepared to leave. Rebekah gave me a hug and thanked me for keeping the firm going while Stan was gone. I assured her everything would go on as usual and promised I'd send her Stan's check each payday so she didn't have to worry about money. After Rebekah and her parents left Agent Logan indicated he wanted to have a private chat with me. We met in my office.

"So, what are you going to do about the Dusty Thomas case now that Stan isn't around to help?" Agent Logan asked.

"I'm handling it until Stan returns. It's not a problem."

"Well, how does your client feel about that? Have you told him?"

"No, I haven't. I think it's a little premature."

"Well, I suggest you tell him before the press conference. Better for him to hear it from you than read about it in the newspaper."

I nodded. "You're right. I'll go see him today."

"And, Paula. You might want to think about the possibility that Stan won't be returning. We haven't had a lot of luck rescuing Americans kidnapped in South America. Odds are that Stan will die."

Logan's words unnerved me. It wasn't just the idea that Stan might die that freaked me. It was Logan's tone of voice. He almost seemed to be enjoying this turn of events. I stood up and said, "Don't bet on it. Stan's a survivor and I have no doubt he'll be back here soon."

Logan stood, smiled, and said, "I admire your optimism, but if I were you I'd start looking for a new co-counsel. You're gonna need it."

I glared at Logan, too angry to respond. *What a son of a bitch.* "Are we done?" I finally said.

"Yes, I guess we are. I'll be in touch."

When Logan was gone I thought hard about his remarks. I *did* need to go see Dusty Thomas and tell him about Stan's disappearance—but I was scared. What if he decided to fire me and find new counsel? After all, he had hired Stan, not me. But I couldn't let that happen. This was my dream case, and I wouldn't let anyone take it away from me.

It was quarter to four when I got out to the Double T Ranch. I had phoned ahead to make sure Dusty and Martha were home. As I was pulling up to the entrance of the ranch I saw that Dusty's neighbors were sitting out on the front porch. Since I wasn't due at Dusty's until four I stopped to talk to them. I pulled up in the driveway, quickly checking my notes as I hadn't remembered their names. Flipping through the pages all I could find was "Emma Lou." I got out and walked up to the porch.

"Good afternoon," I said.

"Howdy," the lady said.

"You must be Emma Lou?"

"Yes, and who might you be?"

"I'm Paula Waters, with Turner and Waters, one of the attorneys for Dusty Thomas."

"Oh, well it's mighty nice to meet you," Emma Lou said. She pointed to the man with her and said, "This is my husband, Ned."

I extended my hand and said, "It's a pleasure to meet you." We shook hands and Ned invited me to sit down on a bench across from them. They both appeared to be in their late sixties. I guessed they were retired. Ned was tall, gray-haired, and wore blue jeans and a brown and white plaid shirt. Emma Lou was much shorter and wore a blue and white sheath dress. They both held a tall glass of lemonade. They offered me a glass but I declined.

"I just have a few minutes, but I wanted to ask you if you were home on the day of Agent Tuttle's murder?"

Emma Lou replied, " Sure, we were home but we didn't see much until the police came."

"Well, if you saw anything I'd be interested in hearing about it."

Ned spoke up. "I saw Dusty come home from cutting out there on the county road. He waved when he went by."

"Did you see anyone else?"

"I saw Bobby Tuttle come by about twenty minutes after Dusty came home. I knew he was after Dusty's tractor, so I called Dusty to warn him."

"You called him?"

"Yes, but he didn't pick up the phone. I left a message. Don't know if he got it."

"What did you do after that?"

"I was about to get in the truck and run up to the house when I heard a gunshot."

"Could you tell where it came from?"

"Not exactly. It was from the general direction of Dusty's house."

"What did you do after you heard the gunshot?"

"Well, gunshots out here in the country are not all that unusual so I didn't think a whole lot about it until I heard the second one."

"Really. How long was it between shots?"

"Ah, maybe five minutes or so."

"So, then what did you do?"

"I got in my truck and was getting ready to head on up to the house when the wrecker showed up and turned onto the road to Dusty's. I started to follow him and nearly collided with a silver Mercedes speeding down the road. I ended up in the ditch next to the road."

"Did you see where the Mercedes came from?"

"Coming from the east at about 75, I guess."

"Did you recognize the driver?"

"No. I didn't get a good look at him. It wasn't a car from around here. Never seen it before."

"The driver was a male?"

"Not necessarily. Like I said, I didn't get much a good look at him—or her."

"What happened then?"

"I was about three or four minutes behind the wrecker. When I got there the wrecker driver was hunched over the body, checking to see if he had a pulse, I guess. When I got out of my truck. I asked him what had happened, and he said Dusty had shot Tuttle. Then he called his dispatcher and told them to call the sheriff."

"Did you see Dusty?"

"No."

"Did you see anybody else."

"No. I just turned around and went home. I didn't figure it was any of my business. I'd just let the police handle it."

"What about you Mrs. . . . Mrs . . . I guess I didn't get your last names."

"Watson," Emma Lou said.

"Right. Mrs. Watson, did you see anything that maybe your husband didn't see?"

"The Mercedes had some minor damage on the driver's side. The side mirror was smashed, too. The driver must have got too close to something."

"Are there any roads into the Double T Ranch other than the main road?"

Ned said, "There's a road around the perimeter of the ranch, along the property line."

"Could the Mercedes have come from that road?"

"It's possible, but I didn't see it come from there."

"Anything else you remember?" I asked.

Both shook their heads. I thanked them and headed on up the road to the house. Dusty was out on the front porch. He came down to meet me. We went into the house without speaking. Martha poured me a cup of coffee and we all sat down.

"I just met your neighbors, the Watsons. They're very nice."

"Yes, aren't they," Martha said.

"Listen, I've got some bad news. I wanted to tell you about it in person before you heard about it on the news. Stan is missing. He traveled to Ecuador to try to locate a missing client and disappeared."

Martha raised her hand to her mouth and gasped, "Oh, my God!"

"It's been over a week since we've heard from him. The police are searching for him, but so far they haven't come up with anything."

"Whatever are you going to do?" Martha asked.

"There's nothing I can do other than keep working on your case. I've done a lot of work already."

I briefed them on my investigation to date and told them what I'd be doing in the next few weeks. They seemed happy with the progress, but I could see they were worried about Stan. I said, "I know you and Stan go back a long way and you really trust him. I hope he's found and comes home soon, but I can't promise you that will happen. If you want to get a new law firm to represent you, I understand. I hope you don't do that, though, as I think I can represent you just as well as anyone."

Dusty looked at Martha. She shrugged, saying, "It sounds like you're doing just fine. What do you think, Dusty?"

Dusty nodded and said, "I don't want another lawyer. If Stan thought enough of you to make you his partner, that's good enough for me."

I smiled and nearly started to cry. "Thank you."

On the way home I turned on the radio to catch the latest news but got only Paul Harvey. I didn't usually listen to him but I figured his show would be over soon and then the news would come on. I was shocked when he started talking about Dusty Thomas.

"You've all heard about the Texas rancher, Dusty Thomas, who is accused of the murder of Agent Bobby Tuttle of the Internal Revenue Service. You know that he was found standing over the body with a shotgun in his hand, and that his case is being funded by the CDA, but you don't know the rest of the story. Don't go anywhere. We'll be right back with the shocking story of the World's Unluckiest Man."

The station cut to a commercial break. I stuck in a cassette tape so I could tape what Mr. Harvey had to say. I couldn't believe our case was the subject of his report. His show was syndicated nationwide; millions would hear it. I waited impatiently for the commercial to end.

"Yes, misfortune first struck Dusty on the day he was born. His mother died of a blood clot while giving birth to him. His father was so distressed by the loss of his wife that he turned to liquor to make it through each day. Three years later he disappeared and left poor Dusty with his grandparents. They raised him as best they could on the

Double T Ranch just north of Dallas. At age seven Dusty nearly drowned when his grandfather's bass tracker struck a stump in Lake Lavon and flipped over. When he was eleven he was riding his pony when a storm blew up suddenly. He took cover under a tree and was nearly killed by a falling branch when the tree was hit by lightning. At twenty-five he thought his bad luck was behind him when he married Margie Bassett of Wylie, Texas. That marriage not only failed but Margie managed to spend Dusty's life savings before she divorced him.

"The only bright spot in Dusty's life was when he met Martha Hill of Dallas, his wife now of 22 years. Unfortunately their life has also been marred by tragedy, starting with the loss of their first child to pneumonia. Then Dusty was lured into the Tax Protest Movement, which has led to his current battle with the IRS, a tax debt over a hundred thousand dollars, and the alleged murder of Revenue Agent Bobby Tuttle. In between all of this Dusty fell off his tractor and broke his leg, had a heart attack, his house was blown away by a tornado, and now . . . yes, just today tragedy strikes again as his defense counsel in his murder trial, Stan Turner, has disappeared while on business in Ecuador.

"If the Guinness Book of World Records had a category for misfortune, Dusty Thomas would surely get that record. So now you know the rest of the story. This is Paul Harvey. Good day."

I couldn't believe multitudes of people would now be talking about Dusty and his propensity for misfortune. I wondered if this would change the general disdain the public had shown toward Dusty after his support from the CDA was announced. Perhaps this was the angle we needed for a temporary insanity defense. Dusty, the world's unluckiest man, had finally cracked. Who wouldn't after what he'd been through? Unfortunately, both Stan and Dusty were adamantly against it, but as the case came closer to trial they might change their mind. *I'll convince them that it's our only hope of saving Dusty's life.*

# THE ESCAPE 12

It had been a week since I had met with General Moya, yet the promised escape hadn't come to pass. It also seemed strange that no one had interrogated me since I had been there other than the General. Then I realized there was no policia. All this was just General Moya's trick to get me to give him Tex's money. But why hadn't we escaped, then? I wondered who he was. Was he in the Ecuadorian military, or was he one of those rebel leaders who seemed to roam the countryside with impunity? I guessed there had been some kind of snag in his plans. If he wasn't part of the government he might be worried about me going to the authorities rather than straight to the airport. I wouldn't do that, but he wasn't stupid enough to rely on my word. Perhaps he was planning his own getaway once I was freed.

Then, very early one morning—too early for breakfast—someone had inserted a key (or something) in the lock but was having trouble getting the to door to open. Finally, it did, and much to my surprise and shock, Monty stepped inside. He motioned for me to come with him. I jumped up and followed him out the door. He was about to turn down the hall when I grabbed his arm and said, "No, this way."

"What?"

"Trust me. I know the way out of here."

Monty frowned, then shrugged and followed me. I went to the door to the courtyard and opened it slowly, looking left, then right. It seemed deserted, so we raced across it to the door where I had been taken to meet General Moya. It was unlocked. A plain white envelope was laying on the table, as promised. I grabbed it as we moved quickly toward our escape route. The door in the back of the room led to another corridor. We went left, as I had been shown, passed a kitchen and then exited outside to an area where trash and garbage were stored for pickup. The smell nearly gagged us, but we pressed on to a gate leading outside the prison walls. It stood opened.

Once outside we traveled several blocks through the streets of the old city until we came to a main thoroughfare. I opened the envelope and found our passports, our airline tickets, a document with wiring instructions to General Moya's bank account in the Cayman Islands, and some local currency. I didn't know how much money it was but I assumed it was enough to pay a cab driver to take us to the airport. Fortuitously, a cab passed by and we hailed it. Monty told the driver to head to the airport and flashed the local currency. The driver nodded, and we got in.

"Okay, what's going on?" Monty asked.

I told him about General Moya and the deal I had struck.

"What about my guns?" he said. "I don't care about the damn luggage but those guns costs me a mint."

As we passed our hotel on the way to the airport we briefly considered stopping for our luggage and Monty's guns, but then decided we didn't have time.

"You can add your guns to your expense report. I'm sure Tex will be happy to reimburse you for their loss."

"Do you think we'll have any trouble at the airport?" he asked. "We'll be sitting ducks waiting for a plane."

The airport did worry me. I knew Rebekah would have filed a missing person's report by now and that airport security and local police would be looking for us. When we got to the airport I went straight to the ticket counter to check in while Monty kept watch. Luckily the next plane to Miami was boarding in less than thirty minutes so we wouldn't have to hang around too long.

I said to Monty, "I'm going to call Rebekah. I'll be right back."

Monty nodded and took a seat. After finding a pay phone, I gave the long distance operator my calling card number, and she placed the call. Rebekah answered quickly.

"Rebekah?"

"Stan! Is that you?"

"Yes, honey. It's me."

"Are you all right? I've been so worried. Oh, my God! I can't believe it's you."

"It's me. Believe it."

"Oh, God! I am so relieved. Where are you?"

"At the airport in Quito. We're waiting for our plane."

"What happened to you?"

After briefly explaining what had happened and assuring Rebekah that I'd soon be home, I hung up and rejoined Monty. At 7:25 AM we boarded the plane and waited as the other passengers came aboard and took their seats.

"I'll feel a lot better when we get off the ground," Monty said. "We'll be damn lucky to leave this country alive. For a while there back in my cell I figured it was all over for us."

"I know. I'm sorry I got you in this mess," I replied. "I guess I never fully appreciated the risk we were taking."

"Do you really think they'll let Tex go?"

"Yeah, the money is much more important to them than killing Tex."

"Do you think he'll be pissed off if you give the general his money?"

"Maybe, but I doubt it. I assume his life is worth more than that money! Anyway, I'll let Toni decide. That way if he is pissed off, he can't say I acted without authority."

"Good idea. You can't trust anyone nowadays."

The plane jerked as it moved away from the gate. A great sense of relief came over me as we taxied out to the runway. We got in line for our takeoff and I looked at Monty and smiled. Suddenly the big engines came to life and we started to move faster and faster down the runway, then suddenly the pilot cut the engines and aborted the take-off. Panic jabbed me like a switchblade in the back. I looked at Monty, who was shaking his head.

"Oh, God!" I said, as the plane taxied off the runway and came to a stop.

Excited chatter erupted among the passengers. I couldn't understand it, but obviously everyone was upset over the delay. The pilot's voice came over the loudspeaker, but again I couldn't understand what he was saying. Monty translated.

"Señoras and Señors, we are sorry for the delay in your flight but the tower has advised us there are unauthorized passengers on the plane. Once they are removed we will get back in line and be taking off momentarily. Our sincerest apologies for the delay."

Everyone started looking around obviously wondering who were the unauthorized passengers. My heart was beating like I'd just finished the White Rock Marathon. Monty had his face plastered against the window trying to see who was coming out to the plane.

"Are they after us?" I asked.

"Who else would they be after?" Monty moaned.

"Shit, now what are we going to do?"

Monty sat back in his chair, took a deep breath, and replied, "There's nothing we can do. Not a goddamned thing!"

A crewman came out of the cockpit and opened the front hatch. A portable stairway was lowered into place. Monty pointed to soldiers who were surrounding the plane; some began boarding. One of them headed our way. He was looking at a photograph he was carrying in his hand and then at each passenger as he went by. When he got to me he stopped, yelled something to the other soldiers, and then put his hand firmly on my shoulder. I was so scared I could scarcely breathe.

# THE GOLF PRO **13**

Stan's disappearance made the headlines in the Dallas Morning News and was the lead story on all the local TV newscasts. Several reporters were waiting outside for me when I got to the office. I talked with them briefly and then went inside. When I walked by Stewart's desk he handed me a thick pile of telephone messages from clients, friends, and other reporters who had called for information or to express their concern over Stan's disappearance.

"Oh, God. I hate all these distractions. I don't have time for this," I moaned.

"Sorry, Paula. Is there anything I can do to help?"

"Yes, let me dictate a short statement and you can return these calls for me."

"No problem, be glad to do it."

I sifted through a large stack of mail on my desk and noticed several handwritten letters. I opened the first and read its content.

> Dear Ms. Waters,
> Sorry to hear of your partner's disappearance.
> I know for a fact the government is behind it. They will do anything, including murder, to protect their revenue sources even if those sources are illegal and unconstitutional. You and Mr. Turner are very courageous for standing up to the IRS and our Congress that have betrayed the American People. We all pray that Stan is safe and soon will be back on the job helping you defend Dusty Thomas. God bless you.
>
> Yours truly,
> Wester

The other letters were similar. It seemed many members of the CDA had come to the erroneous conclusion that Stan and I supported their cause. I felt like writing them back and setting them straight, but I had more important things to do. Now that I had a vote of confidence from Dusty and his wife, I pulled out my notebook to check the next witness on my list: Frank Milborn, a professional golfer from Allen, Texas. The contact information I had on him indicated he was a pro at the Bent Tree Country Club. I called and made an appointment to see him. Since the Watsons had spotted a Mercedes out at the Double T Ranch around the time of Agent Tuttle's death, I decided to pay close attention to what each witness was driving. There were a black Lincoln and a Ford Mustang out in front of the clubhouse when I arrived. I went inside and introduced myself to the man at the counter. It was Milborn.

"I wasn't shocked to hear of Agent Tuttle's death actually. The way he treated people it's no wonder it didn't happen sooner. "

"How *did* he treat people?" I asked.

Milborn looked at me thoughtfully. "He treated everyone who owed taxes like they were criminals. I explained to him that my mother had been diagnosed with breast cancer and needed money to pay for her treatment. She never worked, and when my father died she couldn't afford to keep up his medical insurance. She was too young for Medicare. I gave her the money I had set aside for the taxes. But he didn't care. He was rude, insolent—unrelenting in his efforts to destroy me."

"That must have angered you."

"Of course it did, but there wasn't much I could do about it."

I nodded. "Did Tuttle ever come out to your club to harass you?"

He shook his head and sighed. "Oh, yeah. Many times. He looked for opportunities to humiliate me in front of my customers and friends."

"So, did you just take it or did you fight back?"

"I did call his supervisor and complain about his tactics."

"Do any good?"

He shrugged. "For a week or two. Then he just put more heat on me. I didn't dare complain again for fear he'd retaliate even more."

"Are you married?" I asked.

"Yes, I am. Lorraine is her name. She's a nurse. We've been married eight years now."

"Did agent Tuttle harass your wife as well?"

Milborn made a fist. "Yes, the bastard garnished her wages. She was humiliated at work. I could have—"

"Killed him?"

"Well, not literally. But I'll admit the thought crossed my mind."

"Did you know Agent Tuttle had a hit list?"

"A what?"

"A list of taxpayers that he targeted for special attention. You were on the list along with Dusty Thomas and several others."

He shook his head. "That figures."

"So, did he ever collect anything from you?" I asked.

"Unfortunately. He got a couple of my wife's paychecks, almost a thousand from our bank account, and he seized my bass boat."

"Please don't take offense, but I have to ask you some delicate questions."

"Like what?" Milborn asked warily.

"Like, do you own a shotgun?"

"Sure, I do a little dove hunting each year."

"A Remington?"

"I've got a Remington and a Winchester."

"Have you ever been to the Double T Ranch?"

"No."

"Do you remember where you were on the afternoon of July 11th?"

He grinned. "Watching your partner on TV, just like everybody else."

"Where was the TV?"

"In my office at the clubhouse."

"Were you alone?"

He nodded. "I wasn't giving any lessons, so I was catching up on paperwork."

Milborn had ample motive to kill Agent Tuttle but didn't seem angry enough to do it. Of course, at the time his wife's bank account was garnished his attitude might have been different—particularly if his wife was the emotional type. Whether Milborn was guilty or not, his lack of an alibi could create some reasonable doubt. The thought occurred to me that his wife too could be the perp.

"Did your wife ever hunt with you?"

"No. She didn't like killing animals. Strictly skeet shooting for her."

"What kind of a car does she drive?"

"A Mercedes"

"Gray?"

"No, silver."

It didn't seem likely that Lorraine was the killer, but she did drive a Mercedes. In my experience as an assistant DA I had learned that women didn't kill as often as men but, when they did, a shotgun wasn't the weapon of choice. They would more likely go for poisoning, a knife, or a small handgun. I did note that I needed to find out Lorraine's whereabouts when Agent Tuttle was killed. I thought of Monty and wished he were around to help me with some of this legwork. There was way too much for one woman to handle. I should have hired another investigator already, but that would have given the appearance that I had given up on Stan's and Monty's safe return. That would have upset Jodie and Rebekah, and they didn't need any more trauma right then.

For the umpteenth time I asked myself, where in the hell could they be? Why hasn't the kidnapper called demanding money? Something just didn't add up. What it was, I didn't know. But I did know I couldn't afford to lose my focus. I couldn't let anything distract me from my primary objective: proving Dusty Thomas innocent.

# INTERROGATION 14

Two soldiers rushed toward us. They talked excitedly and then motioned for us to stand. We both stood and they escorted us down the aisle and off the plane. A black Volvo was just pulling up along side the plane when we stepped out onto the runway. Agents Logan and Giles got out of the car and walked over to us. Although they were our adversaries back in the USA, I couldn't help feeling relieved. At least now I knew we'd get home safely. Monty was all smiles as he pumped Logan's hand.

"Boy, are we glad to see you two," Logan said. "Where have you been?"

"Locked up in some dungeon somewhere," I said.

"Really? Who kidnapped you?"

I shrugged. "You got me. They weren't very communicative. I have no idea what they wanted from us."

Logan looked at me warily. "How did you get away?"

I put my hand on Monty's shoulder. "Luckily I brought Monty along. He managed to figure out a way to escape. As soon as we got loose we came straight to the airport."

Logan gave Monty a hard look, then smiled and shook his head. "That's unbelievable. The police, the government—everybody's been scouring the city for you two."

Monty said, "The guards obviously didn't have much training or discipline. I just had to wait for the right moment to catch them off guard. It wasn't difficult."

Giles looked at us with genuine concern in her eyes, "Are you two all right? Do you need any medical attention?"

"No," I replied. "We're okay. They didn't really hurt us, just didn't feed us much. I bet I lost 20 pounds." I smiled and rubbed my stomach. "Luckily I had a little extra stored away. Find us a nice steak dinner and we'll be fine."

"I am sure that won't be a problem," Giles said.

Agent Logan motioned for us to get in the car so we did. The driver drove us back to the terminal and we were escorted to a private lounge. Logan kept pressing for information about our captors but I was reluctant to tell him the truth about our mission to Ecuador so I pled ignorance as much as possible.

"So, why didn't you just let us stay on the plane and catch up with us back in Dallas?" I asked.

"For security reasons," Logan replied. "When the word got out that you were on the way home a mob of people started gathering at Love Field. We have a government jet waiting to take you back to Dallas. We'll land at Addison Airport and avoid the melee."

They led us back out on the runway where a small Lear Jet sat waiting for takeoff. We all climbed aboard and took our seats. A lone stewardess offered us drinks and a snack. Logan continued to question me, but I told him I was tired and wanted to sleep. He finally left me alone and I closed my eyes. The Lear jet rolled down the runway and this time we took off and began our journey home. Although I was exhausted, I couldn't sleep. I was worried about what I was going to say to Logan and Giles when we got back to the States and I was forced to give them a detailed account of our time in Ecuador. I had to concoct a believable story so they would let me get back to work helping Paula defend Dusty. Monty was a problem because he might contradict me and ruin everything.

There was also the problem of Tex. He was still a captive and I was his only hope. I needed to wire money to General Moya so he'd put Tex on the next plane home, yet the FBI was obviously monitoring my account. It was a delicate situation and one miscalculation could be disastrous. As our plane glided effortless through the sky, I finally fell into a shallow slumber. The plane's sudden dissension awakened me. It seemed like we were getting ready to land but we couldn't possibly be back to Dallas. I looked over at Logan and saw him straining to see something out of the window. Curious, I looked out my window but saw nothing but ocean. Then I noticed land in the distance.

Looking at Logan again I said, "Are we landing?"

He looked up and smiled. "Yes, we need to refuel."

I nodded but the explanation didn't make a lot of sense. We'd only been flying a couple of hours and I didn't think we could possibly be out of gas."

Monty whispered, "Bullshit. One of these babies can fly three thousand miles easy before refueling."

Alarmed, I glanced out the window again and saw a large bay and what appeared to be an airstrip on one of its fingers.

"Where are we?" I asked.

"Naval Base Guantanamo," Logan replied.

"We're in Cuba?"

"Right," Logan said as the plane lunged forward into a steeper descent. I didn't know what to think about landing in Cuba. It wasn't exactly on the way to Dallas.

Monty whispered. "This is where they run our antidrug trafficking and anti-terrorism operations for South America and the Caribbean."

"You don't think—?"

My thought was interrupted by the jolt of the plane landing. I gave Monty a worried look. Giles and Logan were whispering something. As we taxied toward a building in the distance I realized we hadn't come here for gas. We were here for our debriefing and whether or not we ever left depended on what we told our interrogators. It was obvious to me now. They perceived us as enemies of the state because of our CDA backing and our mission to Ecuador. If they wanted they could report that we had been killed by our kidnappers and no one would be the wiser. Oh, God. Would I ever see Rebekah and the kids again? I looked at Monty as the plane came to a stop. I regretted that he had been dragged into this mess. I cursed the CDA for their exploitation of Dusty Thomas and vowed someday to pay them back for the chaos they'd brought to my life.

# THE BODYGUARDS 15

On Friday, August 8, Rebekah called and said she'd heard from Stan. I was elated. Finally, he'd be home and we could get down to business. Although I had been at the investigation for several weeks I didn't really feel like I had accomplished much. I needed to brainstorm with Stan and figure out the direction our investigation should be going. But after two days had passed with Stan and Monty still missing, I was devastated. Stan had told Rebekah they were getting on a plane and would be home late that evening. What could have happened to them?

I called Agent Giles to see if she knew anything but I was told she was out of town on assignment. Logan apparently was with her as he was also unavailable. The airlines weren't much help either. They said Stan and Monty were on the plane when it left Quito but they didn't make their connecting flight from Miami to Dallas. Rebekah understandably was beside herself having her hopes raised and then dashed.

Despite a bad case of depression, I had no choice but to keep working. Dusty and Martha were depending on me and I couldn't let them down. As I was flipping through my notebook to decide who I still needed to question, I heard a commotion outside. Jodie went to the door and opened it.

"What the hell?" she said.

I got up and joined her at the front door. There was a crowd of reporters and a TV crew filming two men with shotguns holding an impromptu news conference.

"My name is Nathan Block. I'm the press secretary for Raymond Farr and the CDA. With me here today is Ronald Jack, our chief security officer. We have been advised by informed sources that Stan Turner and Monty Dozier have been taken into custody by agents of the United States government and are being held as political prisoners. The purpose of their detention and illegal incarceration is to obstruct and tamper with the trial of Dusty Thomas. It is clear that the government intends to convict Dusty Thomas without regard to his guilt or innocence and have taken steps to deny him his constitutional right to counsel of his choice."

"Our most honorable leader, Raymond Farr, has instructed myself and Ronald Jack to provide security for Miss Paula Waters during the duration of the Dusty Thomas case. The CDA will not allow the federal government to abduct her as they have her co-counsel, Stan Turner. This flagrant violation of our Constitution will not be tolerated. Thank you."

"Mr. Block!" a reporter yelled. "How do you know Stan Turner was taken into custody by the federal government?"

"We have reliable sources within the federal government who have confirmed that Stan Turner and Monty Dozier were taken off a commercial flight which would have brought them back to Dallas, and taken to an undisclosed location to be held indefinitely."

"Who are these sources?" the reporter asked.

"Obviously we cannot disclose who they are as that would compromise them. But, I will assure you these are extremely reliable sources high up in the federal government. You should ask the FBI to deny that they have Mr. Turner and Mr. Dozier in custody."

Jodie closed the door and we went back into my office. The phone was ringing so Jodie picked it up. She indicated it was a reporter wanting to talk to me. I motioned for her to take a message.

"This is all I need—the damn CDA following me around everywhere I go," I said.

Jodie raised her eyebrows and said, "I don't know. A little security couldn't hurt after everything that has happened."

"I know," I said, "but we've been trying to distance ourselves from the CDA. Having them hanging around isn't good."

"Well, tell them you don't want their help then."

"Somehow I don't think they would take too kindly to that. It would just piss them off and we don't need any more enemies," I said, "especially a bunch of anarchists. . . . I guess I'll just have to live with it."

"Do you think the feds have Stan and Monty?"

I replied, "No, that's ridiculous. Why would they do that? Besides there is a court order prohibiting them from messing with us."

Jodie shrugged. "But why—"

"The CDA will do or say anything if they think it will help their cause. They don't have a clue where Stan and Monty are. As usual, they are trying to take advantage of the situation."

Jodie raised her eyebrows again, shook her head, and went back to whatever she was doing and I started flipping through my notebook again. A notation about a charitable foundation jumped out at me. What charitable foundation? I hadn't talked to Bobby's supervisor Robert Perkins yet so I decided to ask him. Perkins agreed to meet me at his office downtown in the Earl Cabell Federal Building. When I left my office my two CDA bodyguards, an FBI agent and several press vehicles followed me. I felt like I was leading a funeral procession.

Perkins was younger than I expected—late thirties maybe. He escorted me to a conference room and asked if I'd like something to drink. I asked for a glass of water.

"So, now that you've been at it awhile, do you still think your client is innocent?" Perkins asked.

"Absolutely. Dusty Thomas is a very kind and gentle man. He isn't capable of murder."

Perkins chuckled. "Bobby Tuttle could have driven a Buddhist monk to murder. He was our best collector. He put the fear of God into each and every taxpayer who crossed his path. Once they became his target, they would do anything to get the taxes paid just to get him off their back."

"That's what I understand, but any one of those other taxpayers could just have easily murdered him."

"But they weren't found hovering over the body."

I ignored his comment and said, "I'm particularly interested in a charitable organization he was after. Do you know who I'm talking about?"

"The People's Mission. Bobby had been after them for years. They are a so-called church but the organization is really just a front for some high-rollers trying to avoid paying taxes."

"How many people are involved in the People's Mission?" I asked.

"Maybe fifty or so."

"Who's the ringleader?"

"A guy named Riley Davidson started it. He's actually in the real estate business but he operates out of his non-profit corporation. Tuttle was in the process of auditing Davidson's corporation as well as several other members."

"Davidson ever make threats or get violent?" I asked.

"Yes, he's very self-righteous and outspoken about the propriety of what he is doing. One of his relatives, a cousin I think, is an attorney and set the whole thing up. The corporation takes care of all his expenses, both personal and business, so he has no need for a salary. All the real estate income goes to the corporation. Since it claims to be a non-profit corporation it pays no taxes."

"Wow. What a deal."

"Anyway, Tuttle disallowed a slew of personal expenses paid by the corporation and assessed it penalties and interest. Of course, he appealed and I don't think a final ruling has come down yet."

"How did Davidson take it?"

"He screamed and yelled and claimed religious persecution. I think he contacted his congressman."

"Does he really practice a religion?"

"I guess. He talks like a preacher, but I don't think he is affiliated with any reputable church in this country."

Perkins and I talked for quite awhile. I got a lot of background information on Tuttle's service with the Internal Revenue Service and personal life. He also told me how to get in contact with Davidson. I seemed to be gathering quite a list of suspects, each of whom had sufficient motives to kill Tuttle. While I was downtown I stopped into the DA's office to see Bart Williams. It was time for a little intelligence gathering. Bart was glad to see me and invited me to lunch. We went to a little café underneath One Main Place.

"Any word on Stan?" Bart asked.

"No, have you heard anything?"

"No, just what I read in the papers."

"What about the CDA claim that Stan has been taken into custody by the Feds?"

"Ordinarily I would say it was BS, but I heard one side of a conversation between Trenton and Logan. It sounded like they believed Stan had gone over to the Dark Side and would have to be treated accordingly."

"What does that mean?" I asked.

"I don't know exactly, but it didn't sound good."

"Maybe I need to file a writ of habeas corpus and a contempt motion in Judge Stanton's court. I don't think he would take kindly to the government taking Stan into custody."

"He wouldn't, unless there was evidence that Stan was doing something wrong."

"But he wasn't."

"What was he doing in Quito?" Bart asked.

One of the risks in discussing the Dusty Thomas case with Bart was he was just as liable to get confidential information out of me as I was from him. I didn't want the prosecutor to know why Stan went to Quito but if I didn't come up with some plausible explanation Bart would think it was related to the CDA or Dusty Thomas.

"One of his best clients was reported missing by his wife. Evidence at his home indicated he had gone to Ecuador on business. Stan went looking for him."

"Oh, Jesus. Why didn't he file a missing person's report and let the government deal with it."

"His wife wanted Stan to handle it. She didn't think the government would try very hard to find him. Stan agreed just to go down and see if he could figure out what had happened to him. He was supposed to check things out and come right back."

"Your partner is pretty stupid."

"Maybe, but if I was in trouble I'd want him to be my lawyer. He doesn't throw in the towel just because a case is difficult or a little dangerous."

"Well, if I can help out in any way, let me know. I know it must be hell trying to prepare the Thomas case on your own. You look stressed out."

I felt stressed out. Was the government really after Stan? Did I need to go to court with a writ of habeas corpus?

"I'm *am* a bit tired," I confessed.

"Well, take the afternoon off and rest," Bart said as he got up to leave. "I'll drop by tonight and take your mind off your troubles."

I smiled. "Hmm. That would be nice."

"Okay, then—until tonight."

I got up and hugged him goodbye. After Bart had left I sat back down to digest our conversation. Before I could go to court with a writ of habeas corpus, I needed a little evidence. I couldn't act on rumor and suspicion alone. What a mess this was. How did Stan do it all those years by himself? I felt so alone and helpless but I couldn't start feeling sorry for myself. The best therapy for desperation, I had discovered, was work, so I asked for a telephone book and looked up the number for the People's Mission.

# HURRICANE 16

Guantanamo Bay was not on my list of 100 places I wanted to visit. Four hundred miles south of Miami, it was situated strategically in the Caribbean where the U.S. could monitor drug traffickers preying on citizens of the U.S. It was a bargain for the measely $4,028 annual rent the United States paid to Cuba for it, particularly since Fidel Castro never cashed the rent checks. President Reagan had talked of abandoning the facility for being too expensive to maintain and not critical to U.S. security, but the Cuban population of Florida and many members of Congress were so outraged by the idea that he finally abandoned it. Giles narrated a brief history of the base on the way to our quarters. So far we hadn't been put in leg irons.

"So, how long are we going to be here?" I asked. "I'm kind of anxious to get home and see my family."

Logan shrugged. "We just need to ask you a few questions. We can't be letting American citizens get pushed around. We have to know everything that happened to you. It shouldn't take more than a day or two."

"A day or two!" I moaned. "How about an hour or two?"

Logan smiled. "It's not that simple, Stan. The CIA is involved now."

Logan and Giles dropped us off at our quarters and said we would be picked up at 1400 hours for lunch and then our initial round of interrogation would begin. It was fortunate that Monty and I had a few minutes alone to get our stories straight as they would surely try to find inconsistencies in what we had to say. We took a walk while we talked, as we suspected our quarters would be bugged. When we returned we took advantage of the time we had left to take a much needed shower. We felt a little better when the MP showed up to take us to lunch. As promised we were given a nice juicy steak. Unfortunately, I couldn't enjoy it, as I felt like we were just being fattened up for the slaughter. After lunch we were separated and taken to our interrogation rooms.

"This is George Michaels and Rod Hartnett with the CIA. They will be handling the debriefing," Logan said.

I took a seat at a rectangular table in the small stark room painted blue with gray trim. There was a two-way mirror on one wall, a counter to my right with a coffee maker perking away, and a bookshelf opposite where I was sitting. Michaels sat across from me and Hartnett stood in the corner near the door.

"So, Mr. Turner, what brought you to Ecuador?"

"An old client and friend was in Quito on business and disappeared. His wife asked me to go down there and see if I could find him."

"Who was the client?"

"Tex Weller. He is an insurance agent and financial advisor."

"Why didn't she call the police or the FBI?"

"Tex goes away on business a lot and she wasn't sure anything was wrong. She just got worried and asked me to check it out."

"So, right in the middle of the biggest murder trial of your life you just jump on an airplane go to Ecuador?"

"Tex was my very first client, he's a good friend, and he refers a lot of business to me. I needed to find him and make sure he was okay. We didn't figure the State Department would jump on something like this very quickly and we know how quickly a trail can get cold in a few days."

"All right. So who is this guy you brought with you, Monty—"

"Dozier. He's an ex-cop, ex-Army, private investigator who helps me out on cases from time to time. I didn't think it was a good idea to go alone so I brought him along. Besides, he speaks Spanish."

"So what did you do when you got to Quito?" Michaels asked.

"We had a lead that he did business with the United Peoples Bank of Ecuador so we checked it out first."

"What kind of lead?"

"Some correspondence."

"So, who did you talk to at the bank?"

"Oh, God. Ah . . . Lantz? I don't remember his first name."

"What did he tell you?"

"He said that Tex had indeed been there but that he hadn't seen him for several days."

"Did he say what kind of business Tex had there?"

"No, he hadn't handled the business himself. Another officer of the bank—Mr. Alfaro—handled it and he wasn't available."

Michaels stood up and poured himself a cup of coffee. "Would you like a cup?" he asked.

"Sure," I replied and Michaels filled another cup.

Hartnett, who had been very quiet up until now, took a seat across from me. Michaels stood over me sipping his coffee.

Hartnett asked, "So, where did you go from the bank?"

"We had a credit card receipt from a store, I forget the name, so we dropped by there and showed Tex's photograph to the clerk. Unfortunately, he didn't recognize him. After that we went back to the hotel. We had earlier asked about Tex since he had stayed at the same hotel, but were told to ask the afternoon staff as they were more likely to have seen him."

"Did you check with them?"

"Yes, they remembered him but had no idea where he had gone."

"Did you do anything else?"

"Sure, we called the police to see if he was in jail and Monty called all the hospitals. We finally decided he had either left Ecuador or had been kidnapped. That's when the police broke into our room."

I told Michaels and Hartnett about our arrest and incarceration at an unknown location and how Monty had finally taken advantage of an opportunity to escape. I thought everything was going well until Michaels dropped his bombshell.

"Did you meet with General Raul Moya while you were in Ecuador?"

"Moya? I talked to some military type people, but I don't remember their names."

"We know you met with General Moya. An informant advised us that you were taken to see him."

I shrugged. "It's possible. There was a military man who questioned me—tall, dark brown hair, full beard. He said the police had Tex in custody. He didn't say what the charges were. Apparently the police picked us up because we were looking for Tex and were asking questions about him. They mistakenly thought we were business associates."

"That was General Moya. He's a ruthless guerrilla leader who operates in Ecuador. He's been involved in the kidnapping and murder of several U.S. businessmen."

I shook my head. "Really? I didn't know that. I know very little about Ecuador. This was my *first* and *last* trip there, believe me."

"I'd like to believe you, Stan," Michaels said, "but a few things don't add up."

"Like what?" I asked.

"Like how you managed to escape so easily?"

"So easily? I brought Monty along because he was a highly trained, experienced soldier just in case we got into trouble. It paid off because he was able to break us out."

"Right. And then there is the question of the 1.8 million dollars," Michaels interjected.

"What about it?" I said.

"You're laundering money for the CDA, aren't you?"

I let out a gasp. "Oh, Jesus! Give me a break. I hate the CDA. They're nothing but a bunch of scumballs. I wouldn't give them the time of day if they begged me."

"Scumballs who paid you $50,000."

"Listen. That's old news. So, the CDA is funding Dusty Thomas' defense. Big deal."

"Why was $1.8 million wired to your trust account?"

"I don't know. That money belongs to Tex and obviously I haven't been able to talk to him about it."

The interrogation continued for hours. I was so exhausted I could hardly stay awake. I wondered how Monty was holding up. I wasn't too worried about him because he was an ex-cop and knew how interrogations worked. Also, I had kept him pretty much in the dark to protect Tex so he didn't know anything that could really hurt me or Tex. Finally at 1900 hours we were returned to our quarters. We didn't dare say anything about the interrogation so we just engaged in a little small talk until our dinner arrived. After dinner we took a short walk and then went to bed, both exhausted. When I woke up the next morning it was after 1100 hours.

Outside our quarters there were a couple MP's stationed to keep an eye on us. Not that we could go anywhere, as the base was only two and a half miles wide and surrounded by an impenetrable fence. It was windy out and the sky had an eerie glow to it. I walked up to one of the MP's and said, "Looks like a storm is brewing."

"Yes, a hurricane is expected tomorrow morning."

"A hurricane?"

"Yes, we get a lot of them here."

"Wonderful. Are we safe here?"

He shrugged. "It depends on how high the winds get."

"Have you seen Agent Logan or Giles? We were wondering what was on the agenda today."

"Sorry, I don't know. I was instructed to keep you in your quarters until I got further orders."

I nodded and had started back to our quarters when I saw a jeep approaching. It was Giles and she was in a hurry. She skidded to a stop in front of me.

"Get your stuff and get in. We've got to leave now to beat the hurricane."

Elated with the news of our imminent departure, we hurried inside, got our stuff, and took off. Giles drove fast down the narrow asphalt road toward the airstrip. I could see our Lear Jet was waiting for us on the runway. Logan was on the tarmac watching a crew member filling the jet with fuel. We stopped in front of the plane and climbed aboard.

I wondered if our nightmare was over or just beginning so I asked, "So, are we going back to Dallas?"

Logan gave me a stern look. "Yeah, Stan. We're going back to Dallas. Apparently you managed to call your wife at the airport."

I smiled and nodded. My phone call had saved our lives. Rebekah knew we had escaped and were on a plane home. She had obviously told Paula and the press and now we were expected. If the government had planned to detain us and blame it on the kidnappers that opportunity had evaporated. I couldn't wait to get home. Our only problem now was a category five hurricane.

# PEOPLE'S MISSION **17**

The People's Mission was operated out of an executive suite in Carillon Towers in North Dallas. The receptionist told me to have a seat and she would tell Mr. Davidson that I was there to see him. I knew nothing about Reverend Riley Davidson other than the official IRS view that he was nothing but a tax evader. I wondered how people like Riley Davidson figured they could ever get away with not paying their taxes. They must live in a cloud of self delusion or something to think that the government would just let them off the hook because they were self-proclaimed ministers of God.

"Ms. Waters?"

"Yes, I'm sorry to intrude but I was in the neighborhood and thought I'd stop by. I guess you know I'm an attorney and I represent Dusty Thomas."

"Oh, bless you, my child. Now *there's* a man who needs all the help the Lord can give him."

"Yes, he does indeed. . . . I understand you and Dusty Thomas have something in common."

Davidson looked at me curiously. "What's that?"

"Your dislike of Agent Tuttle."

Davidson smiled. "Praise the Lord. Actually I loved agent Tuttle, as misguided a man as he was. I only hope that he is in heaven on the right side of the Father—although I fear he may be in the pits of hell, actually."

I laughed. "I appreciate your honesty, Reverend. Why do you suppose agent Tuttle had you on his hit list?"

"His hit list. Did he really have such a list?"

"Yes, so I'm told."

"Hmm. Well, I suppose because he was an atheist he couldn't understand how anyone could be so immersed in the Lord's work."

"Or he didn't understand how you figured you didn't have to pay taxes."

"Does the Catholic Church pay taxes, the Baptist, or the Lutherans?"

"I suppose not, but aren't you also a stockbroker?"

"Only out of necessity. I would much prefer to do nothing but preach the word of God, but unfortunately I have to eat and pay my rent."

"I see. So you didn't have any animosity toward Agent Tuttle even though he was trying to make your life a living hell?"

"No, not at all. He was a misguided spirit that I tried but couldn't reach."

"Just for the record. Where were you the day of his murder?"

"Training some fellow ministers of the word."

"Other persons who had been ordained in your church?" I asked.

"Yes. Our church is growing rapidly and we need ministers to reach all of the heathens."

"So, the people you were training can back up your story?"

"Yes, of course."

It appeared Reverend Davidson had an alibi but there were others in his organization who I was sure didn't. The only problem was finding time to interview each and every one of them. I doubted Reverend Davidson would be anxious to help but I did manage to get a roster out of him. When I got back to the office I mentioned to Jodie my problem with the lack of manpower.

"I have the same problem. With Stan gone I've had to do a lot of things he would usually do."

"Like what?" I asked.

"Well, today I had to go to a creditors meeting for one of his bankruptcy clients."

"Can you do that?"

"Yeah, the trustee knows Stan is missing so he hasn't complained about me standing in."

"Well, if you need me to do anything, just let me know."

"Okay, I will probably need you to come to court with me tomorrow."

"Oh really, what's going on?"

"GMAC is trying to take away one of our client's cars and Stan is scheduled at a preliminary hearing. I could do it, but I'm not an attorney."

"Gee. I have no clue—"

"It's all right. I'll tell you what to say."

I laughed. "Okay, whatever. Did Stan teach you all this stuff?"

"Yes, he trained me to do all the paperwork and took me to court a few times so I could see exactly how the process worked. He thinks I should go to law school."

"Well, maybe you should."

"I'm thinking about it," Jodie said. "I only have one more semester before I graduate from college."

"You work full time and go to college too?"

"Right. Stan lets me work a flexible schedule so I can attend classes."

"Sounds like you have a great boss."

"He is. I just wish I could do something to help find him."

"Me too."

"Anyway, Stan sometimes sends me out to interview people and do investigations. Maybe I can help you with the People's Mission. Just tell me what you are looking for and I'll be happy to interview some of the members."

It was an interesting idea and I certainly needed all the help I could get. Jodie was a smart girl and she was attractive enough that the other members of the People's Mission would be anxious to talk to her. I figured it would be good for Jodie, too, as it would take her mind off of Stan for a while. I opened my briefcase and pulled out the roster Reverend Davidson had given me.

I handed the roster to her and said, "Okay, we're looking for someone who was particularly angry at Agent Tuttle, angry enough to want to do him harm. Check each alibi and find out what kind of car they were driving—make, model and color."

Jodie smiled and took the roster. "No problem. This will be fun."

When I got home that night the light was flashing on my answering machine. It was a message from Bart telling me he'd be over at 7:30 to take me to dinner. It was 6:15, so I just had time to take a bath and change into something more appropriate for the evening. While the water was running I turned on the evening news.

"Now here is Troy Dungan with the Channel 8 weather report," a reporter said.

"Hurricane Bonnie has changed direction, picked up speed, and is heading toward Cuba as we speak. It's expected to make landfall sometime after 8:00 P.M. Winds have been reported at 118 miles per hour and the Cuban population is bracing for the worst. We'll keep an eye on Bonnie and let you know if it poses any future threat to the Gulf Coast."

"Thank you, Troy. In other news, still no word on attorney Stan Turner, missing now for more than two weeks. It was reported yesterday that Turner had phoned home to tell his wife he was about to board a commercial airplane out of Quito, Ecuador headed for Miami. But that's the last anyone has heard of him. A spokesman for the CDA claimed Turner and his companion, Monty Dozier, had been taken into custody by U.S. officials and flown to an undisclosed location. The State Department denies that Turner is in custody but confirms that according to airport records he did take off from Quito last night in a small jet. There is no word on who owned the plane and where it was headed."

"What a bizarre story. Let's just hope that plane wasn't headed anywhere near Cuba," the reporter said.

I shut off the TV and headed to the bathtub. There is nothing better to sooth a tired, worn out body than a hot bath. I removed my clothes quickly and climbed into the water. The heat immediately began to relax me and the fragrance of the bath oil I had generously poured into the water filled me with energy. I was looking forward to a night out and the companionship and love making that lie ahead. I closed my eyes and drifted off.

But it wasn't Bart who was in my dreams. It was Stan knocking at my door. I ran to it quickly, flung open the door and rushed into his arms. He put one arm around me, swept me off my feet and carried me to my bed. We undressed quickly and—the doorbell interrupted my fantasy. I opened my eyes in frustration and looked at the small crystal clock on the counter. It was 7:25.

"Damn it," I moaned rising from the tub. I grabbed a towel and quickly dried myself, then I put on a robe and went to the front door. Peering out the peep hole I saw it was Bart and let him in. He frowned.

"Sorry, I'm running a little behind. Get yourself a drink and I'll be right with you."

He smiled. "No problem. Take your time."

Luckily I had already laid out a short black cocktail dress to wear for the evening and all the necessary accessories so it didn't take me long to get ready. Bart had finished off a bourbon and was about to pour another one when I made my appearance.

"Oh, wow!" he exclaimed.

"You like my dress?"

"That too," he said with a wry smile.

He was so sweet, always throwing out compliments at every opportunity. Bart escorted me to the parking garage and we got into his silver Mercedes. Seeing his car startled me. I had forgotten he had a silver Mercedes.

"I probably shouldn't tell you this, but we found a witness who saw a car just like this one shortly after agent Tuttle was shot."

"Oh, am I a suspect now?"

"No, of course not. There are a lot of these cars around, I would imagine."

"Probably."

"The one seen near the Double T Ranch had its left side view mirror severed."

"Really?" Bart said.

"Yes. I wonder how it happened."

Bart chuckled. "Well, I happen to have some experience in that regard."

"How's that?"

"Well, you know I have that old antique Model T parked in my garage that I'm restoring. It takes up a lot of room so I have to park far to the left in my garage. One day I was in a hurry pulling out and knocked the frickin' side mirror right off. I had to take the car to the dealer and have them install a new one. They had to take the whole door apart to do it."

I laughed. "Brilliant, Bart. I bet you were pissed."

"Tell me about it."

Bart drove us North on Highway 75 to Richardson and a restaurant called the Swan Court. There was a small band playing and the atmosphere was perfect. We ordered cocktails and listened to the band play. Despite my desire to get my mind off of work I couldn't help but think of the news report about Stan. Why had he switched planes?

After a while we went into the restaurant and ordered dinner. We talked about a lot of things and intentionally avoided anything to do with work or the Dusty Thomas case. It was a pleasant evening which ended in Bart's bedroom. But even while we were making love, my mind was on Stan and I pretended I was making love to him. As long as it was dark it was easy to sustain my fantasy, but when the light of dawn illuminated the bedroom it was Bart sleeping peacefully beside me. It was stupid, I know, to obsess over Stan. Even if he returned safely, I knew I couldn't have him. But I couldn't help how I felt and the more I tried to put him out of my mind, the more my heart ached for him.

# THE RETURN 18

Rain pelted the windows as we began to accelerate down the runway. Lightning flashed and thunder shook us as we picked up speed. We took off in only mild turbulence but once airborne felt the full brunt of the approaching hurricane. The pilot tried to get over the storm but the small Lear jet didn't have the capability to go over 15,000 ft. The plane lurched then suddenly dropped quickly. My stomach felt like it was being ripped from my torso. Giles screamed as we plunged into the darkness below. I smiled at her but she didn't seem to be amused. As we got farther away from the storm the ride became smoother and everyone seemed to relax. It occurred to me that the hurricane would be another way the FBI could get rid of Monty and me. They could simply say our plane went down trying to pass through the storm.

Several hours later I looked down and saw that we were approaching the Texas Coast. I spotted Galveston and the Houston Ship Channel. Relief came over me like a cool breeze. We were actually being taken home. Forty-five minutes later we landed at Addison Airport and deplaned. As I walked down the stairway I spotted Jodie and Paula running toward us. As I stepped on the tarmac Paula jumped into my arms. She squeezed me hard and tears were streaming down her cheeks. Finally she let go and gave Monty a hug. Jodie and I embraced and I noticed she was crying too.

"Oh, Stan, I'm so relieved you're home," Paula said, smiling broadly. "I couldn't believe it when they called and said you were at the airport."

"How long have you been here?"

"They just called us thirty minutes ago. Jodie and I jumped right in the car and came straight here. We didn't even have time to pick up Rebekah. She's waiting anxiously for you at home."

"Let's go. I'm anxious to see her too."

Paula nodded. "Sure. We'll drive you two home."

We followed Paula to her car. As we approached, I noticed two men standing in front of her BMW holding shotguns.

"Who are those men?" I asked.

"Oh, they are my CDA bodyguards."

"Your what!"

Paula explained how the CDA had used my disappearance to bolster their case of a government conspiracy to deny Dusty Thomas a fair trial. As we got to the car several cars pulled up followed by the Channel 5 News van. Reporters quickly scampered out of their vehicles and surrounded us.

"Mr. Turner. Did you just get back?" a reporter asked.

I replied. "Yes, just a few minutes ago?"

"Where have you been all this time?" another reported asked.

"Well, it's a long story. I don't have time to go into it right now other than to say that Monty and I are fine and glad to be home."

"Were you being held by the FBI?" the first reporter asked.

I smiled as I saw Logan and Giles watching us. "Ah.... I have no comment on that at this time. Thank you."

We all got in the car. I sat in the front passenger seat so I could talk to Paula. She eased us slowly out of the growing crowd and then accelerated on to the main road out of the airport. As we drove home I gave Jodie and Paula a brief synopsis of our adventure. Monty filled-in the details I left out. Then Paula updated us on the Dusty Thomas case.

When she was done I smiled and shook my head. "I'm sorry I deserted you. I bet it's been a nightmare working on the case alone."

"It's been hard, but Jodie's been helping out some. I'm just glad you're back so we can talk about what I've turned up so far and decide what to do next."

"Me, too. I've had enough of Ecuador and the Caribbean."

We dropped Monty off at his apartment and finally made it to my house. Rebekah and the kids poured out the front as we drove up. It was pandemonium as Rebekah smothered me with hugs and kisses and the kids danced around us laughing and giggling in delight. Paula watched us in amazement. Finally when the excitement died down, I thanked Paula for driving me home and she left.

"Daddy, where have you been?" Marcia asked. "We've missed you."

"I had to find a friend who was lost down in Ecuador," I replied.

"Where is Ecuador?"

"It's in South America three or four thousand miles from here, on the Equator."

"What's the Equator?' Marcia asked.

"It's the middle of the Earth. Go get your globe and I'll show you."

Marcia left and Rebekah shook her head and said, "I wasn't sure I'd ever see you again. You read all the time about corporate executives and diplomats getting kidnapped and held for ransom. Rarely do they escape alive. Every time the phone rang I cringed in fear expecting it to be a call telling me you had been killed."

"I know it must have been hard. I'm so sorry you had to go through this. I guess it was foolish of me to go to Ecuador."

"Every day I went to Mass and prayed you'd be returned to me safely. Father Bob's got to know me pretty well."

"Well, your prayers worked. When we were taken from our hotel I had my doubts as to whether we'd ever make it out of there alive. But every time I lost hope something miraculous would happen. God must have answered your prayers."

Rebekah came over to me and held me tightly. "Don't ever leave me again, okay? No more rescue missions."

"Okay," I said as our lips met and we kissed passionately. When we stopped to catch our breath Rebekah's eyes lit up.

She said, "Are you hungry? When did you eat last? Come on, Let's go to the kitchen. I'll fix you something to eat."

Rebekah led me to the kitchen and I sat down at the table while she worked. It felt good to be back home. There was so much love here. I had taken it all for granted and almost lost it. While Rebekah was fixing me something to eat I closed my eyes, took a deep breath, and said a silent prayer. *Thank you Lord for watching over me and bringing me home safely. Thank you for protecting and comforting Rebekah and the kids while I was away. Guide me these next few perilous days so that I can bring Tex home safely. And if Dusty Thomas is innocent, show me the way to prove it. I know I am but a weak sinner, but help me gain wisdom and understanding so that I can do thy will on Earth. Amen.*

Rebekah looked up and gave me a worried smile. She seemed to sense my fear and anxiety. We had been married a long time and gone through so much adversity that we had learned to feel each others inner emotions. Our eyes met and she said sadly, "It's not over yet, is it?"

I shook my head and replied, "No, it isn't."

# THE ACCIDENT 19

When I got up the next day I was excited about going to work for the first time in weeks. I had been so lonely without Stan it would be great having him back. I hoped he had missed me as much as I had missed him. It was a special day and I wanted Stan to notice me so I searched through my closet for something memorable. After awhile I narrowed it down to a pinstriped suit with satin lapels and mini skirt, and a two piece red crepe suit, both with plunging necklines to remind Stan I could be so much more than simply his partner. It was a tough decision but I finally went with the pinstriped suit so my intentions would be less obvious. I finished it off with a dangling crystal necklace that would draw Stan's attention right where I wanted it.

I was too keyed up to eat so I settled for a light breakfast of cantaloupe and orange juice. Then I put the final touches on my make-up and left. As I drove out of the parking garage I was expecting to see my two bodyguards but they weren't on duty. I looked at my watch and realized it was only 7:30. I was thirty minutes ahead of schedule. I figured they were probably still at the donut shop.

As I turned onto Keller Springs Road toward Preston Road, a jogger came out of nowhere and ran in front of me. I slammed on my brakes and swerved to the right but it wasn't enough. There was a loud "thud" and the lady went rolling across the roadway. As I came to a halt I opened the door and rushed over to the young Hispanic lady and knelt down beside her. My heart was pounding. She was moaning and rubbing her left hip.

"Are you okay? . . . I'm so sorry. I never saw you."

"My leg, it's killing me. Why did you run me down?"

"I didn't—"

A car stopped and two men jumped out. They rushed over and started talking to the woman in Spanish. To my shock, they picked her up and carried her to their car.

"What are you doing?! She shouldn't be moved, " I yelled.

"It's okay, señorita. We're going to take her the emergency room."

"No, let's call an ambulance. You may make her injuries worse."

The two men ignored me and put the lady into the back seat of their car. I was beside myself, but there was nothing I could do. As the car started to leave I said, "What's her name? Where are you taking her?"

Again they ignored me and drove away. Suddenly I was alone. I didn't know what to do. Should I call the police and tell them what happened? They'd think I was nuts since I didn't know the victim's name or where she had been taken. *Damn it!* For several minutes I stood in front of my car and pondered the situation. Cars drove by and people stared at me standing on the side of the road dressed to kill. Finally, I let out a frustrated cry of despair and got back into my car. As I drove off I noticed blood on the pavement where the woman had fallen.

When I got back to the office I called the Presbyterian Hospital Emergency Room, as it was the closest to the accident scene. No luck. No one matching the woman's description had been seen. Then I called Brookhaven and Parkland Hospital. Still no luck. I got up and started pacing back and forth when I noticed a police car pull up out in front of our offices. Two cops got out and walked over to my car and carefully inspected it. They lingered and my curiosity got the better of me so I walked outside to talk to them.

"Hello, ma'am," one of them said, "Is this your car?"

"Yes, it is. Is there a problem?"

The officer nodded. "Yes, ma'am. It looks like this vehicle was just in an accident."

"Well, it was. I hit a lady and I was just trying to find out what hospital they took her to."

The officer frowned. "Well, that hasn't been determined yet. The ambulance was just pulling up when we came searching for your car."

"What? But some men took her to the hospital. They didn't tell me where they were going so I came here to call and find them."

"Have you been drinking, ma'am?"

"No! It's eight o'clock in the morning."

"Well, we just left the scene of the accident and the lady was still lying in the street. She said you hit her and then ran off."

"What! No way! That's a lie."

The officer rolled his eyes at me. "Listen lady, there are two witnesses who saw you take off just after you hit her. I'm afraid you're going to have to come with us."

Adrenalin flooded through my system. I felt light headed and grabbed the officers arm to steady myself. What was happening to me? I would never hit someone and run. This had to be a setup—a scam of some sort. The officer gently steered me to his car and put me in the backseat. I felt embarrassed and looked around to see if anyone had seen me. Fortunately no one seemed to be around. Then I saw Stan's car coming toward us. He slowed down and frowned when he saw me in the squad car. He parked the car and came over to the officer. They were close enough so that I could hear the conversation.

"What's going on here? Why do you have Miss Waters in your car?" Stan asked.

"And who are you, sir?" the officer asked.

"I'm her partner, Stan Turner. We're attorneys."

The officer raised his eyebrows. "Attorneys. Huh. . . . Well, your partner is being taken in on suspicion of hit and run. She ran down a jogger about a mile from here."

"What? She'd never do that. She used to be an assistant D.A. for christsakes."

The officer shrugged. "Well, I got two witnesses who saw her hit the lady and then drive off. I thought maybe she was drunk or on drugs but she seemed clearheaded. I don't know what to tell you."

"Can I have a word with her before you take her in?"

"Just two seconds. I'm not supposed to allow it, but since you're her lawyer I guess it will be okay."

Stan thanked the officer, walked over and stuck his head in the window.

"You okay?" he asked.

"Yes, I'm fine. Stan, I didn't do it. It's some kind of scam."

Stan nodded. "I know. Just keep your mouth shut and I'll be right over to bail you out."

"Oh, Stan. I can't believe this. After everything that's happened and now this," I moaned, and then started to cry.

Stan took my hand and squeezed it reassuringly. "It's gonna be okay. Just hang in there. I'll have you out in a jiffy."

"Call Bart if you need any help," I said as Stan started to leave.

He nodded and walked back to the officer.

"Where are you taking her?" he asked.

"City jail," the officer replied.

Stan thanked the officer and went inside. The officers got back into the squad car and we drove off. They took me back to the scene of the crime where several crime scene investigators were already at work. I saw the two men who I had seen earlier, talking to a detective. The car stopped and one of the officers went over to the detective. They talked a few minutes and then he came back to the car.

"Okay, we're going to take you in now. I talked to Detective Besch and he confirms that both the victim and two witness confirmed you left the scene of the accident."

"That's a bunch of crap," I said. "They took the woman and left me here alone."

The officer shook his head and we were off. I had been to Dallas City Jail dozens of times usually conferring with the arresting officer to determine if we should prosecute an offender. It felt so strange to be on the other side of the fence. I prayed Stan or Bart would be there so I didn't have to be processed into the system. That would be so humiliating and I didn't know if I could handle it. Fortunately both Bart and Stan were there at the intake desk when they brought me up. Bart came over to me.

"What in the hell happened?"

"Bart, you've got to believe me. I didn't do anything wrong. There's something fishy going on."

"Yes, that's what Stan said."

We embraced and then Bart said, "I'm afraid you'll have to be booked but by the time they are done with you Stan will have your bond arranged. I'll stay with you each step of the way. You should be out of here in an hour."

"Thank you, Bart. I'm so embarrassed. How did this happen?"

"I don't know, but we'll get to the bottom of it," Bart said and then gave me a hard look.

"What?" I said.

"You usually dress like that for work?"

"Ah . . . well, not usually, no . . . but I had a luncheon appointment with a key client."

Bart raised his eyebrows but let my lame explanation slide. By the time I had been booked, Stan's bondman showed up with a $10,000 bond. After completing a little paperwork I was released. With all the stress of the arrest and booking I wasn't feeling so hot, so I asked Stan to take me home. He agreed and we arrived at my condo about noon.

"I'm sorry we weren't able to work on the Dusty Thomas case today. I really wanted to spend the day on it, but I'm in no condition to work now," I said.

"Don't worry about it, Paula. I totally understand. Are you going to be all right?"

"Well I'm worried about the lady I hit. Would you call the hospital and see how she's doing?"

"Sure, where did they take her?"

"Parkland, I think. . . .I just want to take a hot shower and unwind. I'm so stressed out I can hardly think."

"Go take a shower and relax," Stan said. "I'll call you later."

"Well, I really don't want to be alone right now. Why don't you come up. You can order us a pizza and call the hospital while I take a shower. I feel so dirty after being in the jail all morning."

Stan shrugged and said, "Okay, I'll stay a little while but I've got piles of work waiting for me back at the office."

"I know. I really appreciate you being with me today. It has meant a lot to me."

"No problem. Glad to help."

I escorted Stan up to my condo and showed him to the den where the phone was located. He picked it up and started dialing. My bedroom was just off the den and with the door opened he had a clear view of me inside. I started to close the door but then changed my mind. After kicking off my pumps I carefully removed my suit and nylons. I could feel Stan's eyes on me as I removed my bra and panties. When I glanced up at him he turned his head. I smiled, went into the bathroom and turned on the shower. Thirty minutes later I put on my bathrobe and joined Stan in the den.

"I feel so much better, " I said.

Stan smiled and said, "Good. The pizza should be here any minute. I hope you like pepperoni."

"Sure, that's fine. . . . Did you call the hospital?"

"Yes, she was treated for cuts and bruises, a concussion and some broken ribs. She's been admitted and is expected to be released tomorrow."

"That doesn't sound so bad," I said.

"No, it sounds like she should fully recover."

"I'm just so confused," I said. "They took her to the hospital. I was standing next to my car all alone. I'm not crazy."

"So, what do you think we have here, an insurance scam?" Stan asked.

"I don't know. The whole thing was so bizarre I don't know what to make of it."

"It's not unusual at all. Insurance companies pay out millions of dollars every year on bogus claims."

"But why frame me for hit and run?"

"So they can press criminal charges, file a big lawsuit, and force you to pay them a bunch of money. Most people don't want to be dragged through the courts so they settle even if they did nothing wrong."

"Not me, I won't pay those bastards a dime."

"Good. I don't think you should. I'll have Monty do a background check on all three of them. Maybe they've done this scam before. If so, he might be able to find some other victims."

"I hope so. I'd hate for this to drag on and on."

"Just as a precaution you better notify your insurance carrier of the incident. They probably will deny coverage based on the facts alleged, but they will still have to defend you in any civil litigation which will save you a lot of money."

"Okay, I'll call them tomorrow."

The doorbell rang and Stan went to the door and got our pizza. He took it to the kitchen table while I got us some wine to drink. I felt so safe having Stan with me in the condo I didn't want him to leave. We talked and reminisced about old times for quite a while and in the process consumed quite a lot of wine. After we moved back into the den, Stan gave me a detailed account of his escapades in Ecuador.

"God, you're a so lucky to be alive," I said. "When are you going to wire General Moya the money?"

"Tomorrow, I guess. I'm just worried about the FBI though. They've been watching me pretty close and when I wire the money they're going to know about it."

"What do you think they will do?"

"I don't know, but it could open a can of worms."

"Can you get the money to General Moya any other way?"

"No, the wiring instructions are all I have. I wouldn't know where to send a cashier's check."

"Maybe you should just tell the FBI you're paying a ransom. That way they won't go ballistic when you wire the money."

"If I have to, I will. But I don't want to compromise Tex if I don't have to."

"I'm so worried, Stan. What's going to happen to us next?"

Stan smiled and took my hand. "Don't worry, it will all work out. You just have to have faith."

I snuggled up close to him and put my head on his shoulder. He put his arm around me and squeezed me gently. I wanted him so badly, but I knew I couldn't be too pushy. This was the closest I'd come to seducing him and I didn't want to blow it. We sat there quietly for several minutes then I couldn't stand it any longer so I leaned over and gave him a kiss. He didn't push me away.

# BACK TO BUSINESS 20

I felt so badly for Paula. She had been deserted right in the middle of a murder trial and then when I finally came back, she's arrested for a bogus hit and run. I knew she had been traumatized by the arrest and needed my support. The free strip show, the sexy bathrobe, and now the kiss weren't unexpected. But now it was the hour of reckoning. I was attracted to Paula without a doubt. She was smart, beautiful and sexy. But, if I gave in to her it would be an hour of ecstasy and a lifetime of regret. It was time to cool things down so I turned the conversation back to business.

"Did we get a trial notice yet in Dusty's case?" I asked.

"Huh?" Paula said giving me a befuddled look. She sighed and replied, "Ah. . . .Yes, March 2nd. . . .We only have a few months until trial."

"Damn. So, why don't you brief me on where you are in the investigation?"

"Okay, sure," Paula said suddenly seeming embarrassed by her lack of clothing. "Let me go put on some jeans. She left for a minute and returned in jeans and an SMU T-shirt. She filled me in on the witnesses she had interviewed and what she knew of the state's case from visits to their offices and sleepovers with Bart.

"You've done well." I said, "We have what—a half dozen suspects now?"

"At least," Paula said.

"So, I guess we should have Monty check them out too."

"Yes, definitely. We might want to question them once we have background checks in hand."

"Right. . . . So, what's your gut feeling? Is there anyone that you interviewed who is of particular interest to you?"

"Well, there are several, but I'd have to say the People's Mission is at the top of the list."

"I've never heard of the People's Mission," I said.

"They claim to be a legitimate church but Agent Tuttle thought it was a scam and I tend to agree with him."

"So when Agent Tuttle threatened to put them out of business, they decided to beat him to the punch?" I asked.

"Precisely."

"The only way they could get away with it," I said, "would be if it looked like someone else did it."

"Yes, but how would they know when Tuttle was going to seize the tractor?" Paula asked.

"Good point. I don't know."

"Bobby's colleagues at the IRS would have had that information."

"Right. His supervisor and what was that other agent's name?"

"Hurst. Donald Hurst," Paula said. "But he has an alibi, remember?"

"Right. What about the female employee who had his baby?"

"Laura Blair. She denies that it is Tuttle's baby. But she doesn't have an alibi. She or her boyfriend could have done it."

"But the boyfriend wouldn't have had access to Tuttle's schedule."

"True," Paula said, "and it's unlikely they were in on it together."

"Okay," I said. "Let's take a hard look at Laura Blair since she had motive and opportunity."

Paula agreed and I left to go back to the office. She seemed in good spirits when I left and promised to be back at the office the next morning. I told her to take a few days off, but she wouldn't hear of it. We agreed that I would worry about her hit and run and she would concentrate of the Thomas case.

"Jesus, where have you been?" Jodie asked.

"With Paula. She was pretty upset so I had to keep her company for a while until she settled down a bit."

Jodie nodded. "There's a New York Times reporter who has been calling. He wants to interview you."

"Hmm. I don't think so."

"Why not? Jodie asked.

"The situation's too delicate. Tex is still missing and the Feds are all over me. I think it would be best to lay low for a while. Tell them I'm not doing interviews because I don't want to interfere with the FBI investigation."

"Right."

Jodie left to call back the reporter and I sat down at my desk to start sorting through mail and paperwork that had piled up. By the time I looked up it was 4 P.M. I shook my head and suddenly thought of Tex. It was too late to wire General Moya the money that day so I had no choice but to do it in the morning. I pulled out the wiring instructions and studied them carefully. Then I called my bank officer, Billie Jo, to arrange for the transfer.

"You want to send half of the money in the account tomorrow?" she asked.

"Yes. It's a business deal for a client and the agreement is to pay half up front and the balance when the job is done."

"Okay, you'll have to stop by and sign some paperwork for that size of a transfer."

"What kind of paperwork?"

"The request for the wire transfer and some disclosure forms."

"Okay. I'll be there around 9:30."

The paperwork I had to sign bothered me. I was afraid somehow the FBI would get wind of the wire transfer and try to track it. If they tracked it to General Moya I'd be in serious trouble. Hopefully he was an expert in this type of thing and the money couldn't be traced to him. I didn't have any choice either way, Tex's life was on the line. I was pretty sure that General Moya would see to it that Tex was released and put on a airplane home, but the thought occurred to me that he might not be able to follow through with his end of the deal. If Tex wasn't in Moya's custody he might not be able to spring him. In that case he'd take the $900,000 and we'd still never see Tex. Then a horrible thought came over me—what if Tex were already dead?

Before I sent the money I called Toni to make sure she wanted me to send it. After all, it was her money. I was pretty sure what the answer would be, but there was a lot of money at stake and I had to be careful. Beside, if the FBI did come after me, I'd need Toni to back up my explanation as to why I had the money and was wiring it to a guerrilla leader who financed his activities by selling illegal drugs to citizens of the U.S.

"Yes, definitely, send the money. Do whatever it takes to get Tex back," Toni said. "He's all I got."

"Okay. I'll go by the bank and arrange it."

"How long do you think it will be before he is home?"

"I don't know. Hopefully within a few days, but honestly, I have no idea."

"What did General Moya tell you?"

"He just said he would make sure he was released. He didn't go into details and I wasn't in a position to press him."

"I understand. Just send the money and we'll just have to pray he returns soon."

"Rebekah and I *will* be praying hard, believe me."

"I know. I really appreciate all that you've done for Tex and me. Not too many attorneys would have gone down to South America searching for a lost client."

"Hey, good clients are hard to come by," I said with a chuckle.

"The same goes for attorneys," she replied.

After hanging up the telephone I noticed it was almost five o'clock. I wanted to get home early since I needed catch-up time with my family. We were going out to dinner at one of Rebekah's favorite restaurants, Red Lobster. As I left the office there were several reporters waiting for me. I smiled and went straight for the elevators.

"Mr. Turner," the first reporter said. "How does it feel to be back to work?"

"Wonderful," I said. "You never appreciate home until your stranded somewhere and can't get there."

"Does Dusty Thomas intend to plead temporary insanity?"

"We haven't made any decisions in that regard. We're still sorting through the facts and interviewing witnesses. When the time comes to make that decision, we'll let you know."

The elevator finally came and I got in and motioned for the reporters to stay out. They acquiesced. On the way home I thought of how much we still had to do on Dusty's case. I was so far behind and we only had a few months to go. We could try to get a continuance but I knew the District Attorney wouldn't agree to it since the FBI wanted the case over quickly. When I drove into my garage and shut off the engine, I closed my eyes and tried to relax. I wanted to forget about work for a while and concentrate on family. When I went inside Marcia jumped into my arms.

"Daddy! You're finally home," Marcia said.

Rebekah said, "She's been sitting by the door waiting for you for an hour."

"Hey, sweet pea. It's early. It's only five-thirty."

"I know, but I thought you might come home early."

Rebekah said, "Yeah. Fat chance."

"Okay," I said. "Who's hungry?"

By that time all the kids had gathered and they all screamed, "I am! I am!"

Fortunately it was a week night so we didn't have to wait to be seated. The waitress soon brought our drink order, along with a basket of hot bread.

"I'm having lobster," Reggi said.

"Of course, the most expensive thing on the menu," Rebekah said.

"It's all right," I said. "Order whatever you want. We'll talk a little business so I can write it off my taxes."

"Can you do that?" Rebekah asked.

"No, that was for the benefit of my FBI tail. He's sitting two booths behind us. I'm sure he's got some kind of listening device so he can hear whatever we say."

Rebekah turned around and glared at the FBI agent. "You've got to be kidding! We can't even have a quiet dinner alone?"

"Not until this trial is over."

"You want me to search the booth for bugs, Dad?" Reggi said.

I smiled and shook my head. "No, son. That won't be necessary. I doubt there is a bug in the booth since he didn't know where we were going. Well, I take that back. If they were listening to our phone conversation they knew we were coming here. I wonder if the management would let them bug a booth?"

"This is terrible. You want to go somewhere else?" Rebekah asked.

"No, that won't do any good. This is something we'll just have to learn to live with. No more dirty sex talk, I guess."

Rebekah smiled. "Why not? They can't use that against us, can they?"

I shrugged. "I hope not."

The waitress came back and took our orders. While we were waiting, the subject of Paula came up. I was hoping it wouldn't as I was feeling guilty about spending the day with her and Rebekah was sure to sense it.

"How's Paula?" Rebekah asked.

"She's pretty upset."

"I bet. I would be so humiliated if I were arrested. Did anyone see it happen?"

"No."

"You got her out of jail pretty fast."

"It pays to have friends in the DA's office."

"What friend?"

"Her old boyfriend, Bart."

"Did you help get her out?"

"Of course. I got her a bond and Bart talked to the intake people so she wouldn't have to go into the system."

"Were you and Bart with her all day?"

"Bart had to go back to work so I took her home."

"Is that where you were? I tried to reach you several times and Jodie said you were out."

"Ah. . . . Right. I didn't want to leave her alone so I stayed with her awhile."

"In her condo?"

"Yes, we just talked. She brought me up to date on the Thomas case."

Rebekah stiffened up. Now I was going to get the silent treatment for the rest of the evening if I didn't say just the right thing.

"Can you imagine working at the DA's office for all those years prosecuting cases and then to be arrested yourself? She was more than humiliated. She was mortified. You should have seen her. It was terrible. It was either take her to a shrink or try to calm her down myself. Fortunately she's a strong woman and after awhile I was able to get her mind off her arrest."

Rebekah gave me a skeptical look and then said, "Poor girl. I hope she'll be all right."

I let out a silent sigh of relief and said, "Like I said. She's a tough girl. She'll be fine in a few days."

# THE HANGOVER 21

After Stan left, depression engulfed me like a thick morning fog. No matter which direction I looked, I saw nothing but darkness. The burden of the trial had been challenging, but now with my arrest and possible trial for hit and run, I felt like I'd been hit by a jet ski and left to drown. All night I tossed and turned unable to sleep. Finally, just before dawn, I dozed off and didn't wake up until after ten. When I saw the green florescent ten on my clock radio I jumped out of bed.

"Oh, no!" I said as I ran for the bathroom. Halfway there I felt faint and nearly collapsed. I grabbed the door jam to steady myself. My head was pounding and my body felt like it had gained a hundred pounds overnight. I struggled to the sink and looked at myself in the big mirror. My face was pale and there were dark shadows under my eyes. Had I really drunk that much? Apparently so.

After a hot shower, three aspirin, and some breakfast, I started to feel a little better. Then I remembered my blatant attempt to seduce Stan. *He must think I'm a real slut.*

By noon I was sitting at my desk trying to get motivated for an afternoon of hard work. I opened my notebook and started reviewing my to do list. Laura Blair's name popped out at me. She didn't have a great alibi unless her baby learned how to talk soon. It was convenient that she was sick the day Bobby was murdered. She would have had access to his schedule and plans to seize Dusty's tractor. I called Agent Hurst and found out the name of Laura's friends. He knew of two of them, Rita Woods and Samantha Sams. Sams agreed to meet for a drink after work. We met at little sports bar in Addison. She was a short, attractive Asian woman in her late twenties. She insisted I call her Sam.

"How long have you known Laura?" I asked.

"Going on five years now. We started work at the IRS about the same time," Sam said.

"Do you two do things together socially?"

"Sure. We go shopping sometimes and work out together at Presidents."

"So, was Laura excited when she got pregnant?"

"Not exactly. You know how having a baby can ruin your body."

"Yes, I've heard that. So how did she cope with that?"

"She took really good care of herself—didn't eat too much, you know."

"Right. Was she excited when the baby came?"

"Not exactly. You know being a single mom is a bitch."

My interview with Laura suddenly came back to me. She kept asking me if I needed a baby or wanted to take her baby home with me. She was joking, of course, but also expressing her unhappiness with being a mother.

"Oh, yes. I can imagine. All that responsibility and no help from anyone."

"And being tied down all the time," Sam added. "We used to do things together but after she had the baby she never has time anymore."

"What kinds of things did you two do together?" I asked.

"We were both aspiring actresses. We were active with the Metro Theater."

"Oh, really? Have you had roles in any of their plays?"

"Laura did. She played the lead in the musical Oklahoma."

"Wow. Is she working in any productions now?"

"No, she had to drop out on account of she couldn't afford a babysitter."

"That's too bad."

"Are you married?" I asked, wondering if there was more to their relationship than she had so far admitted.

"No, haven't found the right man yet."

I wasn't cruel enough to ask if she was gay, although I was dying to know. I'd pose that question to Rita Woods. Rita agreed to have lunch with me the following day. We met at Steak and Ale across from Prestonwood Mall. She wore her naturally blond hair in a ponytail and I guessed she also worked out at Presidents. We got two Margaritas before ordering lunch.

"I'm trying to learn as much as I can about Bobby Tuttle and the people he worked with in order to get some insight into why he was murdered," I said.

"As far as I'm concerned they have the killer," Rita replied.

"Well, maybe. But we have to be absolutely sure. There are some questions I need to ask you."

"I can't imagine that I'd have any useful information for you."

"Well, you just might, so I'd like to go ahead and ask them.

"Sure. I'll tell you whatever I know."

"Thank you. . . . Are you friends with Samantha too?"

"Sure, we all hung out together."

"I take it you're not married?"

"No, divorced."

"Laura insists that Bobby wasn't the father of her child, but I wonder if she's being totally honest about that?"

Rita hesitated and squirmed in her chair. "How should I know?"

"I'm sure you all must have talked about it."

"Yes, but not with Laura. Sam and I have discussed the possibility, but we have no proof."

"In talking to Sam I get the impression she is more than just a friend to Laura. Am I right?"

"What do you mean?"

"Is Sam in love with Laura?"

"No. . . . Well, I don't know. Maybe."

"How does Laura feel about it?"

"I don't see what this has to do with your—"

"Right. It may not, but I've got to look at this thing from all angles. I'll keep anything you tell me confidential."

"No you won't. I'm not your client. You'll use it whenever it suits you. I think I've said enough."

It didn't matter that Rita had cut the interview short. I had found out what I needed to know. Laura was obviously bisexual and had more than a casual relationship with Sam. That made Sam an official Class II suspect. She had motive but no direct knowledge of Tuttle's schedule the day he died. As I continued to analyze the data I had gathered, the evidence pointing to Laura began to mount. Getting pregnant had destroyed all her dreams and aspirations of becoming a famous actress. True, she hadn't made it yet, but most likely in her mind it was just a matter of time. After being raped and impregnated by someone she didn't even like, she might have been angry enough to do something about it.

When I got back to the office I called Monty and asked him to add Rita and Sam to his list of background checks to be done. I was anxious to see if any of them drove a silver Mercedes. After I hung up the phone Stan walked into my office.

"Hi. How are you feeling?"

"Better," I said and then filled him in on my interviews with Sam and Rita.

"Well, the more suspects you can dig up the better. Eventually we'll have to focus on one or two of them though."

"My bets on Laura," I said.

"Listen, the DA has assigned your case to Martin Silvey."

"Oh, shit. He's a jerk."

"I got that feeling. He was totally unreasonable and indicated that he felt his witnesses were impeccable."

"Wonderful. So, now what?"

"Next week we have to announce your plea. Then we'll get ready for battle. In a day or two Monty should have the background checks completed on the two witnesses and then we can start trying to discredit them."

Before Stan showed up I had been feeling better. Now with the news that my hit and run case wasn't going to go away easily, depression blew over me again like a blue norther. I closed my notebook, cleaned off my desk, and dialed Bart's number. He answered on the second ring.

I said, "Hey, you want to get drunk tonight?"

# WIRE TRANSFER 22

After stopping by the bank and filling out the paperwork to transfer $900,000 to General Moya's bank account in the Cayman Islands, I went straight to the office. I kept telling myself I had no choice but to send the money, nevertheless a feeling of impending doom dogged me. As I sat at my office I wondered if Tex would actually be released or if I had just helped fund the murder of hundreds of innocent citizens of Ecuador. I had to put Tex and General Moya out of my mind and concentrate on a more immediate problem, Paula's hit-and-run case.

The background checks on the three persons involved were sitting on my desk. I couldn't believe Monty had gotten them done so quickly. I guess he was as concerned for Paula as I was. I opened the first file on the victim and began reading. Her name was Maria Cabrillo, age 26, a resident of Dallas, and a student at El Centro College. She was single and lived with her boyfriend, Raul Marcos, in an apartment in Oak Lawn. The report said she was in the U.S. on a green card from El Salvador and had no criminal record. The file included her thin credit report which showed only credit cards with Citibank and Sears. She apparently paid these bills on time.

The first witness was Ernesto Garcia, age 23, of Garland, Texas. Also from El Salvador he was employed by S & T Packing Company as a carpenter. His criminal record included convictions for DUI, possession of marijuana, and criminal mischief. He was still on probation for the DUI. A U.S. Citizen since being sworn in May 1983, Garcia was single.

The second witness Brian Armstrong, age 28, also of Garland, Texas worked with Garcia at S & T Packing Company but as a laborer. Apparently they had been car pooling when they came across Paula's accident. Armstrong had been recently divorced and had no criminal record. His employer reported his income at $28,220.00 per year. Armstrong was a U.S. citizen having been born in McKinney, Texas.

Nothing in the reports seemed to be of much help with the exception of Garcia's criminal history. Since he was on probation I decided to call his probation officer and see if I could get any more information on him. The probation officer's name was Martin Sweeney. I called and his secretary put me through.

"I'm sorry, but I'm not at liberty to talk about the parolees that I supervise," Martin said.

"Well, I don't know if you heard or not, but Mr. Garcia was a witness to an alleged hit and run a couple days ago. He alleges that my partner, Paula Waters, hit a woman jogging and then left the scene of the accident. My partner says Mr. Garcia and his friend took the victim from the scene of the accident to transport her to the hospital. After they left my partner went back to her office to try to figure out where they had taken the victim. She was quite shocked when the police took her back to the scene of the crime and the victim was still lying in the street."

"Really? That's a pretty bizarre story."

"Well, if my partner is telling the truth, and I'm sure she is, your man is involved in some sort of scam."

"That wouldn't surprise me, but you'll need evidence to prove it. I don't suppose you have anything?"

"Not yet."

"Well, if you get any evidence that Mr. Garcia was involved in anything illegal let me know. Otherwise, there's not much I can do."

"You can't tell me anything else about him that might help me figure this thing out?"

"No. Like I said, I'm not at liberty to discuss my cases with anyone outside the court system. You can, however, go down to the court and look through his criminal file yourself. It's a public record. You might find something there."

"Well, I was hoping to avoid the trip, but I guess that's what I'll have to do. Thanks for your help."

"I wish I could do more."

After lunch I went by the county courthouse and pulled Garcia's criminal file. There wasn't much in there that I didn't already know, but I did find a note that Garcia was a member of the 18th Street gang. When I got back to the office I called Bart to ask him if he knew anything about them.

"They're one of the worst," he said. "Their initiation ritual always involves violence. I heard two girls testify once how they were beat up by three of their 'homeys' while the crowd counted slowly to 18."

"Jesus. Why would they want to be in a gang like that?"

"Their parents had pretty much deserted them, I guess. The psychologist who testified at the trial said they had a craving to belong which was so strong they were willing to endure the pain from the beating."

"Boy, that's hard to believe."

"Haven't you seen teenagers with tattoos all over their forearms?"

"I guess."

"Well, that's a sign of their gang membership. The 18th Street gang originated in Los Angeles. They have a blood feud with the Mierda Seca or MS."

"Have you ever heard of these gang members participating in insurance scams?"

"Sure, they're into drugs and will do anything to support their habit. Insurance scams, kidnapping, murder for hire—you name it and they've been there."

"So, it's likely that Garcia and his friends staged this whole thing?"

"Probably. Maybe if you keep digging you'll find another victim. I'm sure Paula isn't the first person this has happened to."

"Would you ask around the D.A.'s office and find out if anyone has ever heard of a scam like this?"

"You bet. I'll check it out and let you know."

"Thanks. I'm going back to the scene of the accident and see if there is anything there that might help us."

"Be careful, if the 18th Street gang is involved they won't like anyone snooping around in their business."

"Right. Maybe I'll get Monty to come with me."

"Good idea."

Monty met me at the scene of the accident. It was a half mile stretch of undeveloped road between Preston Road and the condominium development where Paula lived. The two lane, asphalt road was lined with large cottonwood trees. In the morning it would be pretty dark where the trees blocked the morning sun. A jogger passed by as we were looking around. I watched him as he ran down the road. Apparently this was a popular route for joggers I noticed another one coming toward us from the other direction.

"I wonder if any joggers witnessed what happened to Paula," I said.

Monty nodded. "As popular a route as this is odds are there is someone out there who knows something."

"Maybe we should come here in the morning and talk to some of the joggers who come by. We might get lucky."

"I'll do that for you," Monty said. "I'm sure you've got a dozen other things to do."

"True. I'm so far behind on everything it's getting ridiculous. If I don't get caught up pretty soon I'm afraid I'm going to lose some of my clients."

"Well, if I can help in any way, let me know."

"I will, definitely."

As we were about to leave a beat-up Chevy Impala approached us. As it got closer it slowed down. The car was loaded with a half dozen Latinos who stared at us as they drove by. I could see their tattoos and knew who they were. Bart was right. They knew what we were up to and they didn't like it. Suddenly I wished I had a gun and knew how to use it. Perhaps I'd hire Monty to give me a crash course in self-defense. This case was getting dangerous and the closer I got to the truth the more perilous it would become.

# CASH INFUSION 23

Several days later I was paying bills and realized we had just about exhausted Dusty's retainer. The thought of having to call Raymond Farr and ask for more money made me ill. Stan wouldn't like the idea and might torpedo it if I consulted him on the matter. Since we had already been labeled as "traitors" by some of the more vocal media commentators, I didn't see how we could be hurt by accepting a little more money. Stewart got Raymond Farr at his headquarters in Washington, D.C. on the phone for me.

"Ms. Waters. So nice to hear from you," Farr said.

"Yes, well I just wanted to update you on the case and, well, tell you that we've pretty much exhausted the money you've given us."

"I don't doubt it after all you two have been through. First the FBI kidnapping Stan and now they've set you up."

"What? You think the FBI was behind the hit and run scam?"

"Of course. They'd do anything to keep you from giving Dusty Thomas the best possible defense. They are a bunch of unscrupulous maggots."

"I'll pass on your theory to Stan and maybe he'll look into it."

"You know, Paula, the council is very pleased with you and Stan. You two have demonstrated remarkable courage in standing up to our corrupt government. I want you to know the CDA stands behind you 110 percent.

"Well, our only interest is proving Dusty innocent."

"Fair enough. I'll call our treasurer and have him send you another $50,000. We don't want you to let up. You must prove Dusty innocent no matter what."

"Well, we *have* come up with quite a few other suspects. Tuttle was not a popular guy."

"No, a ruthless agent of our shameful government."

"So, anyway. Thanks a lot. I'll keep you posted if there are any other developments."

"Thank you," Farr said. "Say hello to Stan."

"Sure."

Raymond Farr gave me the creeps. Every time I hung up the phone with him, I felt like I needed a shower. A tinge of guilt made me quiver. I didn't like hiding things from Stan, but I really didn't have any choice. He would find out what I had done eventually, but I'd deal with that problem then. Since he had turned over the checkbook to me he rarely looked at it. He probably wouldn't realize we'd received a new infusion of cash for some time. I'd never known a man who cared so little about money. As long as he had enough to feed and cloth his family and pay his essential bills, he was happy.

Now that the treasury had been replenished, I thought about what I should do next to try to unravel the mystery of Bobby Tuttle's murder. I flipped open my notebook and looked at my list of suspects. Riley Davidson and the People's Mission had been highlighted and underlined. I examined the Mission's roster. The names didn't mean much to me so I called the person designated as the secretary to see if I could get more information. Her name was Mabel Anderson. After I explained who I was, she agreed to a meeting later that day. When I arrived at her apartment on Cole Avenue she opened the door enthusiastically. She was a well dressed, middle-aged black woman, and spoke with a slight English accent.

"Ms. Waters?" Mabel asked.

"Yes. Thank you for letting me stop by,"

"Oh, I'm delighted you called me. I've been following the Dusty Thomas case on TV and in the newspaper. I sure hope you and your partner can get him off."

"Well, we're giving our best shot."

"It was so terrible how the government kidnapped Mr. Turner. You must have been in a frenzy."

"Yes, I was. But it wasn't actually the government. It was—"

"Oh, yes. They just detained him for a while."

"Yes, I'm just so grateful that Stan is back on the case."

"Me too. . . . So, how can I help you?"

"Well, your name came up as the secretary of the People's Mission."

"Yes, one of many charities I support."

"I understand the IRS has challenged your tax-exempt status."

"Yes, but our attorneys think we have a good chance of winning in tax court."

"Really? I hope they are right, but what would happen if you lost?"

"We'd each lose thousands of dollars in tax deductions which would mean we'd owe the government a lot of money."

"How much would you lose?"

"It wouldn't be so bad for me because I haven't taken near the deductions that some of the others have,"

"Who would get hurt the worst, you think?"

"Peter Lowe probably. He owns a used car dealership and has contributed heavily to the foundation."

"Do you know him very well?"

"Yes, I do actually. He's my ex-husband. That's how I got involved in The People's Mission in the first place. I suppose I should consider resigning now that the divorce is final."

"Oh, well. I don't know. Do you agree with their views?"

"Not really. Of course, nobody likes to pay taxes. Peter says the rich have so many tax shelters they don't hardly pay anything and the poor aren't required to pay so that leaves the burden on us—the middle class. It's really quite unfair, don't you think?"

"Well, it's a complicated issue.... How much do you think Peter stands to lose if he loses in tax court?"

"Hundreds of thousands, but that's not his biggest worry."

"Really? What's his biggest worry?"

"If a criminal fraud investigation is instituted."

"Oh, my God! Would they be after you too?"

"I suppose, but like I said, I'm small potatoes compared to some of the others."

Hurst hadn't mentioned to me a possible criminal investigation, presumable because it wasn't underway yet. Peter Lowe seemed to have motive to kill agent Tuttle but killing him wouldn't necessarily stop the criminal prosecution. I was starting to get depressed. It appeared I was on yet another rabbit trail. But before I gave up on Lowe I thought I better talk to him. He was at his used car lot and was just finishing selling a car to a young couple.

As I approached he smiled broadly and said, "Hallelujah! The Lord has blessed this day. Two sales and now he's gone and sent me an angel."

I laughed. "Hi, I'm Paula Waters. You must be Reverend Lowe."

"I am," he said as he closed his eyes. He raised one hand and said, "Okay, don't tell me. I'm praying for inspiration.... yes...it's coming... Buick Riviera. That is your car. The Lord has spoken."

I smiled. "Well, actually I'm not looking for a car. I just need to talk to you for a minute."

He frowned and rubbed his forehead. "What about?"

"Your favorite topic, I'm sure."

"The Lord Jesus?"

"No, the IRS."

He let out a gasp. "Oh, please don't speak of the devil on such a fine day."

"I'm sorry. But I'm afraid I have no choice. I'm an attorney representing Dusty Thomas and I need to ask you a few questions."

"I didn't know Dusty Thomas, but I pray the Lord will forgive him."

"Well, I'm sure that will mean a lot to him, but I was wondering about your reaction to Bobby Tuttle's murder."

"Any senseless death brings me profound sadness," he said. "Bobby was a troubled man, but murder was not the answer. By now the Lord has punished him."

"So you weren't upset by his murder?"

"I never question the will of the Lord."

"So you think the Lord wanted him dead?" I asked.

He nodded. "Apparently so."

"Where were you on the day Agent Tuttle was murdered?"

"Right here on the lot selling cars."

"When did you hear about the murder?"

"Not until that night when I came home from work."

As far as I could tell Reverend Lowe had only one employee. I wanted to go talk to her to verify his story but he called her right after we finished talking and they went into a back room. I debated waiting around for her to come back but finally decided against it. I probably would have to contact her outside work if I was going to get any meaningful information from her.

The next day when I got to the office Stewart told me Stan was looking for me, so I went into his office. It was his birthday so Jodie had decorated his office with balloons and bright streamers made of red ribbon. I wished him a happy birthday and sat down across from him. The only thing on his desk was a newspaper and a cup of coffee.

He thanked me and then began telling me about the 18th Street gang and the probability that they were behind the hit and run scam. I thought of my conversation with Raymond Farr and his theory that the government was behind it. Then he handed me the latest issue of the National Examiner dated August 22, 1986 which I immediately began to read.

### CDA STILL HAS FAITH IN THOMAS DEFENSE TEAM

Despite mounting legal problems for the defense team of Stan Turner and Paula Waters, Raymond Farr, President of the Citizens Defense Alliance announced today that his organization still stands strongly behind them. He reiterated his charge that the federal government was responsible for Stan Turner's abduction and Paula Waters' recent bizarre hit and run case. Farr further indicated that the organization had recently provided additional funding for Dusty Thomas' defense and would continue to do so indefinitely.

Farr called for a national taxpayer's strike urging citizens to burn their form 1040s and demand the IRS quit collecting the illegal income tax. He indicated the CDA planned a national March on Washington the weekend before the start of the Dusty Thomas trial and they expected Dusty and Martha Thomas to lead the parade. They also planned to invite Stan Turner and Paula Waters to participate in the event.

"Oh, my God," I said. "I can't believe this."

"Apparently you've been talking to Farr," Stan said.

"Yes, but just about funding. He didn't mention the march on Washington."

"Is Dusty Thomas really going to lead the parade?"

I shrugged. "I don't know. I haven't talked to him about it."

"Farr didn't mention any of this to you?"

"No, nothing. I'm sorry, Stan. I called him about the money. That's it."

"I thought we weren't going to take any more money from the CDA. I can't believe you took more money," Stan moaned.

"We were out of funds and nobody else was going to give us any."

Stan shook his head and said, "I went to bankruptcy court today and everybody avoided me like the plague. The bailiff wouldn't let me in the courtroom without being searched and Judge Sims chewed me out because I was two minutes late. We were just starting to distance ourselves from the CDA and now I read we're going to be in a damn CDA parade!

"I'm so sorry, Stan. I didn't know anything about that."

"I know it's not your fault entirely. But I wish you would have at least discussed the need for money with me. We might have found another source of funding."

"I guess you're right," I said. "I was just so afraid we'd run out of cash and—"

"I know. I'm sorry I jumped on you. I'm just a little stressed out over Tex."

"You haven't heard anything?"

"No, no word from Ecuador yet."

"Oh, God. I hope he's not dead."

"If he is I just contributed $900,000 toward the overthrow of the elected Ecuadorian government."

I left Stan looking rather dejected. I wondered how much more of this he could take. I wondered how much more I could take. In retrospect I knew it had been a mistake taking money from the CDA and I wished there was a way we could give it back. The reality was we were in bed with them and when this was all over the only clients we'd be defending would be thugs and scumbags like Raymond Farr.

# THE MESSAGE 24

It was mid morning and I was on the phone with an attorney in the consumer fraud division of the Texas Attorney General's office. I had contacted them to see if they were aware of any insurance scams similar to the one perpetrated on Paula. She told me she had researched their records but hadn't found anything remotely like it. I thanked her, hung up and had started going through the mail when I noticed a certified letter from Manuel Ortega, Attorney at Law, addressed to Paula. I didn't recognize the name so I opened it immediately. After the usual introductions the letter got right to the point.

> We have been retained to prosecute a claim on behalf of Maria Cabrillo for the injuries she sustained on August 18, 1986 on account of your ordinary and gross negligence ... Our client has sustained damages including past and future medical expenses, lost wages, pain and suffering, permanent impairment to her hip and legs, and loss of consortium in the amount of $1.2 million ... Please forward this letter to all of your insurance carriers and ask them to contact this office immediately.

This letter didn't surprise me, but the size of the demand did. The last time I had checked with the hospital it didn't seem that Miss Cabrillo's injuries were that serious. I called the state bar to see if there were any active complaints against Manuel Ortega, but there were none. Then I looked in the Yellow Pages to see if Manuel Ortega had a big personal injury add—he didn't. He wasn't even listed. The address on the envelope was a legal office suite in Preston Center. I had been there before for depositions. Any lawyer could rent space on a monthly basis and use the facilities and staff on a fee basis. It was a great way for a new lawyer to get started or a transient lawyer to set up shop.

*What is going on here?* It occurred to me that I needed to hire an investigator to following Ms. Cabrillo and video tape her for a few days. I had to know the true extent of her injuries. If this was a scam then her injuries wouldn't be significant and the investigator would get some good evidence to prove it. The claim, however, complicated matters. Now we had to contact Paula's auto and home owner's insurance carriers and they might want to take over the claim. Insurance carriers often offered money even if the claim was bogus just to get rid of it at an acceptable cost. We couldn't let them settle this case, however, since it might impact her criminal case. We had to prove the entire claim was a scam. As I was continuing my contemplation of the case, Jodie told me I had an emergency telephone call. It was Julie, Monty's secretary.

"Stan, Monty's been stabbed. He's having emergency surgery as we speak."

"What! . . . What happened?"

"He was questioning joggers over near Paula's place and one of them knifed him. They took him to Parkland. I just got here. They say he's in critical condition."

"Oh, my God! I'm on my way."

I felt sick as I rushed to my car. The image of the car slowly passing us the day before went through my mind. That was a warning and I totally ignored it. Now Monty may die because I was sloppy. I wondered how anyone could have gotten the drop on Monty. He was a professional and it wouldn't have been easy to catch him off guard. When I got to the hospital the press was already there. A crowd of them were waiting by the front door. I had no choice but go straight through them. Cameras flashed as I elbowed my way into the hospital. I rushed to the information desk and asked where they had Monty. They directed me to the ICU waiting room. Julie and Paula were already there. I rushed over to them.

"Hey. Any word yet?" I asked.

Paula replied, "No, he's still in surgery."

I shook my head. "This is all my fault. I should have gone with him to question the joggers."

"Do you think his stabbing had something to do with my case?" Paula asked.

"Yeah. I do. This is the gang's doing," I said.

"Why is the gang after me? What did I do to them?" Paula asked.

"Did you ever prosecute a gang member?" I asked.

"I don't know. I might have. I can't think right now."

"It could be a gang member you put away who is out now and trying to get even. You should have Bart check it out. If we could get a name it would make it a lot easier to figure this thing out."

"Okay, I'll ask him to look into it."

We sat in the waiting room for several hours before a doctor came in and told us Monty was out of surgery and in recovery. He said Monty would be moved to the ICU soon. When we asked him if Monty was going to be okay, he shrugged. He said the knife had ruptured Monty's kidney. He lost a lot of blood before the paramedics got to him. They had to remove the kidney and were worried about possible brain damage.

We all stayed until nearly 6 o'clock and then decided to do shifts. Julie would stay until nine. Paula would come back at nine and stay until midnight. Then I'd come at 7 A.M. and stay until 10 A.M. when Julie would return. Paula and I said goodbye to Julie, and we all went home.

It was nearly seven o'clock when I pulled into my driveway. I pushed the button on the garage door opener and then stopped it. There was graffiti all over the garage door. Someone had used spray paint to make some kind of symbol. I got out of the car and walked around the front of the house. The front door had a smaller but similar design painted on it. I unlocked the front door and went inside. Marcia was watching TV.

"Daddy! Daddy!" she said and ran over to me.

Rebekah walked in from the kitchen and asked, "Why did you come in the front door?"

"Some idiot sprayed paint all over our garage and front door."

"What?" Rebekah said as she rushed outside. She looked at the door and shook her head. "What the—?"

"Did Reggi piss somebody off at school?" I asked.

Rebekah took a deep breath and said, "I don't know. Let's ask him."

We went inside and called Reggi down from upstairs. He yelled and said he was on the phone but would be down in just a minute.

"How's Monty?" Rebekah asked.

"He's still in a coma."

Reggi ran down the stairs and stood before us. By this time the entire family had gathered wondering what was going on. "What?" Reggi asked.

"Someone spray painted our front door and the garage door too. Could it have been any of your friends?"

"What? No way. Let me see?" he said as he went outside with all of us following right behind.

"Shit! Oh, my God," Reggi said. "Why did they do this?"

"Why? Who would do this?" I asked.

"The 18th Street Gang."

Fear ripped through me as I reeled from Reggi's revelation. The gang had tried to kill Monty and now they were threatening my family. The message was clear. Stay out of their way or they'd kill me, my family, and anyone else who interfered. I grabbed Rebekah and pulled her close to me. She looked up at me with terror in her eyes.

# A CHANGE IN STRATEGY 25

Since the Dallas Police couldn't guarantee the safety of Rebekah and the kids, I hired a private investigative agency to provide security at our house around the clock. Rebekah still didn't want me to leave them alone, but I had no choice. I had agreed to take the 7 to 9 A.M. watch at Parkland. I walked into the ICU and went straight to the nurses station. I wanted an update on Monty's condition before I went to the waiting room. The nurse told me that Monty had been stable during the night but hadn't regained consciousness since his surgery. I thanked her and went into the waiting room and took a seat at a small desk. I brought my briefcase so I could get a little work done while I waited.

The letter from Miss Cabrillo's attorney was on my mind. Usually in a personal injury case a lot of negotiations go on before a lawsuit is actually filed. These negotiations often go on for as long as two years or until the statute of limitations is about to run out. Normally defense counsel would welcome this delay, but in this case I decided it would be best to get the lawsuit underway. Then I could start taking depositions, doing discovery, and perhaps get some answers as to what was going on. I got Miss Cabrillo's attorney, Manuel Ortega, on the line. We exchanged chilly greetings.

"I got your ridiculous demand letter in the mail yesterday. I can't believe you think your case is worth 1.2 million dollars."

"Well . . . yeah . . . we've got it all documented."

"Yeah, I bet you do. . . . You know, your client's little game isn't going to work. My partner isn't paying a red cent. Your client's claim is obviously frivolous and brought in bad faith."

"What? Are you accusing—"

"I'm just telling you I'm not going to turn this claim over to our insurance carrier. I strongly suggest you drop it. If you don't, we're going to countersue for malicious prosecution and we're going to file a motion for sanctions against you and your firm for participating in a fraudulent lawsuit."

"Fraudulent lawsuit? . . . It's not fraudulent, what are you talking about?"

"I'm talking about perpetrating a fraud against the court and obstruction of justice."

"What! I can't believe your nerve. . . . Let me tell you something, Turner. I *am* going to file the lawsuit and your client *will* pay. Trust me."

"Great. Go for it and see what happens. It's your law license."

I hung up and smiled. It was a little melodramatic but I was pretty sure there would be a lawsuit filed shortly—maybe a grievance too, but I didn't care. I was pissed. I didn't often get angry, but with Monty in a coma, Paula's career in jeopardy, and my wife and family afraid to leave the house, I couldn't control my anger any longer. My arms actually started to shake. Then I felt a tender hand on my shoulder.

"You all right, Stan?" Paula said.

I turned and looked Paula in the eyes trying to maintain my composure. "Yeah. I'm fine."

She smiled. "How's Monty?"

"No change. . . . I've just been sitting here trying to figure out how best to defend you."

I told her about the demand letter and my confrontation with Ortega. Then I filled her in on the graffiti I'd found at home the previous night. She asked me if there had been any word from Tex. I told her I hadn't heard a word and was very nervous about that. While we were talking a doctor walked into the waiting room and motioned for us to come out in the hall.

"I'm afraid I've got bad news," he said.

"What?" I said holding my breath.

"I'm sorry, but Mr. Dozier died a few minutes ago."

Paula let out a shriek. "Oh, no. . . . God no!"

I took Paula in my arms and held her. She was crying hard. The doctor turned and left.

"I'm going to find the son of a bitch who killed Monty," I said. "I'm going to find him and the rest of the sleazy bastards behind his death. They're gonna pay! All of them. I promise you, they're gonna pay."

The funeral was held a few days later at Restland. There were a lot of mourners at the service, which was a bit surprising since Monty's family was small. The police, FBI, and media were also there in force. Paula, Jodie, Rebekah and I were sitting together. I had picked out a seat in the back of the chapel where I could watch the crowd. It was no secret that the murderer often showed up for the victim's funeral. If he was there he was going to get photographed by someone as there were more cameras in the crowd than at Yellowstone.

The service started with a few words from the pastor, some music, and then several testimonials from Monty's family and friends. When the ceremony was over everyone went to the grave site. As we were milling around I noticed a man off in the distance. He looked familiar but I couldn't place him right off. Then I remembered. He was one of the witnesses to Paula's hit and run. I nudged Paula.

"Look to your left," I whispered. "The man across the pond. Do you recognize him?"

Paula looked to her left and replied, "Yes, I sure do. Brian Armstrong. I wonder what he's doing here."

"Curiosity, maybe?" Jodie said.

"Stupidity is more like it," I said. "Now we know for sure there is a connection between the girl Paula hit, the witnesses, and Monty's murderer. That's the only possible reason he would be here."

"Why don't you go tell one of the FBI agents that he's here?" Rebekah asked.

"They already know," I said. "They probably already have the guest list all typed up ready for analysis."

"Maybe they'll see the connection and check it out," Jodie said.

"I doubt it," I said. "The hit and run has nothing to do with them. Besides, I'm sure they are thrilled with all the distractions we've had to deal with since we took on Dusty's case."

"Yeah, it makes you wonder if they didn't have something to do with it."

We all looked at each other. We hadn't seriously considered the idea that the government might be behind the hit and run. The CDA had accused the government of being behind it but I hadn't taken their claim seriously. *Would they stoop so low?* It didn't seem possible, yet why would a gang pick out a high profile attorney as a target? It didn't make sense unless they had intentionally done it to divert our attention from the Dusty Thomas trial. If that was their objective, it had certainly worked. It was hard to believe that the government would go around murdering people, but considering the stakes it wasn't beyond the realm of possibility.

# STAKEOUT 26

As I worked at my desk my mind kept wandering back to the accident, the funeral and the threats against Stan and his family. It was hard to stay focused on Dusty's case with all these thoughts haunting me. I took a deep breath and began leafing through my notebook. *Okay, where was I?* There appeared to be three good suspects: Donald Hurst, Laura Blair, and Reverend Lowe. Hurst was the least likely to have killed Tuttle, I thought. He was jealous of Tuttle and they didn't like each other much, but that didn't seem enough motive for murder. Laura Blair and Reverend Lowe had better motives. Laura had been raped by Tuttle and was probably the father of her child. She was bitter over the rape and having her career squashed to have a baby she didn't want. I thought about who she would have confided in about her feelings—her mother, a sister perhaps but they wouldn't be likely to talk to me. I decided her boyfriend was my best shot. He wouldn't have liked Bobby too much so he'd probably love the opportunity to badmouth him. Once I had him going I'd turn the interview in the direction I wanted it to go.

Chet Conway was a Dallas fireman. He declined at first to talk to me but finally agreed to a meeting after his shift. We met in the bar at Chili's. He was very tall, had blue eyes and jet black hair. Several women in the bar were having trouble keeping their eyes off of him, including myself. We ordered a couple of beers.

"So, I guess you're wondering what this is about?" I said.

"Bobby Tuttle's murder, right?"

"Yes. I guess you know I've already talked to your girlfriend, Laura."

"Yes, she mentioned it."

"Well, I've got to talk to everyone who knew Bobby Tuttle and I understand you met him a few times."

"I didn't kill him," Chet said bluntly. So much for directing the interview. "Don't get me wrong, I thought about killing him a few times."

"Really? Why is that?"

"He was a no good asshole—using his position at work to force her into a relationship she didn't want."

"That seems to be the consensus of everyone I've talked to so far. I was wondering though—weren't you and Laura having some problems?"

"Sure, we got mad at each other a time or two but it was nothing serious," Chet said.

"Really? I thought you had split-up for a while."

"Not a split-up. We just needed a little space for a while . . . you know . . . to think things out."

"Right."

"So, weren't you pissed when Bobby tried to strike up a relationship with Laura when you two were thinking things out?"

"Yes, I was totally pissed. I wanted to tear Bobby a new asshole."

"So, why didn't you?"

Chet looked at me warily. "I know what you're trying to do?"

"What's that?" I asked.

"You're trying to get me upset so I'll incriminate myself."

"No, I'm just looking for the truth. I'm not out to get anyone. I just want to find out what really happened."

"Dusty Thomas shot Bobby Tuttle. Don't you read the papers?" Chet said. "They caught him standing over the body with the shotgun, remember?"

"They can't prove Dusty's shotgun was the murder weapon, so it's possible he didn't do it," I replied.

He shook his head. "Well I guess you're getting paid plenty to believe that, but as for me, Dusty's your man."

"Maybe he did it, maybe he didn't. So, where were you when Bobby Tuttle was murdered?"

"I went dove hunting in East Texas with a friend."

"Dove hunting? You mean with a shotgun?"

"Right."

Chet gave me his friend's name and telephone number and assured me he would verify his alibi. That didn't convince me he was innocent. Old hunting buddies would most likely say anything to protect each other. I asked him what kind of vehicle he drove and he said it was a Ford F150 Extended cab. Laura, however, drove a gray Mercedes. Not silver, but gray and silver were close enough in color that one could be mistaken for the other. It occurred to me that Chet might have borrowed the Mercedes while Laura was home sick. He could have driven to the Double T Ranch, shot Tuttle and brought the car back without Laura knowing it had been gone. I thanked Chet and went back to the office.

Jodie greeted me and said she had completed her research on the other members of the People's Mission. I told her to take a seat and tell me what she had found out. She had a sheet for each of the members with background data and her interview notes. I was very much impressed and made a mental note to give her more assignments in the future.

"All the members of the People's Mission stood to lose plenty if Agent Tuttle was successful in overturning the tax exempt status of the organization. Most of them seemed satisfied with a resolution of the issue in court. But two of the members indicated they would never pay, under any circumstances, an assessment against them if they lost in the Tax Court."

"Who were they?"

"Peter Lowe and Don Harris."

"Peter Lowe, yes, I talked to him. I would agree he had ample motive to kill Tuttle. I don't know this Harris character though. Tell me about him."

"He's a graphic artist. Apparently he's quite good. He designs ads, book covers, logos, that type of thing."

"Really. So why do you think he is a suspect?"

"Besides the losses he would take if the tax deductions weren't allowed, Bobby was threatening to torpedo several government contracts Harris had going if the didn't pay the new assessment. This was bread and butter stuff that paid his rent. He may have decided to take a preemptive strike."

"How could he torpedo the contracts?"

"Simply by garnishing them. If the agency under contract were served with an IRS garnishment they would have to pay the IRS the money due under the contract rather than Harris. He would effectively be put out of business."

"Did you interview him in person?"

"No, over the telephone. He refused to meet with me."

"Did he say where he was on the day of the murder?" I asked.

"Supposedly at his lake house at Lake Lavon. He's living there now while he and his wife are having a new house built in Plano. It's not too far from the Double T Ranch."

"Wow. Good work, Jodie. I guess I'll have to pay a visit to Mr. Harris."

Rather than calling Don Harris and telling him I was coming, I decided it would be better to show up unexpectedly. If he was involved in Bobby's murder, Jodie's phone call would have already shaken him up. My request for an interview would likely prompt him to retrace his steps and destroy any evidence that he might have left behind. I prayed he wasn't already in the process of doing that. It took me about an hour to get to Lake Lavon. I stopped on the side of the road and checked my map. After finding the street I was looking for, I started moving again. It was an old county road that hadn't been maintained very well and there was a lot of dust. Finally I got to a cluster of houses overlooking the lake. The address I had was 2255 Lakeview Dr., St. Paul, Texas.

It was an older house but well maintained. There was an expensive looking ski boat and a red Dodge pickup truck in the driveway. I knocked on the door but nobody answered. I walked around the house. In back was a large patio, a brick barbeque, and several picnic tables. A perfect place to throw a party. I heard voices, and I continued toward them.

"Hello," I said as I approached a man and a woman sitting in two lawn chairs. The man jumped to his feet and glared at me. "Excuse me. I'm looking for Don Harris."

"You're looking at him," he said.

The woman got up and looked at me curiously. "Please excuse the intrusion. I knocked on the front door but there was no answer, then I heard voices."

Harris frowned. "Okay, so you found me. What do you want?"

"I'm Paula Waters—"

"Oh, shit!" Harris said. "I talked to some lady in your office and told her everything I knew about Bobby Tuttle."

"Yes, Jodie told me she had talked to you. I just wanted to ask you a few questions myself, if you don't mind."

"Yes, I do mind. I can't believe you showed up here without an appointment. I'm afraid I'm going to have to ask you to leave."

"I just have a few questions."

"I don't talk to attorneys without my attorney present."

Harris escorted me back to my car. I was mildly upset with his rude treatment. It aroused my suspicion that he was hiding something.

His companion didn't intervene on my behalf, but rather made a dash for the house. After getting in my car I drove off out of view but instead of leaving I parked around the corner where I could observe who came and went from the house. About twenty minutes later the woman I had met came out the front door, got in the pickup and drove off. I didn't know whether to follow her or watch the house. I elected to continue watching the house. A few minutes later a silver Mercedes pulled up in the driveway. Another woman got out and went inside. With a pair of opera glasses I kept in the glove box, I got the license plate number, and wrote it down. I waited a few more minutes but nothing happened so I decided to go back to the office. As I started to pull out onto the road I saw the red Dodge pickup coming straight at me. I froze as it came to a screeching halt in front of me and the woman I'd just met flung opened the door, got out, and strode toward me angrily.

# THE PHONE CALL 27

When I got to the office Jodie told me that Paula had gone to check out a suspect at Lake Lavon. She told me who it was and why Paula thought it was important to go out there right away. I nodded and started going through my telephone messages. As I was about to pick up the phone to start returning calls, Jodie's voice came on the intercom. "Logan and Giles are here to see you."

"Logan and Giles? What do they want?"

"I don't know. They just walked in. Should I ask them?"

"No, I'll be right out."

I got up and walked into the reception area. Logan was smiling. Giles looked grim.

"Hi. What's up?" I said.

Logan pulled out a pair of handcuffs and said, "I've been waiting for this moment for a long time, Turner. You're a traitor and a disgrace to your profession. You'll do anything for money. I've been praying you'd screw up. Wiring that money to General Moya was really stupid. The game is over. You're under arrest."

"Ah!" Jodie gasped.

"It's true I wired some money for a client, but how do you figure it went to General Moya?"

Logan shook his head with a look of disbelief. "It wasn't difficult. We just notified your bank to report any wire transfers to known Moya accounts. If they didn't comply they could have been heavily fined."

"I know you're feeling pretty good right now, Logan, but you've got this all wrong," I said.

"Oh yeah. Tell it to the judge," he said as he threw me up against the wall and put the cuffs on me.

A pain shot through my wrists as he clamped the cuffs closed. I bit my tongue to keep from showing my discomfort. I had feared this moment but somehow had convinced myself it wouldn't happen. I could see the morning headlines in my minds eye—"Stan Turner Arrested for Drug Trafficking—Money Laundering—Treason?" I wondered what the charge actually would be. Then I thought of Rebekah and the kids. The thought of them having to see the headlines and endure the ridicule that would surely follow made me sick.

"Let's talk a minute. I can explain everything," I said in desperation.

"Sorry, it's too late. Besides being wanted by the government of Ecuador, there is a warrant for Moya's arrest out of the Federal District Court in Miami for drug related offenses. You obviously are connected to him somehow and we're going find out exactly how that is."

Logan turned me around and looked me in the eye. He gave me my Miranda warning and escorted me out to a waiting car. Logan sat in the front seat and Giles sat next to me.

"Sorry about the cuffs, " Giles said, "but it's procedure."

I nodded and looked away. My mind was racing trying to figure out what had gone wrong. General Moya apparently wasn't very good at covering his tracks. *What was I going to do now?* My heart sank as I contemplated hours of grueling questioning. How could I possibly explain what had happened without compromising Tex or getting him killed. Just as we started to pull away I heard Jodie's voice screaming. I looked over and she was racing toward our car.

"Stop! Wait!" she screamed.

Logan rolled down his window. "What's wrong?"

"Stan's got an important telephone call. You have to let him take it."

"What? No way. Get away from the car," Logan commanded as his window started back up.

Jodie started pounding on the window. "He has to take this call! You've got—"

"Come on, Logan," Giles said. "Let him take the call if it's that important. Two minutes isn't going to make a difference."

Logan glared at Giles and then threw up his hands. "Okay, okay."

We got out of the car and Logan escorted me back inside. As he passed Jodie he said, "This better be damn important."

Jodie nodded. "It is, trust me."

I picked up the receiver that was laying on Jodie's desk.

"Hello, " I said.

"Stan, this is Tex."

"Oh, Jesus. Am I glad to hear your voice. Where are you?"

"I'm at the Miami airport. I'll be in Dallas by about six tonight. Can you pick me up at the airport?"

"Oh, yeah. You bet. I'll be there. Are you all right?"

"More or less. We've got a lot to talk about."

"Yeah, I guess so. . . . Ah . . . I'm afraid I'm going to have to bring some friends with me."

"Who?"

"A couple of FBI agents. I guess it's about time we leveled with them."

"Oh, Jesus. Do we have to?"

"Yeah, I'm afraid so."

"Okay, whatever. I'll see you soon."

I hung up the phone and looked at Logan and Giles who were waiting for an explanation for the call. I told them that Tex had been kidnapped while in Ecuador and that I had wired the money as part of his ransom. They seemed skeptical but agreed to take me to the airport to pick up Tex. I was still hoping to avoid the issue of Tex's reason for being in Ecuador but didn't know if it would be possible. Despite being in handcuffs I felt great. Knowing Tex was alive was such a relief. I knew it was just a matter of time now before I'd be cleared of any wrongdoing and could get back to practicing law in peace.

When Tex arrived Logan and Giles took us to the Federal Marshall's office for questioning. After several hours of grueling interrogation they let us go. Jodie and Toni were sitting in the waiting room when we were released. Toni and Tex embraced.

"Oh, honey. I was so worried about you," Toni said.

"Ah, you didn't need to worry. You know I always find my way home."

I laughed. "Yeah, well this time it was a little too close for comfort."

Tex smiled. "You're probably right. I suppose I'll have to cool my heels for a while."

Toni nodded. "You better believe it. I'm not letting you out of my sight."

We drove Tex and Toni home but before I let him go I made him promise he'd come to my office the next day so we could sort things out. There was the matter of sending the rest of the money to General Moya and I wanted his account of how he got the 1.8 million dollars in the first place. Although Tex was back, there were still a lot of land mines lurking ahead that we needed to avoid. I just prayed we'd be able to figure out a way to do it.

# THE DEAL 28

My skills as a private investigator were obviously lacking. The big brunette had spotted me spying on them and came to give me a piece of her mind or perhaps her fist, I wasn't sure. My adrenaline level soared as she slammed the door and came quickly toward me. I had taken a self defense course that the Dallas Sheriff's office gave to all the assistant D.A.s, but I wasn't anxious for a test of the skills that I had learned. Fortunately, she stopped without raising her fist.

"Miss Waters. I don't know what you think you're doing, but you're messing with the wrong man. If he sees you spying on him, he'll kill you."

The sudden rush of relief I was feeling quickly fizzled. "Kill me?"

She nodded. "Yes, he's a very dangerous man and I'd hate to see you get hurt. If I was you I'd get back in your car, go home, and forget you ever met Don Harris."

"If he's so bad, why do you stay with him?"

She sighed. "I don't have a choice but you do."

"Why don't you have a choice?"

"He said if I ever left him, he'd kill me."

She spoke with such conviction I was tempted to take her advice, but this was exactly the kind of man who could have killed Dusty Thomas. I had no choice but to pursue this lead. I wondered if I could turn this encounter to my advantage.

"Miss—what was your name?" I asked.

"Jill Murray."

"Jill, maybe we can help each other out here."

"How's that?" Jill asked.

"I'm working on a puzzle and your boyfriend is one of the pieces. I need to figure out where he fits in."

She looked at me curiously. "I know you're defending Dusty Thomas. I've seen you on TV."

"Right. Has Don been following his trial?"

"Oh, God, yes. He watches the news three times a day to see if there is any coverage about it."

"Really? What if I fixed it so he couldn't ever hurt you?"

"Yeah, right," she said.

"I mean it. If you help me I'll give you your freedom."

"But how could you do that?"

"I've got connections with the D.A.'s office. If Mr. Harris is involved in Boby Tuttle's murder and you help me prove it, Don Harris will go to jail for the rest of his life."

"But what if he wasn't involved?" Jill said.

Jill was no dummy. She knew there was only so much I could do to protect her. I didn't want to mislead her so I said, "Well, then I'll help you get a restraining order prohibiting him from contacting you or coming anywhere near you. If he violates the order, he'll go to jail."

"Sure, but he doesn't respect the court. He'll kill me anyway."

I smiled sympathetically. "I don't think so. Most people like him are cowards and wouldn't jeopardize their freedom just to get a little revenge."

"I'm not saying I'll help, but if I did, what kind of help do you need?"

I smiled and said, "Do you spend a lot of time with him?"

"Not a lot. His wife's usually at home. But when he summons me, I come."

"Was that her who just showed up?"

"Yes, that's why I high-tailed it."

"We better go somewhere else to talk. If you spotted me, your boyfriend might too."

"Good idea. If he sees me talking to you, we're both in serious trouble."

We agreed to meet at a bar in Wylie. It was mid-afternoon so it wasn't busy. When I arrived Jill wasn't there yet so I got a table in the corner where we wouldn't be seen. I was thrilled that I had apparently struck a deal with her. She could be instrumental in solving Bobby Tuttle's murder and I'd feel good if I was able to free her from Harris' control. When she walked in the barmaid showed her to my table. After we got a couple drinks, we continued our conversation. She told me that Harris had served eight years in the Army until he got into some kind of trouble and resigned his commission. She didn't know the details but she said he was very bitter about it and had joined some kind of paramilitary group that trained in the Texas hill country.

She didn't know much about his business or the government contracts he had, but she had heard him complain many times about

Bobby Tuttle's obsession with putting the People's Mission out of business. Apparently he had bragged on occasion that if Bobby Tuttle wasn't careful he'd end up with a bullet in his head. I asked her if Harris had a Remington shotgun and she indicated she thought he did. In fact, she said he had quite a collection of weaponry back at the house. Finally, I asked her about the silver Mercedes.

"It belongs to Charlotte, his wife," Jill said.

"Does he ever drive it?"

"Sure. If they go out together, they take the Mercedes."

"Have you noticed any damage to the left side view mirror?" I asked.

She hesitated. "Yes, Charlotte has knocked it off a couple of times backing out of the garage."

"Really? Who told you this?"

"Don. He's always griping about what a klutzy driver she is."

"Do you know where he gets it fixed?"

"Probably at Park Place Motorcars. That's where he usually takes it for repairs."

Jill was too good to be true. Don Harris was looking more and more like the killer every minute I talked to her. I knew I was a long way from cracking the case, but I couldn't quell the excitement I was feeling. Before we parted I found out her address, telephone number, and where she worked so I could find her later. I asked her to try to find out where Harris was on July 11th. She said she would try but wasn't optimistic she could find that out. Apparently Harris was very secretive about his activities and suspicious of any questioning. I couldn't wait to get back to the office and tell Stan what I had discovered.

# THE INJUNCTION 29

The next day Paula filled me in on her new informant, Jill Murray. She was excited about what she had learned about Don Harris and I agreed it was a major breakthrough. My mind, however, was on my next appointment. Tex was due in to explain to me how he got the $1.8 million and what happened to him in Ecuador. I was anxious to send General Moya the final installment and put this chapter of my life behind me. Before Tex arrived, however, Jodie told me there was a constable in the reception room to see me. My heart sank. *What could this be about?*

The constable gave me the paper, I signed for it, and began reading. It was a temporary restraining order, issued out of Judge Lopez' court, restraining me and the firm from sending the remaining nine hundred thousand dollars to General Moya. A chill suddenly overcame me. I remembered General Moya's warning that if he didn't get the second installment he'd send an assassin to kill me and Tex. I showed Jodie the paper and told her to get Logan on the line

"Maybe the judge won't grant the temporary injunction," Jodie said solemnly.

I shrugged. "I hope not."

Jodie left and got Logan on the line for me.

"What do you think you're doing?" I said to him. "I told you General Moya would kill us if he didn't get the rest of the money."

"That was an empty threat. He's not about to send an assassin up here."

"How do you know that?"

"He'll know it wasn't your fault. . . . Don't worry, Stan. We'll protect you."

"How? How could you possibly protect us? Are you going to assign us a bodyguard for the rest of our lives—put us in the witness protection program?"

"No, we'll assign a couple men to watch you for a while, until things die down."

"Well, that's not good enough," I said. "Just as soon as we're left unprotected we'll be dead."

"Listen, Turner. General Moya is an enemy of Ecuador and under U.S. indictment. The President has made a pledge to help the civilian government there get rid of him. There is no way you're going to be allowed to send him another million dollars. This is a foreign policy issue and there's nothing you can do about it."

I knew I wasn't going to get anywhere arguing with Logan. It was up to Judge Lopez and I had a bad feeling about the final outcome. Logan was probably right, this was a political issue that would be dictated by Washington without regard to how it might affect Tex and me. The thought of an assassin stalking me made me uneasy. How could I function knowing someone was out there ready to kill me at any moment?

When Tex showed up I didn't mention the injunction at first. I didn't want him distracted from the purpose of our meeting which was to find out how he got into this situation in the first place and what had happened to him in Ecuador. I sat back in my chair as he began to tell his story.

"When I got the letter I thought it was a joke but several days later Señor Lantz called me. He asked me if I'd read the letter and what my answer was. I told him I had but that I didn't see how it could possibly work. He assured me all the details were worked out and that all they needed was an American to stand-in as Dr. Wells' beneficiary.

"Six hundred and thirty thousand dollars was a lot of incentive to go down to Ecuador and check the situation out. Besides, if I didn't get the money he said some corrupt general would get it.

"Anyway, you know how I am. I couldn't pass up such a great opportunity so I contacted Señor Alfaro and told him I was coming to Quito. He was ecstatic and arranged to meet me at the airport. He said he knew a good hotel and that the whole transaction would only take a few days. He said to come on Friday so he could show me around Quito over the weekend and then we'd transact our business on Monday.

"When I got there he treated me like a long lost brother. I got the grand tour of the city, we went to all the historical sites, and to some great restaurants. Saturday night he showed me some pretty hot night spots. I wish you'd of been there, Stan. You wouldn't believe what those women were doing with their bodies."

I wanted to ask him to clarify that, but then decided it wasn't relevant to the story, so I didn't. "Hmm," I replied.

"So, on Monday I met Victor at his lawyer's office. Victor gave him a folder full of letters, papers and documents supposedly showing that I was Dr. Wells' brother. He reviewed the paperwork and seemed satisfied that I was Dr. Wells' heir."

"Were they speaking English?"

"No, Spanish."

"So, you really didn't know what they were saying?"

"No, not really."

"What happened next?"

"I signed some papers and we left to go to the bank."

"What kind of papers?" I asked.

"I'm not sure. They were in Spanish. Victor said it was an application to have the money transferred to me."

"Did Victor explain how the deal was going to work?"

"He said the bank would wire the money to my account in the Cayman Islands. He and I would then fly there and split it."

"So, how did I end up getting it in my trust account?" I asked.

"Well, I knew Victor might try to take all the money so I figured I'd stay one step ahead of him. On the way to Ecuador I stopped in the Cayman Islands and made arrangements with the bank to wire the funds to your trust account immediately upon receipt. I didn't have it wired to my account because I didn't want anyone to know that I had it. When we got to the Caymans I figured I'd call you and have you wire Victor's share to him."

"Weren't you worried Victor would kill you when he found out the money wasn't in your account in the Caymans?"

He nodded. "Yeah, I knew he'd be pissed off, but I figured as long as I could wire the money to him, he'd get over it."

I raised my eyebrows. "You like to live dangerously."

"Perhaps, but it didn't make any difference, because we never made it out of the country. We were both arrested at the airport."

"What went wrong?"

"I'm not sure, exactly. We were taken to some kind of military base and questioned for hours. I tried to stick to our story, but they obviously didn't believe me. When they started to torture me I came clean."

"How did they take the truth?"

"Not well. Some high ranking officer came to see me and said if I'd send instructions to the bank in the Caymans to wire the money back, he'd let me go."

"General Moya, I bet."

"Perhaps. . . . Unfortunately, because the bank had forwarded the money to you, I couldn't do that."

"Why didn't you just call me?"

"I got to thinking that if I called you and told you to send the money, they'd probably kill me anyway. They wouldn't want any witnesses to what had happened since I'm sure the General was planning on pocketing the money."

"You're exactly right. He had planned to take the money and then you showed up and spoiled his plans."

"Right. So, I figured I'd just sit tight and hopefully you or somebody would come looking for me. I thought my chances were much better if I still had the money."

I shook my head. "You were right. When we got there and put out the word that we were looking for you, it didn't take long for the General to find out about it."

I told Tex about what had happened to Monty and me in Ecuador and about Monty's subsequent murder. Then I showed him the temporary restraining order. He wasn't as upset as I thought he would be. In fact, he said he agreed with Logan. He didn't think General Moya would do anything to either of us. We argued for a while on that point but Tex couldn't be convinced we were in any danger. I advised him as his attorney, and urged him as a friend, not to take any chances but he wouldn't budge on his position. In fact, he told me not to fight the temporary injunction. Then I realized why he was so adamant. He wanted to keep the $900,000!

I couldn't believe the money was so important that he'd risk his life as well as mine to have it. For a split second I wished I hadn't gone down to Ecuador looking for him. My only hope now was that with further reflection he would come to his senses and instruct me to fight the government in their efforts to prevent us from completing the transaction with General Moya. Perhaps if I talked to Toni she could talk some sense into him. I hoped so, because I was quite confident General Moya *would* send an assassin to kill us for double crossing him.

Stan wasn't as excited about my new witness as I thought he would be. He told me about the restraining order and Tex's insistence that he not send General Moya the rest of the ransom. I couldn't believe Tex would do that to him after all Stan had gone through to find him and get him back home safely. So much for gratitude.... Since Stan was too distracted to discuss Jill Murray, I left him and went to my office. I needed to find out as much as I could about Don Harris. I went to the Dallas Courthouse and checked the criminal and civil court records. Don had been in a lawsuit with a former business partner and another one with an ex-employee who allegedly had stolen some trade secrets. Apparently he had trouble getting along with people. There was also a pending DWI case and the divorce records showed Don was in his second marriage.

I had to wait nearly twenty minutes for a clerk to pull the divorce file out of storage but what I found was worth the wait. His first wife, Regina, had divorced him on grounds of physical abuse and adultery and he hadn't contested the proceedings. She got everything. Unfortunately for her, it wasn't much. A rush of excitement came over me. A bitter ex-wife would be another great source of information.

On my way back to the office I stopped by Park Place Motorcars to find out the date of the repair to Harris' wife's car. The elderly man in the customer service department told me he wasn't authorized to give out that kind of information so I put on my charm and tried to sweet talk it out of him. Twenty dollars later I got the information. The invoice was dated July 18—a week after the murder. *This could be the car.* As I was walking back to my car, I got this crazy idea about actually inspecting the Mercedes. Jill had told me Harris' wife worked as a sales representative at J. C. Penney's in Collin Creek Mall so I drove there and went to the Penney's parking lot. There were only a couple silver Mercedes and I had the license plate number so it didn't take long to find the right car.

It had been recently washed so I didn't expect to find much. I looked around to make sure no one was watching me, then I bent down and inspected the side view mirror. Whoever had replaced it had done a good job because I couldn't tell it wasn't original equipment. I continued to inspect the rest of the vehicle not knowing what I was looking for exactly but just hoping I'd find something. I looked inside the car through the windows and noticed a pair of binoculars. At the front of the car, in the recesses of the headlight wells I found some yellow fiber that I didn't recognize so I took a sample. I also found some red mud that had caked below the fender. Thinking it might match dirt from the Double T Ranch I bent down and took a sample of it too. When I stood up a security officer was glaring at me.

"What are you doing Miss?" he said.

"Ah. . . . Ah. . . . Well, I lost my contact lens. I was just searching for it. I know it's down her somewhere."

I bent down and pretended to look for the contact. The officer got out of his electric cart and came over to help.

"Aren't contacts a pain in the ass?" he said. "Mine are falling out all the time too."

"Oh, well. I guess it's lost," I said as I stood up. "Luckily I have insurance. I'll have to stop at the optometrist in the morning and get it replaced."

"You sure," he said. "I'd be happy to help you search a little longer."

I smiled and thanked the officer and walked back to my car. The binoculars interested me. If Harris was the killer he might have used them to watch Dusty's house while he was waiting for Bobby Tuttle to show up. When I got to the office Stan was alone so I went into his office.

"Hey, where have you been?" Stan said.

"Out and about," I replied.

"Hey, I'm sorry about this morning. I was just so shaken up over the TRO that I couldn't concentrate on your new witness—what's her name?"

"Jill Murra. . . . It's okay. Did you talk to Toni?"

"Yeah. She's going to try to talk some sense into Tex. God I hope she can."

"I bet he'll change his mind. He's got to be concerned about General Moya's threat."

Stan shrugged. "Hopefully. . . . So, tell me about your witness."

I filled Stan in on Jill Murray, my courthouse research, and my inspection of the Mercedes.

"You better be careful, girl. I don't want to have to get you out of jail again," he said smiling.

"Don't worry. I promise that won't happen."

Stan inspected the fiber and mud samples and said, "This red mud is pretty common in North Texas and Southern Oklahoma. I doubt it's going to prove the car was at the scene of the murder. This fiber though might be significant. Let's take a trip up to the Double T and see if Dusty knows what it is. I want to take another look around up there anyway."

An afternoon drive in the country sounded relaxing, so I said, "Yes, good idea."

It was late November and the foliage was in full splendor as we drove north along the eastern edge of Lake Lavon. Stan pointed out several good fishing holes that he and his boys had discovered. I didn't know anything about fishing so I just smiled and listened to him talk. When we got to the northern end of the lake he told me about the day he and several hundred other men spent cutting free firewood just before the Corps of Engineers began filling the lake.

"The kids loved playing lumberjack for a day and we brought home enough firewood to last us three years," Stan said. "So, do you like any outdoor activities?"

"Yes, I like hiking and horseback riding," I said.

"Oh really? Do you ride often?"

"Not lately. I haven't had the time. But when I was growing up my parents had a few horses boarded down on a ranch in Red Oak. We used to go down there all the time and ride them."

"That must have been fun," Stan said. "So, you must have a few horse stories to tell."

"Well, yes. There was the time I was out by myself and we ran across a rattlesnake. My horse got spooked and ran off so fast he threw me and I landed on my ass."

"Oh, my God. Were you hurt?"

"Just a broken arm and damaged pride. . . . It was kind of fun having a cast on my arm though. I must have got a hundred autographs."

Our conversation was interrupted by the sounds of a siren approaching. I looked into the rear view mirror and saw a police car behind me with his lights flashing.

"Shit. What's this about."

Stan pulled over, cut the engine and rolled down his window. The DPS officer got out of his car, wrote Stan's license number down on a pad, and then walked to the opened window. His badge read: "P. Curtis."

"Hi, officer," Stan said.

"Did you know you were speeding?" he asked.

Stan frowned and replied, "No, I didn't realize it. How fast was I going?"

"I clocked you at 63 miles per hour," he said. "The limit is 55."

"Oh, gee. I didn't realize I was going that fast."

"Where are you headed?"

"Up to the Double T Ranch."

"What business do you have there?"

Stan told him who we were and why we were going to see Dusty Thomas. He seemed very interested in our mission.

"Well, I'll just give you a warning now, but watch your speed a little closer from now on."

"I will. Definitely," Stan replied.

The officer started to leave and then hesitated. "You know I was on duty that day. I wasn't two miles from the Double T when all hell broke loose."

"Is that right," Stan said. "You didn't happen to see a silver Mercedes did you?"

"Well, now that you mention it, I do recall one. He was driving pretty fast. I would have gone after him had I not heard about the shootings at the Double T. I let him go so I could respond to the call."

"So a man was driving the Mercedes," I asked.

"Yes, I believe so."

"Did you recognize the man?"

"No, he wasn't from around these parts. I just saw him for a split second."

"If you saw him again would you recognize him?"

"Gee. I don't know. It was some time ago and I just saw him for a minute."

"We may want to show you some pictures. We have a suspect who had a good motive to kill Bobby Tuttle but we can't prove he was at the scene of the crime. His wife owns a silver Mercedes that our suspect drives on occasion, so if that's the car you saw it would be a major breakthrough in our case."

"If you have a picture, I'll take a look at it but don't get your hopes up."

The officer let us go and we continued our journey to the Double T. When we got there Dusty and his wife came out of the house and greeted us. Stan showed Dusty the fiber sample. He looked at it carefully and said, "This is alfalfa. We grow four or five acres of it each year for feed." He pointed to the east. "Over there. It's too far to walk. We'll take the four wheelers."

Martha and Dusty went into a shed and came out driving a couple four wheelers. I got on with Dusty and Stan went with Martha. We drove along a dirt road around a large stock pond until we got to a road following a fence line. We took the road about a mile until we came to a fork where we stopped. Dusty pointed to the large pasture that lay before us.

"That's where we grow the alfalfa. It's been cut now, but back in July it was pretty tall. If a car came through this area it would likely get some alfalfa caught in its grille," Dusty said.

"Very good," I said.

Stan looked back toward the ranch house. The land sloped upward to where we were situated. It was a good vantage point for someone watching the house. I wondered what he was thinking. "good vantage point, huh?"

"Yes, now I wonder where he lost his side view mirror."

Dusty scratched his head and then motioned for us to mount the four wheelers. We took off along the fence line toward the main road. Before we got to the highway, the road abruptly ended. We stopped and got off the four wheelers.

"This is the only way to get on and off the ranch without being seen from the ranch house. I don't like surprise visitors so I barricaded all the entrances and exits except the main road."

Dusty pointed to the left where there was a small gap between two fences. "I left a small opening so I could get the tractor through it. It's small, but a car could almost make it through."

Dusty walked over to the two fence posts and examined them. "Well, I'll be damned."

"What is it?" Stan asked.

Dusty chuckled. "There's a streak of silver paint on the fence post."

Stan ran over and examined the streak. He looked back at me smiling. "Nice work, Paula. You're gonna crack this case wide opened."

I shrugged. "Well, hopefully, but we're not quite there yet."

"I know," Stan said. "But we've got proof Don Harris was out here when Tuttle was murdered. That's at least good for reasonable doubt."

I nodded. "We still need that DPS officer to ID Harris as the driver. Otherwise, it could of been anybody out here."

Stan said, "You better call Bart and tell him he needs to get his crime scene unit out here to compare this paint to Mrs. Harris' car."

"Trenton Lee's gonna be pissed when Bart tells him," I said.

"Too bad. He's got to check out all possible leads," Stan replied. "After all we all have the same task—to find the truth, right?"

"Yes, I'll remind him if he complains."

As we drove back to Dallas I was feeling pretty good. Things were finally falling into place and I believed for the first time that we were going to be able to put up a credible defense for Dusty Thomas. Now all we had to do was clear me of the hit and run charges and keep Stan from being assassinated. I took a deep breath and prayed the tide had turned and things were going to start going our way. Then I heard a gunshot. The left front of the car dropped abruptly as the tire blew out. Stan struggled to keep the car on the road. A second gunshot shattered the front windshield. I covered my face with my arms as Stan brought the car to a halt. Stan pushed me toward the door."Let's get out of here. We're sitting ducks," he yelled.

The shots were coming from the woods to our left. We climbed out of the car and scampered down the embankment toward the lake. Another shot ricocheted off a boulder three inches from my hand. At the lake's edge Stan grabbed my hand and we ran toward a thick clump of trees that put us out of eminent danger. There was dead silence as we stood breathless behind an old oak tree.

"That couldn't be the assassin already," Stan moaned.

"No, I'd put my money on Don Harris," I replied. "He must have found out we're on his trail."

"Wonderful. I wonder if he's had enough fun or if he's going to come down here and try to finish us off."

"I don't know," I said as I peered around the tree. The battered BMW sat awkwardly on the side of the road. There was no movement that I could see. Stan pulled on my arm indicating it was time to move on. I was about to follow him when I heard a car coming. Relief swept over me as I realized it was officer Curtis. We were safe—at least for the moment.

We ran to the base of the embankment and yelled up to officer Curtis. He came down to where we were and we told him what happened. He radioed his dispatcher and before long two more DPS officers arrived along with a county sheriff's deputy. My car was a mess—multiple bullet holes, glass everywhere, and a bent front axle. I was sick. Officer Curtis told us to stay away from the vehicle as a crime scene unit was on its way.

Several hours later Curtis took us to the local sheriff's office where two detectives questioned us about the shooting. We told them our suspicions about Don Harris and the possible assassin from Ecuador. They said they would check out Harris' whereabouts but obviously couldn't do anything about General Moya. About an hour later Jodie arrived to take us home. A mob of reporters had gathered outside the Sheriff's office which made getting to her car difficult. The reporters shouted questions at us. Stan assured them we were both fine but declined further comment. What else could we have told them? All we knew was that someone wanted us dead.

# SHAKY WITNESS 31

My strategy with Manuel Ortega had worked like a charm. Paula was served with a lawsuit several weeks after our confrontation. I immediately answered the suit and noticed the two witnesses and the plaintiff for deposition. As a matter of professional courtesy the depositions were set for the offices of Manuel Ortega on Commerce Street just two blocks from the Dallas Courthouse. My usual court reporter, Betty Blake, was setting up in the conference room when I arrived with Paula. Since she was the defendant I felt she should be there when I questioned her accusers. Ortega's secretary served us coffee and five minutes later Ortego showed up with the plaintiff and a man introduced as Raul Marcos.

I said, "I'm going to have to object to Mr. Marcos being present during this deposition unless you have a good reason why he should be here."

"This is Miss Cabrillo's boyfriend. She would like him present while her deposition is taken."

"I'm sorry, but I may need to call him as a witness. I'm invoking the rule."

The rule referred to the option of any attorney in the proceeding to object to other witnesses being present during testimony. You didn't want one witness copying another witnesses' testimony. In this case I didn't want to give the plaintiff the comfort of any moral support or coaching her boyfriend might provide. Ortega complained about my objection but finally told Mr. Marcos to wait outside. After entering our agreements into the record I began questioning Miss Cabrillo.

She confirmed what I had learned from Monty's report that she was from El Salvador and was working here on a green card. I learned further that she was a political refugee and had been granted political asylum. She had met Raul Marcos while attending El Centro College and they had been living together about a year. Marcos was originally from Los Angeles but had recently moved to the Oak Lawn area of Dallas. She indicated he was a bartender at an Oak Lawn sports bar when he wasn't attending classes at El Centro. After a couple hours we got to the day of the incident.

"So, how long have you been a jogger?" I asked.

"Ever since I came to America. My friend, Raul, he is a jogger and he taught me."

"Do you jog every morning?"

"Usually. Yes. Sometimes."

"Okay. . . . How long have you lived in your apartment?"

"Since January. Almost one year."

"So, in the last year how many times have you jogged?"

"Ah . . . I don't know exactly."

"In the thirty days prior to the incident, how many times did you jog?"

"Many times."

"30 times, 20 times, 10 times?"

"More than 10 times."

"Do you take the same route each day?"

"No, I jog different places sometimes."

"Where were you jogging on the date of the incident in question?"

"From my apartment I go to Keller Springs Road. Then I go all the way to Preston Road and back home."

"And were you coming or going when the incident occurred?"

"I was just starting on my way when the lady ran me down."

"Okay, what side of the street were you on?"

"Ah . . . the left side, I think."

"So you were jogging in an easterly direction on the north side of Keller Springs Road?"

"Yes, I suppose so."

"When did you first see Miss Waters?"

"I heard a car and looked behind me and there she was about to hit me."

"Wouldn't she have been on the other side of the street?"

"No, she was right behind me. I tried to avoid her but she came right at me."

"So she was traveling on the wrong side of the road and just ran you down for no reason?"

Cabrillo squirmed in her chair. She looked over at Ortega who didn't offer any help. "I don't know what she thinks but she hit me hard."

"On your left side?"

She looked down at her left side and then her right. "Ah, yes . . . left . . . no, no, right side."

"Were you perhaps crossing the street? Then I could see how she might have hit you on the right side."

"Yes . . . maybe crossing street."

"What made you decide to suddenly cross the street?"

"I don't know. Maybe—"

"Objection!" Ortega shouted. "You're putting words in her mouth."

I frowned at Ortega. "No, I'm not. I'm just trying to understand what happened. She seems confused about the facts."

I turned back to Miss Cabrillo. "You may answer the question."

"What question?"

This line of questioning went on for some time. There were many discrepancies in her story and she seemed very confused about what actually happened. I decided it was time to put some pressure on her.

"Did you know the two men who took you to the hospital?"

"No, I never saw them before."

"Objection!" Ortega said nearly falling out of his chair. He glared at Cabrillo and said, "They didn't take you—"

"What hospital did they—" I said.

"Wait! "the court reporter said, "One at a time please."

"You tricked her," Ortega said. "Let me ask her a question."

"No," I said emphatically. "You can ask her questions when I'm done. Now, Miss Cabrillo. Why did they bring you back to the scene of the accident?"

"What? I don't understand."

"Didn't they, the two men take you away and then bring you back to Keller Springs Road after Miss Waters had left?"

"Ah . . . I don't understand . . . no they never did that. I don't know them."

"You do know them, don't you?"

"Not really."

"Objection!" Ortega screamed. "You're putting words in her mouth again."

"You've met them before, haven't you?"

"No. Only one time."

Ortega ran his hands through his hair, took a deep breath, and shook his head at the witness. He was angry and he let her know it.

"When was that?" I asked.

"I don't remember."

"A day or two before the accident, perhaps?"

"I don't remember."

Ortega had gotten his message across to the witness, but it was too late. She had slipped up and lost all credibility. I continued to question her and used her sudden loss of memory to my advantage. No matter what I asked her from that moment forward, she could not remember the answer. Soon she was sounding like a broken record. Ortega was beside himself and soon asked for a recess. After the deposition Paula and I evaluated her testimony.

"Ortega is in on the scam, obviously," Paula said.

"Yes, I guess we need to start investigating him as well. He may be orchestrating the whole thing."

"I can't believe he thinks he can get away with this. It's so ridiculous."

"Well if his other witnesses don't do better, he won't have a prayer of winning at trial," I replied.

After the deposition we went back to the office. Paula was too wound up to work, so she went home. I dug into my stack of phone messages that had accumulated while I was gone. There was a message from Toni Weller which caught my eye. I returned the call. She apologized and said she hadn't been able to change Tex's mind about opposing the temporary injunction. He was going to keep the money. I wadded up the note and threw it in the waste basket. *Damn it!*

I was tempted to just call the bank and wire the money anyway. After all it was my life that was going to be in jeopardy. Of course, Tex might sue me or file a grievance that would end up costing me my law license. At least I'd be alive. I took a deep breath and tried to relax. Maybe *General Moya will blow it off. A million dollars is just peanuts to him. Damn you, Tex! You greedy son of a bitch!*

# THE KIDNAPPING 32

A few weeks later I decided to call Jill and see if she had found anything out about Don Harris' whereabouts on July 11. I also wondered if she had found out anything about the attempt on our lives a few days earlier. I feared she had been caught snooping around and *that* had triggered Harris' attempt on our lives. She answered the telephone but her voice was very restrained.

"Jill. This is Paula Waters. How are you?"

She didn't answer but I could hear her breathing.

"I guess you heard about the sniper attack on Stan and me."

"I can't talk to you now," she said and the line went dead.

I dropped the phone from my ear and said, "Damn it."

My hunch must of been right. She sounded scared. I decided to go pay her a visit at her apartment up in McKinney, but first I called Bart to let him know she could be a critical witness and needed protection. He was sympathetic but said I'd have to give him a lot more to take that request to Trenton Lee. Disappointed with Bart's response, I called Joe Conrad, one of the detectives we had talked to us up at the Collin County Sheriff's office, and told him about Jill. He said he'd pay her a visit soon and if she needed protection he would make sure she got it.

In the meantime I took my rental car up to McKinney to Jill's place to try to talk to her. As I was pulling up to her apartment complex I saw her leaving with Don Harris. She looked upset and I noticed she had a black eye. He had her by one arm and appeared to be in a hurry. I was glad I was in a rental car because Don didn't seem to notice me. Just as they took off in Don's pickup I eased into the traffic a few cars behind them. I wished I had one of those new mobile phones that were becoming popular so I could have called for help. I obviously didn't have time to stop at a pay phone.

They went west on Highway 380 to Highway 75 and turned south. If they took the Highway 121 exit I knew where they were going—DFW Airport. It looked like Jill was leaving town so she couldn't be a witness against Don Harris. I was a bit relieved that Harris had elected to send Jill away rather than kill her. He probably figured another murder might make things worse. His best bet was for the sheriff's office to come up empty handed when they started snooping into his affairs. When we got to the airport they went to Terminal A and parked. Harris escorted Jill into the terminal and to her gate where they waited. The message board said it was flight 2343 to Baltimore, Maryland.

While they were waiting I went to the phone and called Conrad but neither he nor his partner were available. When I got off the telephone I went back to the gate. They were just calling for pre-boarding when I got there. Jill spotted me approach and I motioned for her to run. Without hesitation she pulled away from Harris and darted off through the crowd. When Harris turned to chase her I slammed into him as hard as I could. We both went sprawling onto the floor. He scrambled to get to his feet and chase Jill but I grabbed a foot and held on for dear life. Harris fell on his face again and this time he kicked me hard in the head causing a lady nearby to scream. I saw two security guards coming at us from the same direction that Jill had fled. The blow to my head caused me to lose my grip on Harris' leg and he ran off, but in the opposite direction. Jill was safe for the moment.

The two security guards helped me up and wanted to know what was going on. I told them I was trying to stop a kidnapping and to call Detective Conrad or Bart to verify my story. I wanted to go looking for Jill but they insisted they would take care of finding her. They never did, nor did they apprehend Don Harris. Two hours later, when Airport Security was about to let me go, Bart showed up. He held my chin up and looked at the gash above my eye.

"Jesus, this may need stitches," he said as he ran his finger over the wound.

I moaned a little to make him feel bad. He deserved it. "It hurts like hell."

Bart smiled sympathetically. "I'm sorry. I should have taken your request to Trenton but I was sure he'd turn it down."

"It's all right. Everything happened so fast you couldn't have responded in time anyway. I'm sure Detective Conrad will provide protection for Jill. Now all I have to do is find her."

"Any idea where she might have gone?"

"No. She obviously isn't going back to her apartment or to work. Maybe she has family or friends close by who she can stay with," I said.

"I'll have someone check all the hotels and motels to see if she has checked-in anywhere," Bart said.

"Thanks. I really need to find her. She's the key to our case, I know it."

"I'll call Trenton and tell him about tonight. Maybe he'll get Logan and Giles involved since there was an attempted kidnapping. So far I haven't been able to convince anybody that Don Harris should be checked out, but with the attempt on your life and now the attempted kidnapping, they'll have to look into it."

"Good. I don't like playing detective. I can't afford the medical bills."

Bart smiled and took my hand. "I don't like you playing detective either. I'm worried about you getting seriously hurt. Can't you guys afford to hire a private detective?"

"Yeah, but we haven't had the heart to since Monty died. Besides, I'm getting pretty good at it, don't you think?"

"Yes, you are but—"

I pressed two fingers against Bart's mouth. "Hold that thought. Come see me later at my apartment, okay? I could use a little company."

He smiled. "Sure. Where are you going now?"

"Back to the office. Jill may be trying to contact me. If not, I'll see if I can find some friends or relatives who might know where she is."

"Be careful," Bart said as we parted.

Back at the office there was no word from Jill. I briefed Stan on what had happened and he made me promise I'd call him for backup before I got into any more skirmishes. He left saying he was going to take a photo of Don Harris to Officer Curtis to see if he could put Harris at or near the Double T on the night of Agent Tuttle's murder. I wished him luck and then started working on finding Jill's friends and relatives.

Jill's employer told me she had a sister who lived in Irving. They couldn't give out the phone number but they did tell me her name, Marty Webster. There were numerous Websters in Irving so I started calling all of them hoping to find the right one. Most were not at home and none of the ones who did answer knew anyone named Jill. Frustrated, I grabbed my purse and headed back to McKinney. Perhaps a neighbor might know something.

The door to Jill's apartment was unlocked. Apparently in their haste to leave they had neglected to lock it. I looked around to be sure nobody was watching me and then slipped inside. I didn't dare turn on a light so I used a small pen light that I kept in my purse in case of an emergency. The house had been ransacked. Apparently Jill had something that Harris was worried about. I wondered what it was and whether or not Harris had found it.

As I gazed around the apartment I wondered where I would go if I were running from someone like Harris. It would have to be someone strong who could protect me or someone so remote that Harris would never figure out who it was. As I was searching, my heart jumped at the sight of an address book. I picked it up and started leafing through it. The name and telephone number of Jill's sister, Marty Webster, was listed so I picked up the phone and dialed her number. After a few rings she answered. I told her who I was and that I was looking for Jill. She said she hadn't talked to Jill for several days but she hesitated like she was being coached on what to say. She quickly hung up.

I didn't blame Jill for not wanting to talk to me but I had to find out what she knew. I felt like if I confronted her face to face she'd talk to me. As I continued to leaf through the address book I came across Don Harris' listing. There were several numbers: home, work, and mobile. There was also a number written in pencil underneath the others. Wondering whose number it was I picked up the telephone and dialed it. A lady answered.

"Hello," she said.

"Oh, Hi. Did I dial the wrong number again? I was trying to get a hold of Don Harris."

"Don Harris? How did you get this number?"

"I'm sorry. Who is this?"

"Who are you?" she asked indignantly.

"One of Jill's friends. I was looking through her address book and came across this number. I take it this is not Don Harris' number."

"I should say not. I've been divorced from him for years."

"Oh, you must be Regina?" I said.

"Why yes, how did you know that?"

"Listen, we've got to talk. Can I meet you somewhere?"

She agreed to meet and talk to me after I explained who I was and what I was doing. She was very suspicious and ultra cautious. I didn't blame her considering she had been married to Don Harris. That must of been a nightmare. We met at a little café off the square in downtown McKinney. Regina was a short brunette in her mid-thirties. She dressed nicely and seemed pleasant enough, but was constantly fidgeting with her napkin, silverware, and left earring. She was making me nervous just watching her. I told her about Jill's abduction and subsequent escape. She told me why her phone number was in Jill's address book.

"Jill called for advice on how to rid herself of Don," Regina said. "She figured I had successfully divorced him so perhaps I could give her some pointers."

"What did you tell her?"

"I told her to forget it. She'd have to wait until Don was through with her. I was only able to get a divorce from Don because he found a new love and she wanted to get married. He was finished with me so he let me go."

"But he didn't contest the divorce. You got everything."

She chuckled. "Yes, everything that wasn't hidden in an offshore bank account or put in someone else's name."

"Oh, I see. So he gave you what he wanted you to have."

"Which was damn little," Regina mused.

"And you didn't do any discovery to locate these assets because you wanted to stay alive?" I said.

She smiled. "Exactly."

Regina told me everything she knew about the People's Mission. She said Harris got the idea for the People's Mission when he did some work for a south Dallas preacher. The preacher ran a lucrative office supply business out of his alleged church and paid no taxes. Harris loved the idea and shared it with some of his friends. Once they got IRS approval for their new church they sold affiliations for $10,000 each—kind of a franchise fee. Everything was going great until Bobby Tuttle audited them and discovered the fraud. The audit took place after Regina and Don divorced so she didn't know too much about Harris' reaction to it.

She also talked about Harris' friends, hang outs, and habits which I was sure would be valuable information later on. She assured me Harris was capable of violence and told me to be very careful which, of course, I already knew. Regina promised to let me know if she heard from Jill. I told Regina to tell Jill I could provide protection if she'd just contact me. It was nearly five when I left the café and headed back to Dallas. It was after six when I got home. There was a message on my recorder from Bart not to eat dinner. He was bringing over Chinese.

At seven Bart knocked on the door. He was carrying our Chinese takeout and a bottle of wine. I let him in and took the bottle of wine. He carried it to the kitchen table, took off his coat, and started unpacking it while I opened the bottle of wine. I got two glasses, set them on the table, and sat down to eat. Bart took a bite and smiled.

"I love Chinese," he said.

"Me too. Thanks for bringing it by. I'm so tired there is no way I could have cooked."

"So, did you get into any more brawls since I saw you last?"

I gave him an exaggerated smile. "No, it was a pretty quiet afternoon actually. I did find a new witness. Don Harris' ex-wife. She gave me an earful."

"Really. Well, speaking of Harris. I talked to Trenton and he doesn't think there is any connection between the sniper attack and the Bobby Tuttle case."

"What? That's ridiculous. Of course there's a connection. It's obvious."

"Well, Trenton doesn't think so and he's not going help you create reasonable doubt. He said you're on your own. He did say he'd talk to Detective Conrad and ask him to keep Trenton apprized of the investigation."

"What a jerk. What do I have to do, serve the killer up on a silver platter?"

"That's about what it's going to take," Bart said. "They're convinced they already have the killer and most everyone agrees."

"But they don't. Dusty is innocent," I protested.

"You don't know that," Bart said. "You just want to believe it. You really have nothing to prove Harris killed Bobby Tuttle, do you?"

I shrugged. "No, not yet. But I know Harris is involved in Bobby's death somehow. He's running scared and I promise you I will find out why. It's just a matter of time."

Bart smiled. "I have no doubt you will.... Now can we cut the shop talk and get down to business?"

I gave Bart a wry smile and replied, "What business did you have in mind, big boy?"

# PRETRIAL JITTERS 33

My meeting with Officer Curtis didn't go well. I showed him Don Harris' photo and he couldn't say for sure that Harris was the one driving the Mercedes the day Tuttle was murdered. Nor was he even positive the driver was male. The lab report that finally came in on the silver paint we found at the Double T Ranch didn't help my spirits much either. Apparently the paint was used on several Mercedes vehicles and wouldn't be enough to prove Harris' Mercedes was at the Double T Ranch.

It was early January 1987 and although Paula's civil case was years away from trial, her criminal case was coming up fast—just 29 days away. The video surveillance report had just come in and it was very disappointing. Miss Cabrillo had been watched and videotaped for 48 hours straight and did nothing inconsistent with her claimed injuries. A jolt of fear went through me. What if we lost? What if Paula was convicted and had to serve time? I took a deep breath and tried to relax. I couldn't get depressed. That would just make matters worse. I had to concentrate and keep plowing ahead. Something would turn up. I closed my eyes and said a silent prayer for Paula. I didn't often pray, but when I really needed help, I did. I knew God would come through if I just had enough faith. When my emotional crisis was over I got back to work.

Shortly after taking Miss Cabrillo's deposition I had taken the depositions of the two witnesses to the accident. They had been better prepared by Ortega and stuck by their stories but I also subpoenaed all their records. Six large boxes of records were sitting in my storage room. The job of going through them was pretty daunting so I had procrastinated in getting to it. Finally I moved the boxes to the conference room and started looking through them. I enlisted Jodie's help to speed along the process.

There were bank statements, deposit books, real estate papers, tax returns, letters, memos, bills, receipts, insurance policies and many other papers. None of them, however, seemed to have any bearing on Paula's case. Miss Cabrillo seemed like a quite ordinary person. But when I got to the records of Ernesto Garcia things got interesting.

His passport showed he had done a lot of traveling—El Salvador, Brazil, Trinidad-Tobago, Grand Cayman, Mexico, Belize, Venezuela, and Ecuador. Seeing the Ecuador stamp in the passport bothered me. Could there be a connection between General Moya and Ernesto Garcia? I didn't think so. It was probably a coincidence but I couldn't get that idea out of my head. There was also a lot of unexplained cash going through Garcia's bank account. He supposedly made $25,000 a year at his job, but he ran nearly a hundred thousand through his bank account during the preceding twelve months. Drug money? I figured he'd be into that being a member of the 18th Street Gang. They were known to deal in just about anything from guns to teenage prostitutes. Garcia was obviously hired to set Paula up, but who hired him? Was this just about money or was there another motive?

I finally broke down and hired another private investigator. His name was Paul Thayer. He had called me a couple times soliciting work and I had put him off, but when he called a third time I told him to check out Cabrillo's boyfriend, Raul Marcos. Marcos also had a record having been convicted of assault and battery stemming from a beating he had dished out to a rival gang member who had reportedly insulted him. He had served six months in the county jail and was on one year's probation. Other than the bartending job his girlfriend had mentioned there was no record of employment. A final interesting piece of information was that Marcos was also a plaintiff in a personal injury suit. Allegedly he had been struck by a limousine in front of the Fairmont Hotel. He was claiming $120,000 for medical expense reimbursement, pain and suffering, mental anguish, permanent impairment to his leg, and lost wages.

As Paula's case got closer I was getting very concerned. We had a lot of circumstantial evidence but nothing to conclusively prove a conspiracy to set Paula up. Our only hope was that Paula could convince the jury that her version of the facts were correct. The problem we had, however, was coming up with a motive for the setup. We could say the lawsuit was the motive but Cabrillo had a perfect right to bring the suit and unless we could show it had been brought in bad faith, we really didn't have much. Likewise, Marcos' personal injury suit would not necessarily be relevant to Paula's criminal case. It was unlikely we'd get it into evidence unless we could prove Paula had been set up and then tied Marcos into it. I finally decided I had no choice but to take Marcos' deposition. Maybe he wouldn't be as slick as his two gang buddies.

# THE LETTER **34**

The lack of progress on my criminal case had me a bit uneasy, but I couldn't let that slow me down. I had to have faith that Stan would get me through the trial unscathed. Dusty Thomas' trial was barely two months away and we had nothing conclusive to prove his innocence. We could create a lot of smoke but when it all cleared Dusty would still be there with the shotgun in his hand looking down at Bobby Tuttle's body. Since the Feds wanted Dusty executed there was no hope of a last minute plea bargain or any other resolution of the case before trial. The momentum I had going in Dusty's case had come to a sudden stop with Jill's disappearance. Where could she be? Why hadn't she contacted me? Was she still alive or had Harris tracked her down and killed her? These were all questions that haunted me and made it difficult to sleep at night.

One missing link in our theory that Don Harris was Tuttle's killer was how he would have known that Bobby Tuttle was coming out to seize Dusty's tractor. Since I couldn't think of anything else to do I decided to try to figure that out. I called Donald Hurst to see if he might shed some light on that issue.

"Sorry to bother you, but I was wondering if you might answer one question for me," I said.

"I guess. What is it?"

"Is there any way someone outside the IRS could have found out when Bobby was going out to seize Dusty's tractor?"

"No, the agent usually keeps that pretty close to the vest so that the taxpayer won't try to hide the asset. The only person who would have known about the seizure was the wrecker service company that was supposed to meet Bobby out at the ranch."

"What wrecker company did Bobby use?"

"In northern Collin County we use A Plus Wreckers in McKinney," Hurst said.

I thanked Hurst and looked up A Plus Wreckers in the yellow pages. It was located on Highway 380 in McKinney. I couldn't remember the wrecker drivers name who found the body so I looked through my notebook. It was Lewis Lance of Princeton, Texas—white male, 38, employed at A Plus Wrecker Service since June 1986. He arrived on the scene a few minutes late and found Dusty standing over the body with a shotgun in his hand.

"Oh, my God! He was in on it," I muttered.

Harris must have arranged for him to go to work for A Plus Wreckers so he would be there when the call came in for the wrecker. He was looking for someone to set up for the murder and Dusty was the lucky pick. When I called A Plus Wreckers to get an appointment to talk to Lewis Lance I learned he didn't work there anymore. That didn't surprise me. I got in my car, that had finally been returned to me by the body shop, and headed for McKinney. Even if I couldn't talk to Lewis I could talk to his boss and co-workers. They might provide some evidence to support my theory. Mason Block was the owner.

"He was an experienced wrecker driver. I was sorry to see him go," Block said.

"How did you happen to hire him," I asked. "Were you looking for a driver?"

"No. He just popped in one day and said he had just moved nearby and needed a job. I didn't have an opening so I took his name and number and told him I'd call if anything opened up."

"So, I guess you eventually did call him?"

"Yeah. Almost right away. One of our drivers was killed in an auto accident."

"Is that right? What happened?"

"It was the strangest thing. He was driving home to Bonham and must have fallen asleep. They found his car twisted around a big oak tree."

"What was his name?"

"Carl Johanson."

I wrote the name in my notebook. "So, how was it that Lewis was working with Bobby Tuttle?"

"Oh gosh. I don't know. I think he volunteered. When Bobby came by he and Lewis hit if off and Bobby always asked for Lewis when there was a job he needed done."

"Lewis was a little late for his meeting with Bobby at the Double T Ranch. Do you know why?"

"No, he left here in plenty of time. I wondered about that. Maybe Bobby would still be alive had he not been late."

After thanking Block for talking to me, I went back to the office and asked Jody to get a copy of Carl Johanson's accident report. She said she'd order it right away. Then I called Bart. I figured since Lewis Lance was a witness the D.A.'s office would be keeping track of him. Bart didn't know but promised to find out. A little later he called and said Lewis Lance was now working in Wylie at Highway 78 Towing. I didn't figure Lance would want to talk to me and I didn't want him warning Don Harris that I was coming to see him, so I went to Highway 78 Towing unannounced. Lance wasn't there so I asked the man on duty a few questions.

"Does Lewis Lance work here?"

"Yeah, he comes on at five," the man said.

I looked at my watch and it was three-thirty. "Shoot. I really wanted to talk to him."

"Why?" the man asked.

"Ah . . . well . . . he was a witness in a murder case and I needed to ask him a few questions. I tried to catch him up in McKinney but I found out he'd quit and went to work here."

"Oh, that was just a part time job. He's been working here steady now for five years."

"Is that right?"

"Yeah, he got behind on his bills and needed some extra cash so he got a second job. It was hard on him working a shift here then driving an hour to Princeton and working another shift. I told him he ought to just file bankruptcy and tell his creditors to take a hike."

"Well, he must be a very responsible person. That's rare nowadays," I said. "I guess, I'll stop by after five some night. Thanks for the info."

"No problem, Ma'am."

"Oh, by the way. Have you seen Don Harris lately?"

"No, not for a week or so. How do you know Don?"

"Oh, he's a friend of Lewis' isn't he?"

"Well, I don't know if they are friends, but Lewis is his mechanic."

My theory was pretty well nailed down so I decided to go home. Then the idea hit me to drive by Don Harris' place and see if anything was going on. Perhaps he had Jill with him if he hadn't killed her. I parked a little farther away than I had the first time. I was sure he couldn't see me from his house. With a pair of binoculars I had in the glove box I watched his house. His truck was in the driveway. After twenty minutes he came out of the house and got in his truck. He drove off and I followed him at a discreet distance.

It felt strange following him, not knowing where he was going. It was exciting though. My heart was pounding and I was feeling a little adrenalin buzz. He turned onto the main highway headed for Wylie. After he drove through town he drove passed his studio and turned into a little commercial district. He parked in front of a warehouse with a sign on the front that read: S & T Packing Company. I drove by and parked around the corner. He didn't seem to notice me.

The warehouse was huge, and there were several eighteen-wheelers parked in the yard next to it. An eight foot chain link fence surrounded the yard and the loading area around the back of the building. A half dozen cars were parked in front. I took down all the license numbers of the cars and trucks I could see from my angle. There wasn't much else I could do and it was getting dark so I finally left and went back to Dallas. It was late, and there was no need to go to the office, I went straight home.

Don Harris was up to something other than designing advertisements. I didn't know what it was but I had a hunch it would eventually answer a lot of questions. I couldn't wait until morning to check with the Secretary of State, State Comptroller, and Department of Motor Vehicles. Maybe by knowing who owned S & T Packing Company and who worked there we'd get one step closer to the truth. When I got to my condo complex I was shocked to see Stan's car was there. He was pacing back and forth in front of my front door. I pulled up next to his Corvette.

"What are you doing here?" I asked as I got out of the car.

"Looking for you. Where have you been? I've been worried sick."

"Following Don Harris around," I said as I unlocked the door. We went inside. "You won't believe what I found out."

"I told you not to do anything dangerous," Stan said.

"I know. I didn't get too close. ... So, tell me. Why are you here?"

"You won't believe what I found in the mail today."

"What?"

"A letter to you from Jill."

"Really? What did it say?"

"I didn't open it. It's addressed to you."

I shook my head. "Stan, you could have opened it. I wouldn't have cared."

"Well, I figured you'd be home soon so I'd let you do it."

I looked over the envelope. It was written on Holiday Inn stationery and the postmark was from Austin. It was dated two days earlier. I ripped open the letter and began reading.

*Dear Paula,*

*Thank you for saving my life. I'm sure had you not shown up at the airport I would be dead right now or imprisoned somewhere with no hope of escape. After your diversion I was able to get out of the terminal and get a cab. I hope Don didn't hurt you too badly. I saw him kick you in the face. You're one brave woman.*

*I'm safe now. I've gone somewhere where Don can't find me. At first I was just going to lay low for a while, but after thinking about it, the least I could do to show my gratitude would be to help you save Dusty Thomas' life. I don't know a lot but there are a few things I have seen that might shed some light on your investigation.*

*Don didn't go to work on the day Bobby Tuttle was killed. I know that because I went to his office looking for him but he hadn't been there all day. That night he called me and wanted to go out. He came by my apartment to pick me up and made a phone call. He called someone in Alexandria, Virginia because later on when I got my phone bill it had the number on it. I don't know who he called, but the telephone bill is what he was looking for when he came and got me the day you followed us. I told him I had thrown it away but he didn't believe me. Unfortunately he found the bill and destroyed it.*

*That is about all I know other than what I've already told you. Good luck and thanks again for all you've done for me.*

*Jill*

"Do you think we can get a copy of the bill from the telephone company?" I asked.

"We can sure try. Detective Conrad can probably get it as part of his investigation of the sniper attack. Just show him the letter and that should convince him of the relevance."

"Good. I'll do that tomorrow. . . . You want a drink?"

"No, I've got to get home. I was just curious about the letter and—"

"And what?"

"I wanted to tell you what a great job you're doing on Dusty's case. You've just forged ahead despite everything that's happened. I've never seen such great focus and determination."

"Thank you, Stan. I appreciate you saying that. It means a lot to me."

"I just wish—"

"Wish what?"

"That I was doing as great a job on your criminal case."

I frowned. "What do you mean? You've been working very hard."

"Yes, but the trial date is so close and I'm not sure we can win," Stan said. "There are powerful forces out there against us. Forces that we know nothing about and can't even see. I'm scared. I'm scared that you might go to jail."

A chill darted through me. I took a deep breath and replied, "I know. I've tried not to worry about it. Even if I lost do you think I'd go to jail?"

"Ordinarily not. It's your first offense. You ought to get probation, but I don't know. This isn't your ordinary case."

I took Stan's hand and said, "I have complete faith in you, Stan. If anybody can get me off you can. If you don't, then . . . well, that's just the way it's meant to be," I said trying to restrain my tears.

Stan smiled, "Jill was right. You are a brave woman. . . . I won't let you down. I'll figure this thing out somehow. I promise."

I smiled and replied, "I know."

This time I couldn't restrain my tears. We embraced for a moment and then he was gone. Was he right? Was I doomed. I wondered.

# THE CONNECTION 35

Marcos showed up for his deposition with the plaintiff, Miss Cabrillo. He was casually dressed in blue jeans and a T-shirt. Ortega looked calm and confident as he joked around with his client and the witness in Spanish. Whenever this happened I cursed the fact I had taken French in high school rather than Spanish. Paula was too busy to attend the deposition so I was on my own. The court reporter asked for agreements and then we got started. Marcos gave me his full name, vital statistics, and current address. We talked about his childhood in LA, his move to Dallas, and his relationship to Miss Cabrillo. He said they had been dating for about six months and recently he had moved in with her. Then I asked him about his employment.

"Before you served time, where did you work?"

"S and T Packing Company," he replied.

Bells and whistles started going off in my head when I heard the name S & T Packing Company. Paula had just observed Don Harris at an S & T Packing Company warehouse. This might be the connection we had been looking for to prove Paula's alleged hit and run was a fraud. I proceeded carefully not wanting to seem more than casually interested in S & T Packing Company.

"What kind of business is S & T Packing Company?" I asked.

"They export fruit and nuts," he replied.

"Where do they export them?"

"I don't know. Lots of places. Japan, Europe."

"Where do they get their products?"

"Different places. Pecans from West Texas. Grapefruit from the Valley. Oranges from Florida. Bananas from South America."

"Where are they located?"

"I worked in the Wylie, Texas office."

"When did you work for them?"

"June 85 to April 86," Marcos replied.

"What were your duties there?"

"Driver . . . loader."

"Where did you drive usually?"

"All over. Sometimes to the Valley to take grapefruit to be shipped out of Corpus Christi. Sometimes to West Texas to pick up pecans."

"Who owns S & T Packing Company?"

He shrugged. "I don't know."

"Who was your boss?"

"Joe."

"Joe. Do you know his last name?"

"No."

"Do you know a man named Don Harris?"

Marcos had a startled look on his face. He didn't respond, so I repeated the question.

"I don't know him."

"You know who he is though?"

Again, he shrugged. "I guess. He's some kind of a supplier. We picked up his shipments and took them to Houston for handling."

"What kind of shipments?"

"I don't know. They were always sealed."

"You have no idea what you were hauling?"

"No."

"Wasn't there an invoice or bill of lading?"

"It didn't show what was in the cargo."

Marcos' deposition went on for several more hours but there were no startling revelations beyond the connection of Don Harris to S & T Packing Company. I wondered what Don Harris was shipping overseas. I was pretty sure he wasn't in the commodities business. And why all the secrecy about the type of cargo being shipped?

When I got back to the office, I asked Jodie if she had received the reports on S & T Packing Company from the Secretary of State, Comptroller and Dunn & Bradstreet. She said they were all in my in-box.

The Public Information report from the Comptroller's office indicated there was just one officer of S & T Packing. His name was John Cox and his address was in Garland, Texas. The company had been incorporated in 1982 according to the Secretary of State, was active and in good standing. A Dunn & Bradstreet report indicated they had commodity sales exceeding five million dollars per year, had a line of credit with the First National Bank of Wylie, and paid their bills on time. I wondered if Harris had hired Marcos to mastermind the hit and run scam on Paula. If so, why? Nothing quite made sense yet but I felt today I'd made a big step in figuring it all out.

# TEXAS MILITIA 36

When Stan told me about Marcos—along with the two witnesses—working for S & T Packing, I was ecstatic. Finally we were making some headway. I got some more good news later in the day when Detective Conrad called and said he had a copy of Jill's phone bill. He said he'd send it to me by messenger and I should have it within a hour or two. I couldn't wait to find out who Harris had called after killing Agent Tuttle. When the messenger came I tore open the envelope and studied the bill. I found the call to Alexandria, Virginia and dialed the number. The call was picked up by an answering machine with an electronic voice. I didn't leave a message. I figured I'd just have to try again later.

As I was pondering the situation Jodie came in with information on the license plate numbers I had written down from the S & T Packing warehouse. None of the car owner's names meant anything to me except Riley Davidson, the preacher who supposedly started the People's Mission. I wondered if the People's Mission was into something more than just tax evasion. After digging through the file, I came up with the members' roster of the People's Mission that I had obtained earlier. Two more of the cars in the S & T lot were owned by members of the People's Mission. I wondered if Bobby Tuttle knew what he had stumbled into before he was murdered. What had he stumbled into? It was something big, I was certain of that.

The thought occurred to me that Bobby might have written a report on the Peoples' Mission or taken notes about them. It was conceivable that he might have written down some valuable information that he had learned during his investigation. I called Bart and asked him if the police had seized all of Bobby Tuttle's notes and files regarding the Peoples' Mission. He said they had some but most were still in the possession of the IRS. I told him I was interested in seeing them. He agreed to meet me at the IRS office and we could go through them together.

I didn't mind going through the records with Bart. There were a lot of them and having his help made the task a little easier. If we found anything I would be duty bound to report it to Trenton Lee anyway so it didn't really matter from a tactical standpoint if Bart helped. Several hours into the task I came across a yellow pad with some notes about one of Don Harris' bank accounts. It looked like Tuttle was getting ready to garnish the account or perhaps subpoena records on the account from the bank. The words "unreported bank account" were written in large letters across the pad and underlined several times. The letters B.C.C.I. were written next to it with an account number. There were notations "WT—1985 $221,733.01, $109,334.07, $88,562.33, and $342,622.87." Wire transfers perhaps? I showed my discovery to Bart.

"These are some pretty big transactions for a graphic artist," I said.

Bart studied the numbers and replied, "Jesus. I'm in the wrong business."

"You suppose Harris paid taxes on this money?"

Bart laughed. "No. That's why Tuttle was so obsessed with pursuing him. I wonder if Harris found out Tuttle had discovered the account?"

We talked to Bobby Tuttle's supervisor, Robert Perkins, and asked him if the investigation of the People's Mission had been assigned to another revenue agent. He said it had not because all Tuttle's records were frozen in case they were needed as evidence in the murder case. If Harris had wanted to derail the investigation against him, he had succeeded. It occurred to me though that the derailment was only temporary and Harris was smart enough to realize that. I assumed he was making plans to disappear or at least relocate.

"Don't you think we have enough on Don Harris to warrant someone keeping an eye on him?" I asked.

Bart gave me a sympathetic smile and replied, "I think we do but I doubt Logan will think so. He'd be the one who'd have to make that decision."

"Try to convince him, would you? We don't have the resources or we'd do it ourselves."

"What about Detective Conrad?"

"They're watching Harris' house and business but if he leaves the county they won't follow him."

Before we left I thanked Perkins for his cooperation and asked him if there was any chance he could go through with the subpoena of

Harris' BCCI bank records. He considered the request, and said that, although he had authority to continue the investigation, he wouldn't want to do it without checking with the IRS. I told him our theory that Harris had killed Bobby Tuttle to derail the investigation against him and that so far it had worked. Perkins looked skeptical but I could tell my argument had got him thinking.

"It couldn't hurt," I said. "Worst case you waste a few hours—best case you're a hero."

The next day Perkins called and said two new revenue agents had been assigned to Don Harris and the People's Mission and that he had made it a priority case. I suggested they be given a security detail. He said *that* had already been done. I felt good. Finally, somebody was listening to me. I knew it was unlikely that the IRS would share any information with me, but at least they would be a distraction to Harris so I could get a little closer without attracting attention. I went into Stan's office and told him the good news.

"That BCCI account is undoubtedly the conduit for his dealings with S & T Packing," Stan said.

"I hope we get those records," I said. "They will tell us who he's doing business with."

"Yeah, that would really answer a lot of questions," Stan replied.

"I wonder how long it will take to get them?"

"Thirty days at least—not soon enough to do you any good."

"I think I stirred Perkins up. Maybe he'll expedite it."

"I hope so," Stan said and took a deep breath. "That would add a lot of credibility to your defense if we found out he was dealing in drugs or laundering money."

"I think I need to pay another visit to Mabel Anderson?" I said.

"Who?"

"Mable Anderson, the secretary of the People's Mission. She was very open with me. I don't think she realizes what the People's Mission is really about. Maybe I should clue her in."

"That should shake things up," Stan agreed. "Go for it."

Mabel Anderson readily agreed to another meeting. I met her at IHOP for breakfast. I told her some of the things we had discovered about the People's Mission and Don Harris in particular. She seemed shocked and dismayed. I told her I liked her and didn't want her to get hurt when my trial started and the People's Mission became front page news.

"Oh, my God. I'm going to resign immediately."

"That would be a good idea. I know you didn't have any idea the People's Mission was a front for illegal activity."

"What can I do to help you? Maybe if I cooperate they won't prosecute me."

"I can't promise that. I don't have any authority to cut deals but if you do help, I'll make sure the right people know about it."

"Good. I'll tell you whatever I know."

My main interest was Don Harris, and I asked Mabel to tell me everything she knew about him. She said when she was married to Peter Lowe they would all go out on occasion. Don Harris, Riley Davidson and Peter Lowe served together in Vietnam and had been friends for twenty years. Like Harris, they had resigned from the Army and had joined a paramilitary group in the Texas Hill Country. I had forgotten about the paramilitary group and asked Mabel if she knew its name. She said it was called the Texas Militia. Apparently they didn't acknowledge the authority of the United States government over the state of Texas. They claimed the people of Texas never voted to become a part of the United States and that the Republic of Texas was seized by military force after the civil war. I had heard of the Texas Militia but never really paid much attention to it. Although I had taken Texas history in high school, I didn't remember much about how Texas became a state. I had just taken it for granted that it had all been done legally. Apparently some people didn't believe it had.

According to Mabel the Texas Militia was heavily armed and was gearing up for a confrontation with the federal government. I chuckled at the thought of insurrection in Texas. It was ludicrous. How could any sane person think they could possibly gain independence for Texas? But apparently there were people like Don Harris who not only believed it, but were determined to make it happen. The scary thing about their movement was that since they didn't recognize the United States government they didn't adhere to its laws and they felt justified in killing anyone as long as it was to further their "just cause."

# PAULA'S TRIAL 37

Paula's long anticipated trial finally arrived on Monday, February 9, 1987. On Monday and Tuesday we picked the jury of eight women and four men. Although it was only a failure to render aid offense the media was treating it like a murder trial. As we stepped out of the car in front of the Dallas County courthouse cameras flashed and the mob of reporters began yelling questions at us. We moved quickly across the sidewalk and into the midst of CDA picketers who were marching and chanting "Set our sister free—set our sister free—set our sister free." I noticed one of the signs said "We love you, Paula," another said, "Dusty needs Paula!" I was moved by the show of support for Paula even if it was for all the wrong reasons. At least somebody cared that she was being falsely accused.

Bart took us to an elevator that was being held for us and we went up to the sixth floor. The courtroom was filled and Martin Silvey was already at the prosecution table. A gray haired man nearing retirement age, Silvey was an impressive looking prosecutor. Paula was wearing a cream color two piece crepe suit with a ruffle on the front. She looked quite pretty but not overly sexy. We didn't want to turn off any of our female jurors. An attorney on trial was always at a disadvantage anyway just because of the natural distrust and hatred some people felt toward attorneys. We had encountered that problem in picking a jury. The judge had dismissed seven prospective jurors for cause simply because of their blatant hostility toward lawyers.

Judge Samuel Jake Justice was on the bench. He was a black judge with little sympathy for those who broke the law. Although considered fair and honest he had a propensity for giving out maximum sentences if an adverse verdict came down against a defendant. I cringed at the thought of Paula being found guilty. Judge Justice would likely give the maximum sentence of five years and a $1,000 fine. I nodded at Paula's parents, Jodie, and Rebekah who were in the gallery directly behind us. Bart was sitting near the door in the back of the courtroom so he could come and go as need be. Representatives of the press, selected by random drawing, filled-out the remaining seats.

The bailiff stood and said, "Please rise for the Honorable Samuel Jake Justice.

Everyone got to their feet as the judge took the bench. "Be seated."

We all sat down and the judge asked Silvey to read the indictment.

"In the name and by the authority of the State of Texas: The Grand Jury of Dallas County, Texas at the June Term, 1986 A.D. of the 333rd District Court, in said court at said Term, do present that one Paula Virginia Waters was driving a vehicle eastbound on Keller Springs Road in Dallas, Texas on August 18, 1986 at approximately 7:10 A.M., when she hit Miss Maria Santos Cabrillo, a pedestrian running along the highway, said accident resulting in Miss Cabrillo's injury. Following the accident Miss Waters intentionally and knowingly failed to stop and render reasonable assistance in violation of Texas Revised Civil Statutes Annotated, article 6701d, §38(d)."

"Thank you," Judge Justice said. "You may present your opening argument, Mr. Silvey."

"Thank you, Your Honor. Ladies and gentlemen of the jury. It is with a heavy heart that I stand before you today. Rarely does the State have to prosecute officers of the court and former members of its own district attorney's staff. But no man or woman is above the law and when one of them strays they must pay the price just as each of you would have to if it were you who had broken the law.

"We will show that on August 18, 1986, Paula Virginia Waters, an attorney and former assistant district attorney with this office, left for work in a hurry. Her condominium is located just off of Keller Springs Road in north Dallas and she turned left onto Keller Springs on her way to Preston Road. Unfortunately Maria Cabrillo was jogging and crossed in front of Mrs. Waters and, despite a last minute evasive maneuver, was struck by Mrs. Waters' vehicle and knocked to the ground. For whatever reason, and only she knows why, Miss Waters stopped briefly and then took off without rendering aid to Miss Cabrillo who had suffered severe injuries to her leg and was bleeding.

"Now Miss Waters, through her attorney, is going to throw a convoluted story at you that this incident was all a set-up. That certain mysterious persons hired Miss Cabrillo and two eyewitnesses to trick Ms. Waters into leaving the scene of the accident. The problem with their story is that they have no proof of it and it is unlikely that Miss Cabrillo would subject herself to serious injury on purpose.

"The judge will instruct you only to consider the evidence presented in this case in rendering your verdict. Remember that. Don't get caught up in the defendant's speculation about a conspiracy against Miss Waters. It's very imaginative and dramatic but don't believe it. Look for the evidence of it. You won't find any. Thank you," Silvey concluded.

"Mr. Turner," the judge said.

"Thank you, Your Honor. Ladies and gentlemen of the jury. This case makes no sense. Why would a young woman who has spent four years in college, three years in law school, passed the Texas Bar Exam and who is sworn to uphold the law and the constitution of the State of Texas do something so fundamentally stupid as to hit someone and run away? It's ridiculous, idiotic, and unthinkable—and it didn't happen. Miss Waters was set-up.

"I know it sounds bizarre and something out of a Hollywood movie, but it happened to my partner, Paula Waters and we will provide substantial evidence of it—enough evidence at least to cast a reasonable doubt as to Miss Waters' guilt.

"As Mr. Silvey said, you must listen to the evidence and render a verdict only on the evidence presented. This is the law and the judge will instruct you accordingly, but he will also instruct you that the State has the burden of proof in this case. Mr. Silvey must prove beyond any reasonable doubt each of the elements of Article 6701d. That is that Miss Waters intentionally and knowingly failed to stop and render reasonable assistance. He will not be able to do that because it's simply not true. Thank you."

The gallery stirred in anticipation of live testimony starting. The judge warned them to be quiet. I looked at Paula and she gave me a thumbs up. I smiled and looked back at Rebekah. She was smiling too. So far, so good. Now the fun would begin trying to shake three very well coached witnesses.

The judge turned to Silvey. "Call your first witness, Mr. Silvey."

Silvey stood and replied, "Yes, Your Honor. The state calls Maria Cabrillo."

Miss Cabrillo was smartly dressed and made a good appearance. Martin Silvey approached her with a big smile and started asking her basic questions about herself, her family, her employment, and her life in general. She came off as a hard working, respectable woman. Then he got to the morning of the accident.

"Where were you on the morning of August 18, 1986?" Silvey asked.

"I was jogging along Keller Springs Road in north Dallas," she replied.

"Tell us what happened on that day, would you?"

"Sure. I was about finished with my run when a dark BMW came barreling around the corner right at me. I tried to jump out of the way but it hit me on the left side knocking me to the pavement."

"Who was driving the car?"

Miss Cabrillo pointed at Paula. "She was—the defendant."

"Did the defendant stop after she hit you?"

"Just for a second. She stopped, looked at me, and then took off and never looked back."

A woman in the gallery gasped. Paula looked over at her and frowned. The judge glared at the woman.

"Now Miss Cabrillo. Did anyone come to your aid after you were hit?" Silvey asked.

"Yes, two nice gentlemen stopped. One of them called the police."

"Did either of these men ever put you in their car?"

Miss Cabrillo shook her head. "No. No way. I was hurt bad. She took off and left me to bleed. She didn't care about me at all."

"You say you were hurt badly. Could you describe your injuries?"

"Yes, my leg was broken and I've had to have two surgeries to repair the damage. The doctors say I might have a permanent injury."

"You won't be doing any more jogging, is that right?"

"Yes, the doctor said, 'No more jogging.'"

Silvey turned and smiled at the judge. "Pass the witness."

The judge nodded and replied, "Let's break for lunch. Report back here at 1:30 P.M."

The judge got up and left the courtroom. The gallery erupted in excited conversation. Paula and I made a quick exit trying to avoid the press. We took the stairs down to the ground floor and exited out a back door. Jodie was waiting for us with her car and we took off just as to reporters came out the same rear exit. We met Paula's parents and Rebekah at Sonny Bryan's restaurant a half mile away. Jodie left to make a phone call while we were seated. Everyone seemed pleased with the way the trial was going and I was feeling optimistic until I saw Jodie's face when she returned.

"The process server can't find Raul Marcos or John Cox. They've disappeared."

"Oh, shit. You've got to be kidding," I said. "Did they try them at home and work?"

"Yes, apparently they both left the state on a fishing trip," Jodie said.

"Well, I was afraid this was going to happen. I told the process server to get them served two weeks ago. Damn it!"

"They've been avoiding service," Jodie replied.

"We don't absolutely need him, do we?" Paula asked.

I forced a smile. "Maybe not."

It was a lie and everyone knew it. We needed Raul Marcos to testify about his previous employment with S & T Packing and connect Don Harris to it. John Cox would be almost as good as he could make the same connection Without this critical link, however, we couldn't present our conspiracy theory to the jury. Martin Silvey would object to it as being irrelevant and he'd be right. Now the only person who could make the connection would be Don Harris himself and he'd undoubtedly take the fifth or have a complete lapse of memory.

"We need a miracle," Paula said, "or I'm going to jail."

"Wait a minute," I said. "Miss Cabrillo testified that you left her on the side of the road to bleed. . . . If she was bleeding then some of the blood might have dripped onto the interior of the vehicle she was loaded into."

"Yes, that's true," Paula said.

"Did the crime scene investigators check the witnesses' car for blood?" I asked.

"I doubt it," Paula said. "It's probably been cleaned by now."

"That doesn't matter. It will still leave some residue," I said.

"Still, it's a little late to be requesting an inspection of the witness' car."

"True. Unless he volunteers to let us test it."

# DESPAIR 38

It was eerie being the defendant in a criminal case. Everyone looked at me when I entered the courtroom and I could feel their eyes staring at me as I sat at the defense table next to Stan. I pulled my dress down, crossed my legs, and looked away from everyone. The courtroom was noisy in anticipation of the trial resuming. Stan was jotting down questions to ask Miss Cabrillo on cross examination, Silvey and a pretty legal assistant were talking and laughing like they were on a date. It irked me that they were so happy when my life was in a shambles. We hadn't talked about it, but everybody knew if I was convicted I might lose my law license along with my freedom. It seemed so unfair that I had to go through this nightmare, let alone lose everything I'd worked my whole life to attain.

The bailiff stood up and announced that the judge was taking the bench. The crowd rose and the room became quiet. The judge walked in, told everyone to be seated and took the bench. He asked the bailiff to bring in the witness and the jury. The bailiff opened the door to the jury room and the jury filed in and took their seats. Then the bailiff went out in the hall and got the witness. After the judge rearranged some papers on his desk he nodded at Stan.

"I believe it is your witness, Mr. Turner."

Stan rose and said, "Thank you.

"Miss Cabrillo. How many times have you jogged along Keller Springs Road?"

"Ah. Many times."

"How many? One, five, twenty-five, a hundred and twenty-five times?"

"Gee. I don't know exactly. Maybe ten times."

"Where else do you jog?" Stan asked.

"I don't know. Ah. . . . White Rock Lake sometimes."

"You don't jog everyday then?"

"No, once or twice a week if the weather is good."

"What made you jog along Keller Springs Road on the morning of August 18, 1986?"

"I don't know. It was a nice day. I just felt like it."

"But why not White Rock Lake? What made you decide to do Keller Springs Road?"

"I don't know."

"Or you don't want to tell us?"

"Objection!" Silvey said. "He's badgering the witness."

"I'll allow it," Judge Justice said.

"I'm telling you I don't know."

"Isn't it true you were told to jog along Keller Springs Road on August 18, 1986?"

"No, nobody told me that."

"Isn't it true you wanted to be hit by Miss Waters?"

"No. Why would I do that?"

"So you could file a civil suit for 1.2 million dollars, perhaps?"

"No, she should pay for hurting me. I didn't want to get hurt."

"On the date you were hit did you know Ernesto Garcia or Brian Armstrong?"

"No. I don't know them."

"You testified they came to your aid after you were hit, right?"

"Yes, they were very nice."

"They were in a vehicle and stopped to help you?"

"Yes."

"What kind of vehicle?"

"Ah . . . a black Chevy, I think."

"Did you get in that vehicle?"

"No, I stayed in the road until the ambulance came."

"You testified you were bleeding, right?"

"Yes, very much. Blood was everywhere."

"Did it get on your clothes?"

"Objection!" Silvey said. "This is all irrelevant. She testified she was injured. That's the only issue before the court."

"Your Honor," Stan said. "I'm laying a foundation for one of our defenses that will be presented later in the trial."

"Very well. Objection overruled," Judge Justice said. "Continue."

"Yes, my pant leg had some blood on it."

"You testified earlier that you live with your boyfriend, Raul Marcos, right?"

"Yes."

"Does he have a personal injury suit going too?"

"Objection!" Silvey said. "Irrelevant and prejudicial."

"Sustained. Mr. Turner. Be careful," Judge Justice said.

"Did your boyfriend ever work for a company called S & T Packing Company?"

The reporters in the gallery stirred, their curiosity obviously aroused by this new name. Our strategy was to get the press to start looking into S & T Packing, Don Harris, and the People's Mission. We needed all the help we could get. The judge banged his gavel and told everyone to quiet down.

"I don't know."

"You don't know? Weren't you at Mr. Marcos' deposition recently?"

"Yes."

"Didn't he testify he used to work for S & T Packing?"

"Oh, right. I remember now. That was his old job."

"Have you ever met a man named Don Harris. I believe he is a customer of S & T Packing?"

She shook her head. "No, I don't know him."

"You're sure?" Stan pressed.

She hesitated. "Well, I don't remember ever meeting him."

"But you might have?"

"I suppose. Maybe when Raul worked there."

"Where is Raul now?"

"I don't know. He went out of town."

"Do you know that he is under subpoena in this case?"

"What's that?"

"Notice that he is to testify in this case."

"He didn't get no notice."

"Did you know a process server has been trying to have him served?"

"No. I didn't know that."

"You know you're under oath, Miss Cabrillo. If you lie you can be prosecuted for perjury."

"Objection!" Silvey said. "Counsel is trying to intimidate the witness."

"Mr. Turner. Are you going somewhere with this?" Judge Justice asked.

"Yes, Your Honor. I am."

"Very well. Objection overruled," the judge said. "Miss Cabrillo you realize you are under oath and must tell the truth, right?"

"Yes, Your Honor."

The judge nodded at Stan. "Miss Cabrillo. Didn't the process server come to your door looking for your boyfriend just yesterday? In fact, hasn't he been at your door numerous times in the past two weeks trying to serve a subpoena on your boyfriend?"

"I didn't know why he was there."

"You never looked at the paper or talked to the process server about it?"

"No, I don't know anything about Raul's business."

"This isn't Raul's business, this is your business. You knew why the process server was there, didn't you? Your boyfriend was avoiding being served so he wouldn't have to testify here today, isn't that right?"

"Objection!" Silvey screamed. "Counsel is badgering the witness, asking compound questions, testifying, and this whole line of questioning is irrelevant."

"Withdraw the question. Pass the witness," Stan said and took his seat.

Silvey took Miss Cabrillo on redirect and made some progress in reestablishing her credibility. Stan attacked her again and when it was all over I'd say it was a draw which wasn't bad since she was the prosecution's star witness. Silvey called his next witness who was Ernesto Garcia. He testified as expected that he and his friend who were car pooling and came up on the accident in time to see Paula take off. He corroborated Miss Cabrillo's account of the accident completely and sounded quite credible. As Stan took him on cross, I was scared. Garcia seemed confident and unshakeable.

"Mr. Garcia. You testified your roommate, Brian Armstrong and you were carpooling on the date of the accident. Is that correct?"

"Yes, we were on our way to work."

"What kind of car were you driving?"

"I drove a pickup truck, actually. A Chevy S10 Longbed."

"Now, you've denied taking Miss Cabrillo in your truck on the morning of the accident, is that correct?"

"Right. We never put her in the truck. They took her to the hospital by ambulance."

"Then you wouldn't mind if we inspected your truck for evidence that Miss Cabrillo had ridden in it."

Armstrong grinned and said, "I wouldn't mind if I still had it."

"What do you mean?" Stan said.

"I mean it was stolen last week."

"You're kidding? . . . Did you file a police report?"

"Yes, it's all been documented."

"I bet," Stan said shaking his head.

"I'm sorry you lost your friend," Garcia said.

"What friend?"

"The private eye guy."

"Monty Dozier?" Garcia nodded. "What do you know about that?"

"Nothing man. I just read about it in the paper."

Stan glared at the witness for a moment and then threw up his hands and said, "I'm through with this witness."

Stan looked at me as he went back to his seat. He was obviously worried. I had never seriously thought I'd get convicted. Somehow I figured Stan would get me off. Now it appeared my fate was sealed. I closed my eyes and took a deep breath. This couldn't be happening. I looked over at Bart for reassurance but he wasn't smiling either. *Oh, God. No!*

By the end of the day both sides had rested and the case went to the jury. At 4:30 P.M. the judge sent the jury home for the night and told them to report back the following morning at ten. Bart took me home after court adjourned. I was in no condition to drive or be alone. Stan voiced his anger at how Garcia had so conveniently had his truck stolen. He was particularly upset at the reference to Monty Dozier. It was obvious to all of us that Garcia had something to do with Monty's murder, yet we'd never be able to prove it.

Bart and I ate a quiet dinner at home. Neither one of us could stomach the thought of an adverse verdict so we talked about other things. We drank a lot and reminisced about old times. Eventually we went to bed. Bart wanted to make love but I just wanted to hold him. He said he understood so we just snuggled up close until we both finally fell asleep.

# THE CIA CONNECTION 39

Fear gripped me as I realized Paula couldn't win. I had never lost a case before and it was hard to accept the fact that it was about to happen. It's not that I believed I was invincible. I knew I would lose plenty of cases during my career, but not this one. I had to somehow pull it out. I racked my brain for ideas. I needed a strategy to save the day, but what would it be?

I was still seated at the defense table after everyone had left. Depression was sweeping over me quickly and I felt like finding the nearest bar and drinking myself into a drunken bliss. But that would have been the easy way out and only seal Paula's fate. There had to be something productive I could do even if it were too late to avoid a conviction. There would be an appeal.

I was sure now that Cabrillo, Garcia, and Armstrong were involved in Monty's death. Garcia had thrown that in my face. They were also somehow connected to S & T Packing, Don Harris, and the 18th Street gang. I needed to figure out how everything fit together. I got up, packed up my briefcase, and headed for home. On the way my mind pondered and calculated every imaginable scenario. What business was Don Harris really in? S & T Packing was obviously his cover. I needed to know more about both of them. It was time to call Mo.

Mo was a client who I had taken through bankruptcy. When the case was all over he informed me confidentially that he was with the CIA and had been instructed by the Agency to go to me and file bankruptcy. I often wondered why the Agency had chosen me as their bankruptcy attorney; why Mo had told me about it; and how many other operatives I had unknowingly put through bankruptcy. As interesting as those questions were they were irrelevant at the moment. The bottom line was I had a resource I hadn't used. When I got home I put a call in to Mo. His wife answered and said she'd have him call me back. Mo had told me the drill. He couldn't accept my phone calls at home but would call me back within two hours. As I hung up the phone Rebekah came up behind me and started rubbing my shoulders.

"Tough day, huh?" she said.

I turned around and we embraced. "Oh, God. I'm so worried about Paula being convicted. I've been sick all evening."

"Maybe she won't be. The jury may see through Miss Cabrillo and her Good Samaritan friends."

I pulled my head back and looked into her eyes. "I hope so, but that's not what I see in their faces."

Rebekah nodded and pulled me close to her again.

"What jury wouldn't relish the opportunity to put the screws to an attorney?" I said holding Rebekah tightly. Tears were beginning to well in my eyes when the telephone rang. I let go of her and grabbed the telephone.

"Hello."

"Stan. It's Mo. You called?"

"Yeah, thanks for returning my call," I said. "How are you?"

"Still kicking. Things have picked up a bit since I saw you last."

"Good. Glad to hear it. . . . Hey, I could use a little help on a case I'm working."

"I bet. I heard you took on the Dusty Thomas case. You seem to like impossible cases."

"Not really. They just seem to fall in my lap."

"I've been reading a lot about you in the paper. Kidnapping? Attempts on your life? Hit and runs? What's the deal?"

"That's what I'm trying to figure out. I think there is a lot more to the Dusty Thomas case than people realize."

"It sounds like it. How can I help?"

"There is a local man, Don Harris. He is supposedly a graphic artist but he runs some kind of business out of a company called S & T Packing. They have a warehouse in Wylie. Two of the witnesses against my partner, Paula Waters, work for S & T. We think Don Harris may have killed Bobby Tuttle and that he's orchestrated the attacks on us to distract us from pursuing him."

"You know, actually everyone at the Agency is supposed to be helping convict Dusty Thomas. The government wants him to fall and fall hard," Mo said.

"Oh. So you can't help me out?"

"I didn't say that. I just wanted you to know what you're up against."
I laughed. "Believe me. I know. That's why I need your help. I'm in
way over my head on this one."

"What would you like me to do?" Mo asked.

"Check out Don Harris for me and find out what you can about S
& T Packing. I need to find out what he's into."

"No problem. It will take a few days. Anything else?"

I told him about General Moya, Tex Weller, the 1.8 million dollar
ransom and the threat on my life.

"I have this constant fear of getting gunned down while I'm walking into my office. And every time I get in my car I'm afraid to turn on
the ignition for fear the car will blow up. I can't sleep at night sometimes. Since General Moya has become a mortal enemy I need to know
as much as possible about him. I know it's a lot to ask, but if you can
help me, I would appreciate it."

"The agency probably has a lot of information on General Moya.
They monitor guerilla leaders and their activities very closely. It's
shouldn't be a problem, but it may take a little time getting it together."

"Well, the Don Harris information is the most vital."

"I'll take care of it. It was nice hearing from you."

"Likewise. . . . Thanks a lot, Mo. I really appreciate it."

"Oh, Stan. . . . Before you go. I'm referring a friend of mine. He
needs to file bankruptcy quickly and discreetly, okay?"

"Sure, I'll take good care of him."

"I know you will."

The referral caught me by surprise. I assumed it was another agent
who'd run up a pocket full of credit cards to the max. I thought it was
an ingenious way to stretch the CIA budget or perhaps fund an unauthorized operation. But that wasn't my problem. I just prayed Mo
would dig up some useful information. Time was running out for Paula
and Dusty Thomas.

# DOWN BUT NOT OUT **40**

By morning I had resigned myself to the fact that I'd be convicted. Bart had spent the night with me and tried hard to keep my spirits up. But I had spent enough time in the courtroom to recognize imminent defeat. Whoever had set me up had done a splendid job and I was sure they were enjoying every minute of the trial. Bart was sure that even if I was convicted I wouldn't get jail time. He had talked to Silvey and got the impression that the D.A. wasn't after blood. He just wanted to put me on the sidelines in the Dusty Thomas case. That got me to thinking that maybe the IRS had something to do with the setup.

Although we tried to avert the crowd of reporters who had assembled in front of the Dallas County Courthouse, several of them managed to spot us heading toward a private entrance on the north side of the building. They blocked the door and stuck microphones in our faces.

"What do you think the jury will do, Miss Waters?" A reporter shouted.

"I don't know. We'll just have to wait and see," I replied.

"If you're convicted will you still be able to assist Stan Turner in the Dusty Thomas case?" Another reporter asked.

I shrugged and slipped inside the building through a door Bart had managed to open. He closed the door behind us. We took the stairs to the second floor and then walked to the elevators to go to the sixth floor. When the elevator door opened, cameras flashed and we were again barraged by reporters. Two bailiffs helped Bart clear a path and we proceeded to the courtroom. The courtroom was locked to spectators so we were escorted through the back hallway and allowed to enter from the judge's chambers. Stan was already there waiting for us.

"Good morning," Stan said.

Bart nodded and helped me off with my coat.

"Well, I wonder how long the jury will be out?" Stan asked.

"Probably not long," I said. "We didn't give them much to work with."

Stan took a deep breath. "I'm sorry, Paula. I really didn't expect our case to fall apart the way it did. I still haven't given up. I've got a friend at the CIA checking out Don Harris and S & T Packing. He may turn up something to connect Garcia to Don Harris. You never know. We might still pull this out."

"It's okay, Stan. You did the best you could. Like you said, we're dealing with some very powerful people. We were outgunned from day one."

"We may be outgunned but we haven't lost the war yet," Stan said. "I won't sit still until I've cleared your name and nailed Don Harris. That son of a bitch isn't going to get away with this."

Stan was a fighter and I believed what he was saying. He wouldn't give up, but I was afraid he had met his match. Whether it was Don Harris or the Federal Government who had decided to attack me personally, it didn't matter. They had one distinct advantage—we were playing by the rules, but they were not. They would do whatever it took to win. They cared nothing about justice or the legal system. This was a matter of winning—of survival at all cost.

At about ten o'clock, the bailiff came in and advised us the jury had reached a verdict. My heart skipped a beat as the moment of truth was at hand. The bailiff opened the courtroom doors and excited reporters and spectators filed in like they were going to a hockey game. Stan put his arms around me and gave me a hug. I smiled and wondered if I'd made a mistake letting him defend me. He had suggested it might be better for me to have separate representation but I wouldn't hear of it. I thought back and tried to think what we could have done differently to prepare for trial. Nothing concrete jumped out at me.

The bailiff announced the judge was entering the courtroom. Everyone got to their feet and watched the judge take the bench. The jury was brought in and the judge asked the foreman of the jury if they had reached a verdict. The foreman said they had and the bailiff took a small piece of paper up to the judge. He looked at it without emotion and then folded it back up and gave it to the bailiff. The bailiff returned it to the foreman.

"How do you find?" the judge asked.

The foreman opened the paper and said, "We the jury find the defendant, Paula Waters, guilty on the charge of failing to stop and render reasonable assistance."

The crowd broke out in excited chatter. The judge banged his gavel and demanded order. The crowd quieted down and the judge thanked the jury and dismissed them. After the judge had left Stan turned and looked a me.

"I'm sorry, Paula. This was all my fault. If I—"

I put a finger on Stan's lips. "Shhh. It was nobody's fault. Just forget about me and concentrate on nailing Don Harris. If you do that then I'll be vindicated."

"Right. I just wish you could still work on the case. You were doing such a great job. I don't know what I'm going to do without you."

"You'll find someone to replace me. Don't worry. Jodie can help you out in the meantime."

Stan and I embraced and then Bart took me home. The judge and the D.A. had agreed I could stay out on bond pending my sentencing hearing. It was a tearful night. One of the worst I've ever been through. I was just glad Bart was there to comfort me.

The following week at my sentencing hearing Judge Justice gave me the maximum penalty the law provided. He scolded and berated me for my conduct and for trying to blame the whole affair on others. I was never so humiliated in my life and just wanted to die.

Somehow Stan got the D.A. and the Judge to allow me to stay out of jail pending my appeal. As a condition of the deal I had to agree to surrender my law license pending a resolution of my criminal conviction. This was particularly painful since it meant I couldn't help Stan nail Don Harris and prove Dusty Thomas innocent—at least officially. There was no way I was going to sit around my condo all day when there was so much work to be done. I'd just have to be discreet.

# THE PERFORMANCE 41

A week later I still hadn't heard from Mo. I wondered why he was taking so long. It seemed like the CIA should have the information I wanted at their fingertips. Dusty's trial was only a few weeks away and I was pretty much at a dead end in my investigation. To make matters worse Raymond Farr and the CDA were making the final preparations for their big march on Washington and mass burning of Form 1040's by each protestor. Farr had called several times to urge me to come to Washington and march with them. I had politely declined on the grounds that I couldn't take the time off with Dusty's trial so close at hand. Dusty also was asked to go but fortunately under the terms of his bond he couldn't leave the state.

As Dusty's trial date approached, the Feds increased their surveillance on me. Whereas in the past there had been only one agent following me around, now I often saw two or three. This was awkward and I had to be careful where I went and what I said to people. With Paula off the case I needed help so I called my new private investigator Paul Thayer in for assistance. He had done well on the few assignments I had given him, so it was time to hire him full time for the duration of the investigation and trial.

He arrived right on time and Jodie showed him into my office. Paul was tall, lean and looked more like an accountant than a private investigator. He was dressed in a dark blue suit and looked very professional. He was familiar with Paula's trial and offered his sympathies. I complimented him on the work he had done so far and told him I needed him to come on board full time.

"Well, I've got some jobs to finish up, but I should be able to start full time in a couple days."

"Good. We have only two and a half weeks to trial and six weeks of work to do. I'm going to be on the job 18 hours a day and I'm going to need you to do likewise."

"Well I charge $50 an hour plus expenses."

"No, problem.... Do you have any associates in case we need additional help?"

"Sure, I've got a few buddies who I can call on if need be."

"Good. You'll need them. Our primary suspect as you know is Don Harris. I want you to watch him like a hawk between now and the trial. Somebody needs to be on him 24 hours a day and I want a daily report of his activities. I'm particularly interested in who he meets and where he goes."

Paul took notes as I briefed him on our case and where I needed help. He seemed excited about the assignment and promised to get right on it. I told him about Jill Murray and how important it was that we find her. He looked through her address book and I had Jodie make him a copy of it. After he left I began looking through my notes to see if there were any loose ends that needed following up. When I came across Jill's telephone bill I remembered I hadn't gotten through to the mysterious number. I dialed it again. The answering machine picked up. I didn't leave a number.

Frustrated, I asked Jodie to call the number and leave a message. I told her to act like she was calling her boyfriend. This was a technique I had learned when I was trying to collect money for clients. If I called the debtor he would invariably be on another line, out of town, or too busy to talk. Of course, I would never get a return phone call. But if Jodie called them she'd almost always get through or get a return phone call. She loved to play this game so she quickly picked up the phone and dialed the number.

When the greeting finished she said in the sexiest voice she could conger up, "This is Jodie. Pick up, please ... come on, honey, pick up the damn phone ... okay, be hard-headed. Call me back when you're in a better mood. I'm at a friend's house. 972-555-5237. I miss ya."

We both laughed when she hung up the phone. "That was good. You're in the wrong profession."

She winked at me and then went back to her office. Ten minutes later the inside line rang. I knew it was our return telephone call so I ran into the reception area. Jodie was smiling broadly when she picked up the telephone.

"It's about time you called."

"Huh, is this Jodie?"

"Well, who do you think it is, silly?"

"I got your message but—"

"I know. You're a busy guy."

"Yeah, but I don't know—"

"Are we still on for tonight?"

"Huh?"

"Don't tell me you forgot?"

"Forgot what?"

"My birthday?"

"Listen, lady, you got the wrong number."

"Really? Who is this?"

"Rob."

"Rob?"

"Yeah, Rob Steakley."

"Oh, I'm sorry. I was calling Tom. . . . Oh, well. Too bad. I guess Tom wrote down the wrong number last night. We were both pretty exhausted. . . after our workout."

There was silence on the line. Finally Rob said, "Well, I'd hate you to be alone on your birthday."

"Yeah, that would be sad."

"Listen, maybe I could fill-in for Tom," Rob said.

"Really. That's an interesting idea. . . . But I don't know you."

"So, how well did you know Tom?"

Jodie giggled. "Oh, Tom and I had talked for hours before—."

"Your workout?"

Jodie giggled again.

"So, I'll buy you a drink and we can talk for hours, too."

"Okay, but tell me about yourself first. There's no use either of us wasting our time if we're incompatible."

"Right."

"How old are you?"

"Thirty-two."

"I'm 22, but I like older men."

"Ten years isn't—"

"You're not married are you?"

"Divorced."

"Good. Me too. Did you and your ex live in Alexandria?"

"Nah, we had a house in West Springfield."

"How long have you been divorced?"

"Two years—October."

"Any kids?"

"Twin boys—Ricky and David."

"I don't have any children," Jodie said.

"I don't see them much. Their mom and I don't get along."

"Umm. So what do you do for a living?"

"Security specialist."

"Oh, really. What's that?"

"You know—bodyguard?"

"Oh, my word. Who do you work for?"

"Does that matter?"

"No. Just curious."

"So, can I pick you up?" Rob asked.

"No, I'll meet you somewhere—you name it," Jodie replied.

"The Raven Club on Mt. Vernon—eight o'clock."

"How will I know you?"

"Six-two, mustache—black hair."

"Hmm, see you later."

Jodie hung up the telephone. We started laughing again. I was overwhelmed by Jodie's performance. "Wow. That was great. Call Lawyer's Aid and have them pull Rob's divorce records. I want a copy of everything in the divorce file. Find out if any depositions were taken and if so, get a copy. That was amazing, Jodie. You are something else."

I started to go back in my office when Jodie said, "Stan. I'll need a new dress for my date."

We both cracked up again, "Yeah, right."

I called Paul and told him I needed someone at the Raven Club in Alexandria, Virginia to wait for Rob Steakley to show up for his date and then follow him. I needed to know who he was working for. Paul said he'd take care of it and get back to me. Adrenalin was pumping again and I was feeling much more optimistic. Maybe I'd crack this case after all. I just had to keep digging until I figured it out. I just hoped it didn't take too long. Time was running out.

# DEFECTION **42**

Sitting around in my condo when there was so much work to do on Dusty's case was driving me crazy. I wanted so badly to go to the office and help Stan. The deal with the D.A. was clear, however. I couldn't set foot in the office. It was so unfair—for me, for Stan, and for Dusty Thomas. I was busy feeling sorry for myself when the noon news came on. The lead story was about the CDA's March on Washington.

"Earlier today thousands of protestors from the Citizens Defense Alliance marched on Washington to voice their protest over the Federal Income Tax. After numerous speeches denouncing the Internal Revenue Service and Congress for enforcing, what they say is an illegal tax, tens of thousands of Americans burned their Form 1040's. It was a site reminiscent of draft dodgers in the 60s.

"Although the crowd wasn't as large as CDA President Raymond Farr had predicted, it was a significant show of strength for this, up until now, obscure organization. Experts credit the Dusty Thomas trial in Dallas for the growing strength of the tax protest movement. The trial is set to start next week in Dallas and the stakes are high for both Dusty Thomas and the government. A loss for the government would strike fear in the hearts of many IRS Revenue Officers and encourage tax protestors.

"Although the CDA has financed the Dusty Thomas trial, attorney Stan Turner denies any connection to or sympathy with the CDA. Turner, however, has not convinced the government of his independence from the CDA and consequently he and his law partner, Paula Waters, have been under investigation for some time.

"In fact, recently Stan Turner's military record has been under scrutiny. In 1970 Stan Turner faced a court martial when his drill sergeant was found murdered. He was cleared of the charge, but later implicated in a drug related incident that resulted in the suicide of his alleged girlfriend, Rita Andrews.

"Speculation is that Stan Turner may have developed anti-government sentiments during these difficult times in the Marine Corps.

Turner, of course, denies any anti-government sentiments and says he supports the Federal Income Tax.

"Security was high in Washington today due to the CDA's history of violence and advocating the overthrow of the federal government. Fortunately, there hasn't been any violence so far today."

The news story infuriated me. I couldn't believe the press was out there digging up dirt on Stan. I felt so bad. It was all my fault for involving the CDA. I had to do something, so I put in a call to Stan.

"Did you see the news?" I asked.

"No. I've been pretty busy," Stan replied.

"They're digging up your military history."

"What?"

"I'm sorry. It's all my fault."

"Oh, God. I never thought that would come up again."

I told Stan about the news report. He was very upset, as he knew it would devastate Rebekah to have that chapter of their lives rehashed.

"Let me help you. I can't stand just sitting around. Isn't there something I can do?"

"I'd love your help, but if you violate the terms of your bail they could revoke it."

"I'll take the chance."

"Well, there are a few loose ends you can follow-up as long as you do it by telephone. Don't leave the condo! Use a fictitious name. I don't want to have to visit you in jail."

"Okay, no problem. What do you have for me?"

"Don Harris had a business partner in a venture that went sour. Find out all you can about it and see if his partner will talk. His name is Ronald Green. The business was called 'Integrated Graphics.'"

"Okay, what else?"

"I wonder what kind of a relationship Don Harris has with his wife?"

"I don't know. I guess it depends on whether or not she knows about Jill."

"My guess is she does and there may be other girlfriends. If you could somehow talk to her that would be great. She may be trapped like Jill and looking for help extricating herself from the relationship."

"How do you think I should approach her?"

"I don't know. You'll think of something."

"Thanks, Stan. I'm so sorry about the CDA. You were right. It was a big mistake getting them involved. I was so stupid—"

"It's water under the bridge. Don't worry about it. Just get to work. I feel like we are on the verge of a breakthough."

"Really? I hope you're right."

Stan's optimistic demeanor picked me up. I immediately got to work on "Integrated Graphics." I looked in the telephone book but there were too many Ronald Greens. It would take hours to find the right one assuming he even lived in the Metroplex. It had only been a little over a year since the breakup of the partnership so I took the direct approach. I called Don Harris' office.

"Is Ronald there?"

"Ronald?"

"Ronald Green? Doesn't he work there?"

"No, he is no longer employed here."

"Oh, do you know where I can find him?"

"No, but I have a forwarding address I can give you."

"Wonderful. What is it?"

She gave me the address and I thanked her. The address was in Irving so I called information to see if I could get a telephone number. Unfortunately, the number was unlisted. I took a deep breath and called Jodie. At the office we had a criss-cross directory. If I had an address I could find out the telephone number at that address. Of course, if the number was unlisted it wouldn't show up on the criss-cross directory but I could get the telephone number for addresses nearby. Jodie gave me the name and address of all of the Greens' neighbors. After two phone calls I got lucky and found someone who knew him. I told her I was a reporter and wanted to interview him. She promised to go next door and leave a message. I hoped Green would be curious enough to call me back.

While I was waiting I called a friend at the district clerks office and had her look up the lawsuit I'd discovered earlier between Harris and his ex-partner. I hadn't had time before to pull the file and read the pleadings. It was a petition to dissolve the partnership filed by Ronald Green. He alleged Don Harris had breached the partnership agreement by failing to devote his full attention to the partnership business. Green asked the court to dissolve the partnership, liquidate the assets, and distribute them to the partners. Of course, he wanted most of the assets himself to compensate himself for Harris's alleged breach of the partnership agreement.

The case never went to trial and it was eventually settled and dismissed with prejudice. The file didn't disclose the terms of the settlement. The lawsuit didn't surprise me. Don Harris' graphics business was obviously just a front for something else. I hoped Green could shed some light on what that was. In the meantime I started thinking about how to approach Harris' wife, Charlotte. If I called Don's house I had to be sure he wasn't there. I called Paul Thayer, who was running a 24 hour surveillance on Don, and asked him to call me when Charlotte was alone. Later that afternoon he called and advised me that Don had left home and Charlotte was by herself. I dialed her number and she answered on the second ring.

"Hi. Mrs. Harris? I'm a friend of Jill Murray."

She didn't respond so I continued. "I think you know Jill. Most wives know when their husbands are cheating on them."

"Who are you?"

"Like I said, I'm a friend of Jill's. She's in hiding. Don tried to have her killed. You may be in danger too."

"How could I be in danger?"

"Don's world is about to come crashing down on him. You probably know too much and he may have to get rid of you."

"They can't make a wife testify against her husband."

"Right, but the key word is *make*. If you wanted to testify, you could."

"This is crazy. Who are you?"

"Okay, I'll come clean with you. I'm working on the Dusty Thomas case. Stan Turner believes your husband actually killed Bobby Tuttle."

There was a moment of silence. "What do you want from me?"

"If you'll help us prove our case, we'll make sure you don't go down with your husband."

"You don't know my husband. I'll end up dead if I help you."

"We can provide protection."

"Right. Like you did for Jill?"

"So you do know about Jill."

"Yes, I know my husband isn't a faithful man. I took him away from his first wife. I was naive to think that he would be faithful to me."

"Will you help us put him behind bars? You know that's where he belongs."

"How? If Don finds out I've even talked to you, he'll kill me."

"Leave the house right now and I'll put you up in a hotel and provide 24 hour security."

"Right now?"

"Yes, do it while you can. Now that you've talked to me Don will notice something is wrong. You have to leave immediately."

"But where should I go?"

I told Charlotte to go to the Fairmont Hotel in Dallas and wait in the lobby where there are lots of people. Then I called Paul Thayer and arranged for security. He promised to have someone there before she arrived. When I hung up with Paul I called Stan to tell him the good news. He was ecstatic.

"What did she tell you?"

"Not much. You'll need to go down to the Fairmont and talk to her. She just agreed to help. I don't know what she knows, if anything."

"That is fabulous, Paula. Thank you. I'm going to head down to the Fairmont right now."

After hanging up with Stan I fixed something for lunch and waited for Ron Green to call me back. I was feeling pretty good about recruiting Charlotte as a witness until I got a phone call from Don Harris.

"Where is my wife? Where did you take her?"

"I didn't take her anywhere. She left of her own free will and volition and I don't blame her from what I've heard about you."

"You and your partner are treading on thin ice. I'd be very careful if I were you."

I swallowed hard. "It's too late. We know you killed Bobby Tuttle and now with the help of Jill and your wife we can prove it."

"Neither one of them know shit. You've got nothing. Now, where is my wife!"

"I'm not telling you. I know what you'll do to her."

Hearing from Harris shook me up. I wondered if he would send someone over to kill me. I called Bart and told him what had happened. He said to lock the doors and windows and not open the door to anyone. After hanging up I did what he said and then waited anxiously. Around two o'clock the telephone rang. I answered it. It was Ron Green.

"Thank you for calling, Mr. Green. My name is ... ah ... Donna Wade," Paula said. "I'm a reporter and we are investigating Don Harris. I understand you two used to be partners?"

"Yes, we were. Why are you investigating him?"

"His name has popped up a few times in the Dusty Thomas murder case and we're trying to find out as much about him as we can."

"We were partners in a graphic arts business. I know he had several other businesses but I'm not really familiar with them."

"Was S & T Packing one of them?"

"Yes, it was."

"Any idea what kind of business that was?"

"Is this off the record? I don't really want to get involved."

"Sure, I'm just looking for information. I'll keep your identity confidential."

"I can't prove this, but I suspect S & T Packing exported more guns than grapefruit."

"Guns?"

"Harris is a military man—a weapons expert. I heard him all the time on the telephone talking about selling guns and military equipment. I think he used S & T Packing as a cover for that purpose. In fact, he was spending so much time doing that he was neglecting the partnership. I finally got fed up and told him I wanted to split up the partnership. He wouldn't agree to it so I finally had to file suit. Eventually he gave in and we settled the suit and split up the partnership."

If it was true that Don Harris was selling guns and military equipment that would give him an even greater motive for killing Bobby Tuttle. It wasn't the People's Mission that Don was worried about. It was his illegal gun running operation. If Bobby Tuttle kept digging into his affairs he would have most likely uncovered Don Harris' real secret.

As I was digesting this new information the doorbell rang. I looked over at the door and wondered who it could be. Had Don Harris come to deliver on his threat? I hoped it was Bart but it didn't seem like it had been long enough for him to make it over to my place. I held my breath as I inched toward the door and peeked through the peep hole.

# THE PACKAGE **43**

Right after getting the call from Paula about Charlotte Harris I headed for the Fairmont Hotel. I couldn't believe that she had bolted from Don Harris so quickly. Obviously she had been wanting to leave him and was just waiting for the right moment. Don Harris had that effect on women. I was especially excited about interviewing Charlotte because she might be able to provide evidence to show that Don Harris went to the Double T Ranch on the day Bobby Tuttle was murdered. He might have even confessed the killing to her. When I got to the Fairmont I called Paul Thayer's office to find out what room Mrs. Harris was in. They didn't want to give out the room number over the phone so they said someone would come down and get me. After a few minutes a security officer found me, took me to her room, and let me in. Charlotte was over by the window looking down at the street.

"Hi, Mrs. Harris. I'm Stan Turner."

She turned and looked at me. "Hello."

"Are you all right?"

"Yes, just nervous," she said.

"Don't worry. You're safe now," I replied.

"Are you sure? My husband is pretty resourceful. He might still find me."

"I doubt it. But we'll have you under twenty-four hour guard just in case."

"Good."

"Are you hungry? I can call room service."

"No, I'm too keyed up to eat."

"Right. Well, if you feel up to it, I have some questions I'd like to ask."

"Sure. Let's get this over with. What do you want to know."

"How long have you been trying to get away from your husband?"

She sighed. "About two weeks after we got married. I didn't realize the kind of man he was. So nice and charming—until I pissed him off. I don't ever remember what I did, but he beat the crap out of me."

"Did you try to leave him then?"

"Yes, but he apologized and promised it wouldn't happen again. So, I didn't leave him."

"How long until he broke his promise?"

"Just a few days. He got mad again about something ridiculous and hit me again. I told him I wasn't going to put up with his abuse and was leaving. That's when he threatened my life."

"Why didn't you go to the police?"

"He warned me about going to the police. He said they couldn't protect me and that I'd be dead before they got to me."

"So, did he keep you prisoner?"

"Not exactly. After a day or two he acted like nothing had happened. I could have run I guess, but I was too scared."

"On the day Bobby Tuttle was murdered did your husband use your car?"

"Yes, his truck wouldn't start so he took my car that day."

"When did he leave?"

"About 8:00 A.M."

"Did you see him during the day?"

"He came home around 9:30 P.M."

"Did you notice any damage to your car?"

"The side view mirror had been knocked off. He said it had happened at the car wash. That surprised me because Don didn't go to car washes. His truck was always filthy."

"Did he say anything about the Tuttle murder?"

"No, but he watched the coverage on the 10 o'clock news and read everything about it the next morning in the newspaper."

"Did you see your husband with a shotgun that day?"

"No."

"Did you suspect he might be involved with the murder?"

"Yes, he hated Agent Tuttle. He complained about him all the time and said more than once that he was going to kill him. I didn't take him seriously until the day he was murdered. I know everyone thought Dusty Thomas did it, but I wasn't so sure."

"Did you ever confront your husband with your suspicions?"

She frowned at me. "What, you think I'm crazy?"

Charlotte Harris was going to be a great witness. All I had to do was keep her alive for a week. I thanked Charlotte and told her to let us know if she needed anything. She said she had left so quickly she didn't have any luggage. I told the security guard to get her whatever she needed to be comfortable. He said he'd take care of it. When I got back to the office there was a package waiting for me. It was from Mo.

Inside was a manila file folder. I opened it and started looking through the papers. The first document was a report on S & T Packing. The document provided the history of the company, officers and directors, a description of its stated business, and financial status. At the bottom there was the following note:

"Secondary unofficial operation—Confirmed weapons supplier to South and Central American guerrillas and drug traffickers."

This confirmed what Ron Green had suspected and provided the names of some of S & T's customers and the dates of transactions that had taken place. The next document was a complete report on Don Harris. It was nine pages long beginning with his high school transcript at Hillcrest High School in Dallas. After graduating from high school the report indicated he went to the University of Texas where he graduated in 1973 with a degree in graphic arts. While at UT he was a member of the Army ROTC. After graduation he reported for duty and served until 1981 when he got a general discharge—not an honorable discharge.

The second document from Mo was part of a report about Harris' suspected illegal activities. Much of the report had been redacted but there was one paragraph that read: "Subject is a member of the Texas Militia terrorist group that advocates the succession of Texas from the Union. He also provides arms and munitions to said organization. Subject under investigation by ATF for RICCO violations and IRS for tax evasion."

A final document contained names of persons associated with Don Harris. Heading the list were Ernesto Garcia and Lewis Lance. My heart jumped with joy. Garcia had lied to us and Lance had been less than forthright. They weren't just casual acquaintances of Don Harris. They were close associates and co-conspirators. Now my only problem was proving it. Mo had been kind enough to get me information, but these documents wouldn't be admissible at trial, and somehow I didn't think he would be able to provide witnesses. Nevertheless, it was a great relief to at least know I was on the right track. I'd find the evidence I needed. I just needed to keep digging.

# THE VISITOR 44

The caller rang the doorbell again and then pounded hard on the door. I looked through the peephole and panicked when I saw it was Don Harris. Backing away from the door I stumbled over a coat rack and nearly fell to the ground. Harris kept banging and screaming. Then there was a loud thud as he tried to break the door down. I ran into my bedroom and got my revolver. After making sure it was loaded, I returned to the front door.

"Let me in you bitch!" Harris yelled. "I'll have you arrested for kidnapping."

"Go away! She's not here."

"You better tell me where she is or I'll break this door down."

"I've called the police," I screamed. "They're on their way."

Harris didn't respond and after a minute of silence I went back to the peep hole. I saw him retreating to his pickup. He took off with a screech. I turned around and took a big breath trying to calm down. A second pounding at the door nearly gave me a heart attack. I turned and looked in the peep hole again and saw Bart. I opened the door with the gun still pointing straight ahead.

"Hey girl. I give up. Point that thing somewhere else."

I laughed and then set the gun down on the table near the door. "Sorry. You missed the son of a bitch. He nearly broke down my door."

"Oh, God. I'm so sorry, Paula. I came as fast as I could."

"I would have killed the son of a bitch had he got in."

Bart nodded and replied, "I can see that."

"I guess he was pissed that I got his wife to leave him."

"Yeah, that is a safe bet. Is she going to help you?"

"I don't know. Stan's meeting with her right now. . . . That reminds me. I'd like to tender her car to the crime lab. Don Harris used it in the murder of Bobby Tuttle."

"Whoa there! Aren't you jumping the gun a little bit? You don't know that for sure."

"Yes, I do. You think Don Harris came over here for a social call? He knows we're getting close to nailing him and he's worried."

"Or he's just pissed off because you turned his wife against him."

"What? I just talked to Harris' ex-partner, Ron Green, and you know what he told me?"

"No."

"Harris is an arms dealer and he uses S & T Packing as a front for his operation. He supplies weapons to Latin American guerillas, drug lords, and the 18th Street gang. Mr. Garcia lied in court. We know now he is one of Don Harris' goons. Harris is responsible for Monty's death and setting me up. You ought to tell your FBI friends to get off their asses and do their job."

"Does he have personal knowledge of all that?"

"Green wasn't a co-conspirator, if that's what you mean. He over-heard telephone conversations and saw guns and military hardware in Harris' warehouse."

"That doesn't prove anything."

"So, what's it gonna take—a signed confession? Or, maybe if you find me dead with a bullet in my head, then you'll believe me."

Bart shook his head. "No, come on now. I believe you. If it were up to me I'd launch a full scale investigation of Don Harris and S & T Packing. But the FBI and the D.A. are not going to lift a finger to help you prove Dusty Thomas is innocent. You know that."

"But if we can prove Don Harris is guilty, what's the difference? They'll still avenge the death of their agent."

"Not necessarily. All you have to do is prove reasonable doubt to get Dusty off. They have to prove Don Harris is guilty beyond all reasonable doubt. That might be difficult even if everything you say about Don Harris is true."

I folded my arms and looked at Bart. "Fine. We'll do the D.A.'s job. We'll prove beyond all reasonable doubt that Don Harris killed Bobby Tuttle. And when this is all over maybe I'll run for D.A. I might as well get his salary if I'm going to do his damn job."

Bart laughed. "Good, I hope you do. I'll definitely vote for you."

We embraced and I closed my eyes finally feeling safe—at least for the moment.

# TRIAL PREP **45**

It had been several days since Jodie had arranged her date with Rob Steakly yet I hadn't heard a word from Paul Thayer about the result of his stakeout. Had they been able to follow Rob Steakley, and if so, what had they learned? Jodie got him on the line for me.

"Sorry, I haven't got back with you on that matter yet. You've been keeping us pretty busy."

"Well, the trial is next week. We're running out of time."

"My man in DC was able to follow Mr. Steakley. It turns out he works for Allied Security Co. It's a big outfit and they have lots of clients including a few congressman, senators, and other important people around the DC area."

"Can your man find out who Steakley was assigned to?"

"He's working on getting a client list and work assignment, but it's not easy being that it is a security firm."

"What about following him and finding out where he ends up?"

"Apparently he's on a new assignment now so we don't know where he was last week."

"What about his divorce records?"

"I've looked through them. I don't think there is anything in there that will be useful."

"Send it to me anyway and call me the minute you find anything else out."

"I'll do that."

It annoyed me that Paul hadn't got me more information about our Virginia connection. I knew it must be important or Harris wouldn't have bothered to destroy the original phone bill. As I was thinking about what to do next, Jodie walked in with three notebooks.

"Here are your trial notebooks. I've organized them like I did the Sarah Winters case—trial, pleadings, evidence. They should have everything you'll need. I made another copy too, just in case."

"Good. I'll go through it tonight. It will be useful in working on my witness questions. Have you got everyone subpoenaed?"

"Yes, there is a witness list in there. If you need anyone else subpoenaed just let me know."

I leaned back in my chair and took a deep breath. "God. I can't believe I've got to try this sucker in less than a week."

"I know. Should I get Dusty Thomas and his wife in to prep for trial?"

"Yes, but wait a day or two. If they come in too early they'll forget everything I tell them."

"What are you going to do for a second chair?"

"I don't know. I don't have time to get anyone up to speed on the case. How about you sitting with me?"

"Me. But—"

"You won't be able to say anything but you know the case as well as I do. It will be a big help having you there to keep me organized."

"Okay. That will be better than sitting around here wondering what's happening."

"Good. That's one less thing I have to worry about."

"Are you going to let Dusty testify?"

"I don't know yet. I guess it depends on how the trial is going and whether or not we are feeling desperate."

"Are you going to meet with the press prior to trial?"

"Do you think I should?"

"Yes, you need to set them straight about the CDA and your military record. I know you haven't had time to worry about it, but the press has been hammering you pretty hard."

"Put that on the list of things to talk to Paula about. I don't usually try my cases in the press but this isn't your typical murder case. It might be a good idea to set the record straight."

"So, how do you see Dusty's chances?"

"We've got a credible defense but we're a little short on evidence. It just depends on how the jury perceives it. It could go either way."

"I just hope they haven't made up their minds before the trial even starts," Jodie said.

Jodie was right. Picking a jury was going to be a big problem. I had thought about asking for a change of venue, but the case had received so much national attention I didn't think it would do much good. I started to make a list of the questions I would need to ask prospective jurors. Who had heard or read about the case? Had they formed any opinions based on the news coverage they'd heard? Did they have animosities toward Dusty because he hadn't paid his taxes? Would any of the publicity about me affect their ability to render a fair and impartial judgment. How did they feel about capital punishment?

The questions went on and on and before I knew it I had five legal pages full of them. I needed Paula. She had so much more experience in picking juries and was so much better at reading people than I was. But I was on my own and Dusty's life depended on getting a fair and impartial jury. I prayed that would happen.

# PRESS CONFERENCE **46**

On the Saturday before the trial was set to begin Stan held a press conference in the lobby of our office building. Since I wasn't allowed to participate in the trial I had to watch it on TV. The lobby was packed with reporters, cameramen, and other interested parties. Stan stood with Dusty and Martha facing the media mob. He tapped on the microphone to indicate he was ready to get started.

"Thank you," Stan said. "Thank you for coming.... We called this news conference on the eve of Dusty Thomas' trial due to the fact that over the past few weeks there have been lots of erroneous information, spurious statements, and innuendo reported in the press. Before Dusty goes on trial I thought it was important to set the record straight or at least present our side of the story. Although we hope to empanel an impartial jury it isn't going to be easy to find twelve good citizens who haven't heard a lot about this case. Since this is a fact we must live with, we want to be sure everyone has accurate information about Dusty and myself.

"First, let me say that neither I nor Dusty Thomas have any affiliation or sympathies with the CDA. They have funded Dusty Thomas' defense for their own purposes and benefit without any strings attached. We have promised nothing in return for their support and nothing will be given. As for me, I love my country and would never do anything to hurt it. I have always filed my income tax returns and paid my taxes in a timely manner. Neither I nor Dusty advocate tax evasion or tax defiance. We believe every American should pay their fair share of taxes set by our representatives in Congress.

"This trial is not about taxes. It's not about the Internal Revenue Service, the Sixteenth Amendment, the CDA, or my military record. It is a simple murder case. Did Dusty Thomas intentionally and with premeditation kill Bobby Tuttle? We believe we can prove he did not. We intend to prove someone else killed Bobby Tuttle and then tried to make it appear that Dusty had done it.

"Now if there are some specific questions I'll be happy to answer them. Obviously I can't delve too deeply into our defense strategy but I'll tell you as much as I can."

Several reporters began shouting their questions. Stan pointed to one of them.

"Will Dusty Thomas be testifying at trial?" the first reporter said.

"We don't know for sure, but there is a strong likelihood that he will."

Stan pointed to another reporter. "Reports are that you will try to prove Don Harris killed Agent Tuttle. Is that correct," the second reporter said.

"Don Harris will be called as a witness. That's about all I can say on that topic."

"You say you have no sympathies for the CDA yet you accept their money and they have been using this trial to promote their cause. Last week there was a big rally in Washington purposely set just before the Dusty Thomas trial. How can you say you don't support the CDA?"

"We don't support the CDA. It's as simple as that," Stan said.

"But Raymond Farr and a contingent of CDA officials will be attending the trial cheering on the defense. Have you told them to stay away," the reporter persisted.

"No, we don't have any control over who attends the trial. The court will determine who can watch it."

"Do you really expect us to believe you're not in bed with them?"

"I agree. It's hard to believe we would take CDA money yet not be beholden to them. The fact is it was Dusty's decision whether to accept the money or not. He didn't believe he could raise the kind of money it would take for a murder defense himself, so he thought he had no choice but to accept their generous offer. At no time, however, did he agree to support the CDA, endorse anything they did, or help them in any way."

After fielding a dozen or so more questions the news conference finally came to a close. When everyone had left, Stan came over to do some last minute brainstorming. There hadn't been any startling developments in the last few days. Paul Thayer still hadn't figured out who Harris was communicating with in Virginia, Mo hadn't come up with any new evidence, and Jill was still missing. The only positive thing that had happened was that Charlotte was still safely tucked away in the Fairmont Hotel anxious to testify against her abusive husband. I had recovered from my visit from Don Harris and was feeling pretty good except for being a little nervous about how the trial was going to turn out.

"Is Rebekah coming?" I asked.

"Are you kidding? She wouldn't miss this circus for the world. She's bringing her mother too. She says it's going to be better than the daytime soaps."

"Yeah, with the CDA and the Vets picketing, the action outside the courtroom might get interesting too."

"Is there anything I can do for you during the trial?"

"No, all you can do is watch, remember?"

"Right. I hate this. I should be helping you."

"Jodie will be there if I need anything."

# DAY OF RECKONING 47

At 7:00 A.M. the alarm went off and I opened my eyes. A sinking feeling came over me as I realized it was the first day of Dusty Thomas' trial. The first few hours of a trial were always the worst. Gripped with fear I'd make my way into the courtroom expecting the worst. But once the trial got underway there wouldn't be time to worry or fret about anything. I'd be too busy presenting evidence, cross examining witnesses, and making my opponent follow the rules by making timely objections. Now, however, I was worried about everything. Would my witnesses show up? Would they testify the way I expected? Would the jury be fair and unbiased? These and many more questions always haunted me those first few hours.

Jodie had loaded everything I needed in my car the day before so I didn't have to go to the office. After taking a long shower I got dressed and went into the kitchen to eat breakfast. Rebekah had made French toast, bacon, eggs and hot coffee. I usually didn't eat this much for breakfast but it was going to be a grueling day and Rebekah knew I might not have time for lunch. She and the children were all very supportive—smothering me with hugs and kisses before I left for the courthouse.

It was a cold and dreary day. It had rained all night and the streets were wet and slippery. Fortunately the temperature had remained above freezing so there wasn't any ice. Dusty, Martha, and Jodie were to meet me at the courthouse at eight-thirty. The trial was set to begin at nine so that would give us thirty minutes to discuss last-minute strategy, get through the crowd of reporters, and get up to the courtroom to set up at the defense table before the trial began.

A tinge of fear ran through me as I got in my car. Ever since the ambush I worried about General Moya's assassin putting a bomb in my car. As I put the key in the ignition I saw in my mind's eye my car exploding. I hesitated, closed my eyes a moment, and then turned the ignition. The engine turned over smoothly and I breathed a sigh of relief as I waved goodbye to Rebekah and the kids. The ride to the

McKinney courthouse was long and grueling through rush hour on Highway 75. As I got close to the courthouse I saw the streets lined with TV vans and trucks with big satellite antennas. A crowd had already assembled in front of the courthouse—sightseers, picketers, reporters, cameramen, and police. I drove past the courthouse parking lot which was full and parked on the street.

Jodie met me at the west door to the courthouse. She said Dusty and Martha were waiting in the snack room. She said she had taken all our files upstairs already so we went in directly to meet Dusty and Martha. They both had dressed modestly as we suggested and looked clean and respectable. I explained to them that the first few days of trial would be spent picking a jury. During that time it was important for them to smile, look attentive, and appear upbeat. Then I went over our trial outline so they would know exactly what to expect once testimony began. As we were getting ready to go upstairs Dusty asked the question that all defendants ask on the eve of trial.

"What are my chances?"

I swallowed hard and replied. "Well, you were found standing over the body with a shotgun in your hand. It's not going to be easy getting past that, but we have developed a strong defense that ought to get the jury's attention."

"So, what do you think? Fifty-fifty? Sixty-forty? Eighty-twenty?" Dusty pressed.

"This isn't Las Vegas. I can't give you precise odds other than to say it's realistically less than fifty-fifty."

Dusty's face dropped and Martha closed her eyes in response to my assessment of their chances of escaping the ordeal unscathed. As we left the snack room, photographers and reporters began crowding around us, snapping our pictures, and asking questions. At this point I simply told them we had no comment. While we were waiting for the elevator with the press crowded around us two bailiffs showed up and told the reporters to move aside. When the elevator opened they commandeered it, shoved us inside, and took us to the sixth floor.

When we got to the courtroom the gallery was filled with prospective jurors talking excitedly. A bailiff handed me a thick envelope as I stepped inside the courtroom. It contained the jury panel list, individual cards on each juror, and an instruction sheet. We sat down at the defense table and started the impossible task of evaluating hundreds of prospective jurors. How could anyone really get to know a juror in such a short time? Their motivations were so mixed and varied it was hard to read them. Few of them wanted to be here. Most were trying to figure out what they could say to insure they wouldn't get picked. I often thought it would be better to put the jury list on a dart board, give each side six darts, and let them throw them at the list. The individuals whose names were hit would make up the jury. A jury picked in this manner would probably be just as good or better than one picked in the conventional fashion.

Before long the bailiff called for silence and announced that court was in session. The judge took the bench and asked Trenton Lee to start voir dire. Trenton got up and introduced himself to the jury and started telling them his version of what had happened on July 11th. The jurors seemed enthralled by the story he was weaving. Of course, they had already seen it on TV but they hung on Trenton's every word like it was the first time they'd heard of it. When he was done with his story he started asking individual jurors questions calculated to illicit any prejudices that they might have, one way or the other, that could unfairly influence their deliberations as a juror.

By the time Trenton finished late in the afternoon it was clear that I couldn't possibly finish that day so the judge called a recess until Tuesday morning. One day was down and I had scarcely opened my mouth. But that would change tomorrow, as it would be my turn to pry into the personal life of the prospective jurors assembled before me and to give them another perspective of the Bobby Tuttle murder. Although these first two days were only a dress rehearsal for the actual trial and no evidence would be introduced, the fact was many if not all the jurors would likely make up their minds those first two days before the indictment was even read.

It's not to say the jurors wouldn't listen to the witnesses and consider the evidence but they would do so predisposed one way or the other. Only something startling or shocking that they had not considered or dreamed possible would change their minds. Fortunately the bizarre story I would soon be telling them had such potential, if they didn't think it so preposterous to have any credibility whatsoever.

That night I called Paul Thayer to get an update on his activities but I couldn't get through to him. The message on his answering machine said he was out of town and wouldn't be back until Wednesday. I wondered where he had gone and why he hadn't called with an update. In less than 36 hours Trenton Lee would be calling his witnesses and I needed more evidence or Dusty's defense would come across as a desperate attorney's pipe dreams. Despite my anxiety I slept soundly that night and when I next opened my eyes I couldn't believe it was already morning.

The scene at the courthouse was a carbon copy of the previous morning except that there were more picketers and press and consequently more police to keep them in line. I took the back stairs to the sixth floor to avoid the press and to get a little exercise to get my blood flowing. Sitting around all day Monday listening to Trenton woo the jury had left me lethargic. The fear and anxiety I had felt on Monday was gone. Today was just another work day and there was much to be done.

The judge nodded at me and said, "Mr. Turner. You may proceed."

"Your Honor. Ladies and Gentlemen of the Jury. Yesterday Mr. Lee gave you his synopsis of the events which led to Dusty Thomas' indictment and the trial in which we are all now engaged. These events were probably familiar to you as this case has received wide publicity in the press and on TV. I must caution you though to the fact that nothing you have seen or heard so far is evidence. There is nothing yet for you to consider. As you know the state has the burden of proof in this matter and at this moment my client enjoys a presumption of innocence. If anyone right now has already decided that Dusty Thomas is guilty then you do not qualify to be a juror today. Who among you has already made that determination?"

Two hands went up in the back of the room. I pointed to one of the gentlemen and said, "So, you've already made up your mind that Dusty Thomas is guilty," I asked.

"Well, it's rather obvious. He was found standing over the body with a shotgun," he replied with a chuckle.

"True enough. But the judge has instructed you that the state has the burden of proof and that there is a presumption of innocence. Will you be able to follow the judges instructions and consider Mr. Thomas innocent unless the state proves otherwise?"

"Hey, I've seen all the proof I need."

I turned to the judge and said, "Your Honor. The defense objects to this juror as he is obviously not impartial and has indicated he cannot follow your instructions."

"The juror will be excused," the judge said.

Turning to the other juror who had raised his hand, I began to question him, but he obviously wanted to be on the jury and knew how to answer my questions. He said he would set aside his personal feelings and follow the judges instructions. I didn't think he was sincere and questioned him at length but he answered each question very carefully. In the end I asked that he be disqualified but the judge refused. I noted I would have to use one of my strikes to keep him off the jury. At this point I began my rendition of the facts of July 11, 1986.

"We are not going to dispute the fact that Dusty Thomas was seen by the wrecker driver standing over Bobby Tuttle's body. But what we are going to ask you to do is not draw any conclusions just yet from that fact. You've all been to see magicians, right? What's so amazing about magicians is their ability to make things appear differently than what they actually are. For instance, you've all seen a magician stick a sword right through a beautiful woman—at least that is what appears to have happened. Yet in the end the woman jumps up without any wounds at all. Well, we are going to show you during the course of this trial that despite the fact that Dusty Thomas looks very guilty he is not. We will show you that a very smart and cunning man killed Bobby Tuttle for his own reasons and then tried to make it look like Dusty was responsible. I know this may seem hard to believe, but all I ask is that you honor the judge's instructions and give Dusty Thomas his presumption of innocence. Keep an open mind and consider all the evidence before you begin to deliberate. We will carefully unravel this complicated conspiracy and show you that it is quite likely that Dusty Thomas was set up and is no more responsible for Agent Tuttle's murder than you or I."

After my summary of the facts I continued to question the jury panel on many issues, some which had been addressed by Trenton and others that he had omitted. By the time I was done it was nearly five o'clock so the judge recessed the case until the following day. Day two was now over and I wondered what the jury was thinking. I would have given a day's pay to be a fly on the wall in the jury room that afternoon when the judge dismissed the jurors. After all, if the case was already decided I certainly wanted to know about it.

# A GOOD LIAR **48**

Watching the trial from the gallery was a unique experience for me. Having tried many cases as a prosecutor, I felt out of place as a spectator. It was difficult for me to sit still those first two days of jury selection. I excelled at picking juries, and I knew Stan hated it. He could have really used my help. It would be even worse when live testimony began. I'd have to be careful I didn't blurt out "objection!" when Trenton got out of line. Dusty looked a little scared as the judge announced that a jury had been selected. He looked nervously at the prospective jurors who were waiting to see if they could go home or would be stuck on the jury for a week or two. He was a good client—generally laid back and easy going. He smiled when he saw me looking at him. As the judge began to call off the juror's names who had been selected I watched their reaction. Most let out a sigh of despair when they heard their names while a few seemed pleased and excited to have been selected.

The judge thanked those who were not picked and advised them they were free to leave. When they were gone the bailiff let in additional spectators to fill the seats vacated by the rejected or unneeded jurors. Many spectators began talking while people were filing in and taking their seats. One of the bailiffs glared at them and motioned for them to be quiet. When everyone was in their seat the judge told Trenton to proceed with the reading of the indictment. When he was done, he gave his opening statement.

"Your honor. Ladies and gentlemen of the jury. We gave you a brief summary of the facts during voir dire. This is not a complicated case. We will show that the accused, Dusty Thomas, had a long history of tax evasion. He failed and refused on numerous occasions to file tax returns and pay the taxes that he lawfully owed. Revenue Agent, Bobby Tuttle, had been assigned to audit him and bring him into compliance. Tuttle had worked with Dusty Thomas and his wife Martha for several years and was forced on several occasions to seize property since Mr. Thomas refused to voluntarily pay the taxes due.

WILLIAM MANCHEE

"Obviously, Mr. Thomas was bitter about this and we will show that on more than one occasion he threatened physical harm to Bobby Tuttle who was just doing his job. On that fateful day, the 11th day of July 1986, Bobby Tuttle went out to the Double T Ranch where Dusty lived with his wife Martha, to seize a valuable tractor that could be sold to satisfy a portion of his tax liability. Agent Tuttle called A Plus Wrecking company that morning and talked to Lewis Lance who agreed to meet him at the Double T Ranch at noon to physically take the tractor and transport it to the auto impound lot where it could be held until an IRS auction could be conducted.

"Unfortunately for Bobby Tuttle, Lewis Lance was late and while Agent Tuttle was waiting for him, Dusty Thomas confronted Tuttle with a Remington shotgun. Now there are no witnesses to the actual murder but Lewis Lance will testify that he arrived several minutes later and saw Dusty Thomas standing over Agent Tuttle who had just been shot. He will also testify that he looked all around in every direction and didn't see anyone else on the ranch.

"The testimony will show that just as soon as Dusty Thomas saw Mr. Lance arrive he ran away. Mr. Lance then checked to see if Agent Tuttle was alive and was prepared to administer CPR. Unfortunately, Agent Tuttle was dead so Mr. Lance called the Sheriff's office. The first two deputy sheriffs pursued Dusty Thomas to the back of his ranch where he had hidden in a barn. They asked him to come out and surrender but he refused to do so. It was only several hours later that his counsel, Mr. Stan Turner, went in and convinced him to surrender.

"Now the defense will be trying to muddy the waters by introducing other persons who had motive to kill Agent Tuttle. It's easy to speculate in a case like this. You have a Revenue Agent who is not popular because he's a tax collector. Sure there may be a lot of people who didn't like him because of what he did, but that doesn't make them murderers. Most taxpayers grumble about paying their taxes but they don't resort to violence to avoid paying them.

"So don't listen to this speculation. That's all it is. Rarely do you get a case where the killer is found standing over the victim's body with the smoking gun. The defense will also be trying to get you to buy into a conspiracy theory. Not only will they suggest there has been a conspiracy against Dusty Thomas, but also against co-counsel Paula Waters, and defense counsel Stan Turner himself. This is ridiculous and simply a sign of how desperate they are to find any kind of a credible defense.

"So don't let the defense complicate this case. It's very simple. Dusty Thomas shot and killed Revenue Agent Bobby Tuttle while he was performing his duties as an agent for the United States Government. It was intentional, premeditated murder and the law dictates that he be punished for his crime.

"Although every murderer should be brought to justice, it is particularly important that Dusty Thomas pay for his crime, as he murdered an agent of the federal government. If we allow him to go unpunished we will be putting thousands of other revenue agents at risk. Don't let this happen. Do your duty as a juror and find Dusty Thomas guilty of murder."

Trenton walked back to his chair and sat down. All eyes now shifted to Stan.

"Thank you, Mr. Lee," the Judge said. "Mr. Turner, you may proceed."

Stan stood up, nodded to the judge, and smiled at the jurors. "Thank you, Your Honor, Ladies and Gentlemen of the jury."

"I will agree with Mr. Trenton on one point. It is important that justice be done. In fact, that is the essence of our judicial system. This trial isn't about protecting revenue agents. This case isn't about preserving the viability of the Internal Revenue Service. This case is about finding out who killed Bobby Tuttle.

"Now we will admit that Dusty Thomas was found standing over the body, but that doesn't mean he killed Bobby Tuttle. There are no witnesses to this murder. At least no witnesses who have come forward. Sure it looks bad that our client was standing over the body, but it was his ranch that Agent Tuttle chose to visit that fateful morning. Anyone could have shot him there that day and it is only logical that if Dusty Thomas heard a shot he would come to investigate—hence being found standing over the body.

"What about the shotgun? The evidence will show that Bobby Tuttle was shot with a Remington shotgun. The evidence will also show that Dusty Thomas' gun was a Remington shotgun. Even so they will be unable to prove that Dusty's shotgun was the murder weapon as a shot can rarely be traced back to the weapon from which it came.

"As Mr. Lee told you we will introduce evidence of many people with equal or better motives to kill Agent Tuttle. In particular we will tell you about one man who was engaged in an illegal business that Agent Tuttle was about to discover. To protect this illegal activity we believe this man killed or was responsible for the death of Agent Tuttle. Although we don't expect him to confess to the murder we believe we will provide you with substantial evidence of his guilt.

"As you've been told, the government must prove its case beyond all reasonable doubt. If we prove to you that someone else may very well have killed Agent Tuttle then that would provide reasonable doubt whether Dusty Thomas did it and you'd be compelled to find him innocent. This is what we intend to do.

"As to the conspiracy that Mr. Lee mentioned let me say this. When two or more persons conspire to do an illegal act that is a conspiracy. We believe Bobby Tuttle's death was not the result of one man's vengeance, but the act of several individuals who conspired together to murder Bobby Tuttle and then make it look like Dusty Thomas had done it. It was a very complicated and brilliant plan, which we hope you will thwart.

"All we ask of you as jurors is to listen carefully to the evidence and only consider that evidence in rendering your verdict. It will be tempting to get caught up in Trenton Lee's patriotic rhetoric and feel like you have to convict Dusty Thomas if you care about your country. Resist that temptation and make Trenton Lee prove beyond all reasonable doubt that Dusty is guilty. We don't believe he will be able to do it. . . . Thank you."

The judge thanked Stan and then announced a ten minute break before testimony would begin. After he had left the bench I joined Stan, Jodie, and Dusty at the defense counsel table.

"Looking good so far, " I said.

"Think so?" Stan asked.

"Yeah, I think the jury got the message that this isn't going to be a slam dunk for the prosecution," I said.

"Good. I hope you're right," Stan said. "How are you holding up, Dusty?"

"Fine. You were exactly right. I heard the shot and came runnin'," Dusty said. "I couldn't imagine who was firing a gun on my ranch. When I saw Agent Tuttle on the ground, I was in shock."

"I know," Stan said. "You'll get your chance to tell the jury what happened. Don't worry."

As we were talking the bailiff signaled that the judge was about to return so I went back to my seat. After the judge had taken the bench and the jury had been brought back in, testimony began. Trenton Lee called the Sheriff's deputy who arrived first on the scene as his first witness. He was followed by Agents Ronald Logan and Jennifer Giles. Just after lunch the medical examiner testified as to the cause of death and then Lewis Lance, the prosecution's key witness took the stand.

"Mr. Lance. What kind of business are you in?" Trenton asked.

"I'm a mechanic and I also drive a wrecker from time to time," Lance replied.

"Did you work for A Plus Wrecking Service in McKinney, Texas in July of 1986?"

"Yes, I drove a wrecker for them part time."

"You had other employment?"

"Yes, my regular job was in Wylie at Highway 78 Towing."

Trenton had obviously worked hard preparing Lance for trial. It appeared he was going to try to explain away all the weaknesses and inconsistencies on direct examination. This was a good strategy and would make it difficult for Stan to cross-examine him. After twenty minutes of background information Trenton got to the murder scene.

"What did you see when you drove up to Dusty Thomas' house?"

"I saw Agent Tuttle on the ground and Dusty Thomas looking down at him. He had a shotgun and he was holding it in both hands like he'd just shot it."

"Objection," Stan said. "The witness is speculating."

"Overruled," the judge said.

"What do you mean "like he'd just shot it?" Trenton asked.

"Well, you know. Like he had just shot it and then pulled the gun back to observe the kill."

"Objection," Stan said again, "This is pure speculation and highly prejudicial."

"Sustained. Just tell us what you observed, Mr. Lance. Don't try to interpret it for us."

"Yes, Your Honor."

"What did Mr. Thomas do when he saw you?"

"He looked around and then took off running toward his house. I thought he was going to go inside but instead he ran around the house and disappeared."

Trenton continued to question him but nothing new came out. After a brief recess Stan took him on cross examination. Lance appeared nervous as Stan began to question him.

"You testified that you worked part time for A Plus Wrecking Service and your main job was with Highway 78 Towing, is that correct?"

"Yes."

"So, why did you go to work for A Plus?"

"I was short on cash—a lot of bills, you know."

"How many hours a week did you work there?"

"Oh, about 15 to 20 a week."

"How far away was it?"

"About a hour's drive."

"Did you work everyday?"

"Weekdays—three or four hours a day."

"So you worked three hours a day and spent two hours driving back and forth?"

"Objection," Trenton said. "I can't see the relevance of this line of questioning."

"Your Honor. It will become clearly relevant but I have to lay a foundation before I can get to the point."

"Overruled. The witness will answer the question."

Lance replied, "Yes."

"How was it that you came to work for A Plus Wrecking Service?"

"I don't know. I think I just looked in the yellow pages and started calling all the wrecking service companies at random."

"Do you know a man named Don Harris?"

Lance squirmed in his chair and began rubbing his chin. "Yes, he's a customer at Highway 78 Towing."

"You're his mechanic?"

"Yes, I work on a couple of his cars."

"Could he have suggested you go work for A Plus?"

"Maybe, but I don't remember it."

"Did he tell you that A Plus Wrecking Service did work for the Internal Revenue Service?"

"Not that I recall."

"But he might have?"

"No, I don't think so."

"He didn't tell you to get to know Agent Bobby Tuttle?"

"Huh? No."

"How did you get to know Bobby Tuttle then?"

"I went out with him on a couple of jobs."

"You volunteered for those jobs, right?"

"I guess. I don't remember."

"In fact, you were the only person who ever went out with Bobby Tuttle from the day you went to work for A Plus, isn't that right?"

"I don't know. Maybe."

"When you first applied for work at A Plus Wrecking Service, was there a job available?"

"I don't remember."

"You don't remember. . . . Do you remember a driver getting killed in an automobile wreck which just happened to create an opening for you?"

"Oh, right. I remember that."

"Did you have anything to do with that accident?"

"What do you mean?"

"Were you a witness? Did you see it happen? Were you involved in it?"

"Objection. Compound question not to mention being irrelevant."

"Withdrawn. I'm through with this witness for now your honor but reserve the right to recall him at a later date."

"Very well. Do you have any re-direct Mr. Lee?"

"No, not at this time, Your Honor."

It was a beginning. I could see several members of the jury were intrigued by Stan's cross examination. He had begun to lay a foundation for our defense without Trenton Lee realizing it. The judge noted it was nearly five o'clock and recessed the case until Thursday morning at nine-thirty. When the judge had left the bench, I joined everyone at the defense table and congratulated them on a job well done. Stan, however, wasn't taking any bows. He was upset that he hadn't been able to ruffle Lewis Lance more. He said if all of Trenton Lee's witnesses were as good a liars as Lewis Lance we were in serious trouble.

# BAD DREAMS **49**

After the judge recessed the case for the night, I went back to the office to work on the presentation of our defense. The way I figured it Trenton would finish up his case on Friday and come Monday morning I would need to be ready to start calling witnesses. First on my witness list was Don Harris. I had been trying to serve a subpoena on him for a month without success. It didn't look like he'd be at trial so I crossed him off the list. It was unlikely he'd admit to anything anyway so it didn't upset me too much that he wasn't going to be there. Fortunately I didn't have to prove he was the killer, just create reasonable doubt.

Paula and I had decided Dusty needed to testify since most everyone presumed he was guilty anyway. He had little to lose. I debated whether to start off with Dusty or bring him on last. In order to keep the focus on Don Harris, I opted to put Dusty and Martha on first and then present all the evidence calculated to show that Don Harris was more likely the actual killer. I looked at my revised witness list.

| # Name | Description | Objective |
|---|---|---|
| 1. Dusty Thomas | Defendant | Show that he is not a killer. Gain sympathy. |
| 2. Martha Thomas | D-wife | Paint Dusty as a good and decent man. |
| 3. Emma Lou | neighbor | Establish Silver Mercedes at the scene of crime; damage to mirror |
| 4. Charlotte Harris | Harris' wife | Show Harris was driving silver Mercedes with damaged mirror; show he had opportunity to kill, also good for motive—hated Bobby Tuttle, IRS, People's Mission |
| 5 Robert Perkins | IRS Sup | Have him explain the People's Mission and Tuttle's investigation of Don Harris |

| 6. Donald Hurst | IRS Agent | Get him to show how Bobby was hated by many |
| 7. Jill Murray ?? | Girlfriend | Opportunity and desire to kill Bobby. Virginia connection? Violent nature, kidnapping by Don Harris. |
| 8. Ron Green | Harris' partner | Show Don Harris' S&T Packing into illegal arms |
| 9. Paul Thayer | PI | ?? Loose ends as needed. |
| 10. Lewis Lance | Driver | Recall after introduction of new evidence–show intentional delay in arriving to give Don Harris time to murder Bobby Tuttle |
| 11. Detective Conrad | CC Sheriff's | Attempted murder of Paula and me—link to Don Harris |

I knew I didn't have enough to prove Harris guilty, but I was sure there was enough to create reasonable doubt. A lot would depend on how well Trenton Lee cross-examined my witnesses. Unfortunately, he was a good prosecutor and I expected him to be no less than an expert at cross. I just prayed all my witnesses wouldn't be intimidated and would stand their ground.

Before I went home I called Paul Thayer to see if he had any news for me. He wasn't in so I left a message for him to call me at home if he had any news. As I hung up the telephone I wondered if I was going to get another report from Mo in time to do me any good. I knew if any of his bosses got wind that he was helping me I'd never hear from him.

Rebekah and the kids were waiting for me when I got home. Rebekah had attended the first day of jury selection but decided she would be imposing on her mother too much to go every day. They had all been watching news reports about the trial and were excited to tell me about it.

"Daddy. I saw you on TV," Marcia said.

"Really?" I replied.

"You were walking into the courthouse with Mr. Thomas and his wife." Mark said. "You looked mad."

I laughed. "Well, they were elbowing me and wouldn't let us get through."

"Everyone thinks you're going to lose, Dad," Reggi said.

I looked at him and shrugged. "Well. As they say, 'It's not over 'til the fat lady sings.'"

Marcia frowned and asked. "What fat lady?"

"Okay," Rebekah said. "Leave your father alone and let him come and eat his dinner. I'm sure he must be famished. Go watch *Alf*. It's about to start."

"Okay," Marcia said and ran off with the boys close behind.

"Sit down. I'll bring you your dinner."

"Thanks," I said.

"So, how is it going?" Rebekah asked as she took a plate out of the cupboard.

"Not so bad. No big surprises so far."

"Good. Maybe you'll prove everyone wrong," Rebekah said. "Dusty Thomas is due for some good luck."

"I feel good about our defense. I don't see how the jury could ignore it."

"They can't. Everything that has happened to you and Paula can't be a coincidence."

"Exactly. But so far the D.A. hasn't been impressed with anything we've come up with and they don't seem too worried about our case at all."

"Really? Hmm. I wonder why."

"What I'm afraid of is that they know something I don't."

"Like what?"

"I wish I knew."

"Wouldn't Bart tell Paula?"

"No. Not if it were important."

"Don't they have to disclose any new evidence that they uncover?"

"Yes. They're supposed to but sometimes they don't follow the rules. The government wants Dusty to go down pretty badly so I wouldn't be surprised if they bent the rules a little or even a lot in this case."

The more Rebekah and I talked the more I began to worry. Trenton has been acting pretty confident. He hadn't put up much of a fight when I cross examined Lewis Lance. As we were talking the telephone rang. It was Paul Thayer and he sounded far away.

"Where are you?" I asked.

"I'm in DC. My man out here wasn't getting anywhere so I decided I'd better come out myself."

"Oh. I appreciate that. Any luck?"

"Yes, I found out the call from Don Harris from Jill's apartment was to a man named Ronald Jack. I haven't been able to find out much about him but I'll be working on that all day tomorrow."

"Great. As soon as you find out something call my office and tell Stewart. He'll be alone but he can send the information to me by messenger."

"All right. Good luck tomorrow in trial."

"Thanks."

The name Ronald Jack didn't ring a bell. But I was sure when I got the rest of Thayer's report it would be quite clear who he was and where he fit into the puzzle. Until then there was no use worrying about it.

I went into the den and joined Rebekah who was watching *Moonlighting*. As the night wore on my exhaustion caught up with me and midway through Johnny Carson I fell asleep and began to dream. I was back in Ecuador face to face with General Moya. He was speaking to me. "I am told you are a man of your word. Very well, we'll do it your way, but do not dare to double cross me. If you do, I will send an assassin to punish you and Señor Weller for your betrayal." Suddenly Monty and I were running through the streets of Quito away from our captors. Then I heard a shot and Monty went down. Blood oozed from his back where the bullet had struck. I knelt down and tried to help him but another shot rang out and I felt the sting of the bullet in my chest. I screamed as pain shot through me. "Ahhhh. Oh, God help us!"

"Stan! Wake up.... Wake up. You're dreaming," Rebekah said.

# THE ALIBI **50**

I got to the courtroom early before Trenton or Stan had arrived. It was Thursday and Trenton had a full slate of prosecution witnesses to go through—crime scene personnel, police and sheriff's deputies who had been on the scene, and a ballistics expert. When Stan walked in I noticed he looked a little pale so I went over to him to see how he was.

"Good morning," I said.

"Oh. Hi, Paula."

"Are you okay? You don't look so good."

"I'm just tired. I didn't sleep well."

"Can I get you anything?"

"No. I'm fine. Don't worry. How are you holding up?"

"I'd be better if I were down here with you."

"I wish you were. Believe me."

"Well, Trenton may wrap it up today. None of his witnesses should take very long."

"Yeah, there's not much to argue about. They saw what they saw. I'm worried about their ballistics expert. What if he claims he can match the shot to Dusty's gun?"

"Then he's a lying son of a bitch. Anyway, I've got another ballistics expert available if need be."

"I know. I just have a feeling they're going to spring a surprise on us today."

"I don't think so. What could it possibly be?" I asked.

"I'm probably just paranoid, don't worry about it."

Stan had got me to worrying. If Trenton had a big surprise up his sleeve what would it be? I couldn't think of a thing that he could do without us knowing about it. As he walked into the room I watched him closely. He was looking very cocky. When Bart came in I went over to him.

"Hey. Good morning."

"Hi, babe. How are you?"

"Great. Listen. There isn't anything coming down that I should be worried about is there?"

"What do you mean?"

"Trenton's been playing it pretty cool. What's he got up his sleeve?"

Bart gave me a stone cold look. I immediately knew we were in trouble.

"What is it? Tell me."

"I can't. It's confidential trial strategy."

"Bart. Don't give me that. What is it?"

"I can only tell you that Stan's about to get his ass kicked. I'm surprised you two haven't seen it coming."

I went back to my seat mortified. What was happening? Stan looked at me and I forced a smile. The bailiff stood up and announced the judge's arrival and everyone scampered to their seats. The judge took the bench and the bailiff brought in the jury. The judge nodded and Trenton called as his next witness the ambulance driver who was first on the scene. All morning Trenton paraded his witnesses before the court. I held my breath expecting to hear some new revelation that would prove Dusty was guilty, but nothing happened. By the end of the day it appeared Trenton had called all his witnesses and I was expecting him to rest but he didn't. He announced to the judge that he had one more witness.

"The prosecution calls Mr. Don Harris."

My heart plunged as Don Harris walked into the courtroom and took the stand. He had a grin on his face that was almost demonic. The fact that Don Harris was appearing as a witness could only mean one thing, he had an alibi and if he had an alibi, Dusty Thomas was as good as dead.

"Objection, your Honor, " Stan said. "This witness is on our list not the prosecution's list."

"That is very true, Your Honor. But there is no reason we can't call him first. Mr. Turner certainly can't complain since he was going to call him himself."

"Overruled. You may proceed."

After the court reporter administered the oath, Trenton Lee proceeded. He asked Harris to identify himself, give his occupation, educational background, and other pertinent information. Then he asked him about the day of Bobby's Tuttle's death.

"Can you account for your whereabouts on July 11, 1986?"

"Yes, I had a meeting in Austin at 11:00 A.M. with two buyers. I also stopped in and saw my CPA in the afternoon. He needed some papers to finish up a tax return."

"So you were gone all day?"

"Yes, I didn't get home until 9:30 or so that night."

"How did you get to Austin?"

"I drove my wife's car. I couldn't get mine started and I didn't have time to get it fixed."

"Did you have any problems with your wife's car while you were on this trip?"

"Yes. My wife is kind of fussy about her car. She didn't really want me to take it. On the way down we got into a couple rain showers and the car got filthy. I didn't want to bring home a dirty car so I went to a car wash on the way home. Unfortunately, I got too close to a security post and knocked the side view mirror off."

"Now, I understand you were also being audited by Agent Bobby Tuttle on behalf of the Internal Revenue Service about this time."

"Yes. I belong to the People's Mission, a local church that was being audited by Agent Tuttle."

"Did you have any animosity toward Mr. Tuttle on account of this audit?"

"No, he was just doing his job. My accountant was dealing with Mr. Tuttle. I only met the man one time."

"Were you involved in any way in Bobby Tuttle's death?"

"No. Absolutely not."

Trenton smiled at Stan and said, "Pass the witness."

The judge responded. "It's nearly five o'clock. We'll adjourn and resume tomorrow morning at 9:30."

When the judge had left the bench I went over to the defense table. Stan was shaking his head and Dusty looked very dejected.

"Well now we know why Don Harris was avoiding us. He was setting a trap and we fell right into it," Stan said.

"I'm so sorry," I said. "This is all my fault. I should have seen this coming"

"It's as much my fault as yours," Stan said.

"So, what's going to happen now?" Dusty asked.

"We're going to have to rethink our defense," Stan said. "It doesn't appear Don Harris killed Bobby Tuttle. We'll have to go back over our investigation and figure out where we went wrong."

"But will there be time?" Dusty asked.

Stan shrugged. "We still have some time. We all just need to stay focused and not panic. The killer is out there and we will find him."

"Or her," I said.

"I don't know, Paula. Women rarely kill with a shotgun. I'd bet it's a man."

That night Jodie, Paula, and I met back at the office to go over all our notes and rethink our defense. We ordered in some pizza and drinks, as it was going to be a long night and we couldn't go home until we had come up with an entirely new defense. In retrospect, it had been foolish to try to pin the murder on Don Harris. But we didn't have time to moan and groan about that error in judgment. We had to move on and come up with something new, and fast.

"Oh, Paula," Stan said. "Paul Thayer came up with the name of Don Harris' contact in Virginia. The name didn't mean anything to me, but maybe it will to you."

"What is it?" I asked.

"Ronald Jack."

"Ronald Jack. . . . Ronald Jack . . . Wait. Isn't that Raymond Farr's chief security officer," I asked.

"Is it? I wouldn't know," Stan said. "I never met him."

"Yes it is," Jodie said. "He hung around here the first week they were supposedly protecting Paula. A lot of good their protection did."

"Yes, wasn't it a coincidence that they quit protecting Paula the day of the alleged hit and run," Stan said.

"You think the CDA has a connection to Don Harris?" I asked.

"Why else would Harris be calling Ronald Jack," Stan said. "We've been set up. I can't believe it."

"But the CDA was financing the trial?" I said.

"You've got to have a fight to draw a crowd. If the feds had crushed Dusty Thomas without a fight it would of been in the news a day or two tops. The CDA wanted publicity, lots of publicity so they could spread their message and get lots of new recruits. They didn't care about Dusty Thomas. They didn't want to save him. They just wanted a martyr."

"Well, it's a moot point now since Don Harris has an alibi," I said.

Stan squinted, stroked his chin a few times, and then a smile lit up his face. "But Lewis Lance doesn't."

I looked at Stan and said, "You think?"

Stan nodded and said, "Jodie, I'm going to need Johanson's accident report. And get in touch with the accident investigator."

# ILLUMINATION 51

The next morning we were in a much better mood and were joking and laughing like we were at a church picnic. It was amazing that we could even stay awake, since we hadn't got more than a couple of hours of sleep. Trenton Lee looked at us curiously. I'm sure he was wondering why were so jovial when our defense had just gone down the toilet. I looked in the gallery and was glad to see Raymond Farr and his CDA contingent had made it. They were going to particularly enjoy today's session, I just knew it.

The bailiff ordered the court in session and Judge Justice took the bench. After he had straightened up his desk and conferred briefly with the court reporter he asked the bailiff to bring in the jury and the witness from the previous day. When the jury was seated the judge looked at me and nodded.

"You may proceed with your cross-examination of the witness, Mr. Turner."

"Thank you, Your Honor. . . . Mr. Harris. What kind of business are you in?"

"I'm a graphic artist," he replied.

"Do you have any interest in a business called S & T Packing, Inc."

"Yes, I'm the majority stockholder."

"What kind of business is that?"

"A commodities export business."

"You mean like fruit and nuts?"

"Well, pretty much. All kinds of vegetables too."

"Has S & T ever engaged in the illegal export of arms?"

The smile on Harris' face faded. "No. Of course not."

"You know you *are* under oath, right? If you lie to this court you could be punished for perjury. You may want to take the fifth."

"Objection! Your Honor, Mr. Turner is badgering the witness and this whole line of testimony is irrelevant," Trenton said.

"Sustained."

"I apologize. I'm not trying to badger you, Mr. Harris, but I've got a witness outside who is prepared to testify that you *do* export illegal arms from S & T Packing. I think you'll remember your ex-partner, Ronald Green."

Harris took a deep breath, looked at Trenton Lee, and then back at me. "I think maybe I would like to confer with my attorney before I answer any more questions."

"Is your attorney present, Mr. Harris?" the judge asked.

"No, Your Honor."

"Well, you're not on trial here. We don't have time to let you go obtain counsel. You have a choice—invoke the fifth amendment if you think your testimony might tend to incriminate you or answer the question."

Harris licked his lips nervously then took a deep breath. I looked over at Raymond Farr and he looked distressed. He got up and started to leave the courtroom. The bailiff stopped him and escorted him to the jury room to wait. I had alerted the bailiff that I wanted to call Raymond Farr as a rebuttal witness and didn't want him leaving.

"I'll invoke the fifth amendment then," Harris said.

"All right. Since you don't want to talk about your illegal arms trade let's change the subject."

"What's your relationship to the CDA?"

"I don't know what you mean?"

"Well, are you a member?"

"No."

"Do you or S & T Packing sell them arms?"

"I'll invoke the fifth amendment again."

"Do you know Raymond Farr?"

"Yes."

"How long have you known him?"

"A long time. We were roommates in college."

"Where did you go to college?"

"The University of Texas."

"So who's idea was it to kill Bobby Tuttle? Yours or Raymond Farr's?"

"Objection!" Trenton screamed. "Assumes facts not in evidence—move the jury be instructed to disregard."

"Sustained," the judge ruled. "The jury will disregard the question."

"Since we know now that you didn't kill Bobby Tuttle let me ask you this: Did you know he was going to be killed?"

"No."

"Didn't Raymond Farr order his death?"

"No. Absolutely not."

"Do you know who killed Bobby Tuttle?"

Harris hesitated one instant too long and then replied, "Dusty Thomas."

"Did you see Dusty Thomas kill Agent Tuttle?"

"No."

"So, do you know who killed Agent Tuttle?"

"No."

"Do you know Ernesto Garcia?"

"Yes."

"Does he work at S & T Packing?"

"Yes, he's a foreman there."

"Is this the same Ernesto Garcia who was a witness against my law partner, Paula Waters, when she was recently on trial for failure to stop and render aid?"

"I . . . I think so."

"Was setting up Paula Winter's your idea or Raymond Farr's?"

"Objection!" Trenton Lee exclaimed. "Assumes facts not in evidence."

"Sustained," the judge said.

"Did you conspire with Ernesto Garcia, Brian Armstrong, or Maria Cabrillo to falsely accuse Paula Waters of leaving the scene of an accident. . . . Feel free to take the fifth."

"Objection!" Trenton yelled.

"Withdrawn. Pass the witness," I replied.

"Any rebuttal, Mr. Lee?" the judge asked.

"No, Your Honor."

"Then call your next witness."

"That was our last witness," Trenton said. "The state rests."

"Very well, Mr. Turner. You may call your first witness."

"Yes, Your Honor. We call Raymond Farr."

The judge looked at the bailiff and said, "Bring in Mr. Farr please."

The bailiff nodded and left the courtroom. A moment later he emerged without the witness and went up to the bench. Trenton and I joined him at the bench.

"Your Honor," the bailiff said. "I've been informed by Mr. Farr that he will not testify and will invoke the fifth amendment on any question that might be asked him."

The judge nodded. "All right step back please."

Trenton and I returned to our seats and all eyes were on the judge. He said, "I've been advised that the witness Mr. Turner wanted to call, Mr. Raymond Farr, has invoked his right under the Constitution of the United States not to testify on grounds that it might tend to incriminate him. Therefore he will not be testifying."

The gallery exploded in conversation and the judge banged his gavel to restore order. When it had quieted down he continued, "Mr. Turner, do you have any other witnesses?"

"Yes, Your Honor. We call Mr. Lewis Lance."

Another buzz went up in the courtroom and the bailiff stood up and glared at the spectators. Finally the bailiff went and got Mr. Lance and escorted him to the witness stand. He looked scared. After he took his seat, I stood and approached the witness.

"Mr. Lance, I guess you realize you're still under oath?"

He nodded and replied, "Right."

"Do you know Raymond Farr?"

He squinted like it was a very difficult question and then replied, "I know who he is. I've never met him."

"Are you a member of the CDA?"

"No."

"How about the Texas Militia?"

"The Texas Militia? Yes."

"Tell us about the Texas Militia."

He frowned. "What does the Texas Militia have to do with—"

"Objection, Your Honor. Non-responsive," I said.

The judge replied, "Just answer the question, Mr. Lance."

Lance looked at the judge then shook his head. "Well for one thing, they don't believe the State of Texas was properly brought into the Union. Therefore, the citizens of Texas don't have to obey federal laws."

"Is that what you believe, Mr. Lance, that you don't have to obey federal laws?"

Lance shifted nervously in his seat, "Well, theoretically?"

"The Texas Militia is a military organization, right?"

"I suppose. You get military training if you join."

"Does S & T Packing supply arms to the Texas Militia?"

"I wouldn't know. I just pack 'em up."

"You're not involved in where the arms go?"

"No."

"Do you own a shotgun?"

"A shotgun?"

"Right. A Remington shotgun to be exact."

"Ah. Well. Probably. I've got several."

"Do you carry this shotgun with you when you go out on jobs in your wrecker?"

"Sure. You never know what kind of situation you might run up against."

"So on July 11, 1986 when you drove your wrecker up to the Double T Ranch to assist Bobby Tuttle you had your shotgun?"

Lance squirmed in his chair and avoided eye contact. "I suppose but I'm not sure it was the Remington."

"Sure it was. You knew Dusty Thomas had a Remington, right?"

"Huh. How would I know that?"

"I'm sure Bobby Tuttle told you. You two were good friends, weren't you?"

Yeah, we got along, but I don't remember talking about Dusty Thomas."

Oh, come on, Mr. Lance. Dusty Thomas was on Bobby Tuttle's hit list. He must have talked about him a lot, right?"

"Maybe he mentioned him a time or two."

"So, you knew to bring the Remington so after you shot Bobby Tuttle you could pin the murder on Dusty Thomas. Isn't that right?"

"No!"

The gallery exploded in excited conversation. The judge banged his gavel and glared at the crowd.

"You killed Bobby Tuttle, didn't you."

Lance nearly leaped out of his chair. "No! He was dead when I got there."

"I don't think so," I said sternly. "You didn't need a second job at A Plus Wrecking Service, did you?"

"Yes I did. I was behind on my bills."

"Didn't Don Harris suggest you hire on with them because he knew there was a strong likelihood you'd get an opportunity to kill Bobby Tuttle and make it look like Dusty Thomas had done it?"

"No, that's crazy. You're hallucinating."

"How much did they pay you for the hit?"

WILLIAM MANCHEE

"Objection!" Trenton exclaimed. "Assumes facts not in evidence. Request an instruction to disregard."

"Sustained. The jury will disregard the question."

"Why don't you just tell the truth? Harris and Farr have already taken the fifth. Do you want to take the fall alone for this?"

"Objection—" Trenton screamed.

"You killed Bobby Tuttle, didn't you?" Stan pressed.

Lance closed his eyes. His hands were shaking and he was breathing heavily. "No. Dusty Thomas did it. It happened just like I said."

"And Bobby Tuttle wasn't your first victim, was he?"

Lance turned pale. "Huh?"

"You ran Carl Johanson off the road so you could get a job at A Plus Wrecking Service didn't you?"

"What?"

"Did you plan on killing him, or were you just trying to knock him out of commission for a while?"

"Objection," Trenton said. "Assumes facts not in evidence. Counsel is badgering the witness."

"Withdrawn," I said. "You're a fine actor, Mr. Lance, but I've got the accident investigator outside who worked the Carl Johanson case. Did you know they took a lot of photographs at the accident scene? There are some particularly good shots of tire tracks and skid marks. Last night he compared the tires on your pickup to tire tracks in the photographs. I guess you know what he discovered."

Lance swallowed hard.

"Do I need to call him in here to tell us about the results of the comparison?"

Lance inhaled and then exhaled slowly. He appeared to be on the verge of tears. Finally, he shook his head and mumbled, "No."

Stan nodded, "Good. It's time we learned the truth. Now, obviously it wasn't your idea to kill Bobby Tuttle. So, who put you up to it?"

"It was Ray's idea.... He said the plan was foolproof—nobody would ever figure it out."

The courtroom erupted in conversation. The judge banged the gavel and demanded order. Dusty Thomas was jubilant. He turned around and smiled at his wife, who was in tears.

"How much were you paid?" Stan asked.

"$50,000 and they said I'd get another $50,000 after Dusty Thomas was convicted."

The courtroom was deadly quiet. Trenton Lee sat down in disgust. All eyes were on Lewis Lance.

"Who paid you the $50,000?" Stan asked.

"Ray. He gave it to me in a plastic bag—small bills."

"So, I'm curious. How exactly did the hit take place?"

Lewis swallowed hard. He took a deep breath and replied, "Bobby called me and said to meet him at the Double T Ranch at noon. When I got there I parked in front of the shack near the front gate so he wouldn't see the wrecker. Then I walked along the fence so he wouldn't see me approaching. When I got real close I crossed over to the driveway and walked straight toward him. He did a double take when he saw me coming but I didn't stop to do any explaining. I just shot him—twice—both barrels. Then I high-tailed it back to my wrecker before Dusty Thomas saw me. After that I just drove the wrecker up to the house and pretended I had just got there. Seemed like a foolproof plan to me."

"It was very ingenious. I'll give you that. No further questions, Your Honor. I move that all charges against Dusty Thomas be dismissed."

The judge took my motion under advisement and recessed the case so all the parties could evaluate what had happened that day. Paula rushed up to me and gave me a big hug and Dusty and Martha couldn't thank us enough. The press mobbed us as we left, and since we were all in a good mood, we took a little time to answer their questions. Paula wanted me to go out with Bart and her to celebrate but I declined. I couldn't wait to get home and tell Rebekah the good news.

# FILLING IN THE BLANKS **52**

Stan had filed a motion for a new trial in my criminal case immediately after I was found guilty. The judge hadn't ruled on it when the Dusty Thomas case came to trial. Based on Lewis Lance's confession, Don Harris' connection to Ernesto Garcia, and a decidedly different attitude at the D.A.'s office, I was granted a new trial and my conviction was set aside. I figured it was just a matter of time before the case would be dismissed all together. With the new trial came an end to my temporary suspension from practicing law. I was glad to get back on the job and anxious to get working again. Fortunately, after successfully defending Dusty Thomas, our services were in great demand so it wasn't long before I had more work to do than I could possibly handle.

In the meantime the D.A.'s office was working on an indictment against Ernesto Garcia, Brian Armstrong, Maria Cabrillo, and Don Harris for the murder of Monty Dozier. They had managed to arrest a member of the 18th Street Gang who they suspected was involved in the murder. In exchange for immunity he fingered Ernesto Garcia as the person who hired him, along with a couple of other gang members, to kill Monty.

Right after Dusty Thomas' acquittal his congressman began a campaign to have any remaining tax liability forgiven. He said it was the least the government could do after they had put Dusty and Martha through hell for six months. With the trial over and a clean slate with the government, it appeared Dusty's fortunes were improving.

Even though the trial was over and it didn't really matter anymore, I was curious about the silver Mercedes. Was it a coincidence that it came along just after the murder? I asked Bart to get someone in the DA's office to ask Lewis Lance about it. Lance confirmed that Charlotte's silver Mercedes had indeed been out at the Double T Ranch on the day of Bobby Tuttle's murder. Don Harris had instructed Riley Davidson to take it and follow Lewis Lance and make sure he got the job done.

Several weeks after the trial I got a call from Jill. She had come out of hiding following Don Harris' arrest and incarceration. I had a lot of questions I wanted to ask her so I suggested lunch. I brought along Charlotte and Regina Harris. I thought between the three of them I could get some answers about Don Harris. We met at Vincent's in Addison.

"I was so glad to hear your voice, Jill," I said. "I was worried Don had killed you."

"He would have if he'd found me," Jill replied. "That's why I had to disappear. I'm sorry."

"It's okay. I probably would have done the same thing. Luckily Charlotte agreed to testify so we didn't absolutely need you."

Jill turned to Charlotte and said, "I'm sorry—"

Charlotte raised her finger to her mouth. "Shhh! Don't worry about it. I never figured Don would be faithful."

"When we first met he told me he was single," Jill said.

Charlotte shook her head. "That figures."

I said. "Listen. There's still one lose end that's troubling us."

"What's that?" Charlotte asked.

"General Moya. We're still worried that he might send an assassin to kill Stan and Tex. I'm sure you read about his threats in the newspaper."

They all nodded.

"Stan got a report from a friend in the CIA that Don Harris sold arms to General Moya. This is quite a coincidence given Stan's kidnapping by General Moya. Did Don ever talk about General Moya?" I asked.

"They met in college," Regina said. "They were a trio—Don, Ray, and Raul. I was dating Don at the time. That's how I know."

"Really?"

"Yes, General Moya's parents were rich and sent him to the U.S. to be educated. They stayed in the same dorm. While Raul was at UT his parents were brutally murdered by agents of the current dictator there. Raul vowed to get revenge. Don and Ray had some kind of beef with the U.S. Army themselves so the three of them had one big thing in common—a hatred for their governments."

"Did Moya stay in school after his parents were killed?"

"Yes, and they all graduated together in 1970. After graduation they all went off in different directions, Don to North Texas, Ray to Washington DC and Raul back to Ecuador, but they stayed in touch. Later on they started doing business together. When Raul joined the guerrillas to fight the government, Don started selling them arms. Then they got the idea of kidnapping American businessmen who were traveling in South America and collecting big ransoms. Don would locate and screen prospective victims to be sure they could pay the ransoms, and Raul would handle the kidnapping, imprisonment, and collection of the ransom. If they couldn't find Americans there to kidnap, they'd lure them there with shady business propositions that promised big rewards."

"Like standing in for lost beneficiaries?" I asked.

"Yes, this was one of their most lucrative schemes," Regina replied. "If a rich person died without heirs they would contact an American and propose that he come to Ecuador as a 'stand-in' beneficiary. They would provide all the documentation to prove the American was the actual beneficiary and when the money was paid they supposedly would split it. However, instead of splitting it they kept it all for themselves, then kidnapped the American, and demanded a ransom."

"Jesus, I can't believe this kind of stuff goes on. It's so unreal," I said.

"Oh, it's real, all right," Charlotte said. "Don went to Ecuador just after Bobby Tuttle's murder. I bet the purpose of the visit was to set up this scam."

"You think? But how did they know Tex was one of Stan's clients? And how did they know he would go to Ecuador looking for him?" I asked.

"I don't think they expected Stan to go to Ecuador. That probably was a big surprise and complicated matters a lot for them," Charlotte said.

"But not as much as when Tex had the money wired into Stan's trust account.," I said.

"He did?" Charlotte said.

"Yes, he instructed his banker in the Cayman Islands to immediately wire the money he received from Ecuador to Dallas into Stan's trust account," I said. "That probably saved his life because had the money still been in the Cayman account, Raul's men would have probably taken the money, kidnapped him, and then locked him away somewhere and demanded a ransom."

"Boy. Raul is one greedy son of a bitch," Jill said.

"Well, that's how he finances their guerrilla war against the government," Regina said.

I shook my head. "Well, thank you ladies. You filled in a lot of blanks for me. I really appreciate you meeting with me."

"Well, thank you for getting rid of Don for us. He's an evil man who hopefully will spend the rest of his life behind bars," Charlotte said.

"I hope they execute him, myself," Jill said.

They all laughed.

After lunch I went back to the office and relayed to Stan what I had learned. I felt badly because had I probed Regina more during my initial interview with her we might have discovered the connection between Don Harris and General Moya a lot earlier. Stan dismissed that notion as nonsense."

"No one had even dreamed of that connection back then," Stan said.

"I guess that's true. . . . I wonder how Don Harris picked Tex to lure to Ecuador?"

"Hmm. I'm not sure."

"How did they even know he was a client?" I asked.

Stan thought about it and then replied, "Actually that wouldn't have been difficult at all. Clients often ask for references, so I have a list of them. Guess who's at the top of the list?"

I shook my head and said, "Son of a bitch. He just called up here like he was a prospective client and asked for a reference before he retained you."

"Yes, and now that you mention it, Jodie told me someone had called and asked for references while I was on vacation. Apparently they stopped by and picked up a firm brochure. Our top ten clients are listed there too."

"Wonderful," I said. "Perhaps we should rethink giving out a reference sheet."

"Perhaps, but we've got a bigger problem to worry about," Stan said.

"What's that?"

"Now that we've put Don and Ray behind bars, General Moya is sure to be angry and has even more reason to make good on his assassination threats against me and Tex."

"I know," I said. "So, what are you going to do?"

"That's a good question," Stan said with a grim look on his face.

# A LOOSE END 53

Although I tried to tell myself General Moya wouldn't go to the trouble to send an assassin all the way from Ecuador to kill Tex and me, I couldn't help but worry about it. Everywhere I went I had this nagging fear that an assassin was lurking around every corner. My stomach was in knots and I had a constant headache worrying about it. I finally decided I couldn't live this way and had to do something about the problem. The only persons I could think of who might be able to help were Agents Ronald Logan and Jennifer Giles of the FBI. They were surprised to get my call but agreed to a meeting. I went to their offices in the Earl Cabell Federal Building in Dallas.

"Thanks for agreeing to meet with me," I said.

"Actually we were glad you called," Giles said. "Weren't we Ron?"

Logan shrugged. "Yeah, I suppose we owe you an apology. We thought for sure you were in Raymond Farr's pocket."

"I know it may have looked that way. It's no big deal. I'm just glad it worked out okay."

"Yes, with all the evidence you dug up and Lewis Lance's confession we have enough to put Raymond Farr away for the rest of his life, not to mention putting an end to the CDA once and for all."

"That's great, but what are you going to do about General Moya? I feel certain he's going to send someone to kill Tex and me."

"Well, we can assign both of you some protection for a while, I suppose. After everything you did for the government they ought to spring for it."

"That's great for the short run but the government isn't going to protect me for more than a month or two."

"Well, there's the witness protection program," Logan said.

"No. I'm not going into hiding," I said. "Why can't you catch the son of a bitch?"

"Well, he's under indictment and we've been trying for several years to arrest him, but he's living out in the jungle and he's protected by his guerilla army."

"Then I want you to let me pay him the rest of the ransom. That's the only way he's going to leave us alone."

"We can't let you do that," Logan said. "He'll just use that money to buy more guns and ammunition to kill innocent citizens."

"Okay. What if we put up a reward?" I said.

"A reward?" Giles asked.

"Yes. Pass the word to all your operatives down in South America. We'll pay $900,000 if they put a bullet in General Moya's head."

Logan and Giles just looked at me.

"If I'm going to have to live with the fear of eminent death, then General Moya's gonna live with it too."

A smile came over Logan's face. He shook his head and said, "You know, that might just work. We'll send a message to General Moya and propose a truce. If he leaves you alone we won't put a price on his head."

"Okay. Let's do it. We don't have anything to lose."

Logan promised to get the message to General Moya and let me know if he got a response. In the meantime Tex and I were each assigned an FBI agent to protect us as best they could. It was almost ten days before we got a reply from General Moya. He said he wasn't worried about having a price on his head—he already had an abundance of enemies who wanted him dead, but he would agree to the proposal because it was well documented in the press that I had been prevented by the government from paying the rest of the ransom and he could hardly hold that against me.

I was glad to get this news but I couldn't help but wonder if General Moya was sincere or just wanted me to let my guard down. I finally decided I'd just have to assume he was sincere or otherwise I'd go crazy worrying about it.

Rebekah was particularly pleased to hear my life was no longer in danger. She had been a nervous wreck for months and finally was starting to smile again. Paula was also relieved, as she didn't enjoy practicing law alone. I was feeling pretty good about how everything turned out, but there was still one unanswered question. Why did Don Harris get kicked out of the Army? What could have happened to him to turn him so violently against the government? After the trial was over I called Mo to thank him for his help and posed that question. He said he was curious about that too so he'd look into it. A week later we had the answer.

The unofficial report on Don Harris' general discharge was that he had been caught engaging in a sexual act with another soldier—Riley Davidson. The Army had zero tolerance for homosexuals, so it was suggested by his superior officers that he resign or face exposure and humiliation. Now I understood why Harris had been so hard on his women. He didn't like them much. They were only around for show. Then it occurred to me.

He may actually enjoy prison.

# EPILOGUE

One Sunday morning nearly ten years after the Dusty Thomas trial I sat down at the kitchen table across from Rebekah to read the Dallas Morning News. There had been terrible thunderstorms the night before and several tornados had touched down in various places in North Texas. One of them had done serious damage in Fort Worth and another one in Wylie, Texas.

With the thunderstorms came hail and I was concerned that our roof had been damaged. I was planning to get up on the roof later that day and do a close inspection but in the meantime I wanted to see what the newspaper had to say about it. The headline was about the Wylie Tornado.

## Massive Tornado Strikes Wylie

A massive cleanup operation was still underway in Wylie, Texas on Thursday after back-to-back tornadoes packing winds of 206 mph or better, smashed through the downtown area, killing four people and causing an estimated $30 million in damage. The death toll from the twisters stood at four, with one person missing and presumed dead. The downtown core of Wylie, a 6-square-block area, remained closed to all but those involved in the cleanup effort.

Softball-size Hailstone Kills Man

The coroner's office said Carl Snyder, 67, was killed by a collapsing wall, and Howard D. Horton, 52, died after a truck trailer toppled onto him. The body of Arthur B. Poole, 24, was recovered Wednesday morning along a creek. John T. Dickens and his grandmother, Adele Wester, 62, were in a car that was swept away by rising waters as they left their Lake Lavon home. Dickens remained missing and was presumed dead. Another victim of the storms, Dusty Thomas, 59 died Wednesday afternoon at Collin County Memorial Hospital. He had suffered severe head injuries when he was hit by a softball-size hailstone in Princeton, Texas while he was mowing grass along State Highway 380. It was a unusual way to die as there have been less than a dozen reported hail deaths in the 20ths century.

"Oh, my God!" I exclaimed.

"What?" Rebekah said.

"Dusty Thomas was killed in that hailstorm last night."

"Oh, no. . . . Oh, Jesus. Poor Dusty."

I handed the paper to Rebekah and while she read the story I thought of poor Dusty being the victim of yet another bitter blow of fate. The thought of being pelted by rocks from the sky was chilling. What had he done to deserve such a fate? The newspaper hadn't made the connection between Dusty Thomas the hailstone victim and Dusty Thomas the murder defendant. But they would soon figure that out and Dusty's tragic life would be talked about for years. There would be no doubt about it now. Dusty Thomas was the world's unluckiest man.

# ABOUT THE AUTHOR

**WILLIAM MANCHEE** grew up in Ventura, California in the Sixties. After obtaining his BA from UCLA in 1965, he and his family moved to Texas where Manchee attended law school at SMU. He began his legal career in Dallas as a sole practitioner in 1976; currently, he practices with his son Jim. Residents of Plano, Texas he and his wife, Janet, have been married for 36 years and raised four children.

Inspired by twenty years of true-life experiences as an attorney, Manchee discovered his passion for writing in 1995. Since then he has written ten books, and he plans henceforth to publish a book every year. In addition to the Stan Turner Mysteries, Manchee is the author of the Rich Coleman Novel series, and has written a nonfiction work, *Yes, We're Open*, a book designed to help small businesses improve their chances of survival.

For more information about William Manchee, visit his website at *http://www.williammanchee.com*

# More Thrills from LeanPress

## ANDROS DRAWS THE LINE

Detective Thriller/Illustrations

BRUCE EDWARDS

Paul Andros just wanted to work quietly at his lucrative private law practice in Seattle and go home each night to his wife, daughter and 25-acre horse ranch. His peaceful life is ruined when the suspicious death of the King County Prosecutor Sherman Falkes results in Andros' temporary appointment to fill the vacancy.

Now forced to push the investigation into his predecessor's death, Andros discovers evidence of drugs and a prostitution ring operating under the protection of a high ranking Seattle police officer and others in the department.

But was Sherman's death related to the corruption? Andros must scramble to get the answers before a new prosecutor is elected and all the evidence is swept away.

Bruce Edwards' unique style deviates from the standard mystery-thriller formula, creating an unusually realistic story and vivid 3-dimensional characters. *Andros Draws the Line* is a great read for both novel lovers and mystery-thriller fans.

ISBN 193247501X

# More Mystery from LeanPress

## DANGEROUS KNOWLEDGE

A Kate Sutherland Mystery/Illustrations

HEIDI BARKER

Struggling to recover from the dark tragedy that claimed her husband and unborn child, lovely Kate Sutherland is ill-prepared to confront a new darkness threatening to claim her as well. Having moved hundreds of miles back to the Pacific Northwest to escape painful memories and unhealthy ties, Kate finds that she is marked for further terror. She has found a home, a new job in Portland, Oregon, and a school for her surviving child Samantha. She has returned to the support of family and childhood friends Scotty, a detective, and Mel, a satire columnist for a local weekly. But someone watching from the shadows has decided to unleash a new wave of fear upon the traumatized Kate. Scorpions in the mailbox, a dismembered cat in the dryer—her watcher will stop at nothing in a quest that baffles the local authorities and can only end in murder.

With *Dangerous Knowledge*, H.M. Barker has made a strikingly competent entrance into the thriller genre. With echoes of the rich character development and nuance of Mary Higgins Clark, *Dangerous Knowledge* is a first-rate read for mystery fans with special appeal for a Pacific Northwest audience.

ISBN 1932475052